A

JASON ELAM
AND STEVE YOHN

NOVEL

PRESENTED BY

*TYNDALE HOUSE
PUBLISHERS, INC.*
CAROL STREAM, ILLINOIS

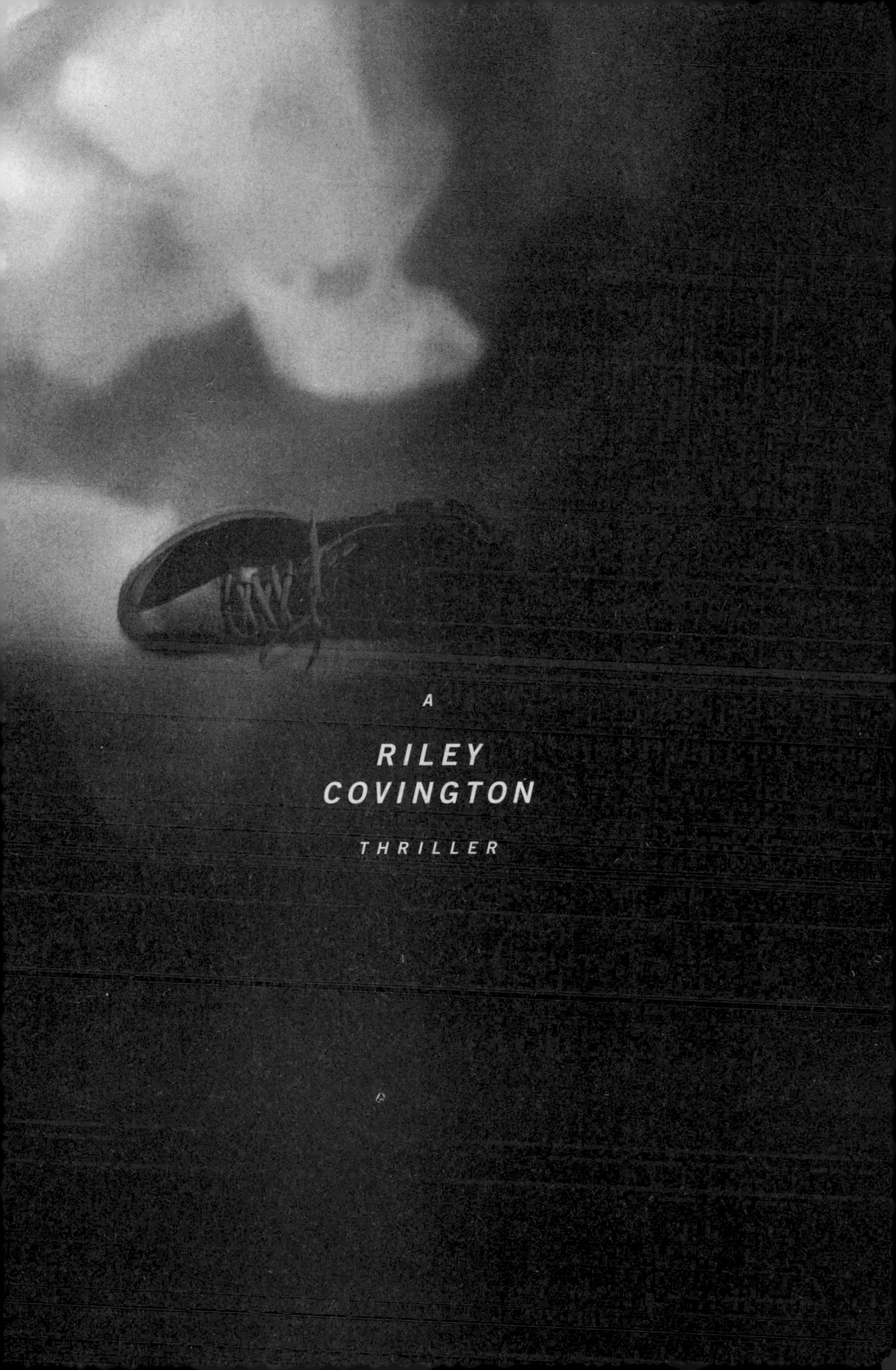

A

RILEY COVINGTON

THRILLER

Visit Tyndale's exciting Web site at www.tyndale.com

TYNDALE and Tyndale's quill logo are registered trademarks of Tyndale House Publishers, Inc.

Blown Coverage

Designed by Dean H. Renninger

Published in association with the literary agency of Yates & Yates, LLP, Attorneys and Counselors, Orange, California.

Scripture taken from the HOLY BIBLE, NEW INTERNATIONAL VERSION®. NIV®. Copyright © 1973, 1978, 1984 by International Bible Society. Used by permission of Zondervan. All rights reserved.

Library of Congress Cataloging-in-Publication Data

Elam, Jason.
  Blown coverage : a Riley Covington thriller / a Jason Elam and Steve Yohn novel.
    p. cm.
  ISBN 978-1-4143-1732-8 (sc)
  1. Football players—Fiction. 2. Terrorists—Fiction. I. Yohn, Steve. II. Title.
  PS3605.L26B66 2008
  813'.6--dc22   2008038117

Printed in the United States of America

15 14 13 12 11 10 09
  7   6   5   4   3   2   1

DEDICATION

LORD, WHEN WE ASKED, YOU ANSWERED. When we trusted, You were faithful. Thank You.

Thanks, also, to our wonderful families. It was your love, patience, advice, and encouragement that kept us going.

We are indebted to LTC Mark Elam for poking holes in our scenarios and filling them with the ways things really work; Troy Bisgard of the Denver Police Homicide Division for feeding us stories that kept us laughing until we were barely sucking air; and Afshin Ziafat for keeping us culturally and linguistically accurate.

We can't leave out Matt Yates and the Yates & Yates team, Karen Watson and our Tyndale House family, and Beverly Rykerd of Beverly Rykerd Public Relations. A special thanks goes to Jeremy Taylor, editor extraordinaire, who has a gift for taking a manuscript and bumping it up to the next level.

Finally, to those friends and fans with whom God has graced us, your support has encouraged us and your prayers have sustained us. We are blessed because of you.

ACKNOWLEDGMENTS

TUESDAY, MARCH 31, 8:45 P.M. CEST
BABROSTY, POLAND

Empty shell casings skittered across the cement floor, propelled by the underside of the mercenary's boots. As he strode down the hall, his eyes remained focused on the door at the end of the passageway—no need to look in the rooms to his right or left; his men were too good to have left any threat on his periphery.

The sooner I deal with this man, the sooner I'm out of this stinking cesspool, thought Lecha Abdalayev, trying hard not to breathe deep the smell of fresh blood and human waste.

Not that he was unfamiliar with those smells. As a veteran of both the First and Second Chechen Wars, he had seen his share of man's inhumanity against man. He himself had once been in a situation while a prisoner of the Russians when death would have seemed a much sweeter alternative to what he experienced in the daily interrogations. *But it wasn't long before I turned the tables and became the one holding the knife,* he gloated with a self-satisfied grunt.

When he reached the end of the hall, one of the two men walking with him slid a key into the lock on the solid metal cell door.

"Wait." Abdalayev took a moment to straighten the black beret that was sitting on his bald head. Then he ran a hand over his fatigues and smoothed his long, salt-and-pepper beard over his chest. "Okay."

The lock protested for just a moment; then the large door slid noisily to the left. Immediately, Abdalayev's senses were violently assaulted. The smell of human waste that had been strong in the hallway was overwhelming in this room. From somewhere in the room a blaring children's song came to an end, then just as quickly began again: "I love you; you love me . . ."

Abdalayev waited a moment for his eyes to adjust to the brilliance of the four floodlights, then entered the room.

In the middle of the cell sat an ancient-looking man. He was FlexiCuffed by the wrists and ankles to a reversed metal chair, while a wide fabric belt held his chest tightly against the chair's back. Except for the restraints, he was completely naked.

The battle-scarred prisoner stared at Abdalayev with his one remaining eye. A crooked smile had spread across his mangled face. Hanging over his back were two I.V. bags—one attached to a line that went into the man's arm, the other positioned to slowly drip down his back. As Abdalayev watched, another drop released from the bag and fell onto a large red welt, causing the old man to wince and a tear to slide from his good eye. But he never lost his smile.

The Chechen renewed his determination to do this fast and get out. Drawing his pistol, he pointed it toward the prisoner. Abdalayev was gratified to see the sudden fear in the elder warrior's face—just a reminder of who was in charge of this operation. He pulled the trigger, shattering the portable CD player in the back of the room and finally putting an end to the music.

Looking to one of his men, he said, "Cover him." The soldier pulled a Mylar foil rescue blanket out of his pack and laid it over the old man's shoulders. Abdalayev settled his eyes upon the man in the chair. Reaching into his shirt, he pulled out a photograph. He examined the photo, then held it out so he could see both the picture and the prisoner's battered face at one time. Satisfied that they were one and the same, he tucked the picture away.

"My name is Lecha Abdalayev," the visitor said in accented

Arabic. "I am the commander of the Chechen Freedom Militia. We have been asked by your friends to assist them in retrieving you. Are you able—"

"Where am I?" the prisoner interrupted.

"You are just outside of Babrosty, Poland, in a prison belonging to the American CIA. Now, I respectfully ask you not to interrupt me. All your questions will be answered in due course. As you can imagine, time now is of the essence."

The old man nodded his acquiescence.

"It is obvious that you will not be able to travel unassisted. Do I have your permission to immobilize you?" Abdalayev asked, knowing he was going to do it no matter the answer.

"Do what you must."

Abdalayev waved to another mercenary who was standing just outside the door. The captive's eyes grew wide as the soldier walked rapidly across the room and plunged a large hypodermic syringe into his neck. Immediately, the old man's head slumped.

"Bundle him up, and let's go," Abdalayev commanded, turning to walk away and wondering how much vodka it was going to take to get this visual out of his mind.

As he left the room, he was forced to step over the body of the man who had been guarding the cell—a quick glance wasn't enough to tell Abdalayev whether he had been American or Polish. *Not that it matters—although there is something about killing Americans,* he thought with a small smile. *It's like the difference between shooting a common deer and hunting big game.*

As he walked, Abdalayev took time to glance at the empty cells around him. Just inside one of these doors, the twisted bodies of two of his mercenaries and a guard were sprawled on top of each other in a spreading pool of blood that crossed the entire hall. Abdalayev didn't bother checking on his men. *Dead or soon to be dead; not much difference today.* He continued on, leaving a trail of bloody bootprints behind him.

When he reached the main courtyard, the four other Arabs who had been held prisoner at the facility were lined up on their knees.

"*As-Salamu `Alaykum,*" he said to them, conveying the traditional Muslim greeting of peace.

"Wa `Alaykum As-Salam," they replied, a look of hope in their swollen eyes.

Abdalayev briefly studied their faces. It was obvious that these men had been exposed to the same treatment given to the old man. He said a silent prayer for them, then told the soldier guarding them, "Kill them."

Abdalayev watched as the men's souls departed for paradise. *Insha'Allah*, Abdalayev thought, *it was obviously their time. If Allah has willed, who can change it? Allah wills some to live and some to die, some to serve and some to be served, some to be soldiers and some to be victims. Insha'Allah—it is as Allah wills.*

One thing every young Muslim learned growing up in Chechnya was that Allah often called the few to sacrifice for the many. These men were too infirm to travel on their own, and he couldn't just leave them here. The very fact that they were in this secret prison meant that they had access to vital information. If they were recaptured and put to the same treatment again, they would break—everyone broke eventually. It was best just to send them to their eternal reward while there was still a possibility that they might arrive with their honor intact.

When the last of the prisoners had stopped moving, Abdalayev said into his comm, "Finish up. Proceed to the rendezvous point immediately." The agreed-upon spot was a large dying oak tree half a kilometer away and just off the road.

After their arrival, the twelve remaining members of Abdalayev's team would clean themselves up and put on casual business attire. They would also do their best to make the old man look presentable—*I'm glad they mentioned the eye patch,* he thought.

From there, the team would divide into groups of four and head northeast for the Belarusian border in three rented Škoda Roomsters. This would hopefully draw any pursuit that might follow. Abdalayev and the former prisoner, meanwhile, would drive a BMW southeast into Ukraine. The mercenary commander was confident that he could make it across the border with his fake passports. It would be difficult for the Americans to raise much of an alert. What could they say—"A man who doesn't officially exist anymore was stolen from a prison that never existed to begin with"?

If only things had been this easy when he was defending Grozny back in 1996. If that had been successful, then maybe he would be home right now with a wife and sons instead of here with mud on his hands and blood on his boots.

But, as every Chechen knew, you took Allah's will as it came. Some days it brought freedom, and another day it brought a bullet in the back of the head for being in the wrong prison at the wrong time. *Insha'Allah.* Allah knew what was best; blessed be his name.

Today Allah's will had brought freedom for al-'Aqran, leader of the Cause.

There was not much that could give Riley Covington the heebie-jeebies—moldy sour cream, chew-
ing on tinfoil, the music of Barry Manilow—but
looking at what was in the tall fountain glass that
had just been placed in front of Scott Ross was
seriously making his skin crawl and his stomach
dance the mambo.

"You try it," Scott said as he slid the glass
across the table with his fingertips.

"You ordered it, you drink it," Riley countered, sliding the sweating glass back across the
polished wood. The two friends were sitting at
an outdoor table at Las Fresas restaurant in San
José, Costa Rica. Skeeter Dawkins and Khadijah
Faroughi rounded out the foursome.

"When I ordered guanabana juice, I thought
I was going to get some sort of guava and banana
mixture. This looks like they took curdled skim
milk, added water, and then took the glass to the
back so that the cooks could each hawk a big,
honkin'—" Scott stopped when he noticed Khadi
looking at him.

Riley grinned. He knew Scott had been trying

really hard to use his verbal filter on this trip, albeit with limited success.

"Let's just say that it looks like the guanabana had a bad head cold just prior to being juiced."

"Thank you, Scott. Although I'm not sure that was much of an improvement over what you were going to say," Khadi laughed. "Just try it. You might be surprised."

"My lips and this twisted tribute to postnasal drip will never meet this side of—"

Scott's pledge was interrupted by a large hand grabbing the glass from in front of him. Bringing the glass to his lips, Skeeter downed the juice in one continuous motion. Riley's huge self-appointed bodyguard slammed the glass onto the table, wiped his mouth with Scott's napkin, then without a word turned back to the spot he had been watching down the street.

"Dude, that was my juice you just drank," Scott whined. "What's up with that?"

Riley took a sip of his fresh pineapple juice as he laughed. At the next table over, a little *tico* girl with enormous brown eyes and her hair in ponytails shyly turned for the fourth time to watch this big, happy American man. She jumped as Riley caught her eyes, then quickly spun back around when Riley shot her a quick wink. The girl's mom gave Riley a smile and a nod in appreciation of his acknowledging her daughter's attention.

These last two weeks in Costa Rica had been exactly what each of the four had needed to physically and emotionally recover from the events of the beginning of the year. This group had experienced a lot of pain and had shed—and spilled—a lot of blood in the search for Hakeem Qasim. Only now was Riley finally feeling ready to go back to Denver to face life again.

Riley Covington knew he faced a decision when he got home. Three months ago, he was an all-pro linebacker for the Colorado Mustangs. Then, suddenly, his old life had literally blown up in his face when a terrorist group bombed Platte River Stadium in Denver during a Monday night game. Nearly two thousand people were killed in that suicide attack.

Because of his post-Academy years in Afghanistan as part of the

Air Force Special Operations Command, Riley had been pulled back into the Special Forces life of guns and death. *Can I really go back to the Professional Football League as if nothing ever happened? I've been franchised by the team, so it's obvious they still want me. But do I have the passion anymore?*

"Riley . . . earth to Riley," Khadi's voice drew him back from his thoughts. She motioned to the waitress who was trying to put his food down.

"Oh, sorry," he said to the woman as he dropped his elbows off the table. His jaw immediately followed his elbows when he saw the plate that was put in front of him.

"Holy Mother Russia, what is that monstrosity?" Scott asked before realizing that two more were being delivered to him and Khadi.

"Pastor Jimenez told me, 'Order the *Ensalada de Fruta con Helado,*'" Riley said. "He told me it's just a simple fruit salad with ice cream." But Riley had never seen so much fruit. His plate was overflowing with strawberries and huge chunks of pineapple, watermelon, and mango. And if that wasn't enough, three enormous scoops of ice cream topped off the tropical explosion.

"I'll never be able to finish this myself," Khadi complained. "In fact, I would never forgive myself if I did."

"Don't look at me. He never told me to get just one for all of us. I just assumed."

"Yeah, well we all know where that gets us, Pach," Scott said. *Pach* was Riley's nickname back from his Air Force football days, when his speed and hitting power drew comparisons to the AH-64 Apache attack helicopter. "If I try to eat all this, it could make for a long, painful flight home. This stuff will shoot through me like . . . like . . . like refuse through a Canadian waterfowl," Scott finished lamely. "Khadi, this whole verbal filter thing is really a pain."

Khadi reached over and patted Scott's arm. "I know it is, and I appreciate it."

Scott called the manager of the restaurant over and had him take a picture of the three of them with their fruit salads and Skeeter with his Cuban sandwich.

"Nice smile, Skeet," Scott said as he checked out the picture in the digital viewer of his camera. "You look like someone just stole your brass knuckles."

"Mmm," replied Skeeter, who turned his attention back up the street.

"It's always great having you part of the conversation, my friend."

Riley, Khadi, and Scott attacked their fruit salads, effectively halting conversation other than the occasional "Oh, yeah" and "That's good."

A passing box truck spewed black diesel exhaust into the sidewalk café, causing Riley to cough and look up for the first time in five minutes. As he waved his hand in an attempt to clear the air in front of his face, his eyes were drawn to Skeeter, who was so intent on something up the street that he had completely ignored his plate. "Hey, Skeet, you okay? What's up?"

Skeeter turned around and noticed his sandwich but didn't take a bite. "I don't know, Pach. There's a couple of guys halfway down the block. Caught them looking this way a few times."

"Where're they at?"

"Your eleven."

Riley casually looked around Skeeter's big frame and saw the two men. One was sitting on a car, and the other was leaning against a building. Their close-cropped black hair and full beards seemed out of place on a Costa Rican street. Both men were smoking. As Riley watched, a third man walked out of a *farmacia* and joined them. "Don't look now, but your two have turned into three."

"Will you two relax?" Scott said as he turned around to look at the men. "You guys have been seeing bogeymen behind . . . Whoa, hold on. They do look a little more *hajji* than *tico*."

Khadi spotted the men also. "They sure do. And I've asked you to please quit using that term."

"What? *Hajji*? That's just what we called all the Middle East folk when we were out on patrol in the 'Stans."

"First of all, this isn't the 'Stans. And second, if that's true, then I'm a *hajji*, too." Khadi was from a Persian family who had fled Iran just prior to the fall of the shah.

"Come on, Khadi, that's ridiculous. *Hajji*s are guys. You'd be like a *hajjette* or something."

"Thanks, Scott. That's far less demeaning."

"They're moving," Skeeter broke in. As the four watched from the table, the three men walked to the far end of the block and turned out of sight.

"There! Did you see that last guy take a quick glance back before he rounded the corner?" Riley asked.

"I'm kind of getting a bad feeling about this," Khadi said. "We need to think about making ourselves scarce."

"Good call." Riley caught the waitress's attention and made a scribbling motion on his hand indicating he was ready for the check. "Skeeter, what are you packing?" As Riley's official bodyguard, Skeeter was the only one allowed by Costa Rican immigration to bring in firearms.

"Got my HK45 and a Mark 23."

"Good. Pass your Mark to Scott under the table. Now, there's no way anyone could know we're here, so this is probably total paranoia. But still, it's not worth taking chances. Scott and Khadi, as soon as I settle up, I want you two to walk to the corner and hang a left. Skeeter and I will cross and head up the next street to the right. We'll meet back at the hotel as soon as we can get there."

Khadi laid her hand on Riley's wrist. "I don't feel good about us all splitting up."

Riley knew that by "us all," Khadi meant the two of them. The feelings between Riley and Khadi had continued to grow over the months since they had met in the aftermath of the Platte River Stadium attack. The only thing separating them now was the only issue big enough to keep them apart—their religious beliefs. Both Khadi's Koran and Riley's Bible prohibited cross-faith unions. But, while both could control their actions, it was much harder to control their emotions.

"I understand, Khadi. But if these really are *haj*—bad guys, I don't want you or Scott anywhere around me. Skeeter can take care—"

A screech of tires made Riley jump.

"Don't matter now! Here they come," Skeeter yelled as he pushed Riley to the ground. Scott and Khadi dove for cover.

"Get inside," Riley yelled to the next table. The mother grabbed her daughter and ran through the front door.

A rusting red sedan tore around the corner where the three men had disappeared and sped up the street. One masked man was leaning over the roof of the car, and a second was hanging out the rear driver's-side window. Both were armed with AK-47s.

The sound of the assault rifles combined with the shattering glass of the windows sent screams up all around the restaurant. Riley prayed that the mother had made it to the ground in time. Scott and Skeeter returned fire with their handguns. A shot from Scott put a hole in the knit mask of the man leaning over the roof. He flew off his side window perch and exploded the rear glass of a parked car.

All of Skeeter's shots were directed at the driver, with one finally hitting its mark. The car swerved, caught a tire, and began to roll. On the third spin, Riley could see the other gunman ejected from his window. The last Riley saw of him was when the car landed on top of him then skidded up against a delivery truck.

Riley quickly turned toward Khadi. Blood streamed down her cheek from a shard of glass. "You all right?"

"I'm fine. How'd they know we were here?"

"I have no clue. Scott, Skeet, you guys okay?" Before they could answer, all four heard the familiar *whoosh* of an RPG launch. "Incoming!" Riley yelled.

They dove to the ground just as the rocket plowed into the restaurant, showering them with pieces of the building. The explosive wave slammed hard into Riley's body and drove the air out of his lungs. Plaster dust hung like a fog, burning his eyes. He lay there gasping for breath, trying to clear his brain. People screamed around him, but they sounded like they were down a long tunnel.

He didn't know how long he remained in that state before the sound of automatic weapons fire snapped him back to full consciousness. He looked to his left and saw Khadi moving slowly. Beyond her, Scott knelt behind two large fern planters, returning fire. Next to him, Skeeter was stretched out. There was blood on his forehead, and he wasn't moving.

"Scott, sit rep," Riley called out, looking for a situation report.

"Minimum three bogies with AKs hoofing it down the opposite

direction from our first batch. Skeet's out but breathing. I've got two more clips for his Mark, and three for his .45."

"Got it! Slide me the .45 and the clips!"

Scott complied.

Riley picked up the weapon and lost his fingers in the thick grooves of Skeeter's custom-made grip. However, Skeeter's gun was not unfamiliar to Riley, and he made a quick adjustment to his hold. Turning to Khadi, he said, "Scott and I are going to press these guys back. Soon as we're forward, I want you to check on Skeet."

Khadi tried to respond but started coughing instead. Tears from her grit-filled eyes were making streaks down her dusty face. She put a thumb up instead.

Turning back around, Riley said, "Okay, Scott. Just like back in Afghanistan, except this time we're outnumbered, outgunned, and surrounded by innocent civilians."

Scott grinned, "Look out, *hajji*, here we come!"

"On *go*, you cross the street and split the fire! Three—two—one—GO!" Riley began firing up the street as Scott bolted across. His peripheral vision caught Scott suddenly veering course. He turned in time to see Scott grab the first casualty's rifle off the pavement and dive behind a car. *The guy's good,* Riley thought.

He signaled Scott, who began to lay down cover fire. Running past the corner restaurant and across the intersection, Riley could hear the whiz of bullets all around him. The discordant scents of fresh baked bread and gunpowder hung in the air as he flattened himself against the side of a *panadería*. Chunks of pulverized brick showered his face from the corner of the building.

Riley looked back to see Scott ejecting the magazines that had been taped together and shoving the fresh box into his AK-47. *That'll give him thirty more rounds,* Riley thought as he slid a new clip into his handgun. *Not much, but it'll have to do.*

Suddenly, he saw Scott's eyes get big. Scott quickly signaled to him that there was another RPG ready to fire but that he wasn't in position to get a shot at it.

Riley leaned out just a touch and used the glass of the buildings up the street to give him a picture of where the gunmen were. His eye caught a dark shape with a long cylinder stepping out into the street.

Riley signaled Scott to lay fire and then spun around the corner. His first two shots were wild as he tried to get his bearings, but the next three hit their mark. As the man fell back, his RPG fired wildly into the sky. *Lord, don't let that land in a school yard,* Riley prayed as he quickly advanced. Running ahead, he saw another bogey lose half his face courtesy of Scott.

Where's the third one? Riley thought as he ran. *Scott said there were three. There!* At the next corner, a man was pulling off a mask as he rounded a corner at top speed. Riley signaled to Scott, who was now across the street and trying his best to match the linebacker stride for stride. Scott nodded, and they both went toward the corner.

Just before they reached it, the sound of a motorcycle engine kicking to life echoed down the narrow side street. Scott and Riley made a wide turn around the corner just in time to see the third gunman speeding away.

The sounds of sirens began to fill the air. The two men slumped against the building and tried to catch their breath.

"How'd they know, Scott?" Riley panted. "How could they possibly have known I was down here?"

"I don't know, man. But, believe me, I'm going to find out."

SATURDAY, APRIL 25, 4:18 P.M. MDT
ENGLEWOOD, COLORADO

The war room was divided. Less than three minutes remained, and tensions were high. Sweat and
stale coffee hung heavy in the air. The snap of a
pencil breaking between someone's fingers rico-
cheted through the room.

Exasperated, Todd Maule couldn't take it anymore. "How could you even think of pulling the
trigger on this one?" His tone made it more of an
accusation than a question.

"Son, watch your tone!" fired back the man in
charge, staring down Maule.

After an uncomfortable silence, Maule finally
looked away, trying to regain some semblance of
composure.

"Give me the biographical sketch again," the
team leader called out. Almost instantly the mam-
moth monitor displayed the image of a young
man. To the right of the picture was his life history right down to the latest videos he'd rented
from Blockbuster.

So much was riding on this decision. Guys had
been falling all afternoon, and the people in this
room never thought they'd be in this position. If

they let this man out of their grasp, they could potentially be paying for it for years to come.

"Boss, are you sure on this one? The political fallout if you make this move could be a lot more than we want to deal with," Mark Schlegel said, giving the voice of reason.

Less than one minute remained on the clock. The phones were ringing off the hook. All around the room legs were shaking and pens were tapping—anything to give vent to the nervous energy.

The man in charge stood stoically, glaring at the picture on the screen. Without moving, he verbally made a circuit of the room. "Adams?"

"I'm with you."

"Cherapy?"

"If you're okay with the fallout, then I'm okay with the decision."

"Schlegel?"

"I've got major reservations, but you're rarely wrong. I'll support you on it."

"Should I even ask you, Maule?"

"I think it's insane. Absolutely the worst decision you could make!"

Schlegel interjected with urgency, "Boss, fifteen seconds!"

Exhaling deeply, the decision-maker made up his mind. He picked up the direct line and said into the phone, "Do it!"

6:21 P.M. EDT
NEW YORK CITY

Jerome Taylor waited backstage by the curtains. He had been PFL commissioner less than one year and was still reeling from the Platte River Stadium attack in December. Many people had wanted him fired for not having better security in place for the big game. And he had been shredded in the press for his handling of the aftermath of the attack. On top of that, teams were already beginning to panic about the potential loss of revenue due to fan apprehension about attending upcoming games. Usually a man who thrived under pressure, he wasn't sure how much more of this he could take.

Taylor let his mind wander back to that dreadful day at Platte River Stadium. *What more could I have done? Who would have ever dreamed Sal Ricci could do such a thing?*

One of his first moves following the incident had been to institute a mandatory, highly detailed background check on every player, coach, front-office person—everyone, right down to the people who cleaned up the stadium after the games. Although the teams had fought back because of the huge expense, Taylor had pushed the decision through. Somehow the PFL had to get fan confidence back.

Taylor's assistant woke him from his fog telling him it was time. Taking a deep breath, he walked out onto the stage. Halfway across he was met with a slip of paper from the Mustangs' representative. Taylor read the paper and couldn't believe his eyes. *You have got to be kidding! Burton, what are you doing to me?* he thought angrily.

"Are you sure?" Taylor asked the man who had given him the paper—a little more bite was in his voice than he had intended.

"Down to the letter, sir."

Without saying another word, Taylor finished his walk to the podium. The heat from the lights just added to the sweat that had already begun streaming down his back. Grabbing the microphone, he briefly hesitated, then said, "With the twentieth overall selection in the first round, the Colorado Mustangs select out of the University of Texas, linebacker Afshin Ziafat."

4:23 P.M. MDT
INVERNESS TRAINING CENTER
ENGLEWOOD, COLORADO

Normally the Colorado Mustangs' war room at the Inverness Training Center exploded with jubilation after such an important pick was made—a pick that represented hours upon hours of research and work for everyone in the personnel department; a pick that meant an enormous investment on the part of the team to a player they really didn't know; a pick that would guarantee this young man millions of dollars and the assurance he would probably never have to work again after signing his name on the dotted line; a pick that would likely make that player an overnight household name—jerseys would be made, billboards would be erected, and endorsements would be signed.

Now, only four months after the attack by the Cause during a Monday Night Football game, the question was whether this organization, this locker room, and this city were prepared to embrace a player with a Muslim name. Within minutes of the announcement, blogs and online message boards filled with people giving their opinions of the Mustangs' move. Most of them were calling for Burton's job, if not his head.

A bevy of sports reporters waited desperately for Mustangs head coach Roy Burton to emerge. Some saw the selection as disturbing, while others saw it as an act of redemption or tolerance or maybe just insanity. All, however, saw it as a story that wouldn't die for a long time.

Burton burst through the door and mounted the podium as the room lit up with camera-mounted lights. The questions came crashing down like an avalanche.

"Whoa, whoa, whoa," Burton recoiled. "I know precisely what the question is going to be, so let me be clear. We held the twentieth overall selection, and our greatest need was at linebacker. We had to address that position, especially with the uncertainty of Riley Covington's status.

"Afshin Ziafat was the top collegiate linebacker. In fact, he was ranked as the fourth-best player in this year's draft. We never expected he would have dropped to number twenty. Face it: if the kid had a different last name, we wouldn't be having this conversation.

"As our pick came closer, we were faced with quite the dilemma. The next-best linebacker was ranked twenty-seventh overall on our board. You tell me one coach worth his salt who would bypass the fourth best player in the draft for the twenty-seventh. I don't care if the kid's mother named him Osama bin Laden; that's just simple math.

"Our other option was to draft not according to our need at linebacker but to go with the best available player after Ziafat, no matter the position. That player was a quarterback. Obviously, with Meyer we don't have a need at the quarterback position. After that was a center. With the production we've had out of Gorkowski, that wouldn't make much sense either. Our only other choice would have been to hope to get something worthwhile by trading down to a lower pick, but the offers we had were not in our best interest.

"So, we had the opportunity to select a number-four player with a number-twenty pick at a position that addressed our greatest need. Any other time in our history, this pick would be a no-brainer. We've pulled everything on this kid that we could find. He's a good kid—a bright kid."

Burton paused for a moment. "Look, bottom line is yes, he's from a background that scares some people, and we do have a wound that is still raw. But I see this as the next big step in the healing process for this team, this city, and ultimately, for this country. So, I made the pick, and I need to go call Ziafat to welcome him to the Mustang family. I hope all of you will extend him that same courtesy." Before the media could rebound, Burton sprang from the platform and was through the door.

/////////////////////////

Back in the Mustangs' war room, Burton called out, "Anything new?"

"It's been pretty quiet, Coach. We don't pick again until number fifty-two, so things will start speeding up around number forty-five," responded Mark Schlegel, Burton's right-hand man.

Burton dropped into his chair and heaved a deep sigh. The first round of the draft had been agonizingly slow. Virtually every team had taken its full ten minutes to make a selection or trade its pick. The second round would proceed much more quickly since each team received only seven minutes per choice. However, speed didn't equate to carelessness. Most organizations would continue to be very calculated with their selections; millions of dollars would still be at stake on a second-rounder.

After the first day, though, rounds three through seven would be much faster. The risk and the investment were far less, and the greatest hope was that a team could find a diamond in the rough during their allotted five minutes.

Everyone in the war room was watching the ESPN reports and speculating on who would be picked next. Two large, white boards flanked the giant television screen. The board to the left listed on thin magnetic strips the top one hundred offensive players. The board to the right did the same for the defensive prospects. Each strip listed a player's name, ranking, college, height, weight, and forty-yard-dash time. Once a player was selected, his strip was taken away, and the waiting game continued.

As Burton looked around the room, he could see that Todd Maule was still visibly upset.

Just then, Liberty University left tackle Bob Fiala, a player Maule had wanted, was selected with the twenty-eighth overall pick.

"That's perfect," Maule cried out. "We pass on Fiala for Ziafat! That's like passing on Riley Covington for Mahmoud Ahmadinejad."

Burton realized it was time to take control of the room again. Ignoring Maule's outburst, he said, "I want to make sure we have plenty of depth at linebacker, fellas, so over the next few rounds I want to stay defensive. Of course, if someone else has a significant drop, we'll need to consider that."

Again Maule couldn't resist. "Why do we need more at linebacker when we've got the Hezbollah Kid? I can see the headlines now. 'Ziafat Terrorizes the Quarterback'. Or 'Ziafat Intercepts a Bomb'. Oh yeah! The press is going to love this!"

"Son, I've had enough of you. This isn't a democracy around here," Burton said with authority. "I'll have your office boxed up and sent to you. Now get out of my war room."

With that Burton motioned to the off-duty Denver policeman who had been watching from the rear corner. Within seconds, Todd Maule found himself being escorted from the Inverness Training Center—permanently.

8:41 P.M. CRST
EDUARDO CASTILLO MEMORIAL HOSPITAL
SAN JOSÉ, COSTA RICA

"I expect a call back within the hour, and you better have some answers! Otherwise, I'll be on the phone with my *jefe*, and before you know it, he'll be on the phone with your *jefe* threatening to turn this into an international incident. So, how about you save us all some trouble, *amigo*, and get back to me with some names!" Khadi had been on the SatCom phone nonstop since yesterday's attack. She was trying to get identities on the gunmen from Costa Rican authorities, but that information was not coming easily.

Riley had been working out of Skeeter's hospital room, planning their return to the U.S. with help from his connections at Homeland Security. Whenever he wasn't on the phone, Riley was trying to calm an increasingly agitated Skeeter.

"Pach, I'm telling you I'm fine. Now get me out of here."

"Quit your bellyaching, Skeet. And while you're at it, leave the poor hospital staff alone. They're just trying to do their jobs, and they don't need you harassing them at every move. I told you I'd get you out just as soon as we've covered all our bases. Until then, I can't risk everyone's safety."

Scott had set up camp across the room next to the second-story window. The Regional Security Office of the U.S. Embassy had set up a perimeter around the hospital and had assured anonymity for the four friends. Scott had been alternating between keeping watch on the security detail outside and following a soccer game on ESPN Deportes on the wall-mounted television.

One of the nurses brought in a concoction that looked even worse than the guanabana juice the team had ordered the day before. She motioned for Skeeter to drink it.

"Down the hatch, tough guy," Scott teased.

Skeeter glared at the drink and then at Scott. "I've got something real special planned for you soon as we get home."

Scott smirked and glanced back up at the television. Watching the crawler reporting on the PFL draft creep along the bottom of the screen, he suddenly bolted upright. "Riley, you are not going to believe this!"

TUESDAY, MAY 5, 7:05 P.M. EDT
NEW YORK CITY

Summer had come early to New York. With the temperature pushing ninety, it had been all Ishaq Mustaf Khan—known by his friends as Isaac—could do to keep himself hydrated. Shunning the highly sugared electrolyte drinks preferred by his fellow workers on the Eudy & Sons warehouse loading docks, the fifty-three-year-old typically brought a two-liter bottle filled with a homemade tea brew that he had grown up on in Pakistan. Usually it did the trick, but not today. Whether it was the unexpected heat or just the fact that he was getting older, for the first time he could remember, Isaac struggled to keep up with the younger men.

Finding an unused bay as the next shift came on, he sat down with his legs hanging off the side. *It wasn't like this when I was young,* he thought. He absentmindedly tapped the empty two-liter against the edge of the loading bay and let his mind drift back to his hometown. Bela was an ancient village set in the middle of a fertile plain surrounded by hills. Isaac had been something special there. All the men had respected him for his size and strength. And all the women . . . Isaac's mouth curved into a small smile. *Yes, all the women.*

But then came the move. Eighteen years ago he had left his home and his family to come to America. Although he had no desire to do it, he still came without a fight. *Sometimes Allah's plans are a little different from our own.*

Since that time he had endured year after year of waiting. Now, as he felt the strength of his body beginning to fade, he wondered if his chance for glory would ever come. *Or have I simply been forgotten? If I have, so be it. Allah knows. Allah sees.*

"Isaac, there you are!"

Isaac turned to see Jimmie Holliday coming his way. Jimmie was in his early thirties but had the energy of a teenager. The younger man dropped next to Isaac and held out a Gatorade Cool Blue. "Yeah, I know it ain't that Pakistani potion you're always drinking, but you need something."

Isaac reluctantly accepted the plastic bottle, then turned his eyes back toward the ground. "Thanks."

"You okay? Don't mean to be slamming you or nothing, but you were kinda dogging it today."

Isaac took a sip of the Gatorade and grimaced at the sweetness. "Don't ever get old, my friend."

"Don't worry; I don't plan to."

They both sat lost in their own thoughts for a moment. Then, suddenly, someone flipped Jimmie's "on switch" again, and he said, "Hey, me and Hector and a couple other guys are going to catch that new Jackie Chan movie. Wanna come along and see some dudes get all chop-a-sockied?" Jimmie's hands flailed at the air.

Isaac smiled and looked at his friend. "Thanks, but I think I'll pass. I'm just going to sit here a while longer and see if my car will drive itself to me."

"What? Hey, how about I run and pull your car up for you? Seriously, I can do it for you, no problem."

"Careful, my friend, or you will insult me."

"No . . . what . . . man, I didn't mean anything by it. I was just—"

Isaac held up his hand with a grin. "It's a joke. You're fine. You go. And thanks for the drink."

Jimmie stood. "Okay. As long as you're sure you're all right."
Isaac held up his hand again in response.

"Okay, man. See you tomorrow."

Mohsin Ghani kicked his feet up on the corner of his new glass and hardwood executive desk. Tilting his chair back, he enjoyed the rich smell of the futuristic-looking leather chair.

The sailboats are out in full force this evening, Mohsin thought as he stared longingly at Lake Michigan. The only place he loved more than the law firm where he was just made junior partner was the water—a passion born out of his early years growing up in Al Mukalla in the Hadramawt coastal region of what was then South Yemen. *Only four more days until the weekend.*

Accepted into Northwestern University as part of an international scholarship program, Mohsin had decided early on to make the most of his chance in America. The first few years were miserable. It seemed he had to work as hard at his language skills as he did his coursework. Eventually, though, he graduated magna cum laude and gained entrance into the University of Chicago Law School.

That began another purgatory in his life. The international scholarship had covered his undergraduate degree only, and now Mohsin faced $35,000 a year in tuition plus living expenses. His schedule had become one of spending his days in class, his afternoons clerking for a local hack lawyer, his evenings waiting tables at an upscale steakhouse, and his nights studying case law. Somehow he had survived and was recruited right out of school by the prestigious law firm of Novak, Novak, & DuCharme.

Was it worth it? Mohsin asked himself for the hundredth time. The smell of the fresh paint, the coolness of the frosted glass under his arm, the enormous window facing Lake Michigan, and the keys in his pocket to the little black Mercedes SLK350 Roadster all seemed to scream, "Yes!" And Mohsin was inclined to agree with them.

There was only one event that could destroy the perfect life this thirty-two-year-old immigrant had worked so hard for. Mohsin prayed it would never come.

5:05 P.M. MDT
DENVER, COLORADO

Abdullah Muhammad was still sore, but the pain was well worth the story that he could now tell to his buddies. The three friends all sat on metal benches and were in various stages of undress. Loud voices echoed off the cement and tile surrounding them, and the steam from the showers hung heavy in the air.

"So, I'm on foot chasing this guy down Kentucky, and he is *moving*. He splits off Kentucky and starts heading down Clayton. I'm still keeping up with him pretty good, and he knows it. So, he heads for the fences."

"Ohhh, the fences," said Reggie Brooks, laughing. "I hate the fences!"

"Yeah, but get this—he gets to the gate and he literally flips into the backyard. I mean, one step and over! And check this out—I actually make eye contact with him as he's flipping over."

"Serious?"

"Dead! Totally freaked me out. So I'm thinking, 'Great, I'm chasing one of those . . .' what do you call those dudes who go running and jumping all over buildings and parking garages and stuff?"

"Free runners?" offered Dan Elijah.

"Yeah, I'm chasing one of those free runners. So I get to the gate, and I say, 'Forget this,' and I crash the thing just in time to see him flipping over the next fence. I hightail it across the yard, but while I'm doing my Abdullah the Magnificent over the fence, I see the birdman launching into the next yard."

"I'da just shot him," Reggie laughed.

"Believe me, I thought about it. So we do this for a couple more yards. Then, all of a sudden after a particularly graceful flip, the guy lets out a scream. I'm thinking, 'Cool, the bad guy's landed wrong and broken an ankle or something.'

"I catch up to him and look over the fence. Turns out the old lady who owns that yard is big into metal sculpture and has built herself a little forest of very pointy evergreen trees."

By now the three friends were laughing so hard they could barely speak. Reggie finally got enough control to ask, "Just how big were the trees in this little forest?"

"Big enough to slice the guy's Achilles and impale him in three separate places!"

"Ohhh," Reggie and Dan exclaimed together.

"The guy's lying there screaming and bleeding. I radio for medics and hop the fence, and I'm trying to calm him down a bit while we wait for the EMTs, but I was laughing so hard I don't think I was much help," Abdullah laughed, rubbing his shoulder where he had hit the gate.

"You get that checked out?" Dan asked, finally calming down.

"Nah. I'll probably pay for it in the morning, but it's all good."

This was Abdullah's fifth year with the Denver Police Department. Born and raised in Denver, he knew this city like only a native could. When told to join the police force, he had jumped at the opportunity. What could be better than to cruise the streets—his streets—with a gun and a whole lot of power?

Abdullah watched his friends as Dan began a story of his own. Why didn't they understand? Why couldn't they see how messed up things were? There were times when Abdullah wanted to tell them everything just to see how they'd react. But he knew he couldn't. They were brainwashed just like everyone else.

Abdullah knew he had a special calling. And part of that calling was isolation, pretending, never letting anyone get close enough to see who he really was.

But someday . . . he thought. *Someday my time will come. Then my true identity will be revealed.*

4:05 P.M. PDT
SAN FRANCISCO, CALIFORNIA

The pepper white MINI Cooper S convertible tucked into a parking spot on the third level of the garage. Immediately, the top began closing. Naheed Yamani checked her face in the rearview mirror, then bent her five-foot-ten-inch body through the car door as the roof snapped into place.

49 Geary Street was one of Naheed's favorite places. This one building held more than twenty art galleries and a number of rare-book dealers. Naheed could spend days in here without it getting old. But today was not the day for browsing. Her friend June Waller had an exhibition opening in just under an hour at the prestigious Vorreiter Gallery, and Naheed had promised to be there a half hour ago to help make sure everything was just right.

The granddaughter of a Saudi prince, Naheed had always known the finer things. But life in Saudi Arabia—even a privileged life—wasn't for her. Six years ago, when she turned eighteen, she'd begged her grandfather to let her move to San Francisco on the pretense of pursuing her sculpting in a place that truly appreciated art. Grandfather, always a pushover for his many granddaughters, had happily obliged. He had set Naheed up in a Nob Hill loft that doubled as her studio and had given her a generous allowance. So far she hadn't sold a piece, but that was okay. Becoming a great artist really wasn't the ultimate purpose of her being here anyway.

Her heels clicked loudly on the tile floors as she brushed past people she didn't know and nodded to people she did. Naheed was used to being noticed. Her midnight black hair contrasted with her light mocha eyes in a way that often made people take a second look. Today, her clinging designer T-shirt and skintight jeans gave two more excuses for double takes.

A friend from FiftyCrows stepped out of his gallery and grabbed Naheed's arm. "Sweetheart, I've got that—"

"Sorry, can't right now, Richard," she said apologetically, shaking herself free of his grasp. "I'm late for June's setup."

Three galleries up was her destination; June stood out front. Racing up to her, out of breath, Naheed threw herself on her friend's mercy. "June, I'm so sorry. I just totally lost track of time."

June was laughing. "Girl, when have you ever been *on time*?"

"Unfortunately, that is only too true. Now, hurry, if we start setting up now we can make up for lost time."

"Setting up? Pardon me, but this is the big time. I don't do setup. I now have people who set me up," June said, trying her best to sound pretentious. Unfortunately, she was just too nice and down-to-earth to pull it off. "Actually, the gallery took care of the layout."

Naheed was confused. "Then why did you ask me to come down here so early?"

"What time would you have shown up if I had told you the exhibition *started* at five o'clock?"

"Four thirty?" Naheed attempted.

"You lie like a rug! You would have come rushing in here around six at the earliest."

Naheed grinned sheepishly. "Okay, puppet-master, how are you going to manipulate my life next?"

June danced her hand above her friend's head and said, "The puppet-master says we must go in and have a drink. Come on, my nerves are on hyperdrive."

The two walked arm-in-arm into the gallery and headed to what would soon be the open bar. The bartender was just polishing the last of his glasses.

Naheed flashed her best flirty smile, put her hand on his arm, and said, "Any chance of mixing the artist and her best friend a couple of Gibsons, two onions each?"

The bartender, looking into her eyes and then letting his gaze slowly slide down until it hit the floor, took the bait. "Can I see a couple of IDs from you little whippersnappers?" he asked with a smile as he began mixing the drinks.

"I'm so sorry, young man," Naheed said, playing her part to the hilt, "but I left it in my car. You'll just have to trust me when I tell you I'm sixty-three."

"Wow, you sure have aged well."

"It's because I'm well preserved," she said, picking up her glass. "Ta-ta."

The two friends walked away with drinks in hand. "How do you do that?" June whispered.

Naheed knew June had always been a little jealous of her ease around men. "You just have to remember who has the power."

As Naheed looked around the gallery, she was again struck by

June's photographs. The subjects' eyes were what always got to Naheed—the emptiness and pain of the eyes. June was very socially conscious, and most of her pictures were of women and children who were victims of poverty or abuse. "You amaze me. I don't know how you do it, but somehow you seem to capture a person's whole life in one photo."

June blushed, then said, "I think it's because I just feel them— you know, hurt with their hurts—and it somehow comes out in the picture."

The two continued to walk quietly, looking over the exhibit. The sound of a ring interrupted their thoughts. Reaching into the very tight gap in her front pocket, Naheed pulled out her phone. "This is Naheed. Speak."

"Awake, O Sleeper," came a deep, accented voice, and then the signal abruptly cut.

Naheed's martini glass shattered on the tile floor, while a tremble that began deep inside her soon shook her entire body.

Riley saw the twinkle in her beautiful brown eyes. He knew what was coming next but felt himself powerless to stop it. Slowly she moved her face toward his. Riley couldn't help but smile in anticipation.

When they were just a few inches apart, she stuck out her tongue and proceeded to blow the biggest, wettest raspberry Riley had ever experienced.

"Alessandra Ricci, what are you doing?" a mortified Meg Ricci scolded her fourteen-month-old daughter. "Riley, I'm so sorry!"

"That's okay," he replied, more to the little girl who was lying on top of him as he was stretched out on the living room carpet. "As long as she doesn't mind being my towel!" In a flash, Riley's big hands snatched Alessandra off his chest and dropped her stomachfirst onto his face, rubbing her all around to dry off the spit. This quickly deteriorated into a five-minute-long belly-furber fest that eventually left both Riley and Alessandra exhausted.

Ever since his friend and former teammate Sal Ricci had been killed last February, Riley had been coming regularly to spend time with Sal's widow, Meg, and little Alessandra. "Just because a man doesn't turn out to be who you thought he was doesn't mean that his wife and daughter should pay the price, too," he'd often told naysayers who criticized him for his loyalty to these two innocent victims.

After giving one more kiss to the black hair on the top of the little girl's head, Riley rolled himself up off the floor and dropped down in a leather chair. Opposite him, Meg set down the crossword puzzle book she had been working on. Riley noticed that none of the squares had been filled in.

"You are so good with her," Meg complimented him.

"It's hard not to be." Riley tossed a soft throw pillow from the chair onto Alessandra's back. She giggled and continued to crawl away.

"So, tell me what really happened to you down in Costa Rica. The news tells all these stories, but the former reporter in me doesn't fully believe anything I hear from them."

Riley sighed. "You know, Meg, I'd really rather just forget about it. I'm having too nice a time to bring that junk up. Besides, what I really want to know is how you're doing."

"That's fine, Riley, you can tell me your top secret stories another time," Meg responded with a little irritation in her voice. "As for me, that lawyer you sent to me has been a huge help. She's blocked anyone from seizing our assets, and she made sure the life insurance is paying up. I don't think we'll have anything to worry about."

"Excellent. So, back to my original question—how are *you* doing?"

Although Meg's voice remained steady, Riley could see her eyes begin to tear up as she answered, "I'm fine, Riley. Really I am. Other than the loneliness, the fact that all my neighbors hate me, and the well-deserved reputation I now have of being the stupidest woman in the world, everything's just dandy." Her tears finally let loose, and Meg covered her face with her hands.

Riley leaned forward in his chair. "Meg, if you're the stupidest woman, then I'm the stupidest man. We were all taken in by Sal."

Dropping her hands, she cried, "Yeah, but I married him; I slept with him; I had his child!"

Silence filled the room, except for the soft sound of Meg's sobs. Riley, feeling very awkward, said, "You mentioned your neighbors. Have you been harassed at all? Gotten any threats?"

"No, nobody is that blatant. But I can see it in their eyes—that is, when they will at least look at me. Even Jill from next door has become cold toward me." Meg pulled a couple of tissues from a nearby box and began dabbing her eyes.

Oops, Riley thought, *I probably should have offered those to her.* His mind raced to come up with some other conversation to break the silence.

"Have you ever thought of moving? You know, starting fresh again somewhere?"

Meg sighed and dropped the tissues on a side table. "Of course. My folks have even invited me to come live with them up in Fort Collins. But Alessandra and I have been through so much, I just don't think I'm ready to pack everything up and leave home. Besides, if we tried to sell this place, we'd end up taking a huge hit. Who'd want to buy Sal Ricci's old house?"

Riley saw his opportunity to hop back on his white stallion. "That kind of stuff, Meg, you don't worry about. You let me worry about it. You just do what you need to do."

"I know, Riley. Thanks." Then, bravely trying to brighten things up, Meg asked, "So, do you want to stay for dinner? I make a mean peanut-butter-and-banana sandwich. Just ask Alessandra."

Riley laughed. "No, I better get going. I've got to—"

"No, no, you don't need to explain anything to me," Meg interrupted.

"What? No, seriously, Meg. I've got to go meet—"

"Riley! I said you don't have to explain," Meg insisted as she stood up to find where Alessandra had wandered off. "We're just thankful for any time we can get with you."

Meg found her daughter crawling under the baby grand piano tucked in the front corner of the room. She picked her up off the floor and said, "Alessandra, give Uncle Riley a kiss before he goes."

Riley took Alessandra from Meg's hands and gave her a quick tickle and a kiss. Alessandra, for her part, tried to start the previous game again by spraying raspberries all over Riley's face. Meg reached around and covered her daughter's mouth, then set her back down on the ground.

After walking Riley to the door, she put her arms around him. Riley responded to the hug, but when he began to break off the embrace, Meg kept holding on. Sensing that she must be a little emotional, he held on to her longer. He could feel her breath against his neck, slow and steady.

Finally, just as it was really beginning to get awkward for Riley, Meg pulled back. She looked at him with dry eyes and said, "Thank you, Riley, for being the man in our lives."

Riley stammered something like "Sure" and "No problem" and went out the door.

As he walked to the car where Skeeter was waiting in the passenger seat he began trying to process what had just happened. But as soon as he started his Denali and TobyMac's *Portable Sounds* began blaring through the speakers, the incident was quickly filed away in the "To Be Reviewed Later" section of his brain.

5:17 P.M. MDT
DENVER, COLORADO

"I walk up to the kid and motion for him to roll down his window." Reggie Brooks had taken the floor and now had Dan Elijah and Abdullah in stitches. "He's all nervous, and I can tell his mind is trying to figure out what to say to me. I ask him for his docs, and as he's fumbling through his wallet, he says, 'I just want you to know right off, officer, that these are not my pants.'"

The two-member audience completely lost it.

Reggie continued, "I'm like, 'Not your pants?' And he's all nodding and saying, 'Yeah, they're my friend's, so any drugs or anything that might be in them belong to him and not me.' So, I'm like, 'Uh, son, you probably ought to step out of the car.'"

Abdullah's cell phone drew him away from the story. Still laughing, he reached into his locker to grab the RAZR out of his jeans pocket. Flipping it open, he said, "Abdullah."

"Awake, O Sleeper."

Abdullah sobered up in an instant. He had rehearsed so many times in his head what he would do if he ever got this call that he kicked into autopilot. He quickly slipped his shirt over his head and grabbed his jeans.

"Everything okay, man?" asked Dan. "You look like you've seen a ghost."

But Abdullah didn't hear him. "Sorry, boys, gotta go," Abdullah said to Reggie and Dan and ran off before the other two had a chance to protest.

6:19 P.M. CDT
CHICAGO, ILLINOIS

Mohsin played with the remote control, lowering and raising the projection screen at the far end of the mini conference table in his office. He tried a new button, and suddenly vertical blinds shot out of a hidden door, causing him to jump and then burst out laughing. The blinds swept across the windows. Another button twisted the blinds closed, and still another twisted them back open.

His cell phone rang. Mohsin checked the caller ID on the front of the phone. *Unavailable* was written across the screen. This was the third unavailable call in the last three minutes. He silenced the ringer and began looking for the remote button that would open his television cabinet.

His phone rang again. Exasperated, Mohsin snatched the phone up, hit Send, and yelled, "What?"

What he heard on the other end caused the phone to slip from his hand onto the glass desktop. A tear rolled down his cheek.

Suddenly, he reached under his $4,000 desk, snatched up his leather-wrapped waste can, and purged every ounce of food from his body.

7:23 P.M. EDT
NEW YORK CITY

Isaac Khan forced himself to finish the last of the Gatorade. Although he still felt a little weak, he was definitely on the upswing. Looking at the empty bottle, he thought, *If they could just make a flavor that didn't taste like a three-year-old's birthday party.*

He launched the empty at a greasy metal barrel that served as a trash can. The bottle clipped the rim, bounced to the ground, then circled to a stop. *I probably ought to get that. . . . Nah, somebody will pick it up eventually.*

He willed himself to slide off the loading bay so he could make his way to the car. His cell phone stopped him. Reaching into his shirt pocket with his grimy hands, he pulled out an eight-year-old Motorola flip phone that was stained the color of the grungy fingers that held it.

"Hello?"

Isaac stopped in his tracks. After hearing the words on the other end, Isaac dropped to his knees on the hard cement and wept.

Awake, O Sleeper! Awake! Awake! he sang in his head. Isaac turned his face up and raised his hands to the sky. "After all these years of slumber, I am finally awake. Oh, Allah, you are so merciful to take notice of your servant. Whatever you want of me, I will do. All you need do is ask. Thank you for not forgetting me. You truly are great."

His prayer complete, Isaac jumped to his feet and ran to his car. The years fell off him with every step he took. By the time he put the keys in his car door, he felt like the eighteen years he had wasted on the docks had been given back to him by Allah as a reward for his long-suffering patience.

MONDAY, MAY 11, 8:30 A.M. MDT
ENGLEWOOD, COLORADO

Is dread *the right word?* Riley asked himself. *What about* disgust*? Or maybe* revulsion*? Or maybe something not quite so strong, like* hesitant*, or a fancy word like* trepidation*?*

Driving to his first day of minicamp, Riley tried to put a name to how he was feeling. *No, nothing fancy.* Dread*'s the right word. Pure and simple dread!* Riley's reluctance to start minicamp was an entirely new phenomenon. He had always loved football. And days like this used to really get him excited. Minicamp was a time to enjoy the workouts and the game without having to deal with all the pressures that came during the season.

Even back in high school, Riley had counted the days until the summer practices started. The competition, the challenge of meeting and exceeding his personal goals, learning new team systems, and everything else that embodied football were things that had gotten his adrenaline pumping from the time he was a kid. But now . . .

Riley hit the brakes hard at a yellow light, causing the car behind him to screech to a halt. When the guy laid on his horn, it was all Riley could do to keep himself from getting out of the car and explaining to the man—in no uncertain terms—that yellow means slow down. He resisted the urge, though, because first of all, he didn't need the added drama in his life, and second, any other day he would have just blown through the light. *It's not that guy's fault I'm trying to stretch my drive to take as long as possible.*

"You want me to go back there and shoot him?" Skeeter asked from the passenger seat.

Riley glared at him in response.

Deep down, Riley knew the reason for his dread. There were still deep wounds from the end of last season—the attack on Platte River Stadium, his own experience of being held hostage and tortured, the betrayal and death of people he loved. *Lord, please give me the strength to follow through with the calling You've given me. Help me be a light, even when I feel the darkness permeating my very soul.*

Riley turned on his stereo and pushed the button for disc five. The stark snare-drum opening of U2's *War* album filled the interior of his black Yukon Denali. Riley used the steering wheel as his own snare and began singing along when Bono's voice launched in.

Out of the corner of his eye, he could see a smirk form on Skeeter's forward-looking face. Riley pretended to ignore him. *If I'm going to have to live with this giant walking shadow, he's going to have to deal with my habits. I've already lost my privacy. I'm not going to sit here and shut up just because he's riding shotgun.*

Riley kept singing in his off-key baritone, slipping into an auditorily uncomfortable falsetto when Bono rose out of his range. However, when the song reached its chorus, Riley quickly hit the power button. "Sunday Bloody Sunday" ventured a little too close to what he was trying to forget.

Unfortunately, the silence left him alone with his thoughts.

Another issue that concerned him was having to face the coaching staff and Robert Taylor, the Mustangs' public relations manager. It had been two weeks since Riley had returned any of their phone calls—something he was sure he'd have to answer for this morning.

The reason for his prolonged silence was that as late as this morning, he still wasn't sure what he was going to do about football.

At 7:30 a.m., Riley had been on a conference iChat with his parents and his grandpa. During the off-season, he had purchased MacBooks for all of them so that they could better keep in contact through the video-chatting program.

From the left side of his laptop screen, Mom and Dad had both wished him well for the day and said they'd be praying for him. But it was Grandpa's words from the right side of the monitor that had stuck with him.

"I know today is going to be a tough day for you, son. Your folks and I just want you to know how proud we are of you. As you head out today, try to keep your eye on the big picture. We've talked before about how, from time to time, you're going to face situations that may seem too much to take. It's times like this you've got to remember that God won't give you more than you can handle. He's promised that, so you can take it to the bank."

"Yeah, I know, Grandpa," Riley had replied. "I just don't know if I still have football in me."

Grandpa had smiled and said, "I understand. A lot has happened. I was just thinking back to the day you were drafted. Remember the excitement you felt? The feeling of a dream coming true? The Mustangs fulfilled that dream of yours. When you finally signed that contract with them, you were telling them that in return for that dream, you would give them your best. Riley, as long as you are out there giving your best, your best will always be good enough."

After disconnecting the videoconference, Riley had sat at his kitchen table rubbing his face with his hands. Riley knew Grandpa was right. He had made a commitment, something he didn't take lightly. A quick prayer later, he had gathered up Skeeter and his gear and headed toward the garage.

Now that he was so close to Inverness Training Center, the apprehension was growing stronger than ever. He knew there would be unpleasant people he would have to see and verbal lumps he would have to take. But there was one group of people that he just didn't have the strength to deal with this first day back. So for the last five minutes of his trip to the training center, Riley turned his thoughts toward plotting all the creative ways he could avoid facing the media today.

It had been less than a month since Whitney Walker had joined Fox 31 News. The competition among reporters was fierce, and she knew there were hundreds of other applicants who would jump at the chance to take her job. The window for her to step up and make a name for herself was small. So she had decided to "catch the worm" and had gotten to the Inverness Training Center early with her cameraman, Mark Sandoval, to begin gathering sound bites from Mustang players as they straggled in.

Unfortunately, things were not going well. Sure, she was getting all the usual comments: "We're just looking for a fresh start" and "I think we have what it takes to go all the way this year." But that was the problem; they were just the *usual comments.* Every other reporter was hearing the same thing. There was absolutely nothing that would help her stand out in the crowd. Whitney hated to admit it, but she was bored with her material.

She sat down at one of several green picnic tables that were located under a covering next to the east practice field. Sandoval sat at the next table over, which was a relief. All morning, anytime she looked at him, he'd been staring at her. He would quickly look away, but it was still giving her a bit of the creeps.

It was hardly as if she wasn't used to the attention. Whitney Walker was a knockout, and she knew it. Her long blonde hair framed a face that on anyone else might be considered a little long. But the perfect balance of her features, along with the surprisingly rich emerald green eyes that everyone was constantly accusing her of aiding with contacts, created in her a beauty that was difficult not to stare at.

While Whitney was not averse to using her beauty to her advantage—whether it was to further her career or to get out of the occasional speeding ticket—she also wanted to be taken seriously, something men seemed to have difficulty doing. To this end, she had graduated from UCLA in the top 5 percent of her class and was now working hard to develop an on-air personality that showed true professionalism yet still drew the viewers in.

That desire to be taken seriously was what was plaguing her today. The one thing that would brighten Whitney's day today would be to talk to Riley Covington. He was *the* story of minicamp. *Football star, national hero, and let's face it, extremely good-looking guy—a few minutes with him would brighten any girl's day,* Whitney thought with a smile.

The problem was that getting to him seemed near impossible. The Mustangs' media relations department was already busy earning their salaries for the day trying to keep the mob of reporters away from the players' parking lot in anticipation of Riley's arrival. *If I try there, I'm just another goldfish in an already crowded fishbowl. Think— what would Riley do?*

Whitney had spent a lot of time researching Riley since taking this job, and in many ways she felt like she already knew him. *He's always ready to do a scheduled interview, but he still avoids media whenever he can. He has to know what's waiting for him here. If I were him, you couldn't catch me dead driving into the insanity of the players' parking lot.*

Then an idea popped into her mind.

"Come on, Mark," she said to her cameraman, "let's try something different."

Sandoval, who was in the middle of a Butterfinger bar, stuffed the uneaten half of the candy into his pocket and enthusiastically followed Whitney, no doubt hoping for something to break the minicamp routine.

Walking quickly, they passed the crowd in the parking lot. Whitney motioned for Sandoval to slow down so they wouldn't attract notice as they exited the gates and excused their way through the crowd of fans who had gathered to try to get autographs when the players pulled up to punch in the gate code.

Once through the fans, they sped up again, going all the way around to the front of the main building. Just as they rounded the front corner, Whitney saw that her hunch was going to pay off. Fifty feet in front of her, Riley Covington was stepping out of a black Yukon Denali parked in the guest lot.

"There he is!" she shouted to Sandoval and began hustling over until she saw another person step out of the passenger side.

This other man was, as best she could tell, six feet seven and solid as a tree trunk. His hair was shaved tight against his scalp, and his dark skin showed lighter scars in a number of areas around his face and head. He was dressed all in black, and as he stepped out, his right hand was tucked in the left side of his sport coat.

Gathering all her courage, Whitney moved forward to intercept Riley before he made it to the building's front door. She knew he had spotted her when he answered his cell phone even though she hadn't heard it ring. A bigger problem was that the other man had spotted her too, and with surprisingly few strides cut off her progress with his body.

"Riley, please?" she called out, trying to look around the human roadblock. When he looked at her, she made a dainty little dip with her knees, and pled with her eyes for him to stop. Riley paused, smiled thinly, and put his cell phone away.

"It's okay, Skeeter," he said as he walked up to her.

Whitney held out her hand to him, knowing the value of physical contact. "Hi, Mr. Covington. My name is Whitney Walker with Fox 31. Is there any way I could talk you into just a quick interview?" She could see that he was annoyed at having to stop, so she was laying the charm on thick.

"Sure, Miss Walker, a very quick one. I have to get in," Riley said matter-of-factly.

"Please, call me Whitney," she said with a flash in her eyes.

When Riley didn't respond, it threw her off her game a bit. She had the interview all planned out—flirt a little to loosen him up, ask him about his off-season, get him to talk about the tragic and heroic events surrounding his time with the counterterrorism division, then transition to discussing the selection of Afshin Ziafat in the first round of the draft—a perfect journalistic coup that was bound to get her noticed by her higher-ups.

But there was something about Riley that made her uneasy. Whitney had never felt so much pain and struggle in one person before. There was a sadness in his eyes that made her want to wrap her arms around him and tell him everything would be okay. She tried to ask the first question but couldn't get it out. The silence became awkward.

"Miss Walker?" Riley asked.

After a few moments, Whitney finally spoke, amazing herself with her words even as they came out of her mouth. "Mr. Covington, I know you've been through a lot. I want you to know how sorry I am for what you've experienced. I was just hoping that . . . that maybe you would be willing to give us a station tag?"

Riley's shock showed in his eyes. "Uhh . . . sure."

Whitney quickly wrote out some words on a slip of paper and handed it to him.

He read it over, then smiled at the camera and said, "Hi, I'm Riley Covington of the Colorado Mustangs, and you're watching Fox 31 Denver."

Whitney smiled. "Thank you, Mr. Covington. I hope you have a great day."

This time Riley reached for her hand and shook it. "No, thank you. And please, call me Riley."

"Do you mind if . . . ?" Whitney asked shyly, holding out her business card to him.

Riley took it with a smile, then turned and walked toward the entrance of the training center. Whitney watched until the doors closed behind him and his friend.

Sandoval's angry voice interrupted her reverie. "You just had the interview of a lifetime! I mean, that was one that people would be telling stories about for years to come! What happened?"

Without looking at him, she said, "I don't know, Mark. I honestly don't know."

As she walked back around the building, she couldn't help but wonder two things—whether that card she had handed Riley would ever produce a call, and whether or not her heart would ever slow down.

MONDAY, MAY 11, 9:00 A.M. MDT
INVERNESS TRAINING CENTER
ENGLEWOOD, COLORADO

Heads turned and conversations died when Riley
and Skeeter passed through the frosted glass doors
into the Mustangs locker room. Riley suddenly
felt like he had walked in wearing his mother's
housecoat. Never had he felt uncomfortable in a
locker room . . . until now.

"Skeet, I think I'm okay in here," he whispered
to his friend. "Would you mind putting an eyeball
on the media folk outside?"

"Yes, sir," Skeeter replied. He gave the staring
faces one last look over, then walked back out the
doors.

Activity slowly returned as Riley made his way
to his locker. Most of the players were already sitting under their nameplates performing various
prepractice rituals. Some taped their wrists; others rubbed lotions on their legs. More than one
man had his playbook on his lap while he tried
to memorize new codes and their corresponding
actions.

Riley felt out of place as he walked past the
lockers. Most of the players that he knew greeted
him with a "What's up, Covington?" or "Hey,

Pach." But since he hadn't shown himself around the Mustang facility for any of the precamp workouts, there were a lot of faces he'd never seen before. It was a little disorienting being somewhere so familiar but seeing new people sitting in old friends' places.

At least thirty or thirty-five of the players here were new to Riley, but he knew he wouldn't take time to get to know many of them. The reality of the PFL was that stints with teams tended to be quite short, and careers typically ended sooner rather than later. A vast majority of those thirty or thirty-five new faces would not still be here by the time the season rolled around.

Riley continued his journey, but when he passed by Keith Simmons's locker, he stopped and did a double take. Sitting back by his street shoes were books by C. S. Lewis and Lee Strobel. Then, set out proudly so everyone could see, was a beautiful two-tone leather New Living Translation Study Bible with *Keith Simmons* embossed in gold lettering right on the cover. *I think Keith's got some 'splaining to do,* Riley thought with a surprised smile.

His smile was short-lived, though. The locker three down from Simmons's belonged to Riley. The one just past his had, until the end of last season, belonged to his best friend, Sal Ricci. Memories of conversations, jokes, and pranks flooded Riley's mind—like the time he had filled the toes of Sal's new ECCO Supercross shoes with shaving cream. Sal was quick to avenge himself, substituting Riley's aftershave with Johnnie Walker Red.

Riley smiled sadly at the memories. But then reality set in—grief, betrayal, torture, all culminating in a final gun battle. Riley closed his eyes and felt again the warm wetness of Sal's—Hakeem's—shattered head on his face. His stomach turned.

Riley took a deep breath to steady himself, thankful that everyone seemed to be giving him the space he needed. He took the final steps to his locker and stood in front of it, trying hard not to look next to him. But the more he tried to avoid looking, the more he felt drawn that direction. Finally he gave in, and what he saw took his breath away a second time.

On the nameplate above the locker was a piece of white athletic tape—a sure indication that the player was a rookie. And on that piece of tape was written *AFSHIN ZIAFAT #59.*

Oh, Lord, what are you doing to me? This was too much, even for the normally easygoing Riley. He felt his face reddening with anger. *What am I even doing here? You know, I gave it my best shot today! If I bolt out now, I can try to explain tomorrow. If they fine me, they fine me!*

He turned to leave the way he had come but was met by Robert Taylor, head of Mustangs public relations. "Hey, Riley, how've you been?" Taylor asked with a big smile on his face. Without waiting for an answer, he continued, "Listen, buddy, there's a group of national guys outside aching to talk to you. You got a quick second?"

"Not right now," Riley shot back a little more aggressively than he had intended.

Surprise showed on Taylor's face. "Okay, what should I tell them?"

Regretting each word even as he said it, Riley leaned into Taylor's personal space and said, "Tell you what, I'll let you know when I'm ready. Until then, I don't really give a rip what you tell them." Riley turned to his locker and began fiddling with his workout clothes until Taylor walked away.

Once he was alone, he placed his hands on either side of his open locker and slowly began doing standing push-ups with his head down. *Come on, man, Robert's your friend. After all he's done for you, you're going to treat him like that?* Slowly he moved in and out of his maple-wood locker, his head brushing against his workout uniform with each pass. *Father God, if I'm going to survive this, I'm going to need Your help. Protect me from any more surprises, and please help me to get a grip.*

"Riley?" came a voice from behind him, stopping him halfway through another descent. While he couldn't know for sure who had said it, with the way his day was going he had a pretty good idea.

Riley straightened up and turned around.

There stood a young guy with a huge white smile on his face and his hand held out. "Riley, I'm Afshin Ziafat. It's an honor to meet you."

Riley slowly met Ziafat's hand and said coldly, "Likewise." *'Likewise?' Brilliant!* Riley silently chastised himself.

Suddenly, something very large slammed into him, knocking him back into his locker. Riley looked up to see another big smile beaming down at him.

"Keith, what's up?" Riley managed.

"What's up? Bro, you can't even begin to imagine! We seriously have to talk."

"No doubt. I saw you were reading C. S. Lewis's *Screwtape Letters*. Not exactly what I would have pegged you to have on your library list."

Keith pretended to be offended. "What? Do you think all I do is sit around playing Xbox and reading back issues of *Modern Black Male*? Wait, modern blackmail! Get it? I crack myself up!"

"I'm glad to see you amuse yourself," Riley said, smiling despite himself.

"I'm a regular one-man comedy show," Keith said proudly. "But seriously, we do need to talk. That little brush with death in December really got me thinking. I ended up going in to see my sister's pastor, and next thing you know I'm on my knees in his office giving my life to the Lord."

"Simm, that is so awesome!"

"Isn't it, though? But I've got so much more to tell you about. Why don't we grill out at your place this week? You do the cooking, and I'll do the talking and the eating."

"How could I pass up an opportunity like that? How about Friday night after practice?"

"I'm on it like Gorkowski on a pork chop!"

Without warning, the heavy thump of Buju Banton echoed through the locker room's sound system, causing many of the players to instinctively jump up and break into a reggae dance.

"Speaking of . . ." Riley said, pointing to center Chris Gorkowski, who was deep into his own artistic interpretation of the song that looked very much like a Samoan fire dance, complete with extended tongue.

"I see you, Snap," Riley said, laughing.

Gorkowski smiled in return, revealing his tobacco-stained teeth. Riley hadn't seen the big man since the attack at the stadium when he had had to slap some sense into the center in order to get him to safety. Although the two had never gotten along in the past, Riley hoped things might be a little different now.

"Two minutes! Two minutes!" came the voice of one of the coaches, sounding the alarm for Coach Roy Burton's team meeting. The impromptu beach party quickly broke up. No one wanted to be late for the first formal meeting of the year.

Most guys were walking on eggshells around the coaches, trying hard to make the best possible impression. They knew that today was the beginning of a long four months of continuous evaluation that would culminate in massive cuts at the end of training camp. Any little slipup could cost an already iffy player his chance at fulfilling his dream.

Although the positions of most of the starters were secure, their motivation for an on-time arrival was a hefty fine for being late. As a result, the two-minute warning caused a mass exodus from the locker room into the large, tiered meeting room where Coach Burton was already waiting to address his reconstituted team.

As Riley entered through the meeting room's door, he heard Coach Burton shouting, "What do you mean there're four helicopters up there? Shoot 'em down if you have to, but get them out of here by practice time!"

"Sir, according to federal aviation regulations, as long as they stay five hundred feet clear of people or buildings, they are perfectly within their rights to be . . ." Robert Taylor's words faded as he realized that Burton didn't give two hoots about his legal explanations. "I'll take care of them, Coach."

On the way to his seat, Riley turned to Simmons and asked, "What helicopters?"

"What helicopters do you think, Captain Hollywood? It's the newsies, and they're all here for the Riley watch," Simmons laughed.

"Yeah right."

"Oh, you better believe it, boy. You've got the paparazzi saying, 'Britney who?' They all just want a glimpse of our very own American hero. Better get used to it."

Riley shook his head as he sat, not wanting to believe anything that Simmons was telling him. His worst fears seemed to be confirmed, though, when Coach Burton spotted him in the audience. Coach just glared at him, then turned away.

Swell, Riley thought.

Burton moved to the center of the mini stage, and all the conversation immediately died. But before he had a chance to say his first word, the door burst open.

An entourage of men in suits came bounding down the stairs to the front of the amphitheater. Out in front of the group was A. J. Salley. Mr. Salley had owned the Colorado Mustangs for just five years, but it was apparent that he had spent every one of those 1,826 days working to put his mark on the organization. Having made his millions in the global telecom industry, he was a fair, no-nonsense businessman, and today he seemed clearly agitated.

A brief conversation was held between Mr. Salley and Coach Burton. Then the team owner quickly left the room, followed by his team of suits.

Coach Burton, obviously angered by the intrusion on *his* meeting, said, "Covington, Mr. Salley would like to see you in the hall."

Embarrassed and irritated, Riley muttered under his breath, "Don't these guys have anything better to do?" As he made his way to the door, he was serenaded with calls of "Oooooo" and "Busted."

Apparently that was enough to send Coach Burton over the top. "Baskin," he called out to the conditioning coach.

"Yes, Coach," came the reply.

"Obviously these boys have some extra energy. Tack on an extra sprint series to their run today."

A chorus of groans drowned out Coach Baskin's answer of "Yes, Coach."

In response, Burton said, "Make that two series."

This time Coach Baskin's answer could be clearly heard in the dead silence.

/////////////////////////

As soon as Riley stepped into the hallway, Mr. Salley tersely said, "Riley, what are we going to do about this? We have choppers overhead. Our phones are ringing off the hook. And there are over five hundred photographers and journalists outside this building right now. We've called in the police and made contact with the FAA, but this is getting out of control quickly."

"Yes, sir. I'm sorry, sir," Riley responded, feeling a bit like he was in the Air Force again getting chewed out for something he hadn't done. "What would you like me to do, Mr. Salley?"

"I want you to go home for the day. You had someone come with you today, didn't you?"

"Yes, sir. Skeeter Dawkins. He was one of—"

"Good," Mr. Salley continued, not interested in Riley's story. "Have him pull your car around to the loading dock for the team store. We'll send you out that way."

This was one of the first pieces of good news that Riley had heard today, especially knowing that he was going to miss those extra sprint series. "Yes, sir. And what about tomorrow?"

Exasperated and obviously done with the conversation, Mr. Salley answered, "I have no idea. You're going to be a distraction any way we cut it. We need to figure out how we're going to deal with all of this. We'll call you when we get a plan. Until then, you work out at home." That said, Mr. Salley turned and was gone.

Riley stood there for a moment trying to process what had just happened. Part of him wanted to laugh, while another part wanted to haul off and punch somebody. *Where does Salley get off coming down here and tearing me a new one for something I have absolutely no control over? At least he got one thing right: I am definitely out of here!*

A guy whose name Riley couldn't remember from the Mustangs video department rounded a corner and came toward him. "Hey," Riley called out to him.

"Hey, Riley. Great to see you back!"

"Yeah, good to be back. Listen, can you do me a favor? You know my friend—the one who came with me this morning?"

"You mean . . . ?" The guy lifted his hand way up in the air.

"That's him. Could you find him and ask him to bring the truck around to the loading dock behind the Mustangs store in five minutes?"

The video man seemed eager to help. "You got it, Riley," he said before sprinting out to the practice fields.

Riley walked back to his locker, decided there was nothing he wanted out of it, and headed to the hallway. Right outside the front locker room doors was a line of mail cubbies. Most of the little nooks had at least a few letters in them. A number of them were pretty packed. Riley's was stuffed full, and there was a white U.S. Postal Service tub sitting on the ground and a sticky note attached with his name on it. He stopped, looked at it, and then walked on.

Stopping by the equipment room, Riley picked up a Mustangs cap. Pulling it low on his head and putting his sunglasses on, he walked through the back room of the team store and out into the May sunshine. Immediately, he heard a mass of loud shouting. The only discernable word was *Riley*.

Thankfully, Skeeter had the Yukon right there with the rear passenger door open. Riley saw a huge wave of reporters and cameramen racing toward him as he dove into the back of the vehicle. His hand scraped against something hard on the leather seat. Looking down, he saw it was Skeeter's Heckler & Koch MK23.

"Left a little something for you, just in case," Skeeter said as he slowly pulled out into the growing mass of people.

Riley quickly sat up and tucked the gun under his right thigh. The last thing he needed was a picture published of him defending himself against the media by holding a handgun in the back of his SUV.

Suddenly cameras, microphones, and faces were pressed against his side windows. Riley instinctively pulled the cap a little lower on his head. Hands began grasping at the handles and banging on the doors. The truck dropped in the back, and Riley turned to see three men standing on his rear bumper shooting their cameras through the tinted glass of the gate.

While all this was going on, Skeeter kept the vehicle moving— slow and steady, never speeding up but never slowing down, like an icebreaker making its way through the early thaw of Hudson Bay. Insanity was all around the outside of the truck, but inside it was peace and harmony. Riley noticed that Skeeter had even tuned to public radio's classical music station.

"Skeeter, you are amazing," he said with genuine admiration. Riley couldn't be sure, but he thought he might have seen a slight expansion of Skeeter's cheeks at hearing the comment.

Finally Skeeter got to the street and gunned the Yukon. *Oh man, did that just happen?* Riley asked himself. *That was complete insanity.* He looked behind to see the size of the crowd but instead saw three vehicles rushing to catch up to them.

"Hey, Skeet? We're not done yet."

Riley saw Skeeter's eyes look into the rearview mirror. Then the big man pulled out his cell phone, hit a speed-dial number, and said a few words before hanging up. "Done," he said to Riley.

Within four minutes, Riley watched each of the chase cars being pulled over to receive tickets for various traffic infractions, real or imagined. "What about home?" he asked Skeeter.

"Taken care of. The security team's not allowing anyone on the block who doesn't live there."

"Excellent. Thanks again, my friend."

"Mmmm," came the reply.

Riley stretched himself out in the roomy backseat and began processing what had just happened. The day had been so emotional and so downright bizarre, he felt like he needed to debrief with somebody. But he knew that Scott and Khadi were busy at CTD. Talking to Skeeter was just one small step above talking to himself. Keith Simmons was at practice. Mom and Dad and Grandpa? No, there was too much distance. He wanted to look someone in the eyes while he spoke.

Hmmm, look someone in the eyes. Riley thought for a moment, then reached into his pocket and extracted a now-crumpled business card. He pulled his cell phone out of his shorts and dialed the number.

"Hello?" a woman's voice answered after the first ring.

Riley took a deep breath. "Whitney?"

His right foot gently tap, tap-tapped to an old Tommy James & The Shondells song that had been stuck in his head for the last two days. Unfortunately, the only lyrics he could remember—"Crystal blue persuasion, mmm-hmm"—were looping in his mind over and over and driving him crazy.

Jim Hicks stood up from his desk and walked to the interior window of his office, hoping the change of location would purge the song from his brain.

The room into which he looked was filled with the varied pulse of blinking lights and the soft glow of computer monitors, all of which reflected off the glass and metal furnishings, giving the room the feel of a high-tech Christmas display.

Gathered around a conference table in the middle of the large space just beyond his door was Hicks's team: Scott Ross, Tara Walsh, Khadi Faroughi, and the genius misfit quartet of analysts—Virgil Hernandez, Evie Cline, Joey Williamson, and Gooey . . . whatever his last name was.

Scott caught Hicks looking out. He smiled, tapped his watch, and held up two fingers. Hicks gave a wave of acknowledgment in response.

Guilt grabbed his insides as he watched Scott and Khadi talking. He would give anything to be able to go back in time and accept that invitation to the Costa Rican vacation. When Hicks first heard about the attempt on Riley and his friends, it was the closest he had come to emotionally losing it since his second wife had left him. But when it came down to it, Riley and Scott had handled the situation beautifully, even without him. Everyone had survived, and now Scott and Khadi were here as part of his new team.

Two months ago, Hicks had been approached by Stanley Porter, chief of the Midwest division of Homeland Security's counterterrorism division (CTD). Porter had been tasked with creating smaller, more action-oriented subsets of the larger departments. Hicks, after showing extraordinary leadership during the recent Hakeem Qasim manhunt, had been pegged to head up the new Denver-based CTD Front Range Response Team.

At first Hicks had balked. He was an *ops* guy, not a suit, he had said to them. In his mind, rules were there simply as a guideline for the less creative. But when Porter told him the amount of autonomy he would have in running his team, he had actually begun to consider the leadership position. Finally, Hicks had accepted on the condition that he could choose his own people. Scott and Khadi had been obvious choices.

As for the analysts, he'd left that to Scott. The gang of misfits his number-two man had brought in were an odd bunch, and Hicks figured the less direct contact he had with them, the more peace would reign.

But now he had to go out and face this group, and he had no idea what to do with them. He could lead any team into battle with strength and confidence. But this was a whole new ball game.

Taking a deep breath, Hicks opened his office door and walked into the very first meeting with his new team. Scott, seeing him come out, began clapping. The four analysts, apparently recognizing a chance to burn off some of their sugar calories, took it to the next level by standing and cheering. Khadi and Tara just sat there shaking their heads, although Khadi at least did it with a smile.

Hicks took his chair at the head of the table and, after Scott finally got the analysts to sit back down, said, "Okay, that will never happen again."

"Sorry, Jim," said Scott with a mocking grin on his face. "I guess we're all just a little enthusiastic."

"Well, enthusiasm can be a good thing when it's directed properly," Hicks responded, immediately realizing that he was already sounding like the stuffed-shirt political bureaucrat he was afraid of becoming.

Khadi stifled a laugh, and Hicks glared at her, though he softened his look when he spotted the slowly fading scar on her cheek that she didn't bother trying to cover with makeup.

He continued, "I want to welcome you all to the Front Range Response Team."

Hernandez, Cline, Williamson, and Gooey all started to giggle.

"What's so funny?" Hicks called out, his nerves causing his already short fuse to burn at double time.

Tara Walsh responded for them. "Sorry, sir, but about an hour ago they finally figured out our team's acronym, and they've been this way ever since."

"Coulda been worse. What if we were the Bureau for Uncovering Terrorist Threats?" Williamson said innocently, causing the other three analysts to burst out laughing.

Hicks turned to Scott for some help, but his right-hand man was looking intently at the glass tabletop and drawing on every ounce of self-control to not laugh. He looked at Khadi, who had her hands folded properly in front of her and was sporting a huge grin on her face. Tara was staring at him with an expression that said, *"See what I have to put up with every day?"*

Finally, Scott jumped in. "Come on, gang, knock it off. Jim is trying to speak."

"Thanks, Scott. Now I—"

"And I certainly don't want anyone suggesting the Departmentally Utilized Military Bureau and Systems—"

"Scott!" Jim yelled.

Everyone lost it. Even Tara joined in. Hicks leaned back into his chair, heaved a deep sigh, and then slowly began to chuckle. His laughter built up momentum until he was wiping tears away from his eyes like everyone else.

All the stress and anxiety Hicks had about his new position was released at that moment. He raised his hand, trying to get control of the group even as he struggled to get control of himself.

"Okay, everyone, enough. Let's have a little chat."

As Hicks spoke, he kicked his feet up on the table, then motioned for everyone else to do the same. "I have no clue what the suits were thinking when they gave me this job. I have a feeling that before long they'll be asking themselves that same question."

A chorus of chuckles sounded around the table.

"The one stipulation I gave in accepting this job was that I be allowed to pick my team. I figured if I was going to give this a shot, I wanted the best around me. In my opinion, you folks and our boys on the ops side are the best."

"Gawrsh," interjected Hernandez.

"Although I'm beginning to understand why Stanley Porter didn't give me a fight when I stole you away from him."

"Mr. Porter's bad! He's bad!" said Williamson, doing his best impersonation of Dana Carvey impersonating George Bush.

"Yeah, well you'll find that I run things a little differently than Porter. As you can tell by my friendship with Scott, I don't care what you look like or how you dress."

Scott feigned offense.

"I don't care how you act or what rules you need to break. Gooey, I don't even care how you smell."

Gooey responded with a thumbs-up and a stifled belch.

"All I care about are results. You guys do your jobs, and you've got free rein. You don't, and it's back to Porter with the lot of you. Any questions?"

Evie Cline's hand went up. "Yes, Evie?"

"Mr. Hicks, sir, I know this is technically called a 'war room,' but that makes me uncomfortable. It just sounds so violent. So, instead of calling this the war room, could we call it something different? Our old place was called—"

"Yeah, I know all about the Room of Understanding. Listen, you can call this Tinky Winky's playground for all I care, as long as your work gets done."

Seeing Hernandez's hand go up, Jim sighed and said, "Yes, Virgil?"

"Sir, I don't think Tinky Winky had a playground. Unless maybe the rest of the Teletubbies had a playground that they shared."

"Barney had a playground," Evie pointed out.

"I think Mickey Mouse might have had one, too. Or maybe that belonged to the Mouseketeers," said Williamson.

Scott jumped into the action. "You know, that Teletubbies baby sun always creeped me out. Why was it always laughing? Was that supposed to mean something?"

Hicks shot Scott a "you're not really helping" look, which Scott caught out of the corner of his eye.

"I mean, let's rein this in, people! Jim?"

"Thank you, Scott. Now, enough of that intro stuff. Tara, tell me what you've got on Costa Rica."

"Thank you, sir. And let me just tell you what an honor it is to be working with you."

A chorus of wet-sounding kisses came from the analyst end of the table.

Doing her best to ignore them, Tara continued, "Truthfully, we don't have much that's new. The bad guys were all Middle Eastern of one stripe or another. They flew to Havana; boated to Nicaragua, where they got their weapons; then went down across the border."

"Any sign of the last gunman?"

"No, sir. He's just vanished. And the Costa Rican authorities are not being overly cooperative."

Hicks's frustration was beginning to show. "Are we getting any pressure from our higher-ups on their government?"

"No, sir. They seem to want to treat this as a random incident."

"They what?"

"Tara, if I may," Scott broke in. "Jim, the higher-ups are idiots. You know that, and I know that. The only good information we're going to get is what we dig up ourselves. Right now Khadi and I are working on finding out who fed the bad guys Riley's location."

"And is Riley safe right now?"

"Skeet's his shadow, so he's probably safe as he can be."

"Fair enough. You know to keep me up-to-date with everything on this."

"Will do," said Scott.

Hicks turned back to Tara. "Tell me what else you're working on."

"Over the last week, there has been a remarkable spike in the amount of intercepted chatter. As you know, all of our intelligence branches are woefully lacking in Arabic, Farsi, Urdu, and Pashtun speakers, so much of our COMINT—that's communications intelligence—"

"I'm familiar with the term."

"Of course; sorry. Much of our COMINT remains untranslated and is therefore useless to us. So what we've done is set up filters to catch often-repeated phrases in those other languages. The computer doesn't necessarily recognize the words, just the sounds. When we get something, we send it to Khadi, who gives us the translation."

"Okay, probably more information than I needed, but that's fine. What about it?"

"There has been one new phrase that has hit at least twenty-five times in the last seven days. Its translation is 'Awake, O Sleeper.' We think it might have something to do with awakening sleeper cells."

Scott jumped in. "I, on the other hand, have a hard time believing this. Waking up sleeper cells with the phrase 'Awake, O Sleeper?' Could they be a little more obvious? The only thing more blatant would be a knock on the door by someone with a suicide vest on a hanger, calling out, 'Terrorgram for Mr. Ahmed!' I mean, let's give these guys a little credit."

Tara immediately countered. "Listen, Scott, it's not out of the realm—"

"You mean 'boss'."

"What?"

"Chain of command. You need to call me 'boss' from now on," Scott said with a grin on his face.

In response, Tara picked up her cell phone and began dialing. Jim asked, "Tara, what are you doing?"

"I'm calling the devil to see if I can get a weather report."

The analysts showed their appreciation for the slam with an "Oooooo" and some light applause. Tara was typically known for her well-rehearsed and poorly executed attempts at zingers. She sat back in her chair with a smug smile on her face. Her celebration was short-lived.

"I'm surprised you had to dial so many numbers," Scott responded immediately. "I always figured you'd have him on speed dial."

The analysts all jumped to their feet and began a chorus of "Scott, Scott, Scott!"

Once the cheer died down, it was Khadi's turn to finally weigh in. "Scott, I agree that it would be unusual to use that blatant a phrase. But you'll agree it's not out of the realm of possibility."

"Of course. Nothing's out of the realm of possibility."

"Cubs winning a World Series," Williamson reminded Scott.

"Ashlee Simpson winning a Grammy," added Hernandez.

"True, but I took those as givens."

"Stay with me, boys," Khadi said. "Let's just play this out a bit. What possible reasons could the bad guys have for using an obvious code sign?"

"They're stupid?" offered Scott.

"Try a little harder, Mr. Wizard," countered Khadi.

"To show power?" said Evie. "You know, 'Look how strong we are, we've got all these sleeper cells activating.'"

"Maybe it's a distraction," suggested Gooey. "We're all looking for these cells—maybe real, maybe not—while they've got some big thing planned."

"Could be fear," said Scott. "Imagine what would happen if the media got hold of this. Twenty-five sleeper cells ready to wreak havoc on America. Think of what would happen to the stock market."

Khadi was nodding. "Fear fits. Remember Hakeem Qasim's big thing was to create fear. Fear in your city. Fear in your neighborhood."

"And not just in your neighborhood, but of your neighbor," said Tara.

Hicks jumped in. "Okay, sounds like we've got reason enough not to rule out a mass sleeper awakening. Tara, I'm guessing they've disguised their tracks fairly well on those calls, but I'd still like you and the kids to try to get me sources and receivers on each one of them."

"You got it, boss."

"Scott and Khadi, I want you to run out the scenarios for each of these options—power play, distraction, and fear."

"And stupid?" asked Scott.

"And stupid. We all know that isn't out of the realm of possibilities either with these guys. I want to take reports home with me tonight, so that means you have exactly six hours and twenty-nine minutes to get them to me." Hicks got up and walked to his office. Just before going in, he turned and said, "Good work, gang."

But everyone was already too involved in their discussions to hear him. Hicks went into his office, sat down, and kicked his feet up on the desk. A satisfied smile spread across his face. This was exactly what he had hoped for when he brought this team together. *Maybe being a suit isn't that bad after all.*

The fan slowly cycled back and forth, causing the collar on Isaac Khan's work shirt to flap up and tap him on the jaw every ten seconds or so. But rather than shift positions or adjust the fan, he sat perfectly still on an old chair in his tiny studio apartment, staring.

A cockroach skittered across the small kitchen table and stopped when it detected Isaac's thick right forearm. A standoff ensued, the cockroach staring at the hairy arm, Isaac staring at his bed. Finally, after sensing no movement, the insect pushed ahead, lightly brushing against the man's elbow, causing Isaac to absentmindedly sweep the fingers of his left hand across his arm.

At last Isaac emitted an incredulous sigh, stood up, and walked to his front door. Opening it, he examined the locks and the doorjamb. *No sign of forced entry. Then how?* He closed the door, relocked the three dead bolts, and returned to his chair.

A smile came to his face. *I guess this means that I truly have not been forgotten.*

The past week had been torture for Isaac. The elation he had experienced following the initial phone call had gradually turned to frustration as he waited day after day for instructions.

Soon the frustrations had turned to doubt. Had he really heard those words: *Awake, O Sleeper?* Had something happened to the person who was supposed to tell him his next steps? Had he forgotten some special orders from long ago? Had he been contacted only to be forgotten *again?*

All these questions and doubts had been answered today by the three mysterious backpacks that sat across the small room on his bed. They hadn't been there when he left for work this morning, yet there they were now. *What do they contain? What are they for?* He knew the answers to these questions would be in the envelope propped against the center backpack. There was one word written on the bright white paper—*Warrior.*

Isaac started to get up to retrieve the envelope but then sat back down. Fear and excitement battled each other in his mind. *Warrior. Can that really be me? It's been so long since I've fought—so long since I've killed. Warrior? Oh, Allah, please forgive my unbelief.*

Finally, Isaac took the two steps from the table to the bed. He reached for the left backpack, wanting to feel its bulk, but then quickly drew back his hand. *Patience! What if there is something in the envelope telling you not to pick up the backpacks?*

Feeling like he just dodged a bullet, Isaac lifted the envelope. It was thick and heavy. He stepped back to the table and laid it down on the chipped Formica top. *Tea,* he thought, leaving the envelope and walking around to his kitchenette. *Something like this cannot be started without tea.*

Isaac filled the teakettle and put it on a hot plate. After getting down a glass mug, his can of tea leaves, and two sugar cubes, he began chastising himself. *What are you afraid of? You are a grown man, but you are acting like a child!* Shaking his head, he sat in his other chair, reached across the small table, and picked up the envelope. He slid the handle of his teaspoon into the corner of the seal and roughly pulled it across.

A gasp escaped his mouth when he pulled out the contents. There were five thin packets of one hundred dollar bills, each with a band stamped with *$1,000* wrapped around it. Isaac had never seen that much money in one place at one time. He resisted the urge to count through the money and instead lifted the rest of the contents.

In his hand he held three documents. Unfolding the first, he found a computer-printed map with a large *X* on it. The second and third documents were similar to the first but displayed different locations. A shudder went through his body as he realized what he was being asked to do. He fell to his knees and raised his hands to heaven.

"Oh, Allah, I declare that you are one! Thank you for calling me to your service. Give me the strength and the determination to carry out whatever tasks you lay before me. There is no God but you. There is no God but you. There is no God but you. . . ." Isaac repeated these words over and over. His prayer blended with the steam from his whistling kettle, and they both slowly ascended to heaven.

TUESDAY, MAY 12, 8:30 P.M. CDT
CHICAGO, ILLINOIS

Mohsin Ghani breathed into a paper bag that still smelled of his breakfast egg and cheese biscuit. It had been four minutes since this bag had become his primary air source, and he was only now beginning to get himself under control.

Somehow in the past week, Mohsin had convinced himself that they had decided not to use him. Maybe they had gone a different direction. Maybe they had realized how much more he could benefit their cause by remaining in the position he was in. Maybe they discovered what a coward he really was. However, all those hopes had crashed to the ground the moment he sat down in his Mercedes Roadster. There, on the steering wheel, resting against the protruding speedometer and tachometer, was an envelope.

Mohsin slowly opened his eyes, praying that maybe he had been mistaken. Maybe he was sick and didn't know it and was simply having a hallucination. Maybe he had forgotten that he had placed a bill there that needed to be taken care of after work. Maybe . . .

maybe . . . But there it sat. "'Warrior!'" he screamed. "Who are they kidding?"

Angrily, he snatched the envelope off the steering column and ripped it open. Inside were four sheets of paper. The first was a Google map with an *X*.

"What is this? Am I supposed to meet somebody here? Do they think I'm a pirate looking for buried treasure? Idiots!" He angrily tossed the first sheet onto the passenger seat and saw that the second was a map like the first. "Could you people have at least left some instructions? I'm not a mind reader! This is ridiculous!" The second map joined the first, and a third map was about to meet the same fate when he stopped cold.

His hand began to tremble as he looked at the fourth sheet. There was no map on that page. There was only the hand-printed word *Trunk*.

Sweat broke out all over Mohsin's body, and he could feel his breathing rate beginning to increase. He loosened his tie and undid the top button of his shirt. "No . . . No . . . No, no, no!" Mohsin slammed his fist into the passenger seat with each word. He grabbed the wheel with both hands and cried out, "Oh, God! What should I do? Help me, help me, help me!"

Leaning forward, he rested his head against the warm leather of the steering wheel. After a couple of minutes, Mohsin said, "Come on, you can do this. You can do this!" Mustering all his courage, he reached out and pressed the trunk release.

His legs felt rubbery as he stepped out of the car, and he steadied himself on the roof, leaving streaky fingerprints on the glossy black finish. Before going to the rear of the sports car, he reached back in and grabbed his paper bag.

"Come on, Mohsin, you know you can do this," he muttered to himself. "What could be back there—a body?" He tried to chuckle, but the resulting wet spurt betrayed his anxiety. "Quit being ridiculous. It's probably just more instructions. Be a man!"

With the bag in one hand and the lid in the other, Mohsin thrust open the trunk. Inside were three large backpacks laid side by side. A dull matte black handgun lay on the middle pack.

Mohsin's knees buckled, and his weight drove the lid down,

sealing away the trunk's contents. Spinning himself around, he leaned against the back of the car and began again to breathe in the stale smell of breakfast.

Abdullah Muhammad's contact had come earlier in the day via a series of coded text messages. When the first one had beeped through and he had seen the gibberish written there, a surge of adrenaline had rushed through his body. After all the waiting, waiting, waiting, with a flick of Allah's hand and a message across his cell phone screen, his time had finally come!

Abdullah had immediately pulled his patrol car into a Burger King parking lot. After copying the messages down in his notebook, he had quickly deleted the texts from his cell phone. The page was then torn out of the notebook and tucked down deep in his wallet.

Finishing out his shift that day had taken what seemed an eternity—making the stops, writing the tickets, taking the reports. When he finally walked out of the precinct, he did it knowing that he would never step foot back in.

At first, rather than just not showing up anymore, Abdullah had thought of quitting the police force or taking a leave of absence. However, both of those options would require him to give up his badge, and he really wanted to keep that useful piece of hardware for the activities to come. So Abdullah simply became a ghost instead.

He drove his car from the precinct out to Denver International Airport, where he parked it in a long-term lot. After changing clothes in his car and stuffing his old clothes under the seat, he pulled a baseball cap low onto his head and walked to the terminal. There he caught a cab. He directed the taxi to drop him off downtown, where he picked up the light rail F line and rode it south to its termination in Lone Tree. From there it was a quick walk to an apartment he had kept rented for the past two years but had as yet never slept in.

This trendy singles location served Abdullah's needs perfectly.

The area was filled with high turnover apartments and condos that were populated by young professionals who cherished their anonymity. And because of the nearby light rail, Abdullah could keep the car he had purchased for this second life parked in the same place for a week at a time without raising any suspicions.

As the key turned the lock and the latch clicked, Abdullah felt that he was opening the door to a new beginning—his true person. Without bothering to lock the door behind him, he strode through the entryway, past the bare living room walls, and right to the bookshelf by the sliding glass door. He pulled out his Everyman's Library edition of Naguib Mahfouz's *The Cairo Trilogy* and picked up a yellow pad of paper that he kept on the bookshelf. Both items he took to the glass dining table. Abdullah then pulled out his wallet and retrieved the coded message. Impulsively, he pressed the piece of paper to his lips. *All the years of waiting have finally come to an end.*

The first two numbers told him to open to chapter 57. Then, using the text of the book as his key, he proceeded to decipher the code. His heel tapped rapidly in anticipation as he worked. *Slow down; slow down,* he chastised himself. *Now is not the time to be making mistakes.*

With each new phrase his excitement grew as his destiny was revealed to him. It wasn't until he got to the end of the fifty-plus-word message that the full brutal force of what he was being asked to do hit him.

Abdullah was ashamed to admit it, but he was rocked. He had known he would be asked to do something terrible, but this was violent beyond anything he had imagined. *Stop it! Can you really be surprised? You are a warrior, and you are being asked to act like a warrior. This is not a time to question.*

But, oh, my Lord, this is so . . . so . . . hands-on! This is so bloody! Oh, Allah, can this really be in your will? Abdullah began pacing around the apartment. *Remember who you are,* he chastised himself again. *You are simply a tool in Allah's hands. People greater than you have been given the words of truth. They are the ones who can discern his will. Who are you to question them? You can do this! You will do this! Allah will give you the strength.*

Sitting back down, Abdullah reread the message, committing

it to memory. Then he took the original notebook page and all the pages underneath, as well as the entire yellow pad, into his bedroom and ran them through the shredder.

Naheed Yamani put the copy of *The Cairo Trilogy* back onto the bookshelf. After rereading then destroying the message, she flopped herself down on her overstuffed Payton sofa and tucked her feet up. She ran her hands over the khaki linen material and enjoyed its coolness.

Do I really believe in what I'm doing, or am I just bored? Naheed had always been somewhat of an adrenaline junkie. Summers as a rich, spoiled, semiroyal teenager on the French Riviera usually found her Jet Skiing, parasailing, or shoplifting worthless junk from the tourist stores. But no matter how much she tempted fate, it was never enough.

Then one day she had been approached at a family gathering by her cousin, Saleh Jameel. Saleh had always been the one about whom the rest of the mothers told their children, "Why can't you be more like him?" Good grades, impeccable manners, never forgetting to hold the door open for giggling old ladies—you name a positive quality, Saleh possessed it.

But Naheed had always been suspicious of her cousin. Somewhere beneath that sickeningly sweet exterior, she knew there was a different Saleh. It could have been the quick flashes of anger on the soccer field or the way he sometimes was unnecessarily harsh to the servants. Whatever it was, it was enough that when Naheed and Saleh were sitting together on a bench at another overdone family feast, she was ready to hear him out.

Saleh began by telling her that he had been watching her for a long time. He followed that with a long description of his recent involvement in a secret paramilitary organization. He finished by telling her, "You're just the kind of person we need to defeat the Great Satan and to end the oppression."

Naheed's interest had been piqued. Maybe this was the ultimate adventure she had been searching for. Maybe this was the piece of her life that had been missing—a purpose, a cause.

Soon she began spending two days a week after school at Saleh's family compound. His parents, who helped finance a budding terrorist group, willingly confirmed the lie that Naheed told to her father about being there to study.

For Naheed, the only drawbacks to the training were the ranting sermons with which the mullahs began each session. Despite joining up with Allah's army, she was not particularly religious. Of course, Naheed believed there was a God. She just didn't buy the fact that he was quite so unforgiving with his people.

So she had endured the preaching with an appropriately pious look on her face. She shook her fist and chanted when necessary. She endured the lengthy, repetitive tirades because she knew that afterward would come the training—how to kill with a gun, how to kill with a knife, how to kill with one's hands. Naheed excelled at stealth, cunning, treachery, and violence. For once in her short life, she felt totally alive and in her element.

Finally, the time had come when her preparation was at an end. She had far exceeded the others in her group, including Saleh. There was no graduation ceremony; *I guess this is not really a cap and gown kind of event,* she had thought, laughing to herself.

But there was a meeting—a very special meeting—with an old one-eyed Iraqi.

For someone who prided herself with being fearless, Naheed was terrified in this man's presence.

"Are you ready to fight for your God?" this man had asked.

Calling on all the religious fervor she could fake, Naheed had replied, "I am ready to die for my God. *Allahu akhbar!*"

A twinkle in the old warrior's eye had told her that he knew her religious talk was just bluster. His next words still made their way into Naheed's dreams at least once a week. He had reached his damaged right hand up and lightly patted her cheek. "Such a beautiful young woman," he had said with a smile. "Rest assured, my dear, you will die. But whether it will be for God or for reasons of your own, that you must decide." The old man had then moved on to the next graduate, leaving Naheed weak-kneed and flushed.

Three days later she had been told to go to America and build herself a life. She would be told when it was her time to act. So she had gone to her grandfather and begged him to set her up in America. He had agreed and unknowingly placed a ticking time bomb into the heart of the art culture in San Francisco.

What will *be my reason for dying?*

As Naheed sank deeper back into the pillows of her couch, her hand lightly touched her cheek where the old man's hand had been. *Is it a love for God? Is it a disdain for others? Is it because death is the final and greatest adventure?*

Whatever it is, you better spend some time thinking about it now, she told herself, *because the time for coming up with an answer is rushing to a close.*

WEDNESDAY, MAY 13, 2:30 P.M. MDT
ENGLEWOOD, COLORADO

"You mean being franchised isn't a good thing?"
Khadi asked Riley. "I thought it was a compliment. Like it was their way of saying we really,
really want you."

Riley and Khadi were enjoying the May Colorado sun in front of Caribou Coffee. Skeeter sat
two tables over. Riley took a sip from his ceramic
mug, placing it back on the black metal table
before answering.

"Yeah, most people think that. But in reality,
most players dread it. Since I'm franchised, I'm
not going to be able to become a free agent like I
was supposed to."

"Do you really want to be a free agent? Doesn't
that mean that there's a good likelihood that you'd
be moving to another team?"

Riley sighed. He really didn't want to talk football, especially with someone who didn't know
football. His gaze shifted to another outdoor table
where a man in running attire was sitting with
his black lab stretched out next to him. Two days
ago, Riley had sat at that same table with Whitney
Walker.

That had been a very enjoyable conversation.

Whitney knew her football. She'd asked great questions, and she'd proven that she could be trusted to distinguish "on the record" from "off the record." After the two of them had talked for an hour, they'd gone across the street to the wildlife museum and shot a quick interview for television.

It was a huge asset for a player to have a go-to media person, someone he could trust if he had information he wanted to get out. Riley wondered if maybe Whitney could turn out to be that person for him.

Part of Riley thought he should tell Khadi about his time here with Whitney. But then he thought maybe that would end up being more trouble than it was worth. *Why open that can of worms? It was just an innocent coffee—wasn't it?*

"The goal in free agency," Riley continued, shaking the picture of Whitney Walker's green eyes out of his mind, "is to start a bidding war. That helps to drive up the terms of a player's contract, especially his signing bonus, which is the only part of the contract that's really guaranteed."

"Seriously? So a contract isn't really a contract."

Riley smiled. "Well, yes and no. A team can release a player at any time without having to honor future salaries. That's why guys want the big signing bonus. The teams have to pay that. But since I've been franchised, it means no signing bonus for me, and I'm being forced into a one-year contract that only pays the average of the top five players in my position. Basically, it's going to cost me between five and seven million this year."

Khadi almost spit out her mouthful of coffee. "Ouch! That's harsh. So are you going to stay with football?"

Just then, Riley's cell phone rang. He picked the phone off the table, quickly looked at the caller ID, and then silenced the phone.

"I don't know. I mean, I understand where they're coming from. There are still a lot of question marks in my own mind about football. I'm sure they've got even more. They don't want to dump a seven-figure bonus on me and have me leave football or end up dead in some foreign country."

"You're not going to end up dead in some foreign country," Khadi corrected him.

"Sorry, I guess I'm just feeling a tad pessimistic right now. But as for football? For right now, yeah, I think I'll stay with it. I mean, what else is there for me? I don't really want to go back full-time into the Air Force. And I'm not going to go into the CTD. I'm not really the analyst type."

"And just what is the analyst type?" asked Khadi the analyst.

"Smart and beautiful," Riley said with an embarrassed smile. "Unfortunately, I'm just beautiful."

"Oh, I wouldn't say that." Then seeing Riley's feigned look of shock, she corrected herself. "I mean, you know you're smart."

"But not beautiful?"

"Shut up!" Khadi said, laughing.

Riley took another sip of his coffee. "So anyway, I don't see myself doing the analyst thing, and long-term ops holds no appeal for me either. Too much shooting and getting shot at."

"So, it's football by default?"

"Looks that way."

Khadi's cell phone began ringing. "Feel free to get that," Riley said as Khadi checked who was calling.

"No, it's fine," she said, silencing the ring. "Hey, didn't you go visit Meg last week? How are she and Alessandra doing?"

Before he knew it, Riley told Khadi all the details of the visit, including the final few minutes of their time together.

"You know she's interested in you," Khadi said matter-of-factly.

"Oh, please! She's a lonely, grieving friend." Riley had known it was a mistake telling Khadi about the hug as soon as the words left his mouth. But for some reason, around Khadi his mouth often took the lead while his brain played catch-up. "Seriously, her husband's less than five months dead. Now you've got her on the prowl for a replacement."

Khadi looked at him for a moment, then said, "Riley, tell me about the things you know."

Although he couldn't see Khadi's eyes clearly through her Salvatore Ferragamo sunglasses, Riley could hear their sparkle in her voice. "What are you getting at?"

"Come on. What are the things that you are an expert in?"

Leaning back in his metal chair, Riley said, "All right, I'll play along. Let's see, I know a lot about professional football defense. Military operations. Various guns and weapons. . . . Uh . . . I've seen all of Clint Eastwood's spaghetti westerns at least a dozen times each. I rock at recipes involving fire and large pieces of dead animals. . . . I do a mean Sean Connery impersonation. And I used to be the neighborhood expert on the Justice League of America—although I'll readily admit that my prowess here has slipped a little over the years."

Khadi was laughing. "Okay, other than the Sean Connery imper- sonation, I agree wholeheartedly."

"Hey—"

"Riley, we've had this discussion before. An impersonation needs to be more than a benign hand gesture and the repetition of the word *Scotland*. But we digress. The subject you did not mention, my dear sir, is women."

Straightening up, Riley said, "You're right. My oversight. I am an expert on all things female!"

"Yeah right. Just like I'm an expert in that League of Justice thing."

"Listen, the Justice League of America was a very well-respect- ed team of superheroes who battled evil and injustice for many years."

Khadi just stared at Riley.

"Well they were," he said defensively.

Riley was saved by Khadi's phone going off again. "Sorry," she said as she silenced it. "So, back to my point. You have great wis- dom about a lot of things, but you're clueless when it comes to women."

"Fair enough. But you weren't there when Meg gave me the hug."

"I didn't need to be. All I'm saying is be careful. She may be look- ing for more from you than you're ready to give. At least more than I think you're ready to give." Khadi now began sounding a little bit flustered. "If you *are* interested in her, there's nothing standing in your way, since I'm . . . I mean, we're not—"

"No, of course we're not," Riley jumped in trying to save her. Unfortunately, he instead found himself falling into the same verbal pit. "I mean, not that if things were different with us it wouldn't mean that things would be . . . uh, different with us. But, no, I'm not interested in Meg. I'm just trying to help her and Alessandra get through this."

"Sure, that's what I figured. I just wanted you to know that *if* you felt, you know, different, that I wouldn't blame you. She is a very beautiful woman," Khadi said, leaving that last statement hanging there as if some sort of response were required.

"Khadi," Riley said instead.

"Yes."

"Can we change the subject?"

"Please."

"So . . . how about this weather?"

Riley and Khadi looked at each other silently until they both broke down laughing. Shaking his head, Riley picked up their mugs to take them for refills, then swung by Skeeter's table and grabbed his empty before going inside. As the air-conditioning hit his face, he smiled and prayed, *Lord, why did You place the most perfect woman I know so far out of my reach? It just ain't right, Lord; it just ain't right.*

ELEVEN

His words were directed to God, but behind his closed eyes, al-'Aqran saw someone else entirely. This man was asking him questions in butchered Arabic spoken with an American accent, slowly, with the vowels drawn out. He was tall, well built, and was wearing a khaki green shirt splattered with blood—al-'Aqran's blood. Over and over, this agent of Satan kept asking the same questions: *Who is in America? Give me names! Who is in the U.K.? Give me names! Who is in central Europe? Give me names!*

At first, al-'Aqran had responded by spitting in the man's face or yelling curses back at him. But with each act of defiance, a belt-wrapped hand would land across his face or a blackjack would connect with a joint. His body had screamed out in pain. He had prayed for Allah to take his life. Eventually, the old man was so broken down that all he could do was respond to the questions with a look of contempt. *But I never talked! Before Allah, I swear I never talked!*

Pop, Pop! rang out like rifle shots in the quiet room. Although the other men politely gave no indication that they had noticed, al-'Aqran silently cursed his aging body—especially the way his knees seemed to find it necessary to remind both him and anyone around him of their constant deterioration.

Prior to his time in captivity, these percussive protestations had happened only occasionally. But now he had audible accompaniment to his physical movements multiple times every prayer session. His joints mocked him whenever he shifted from prostrate to kneeling. And they downright rebelled whenever he tried to rise to a standing position.

Sitting back on his heels at the end of the *Dhuhr*, or noon prayer, al-'Aqran turned to his right and muttered, *"As Salaamu 'alaikum wa rahmatulaah"* to the angel over his right shoulder who was there to record all of his good deeds. He then repeated the blessing of peace—although with a little less feeling—over his left shoulder, where the angel spying for his sinful actions resided. Someday, the lists these two were creating would be weighed against each other on the great scale. The old man prayed that when that happened, things would go "right."

The prayer having ended, al-'Aqran willed himself to rise. Immediately four hands grasped his arms to ease his journey up. Roughly, he shook them off as his anger flashed. But then words from the Koran flashed into his mind (ten years ago, he could have recited the exact Surah and verse) and stayed his temper. *"Today you will be paid back with humiliation, for you were unjustly proud on earth."*

"I am sorry, my brothers. Please—your assistance?" Al-'Aqran resigned himself to the help but pulled himself away as soon as he was fully upright.

Babrak Zahir, the youngest of the men with him, carefully began to roll up the *sajjada* as soon as al-'Aqran stepped off of it. A gift from the five men with him, the prayer rug was colored a rich red with an intricately embroidered black and gold outline of the *Kaaba* covering its center. Al-'Aqran used a craggy and pitted old wooden walking stick to help him shuffle his way across the faded linoleum floor, again cursing the Americans for what they had done to his body. Coming to a small, rectangular table around which were crammed six chairs, he took his place at the head of the table, hearing the air whistle from the bottom cushion as he sat.

The five men with him immediately began a subtle jostling as several of them tried to maneuver themselves to the places of honor at their leader's right and left. The sight reminded al-'Aqran of a game he had played as a child called Dance of the Chairs, in which the children walked around a group of chairs while someone sang. The only difference here was when the music stopped, there would be chairs enough for everyone—just not necessarily the chairs they wanted.

Al-'Aqran closed his one good eye and thought back through the weeks since he had come to Istanbul. While it was good to get back to his people, he could sense the general disarray that had beset the Cause since he had been gone. The days since then had been spent in honing the leadership, reestablishing lines of communication, and preparing for the next big operation.

After the glory of the Platte River Stadium attack in Denver, Colorado, things had begun to go wrong for the Cause. Al-'Aqran was determined to make those responsible for the organization's black eye pay and to place the terror of the Cause back in the heart and mind of every American.

The sound of air shooting out from the five other cushions drew his thoughts back to the meeting at hand. However, just because the seats were taken, that didn't mean the loud discussion had ended.

And these are my leaders? al-'Aqran thought. *These men who can't even sit around a table without an argument?*

Opening his eye, he saw one man who was not participating in the bickering. Hamad bin Salih Asaf sat at the opposite end of the table, staring at al-'Aqran with the slightest of smirks on his face.

Asaf was the one who had masterminded al-'Aqran's rescue and the brilliant but unfortunately failed attempt on Riley Covington in Costa Rica. Saudi-born, Asaf had been given an excellent education. Following graduation, he had fulfilled a short commitment with the Royal Saudi Naval Forces before being recruited to the *Al Mukhabarat Al A'amah*.

For the next ten years, Asaf had worked in this Saudi Arabian version of the CIA. While the secrets he learned about his country and the rest of the Middle East were helpful in his new life as part of the Cause, the greatest assets he had come away with were connections.

Asaf had ties into all the major terrorist organizations and most Middle Eastern governments. It was one of these relationships that had allowed him to broker a deal with the Chechens through Hezbollah, despite its being a Shi'ite organization. Asaf was the one al-'Aqran counted on to clearly analyze the economic, political, and social fallout of any attack the Cause might be planning.

As if in direct contrast to Asaf, the man who had managed to plant his sizable bulk into the seat of honor was Kamal Hejazi, an Egyptian who had somehow found a way to weasel himself into the upper leadership echelon during al-'Aqran's incarceration. As soon as Hejazi noticed al-'Aqran looking at him, a wide smile broke out on his face.

"Would you like me to call this meeting to order for you, *sayyid*?"

Rather than answer Hejazi, al-'Aqran looked back to the opposite end of the table. "Hamad, my brother, why are you so far away from me? Come to me. I need your counsel. Kamal will gladly give up his seat for you, won't you Kamal?"

Al-'Aqran locked eyes with Hejazi. Surprise, then anger flashed in the Egyptian's puffy gaze. Then resignation and shame washed out all other emotions. Hejazi answered with a slight bow. "Of course, *sayyid*. After all, a chair is just a chair."

Al-'Aqran watched the other three men at the table as Asaf and Hejazi swapped positions. All three seemed to be diligently studying the embedded gold glitter pattern on the faded white tabletop.

Silently, al-'Aqran assessed the leadership council of the Cause. To his left sat Arshad Hushimi, an Iraqi, al-'Aqran's oldest confidant, valued both for his skill with munitions and for his friendship.

Next to Hushimi was Tahir Talib, another Iraqi. Talib was in charge of communications—internally to the members of the Cause itself, to other organizations who shared the same goals, and ultimately extending out to the media of the world.

Quickly passing over Hejazi, whose only contribution al-'Aqran could discern was contradicting and nay-saying the leadership council's decisions—*something I'll put a stop to today if the opportunity presents itself,* he thought—he came to Babrak Zahir. Zahir's father, Mohammad Zahir, had packed up his family and left (not *fled*, he was always certain to insist) Afghanistan in 1996 after the Taliban took control of the capital city of Kabul. While the elder Zahir had been no fan of President Burhanuddin Rabbani, he also hadn't cared for the leadership of the new extremist Islamic regime. "It's like a stupid little ten-year-old stealing the key to his parents' car," he used to say. "He'll drive hard and fast—running over some pedestrians along the way—but eventually he'll crash and crash hard." His words proved prophetic when Kabul fell to Western forces a mere five years later.

Mohammad Zahir had been al-'Aqran's closest friend for the past ten years, ever since they had been introduced to each other in Algeria. That friendship had abruptly ended when Zahir was killed earlier that year during the Americans' rescue of Riley Covington in Italy. Only the news of Hakeem Qasim's failure in his attack in California had shaken al-'Aqran more upon his arrival in Istanbul than had the news of his friend's death.

Upon learning of Mohammad's martyrdom, al-'Aqran had immediately promoted twenty-five-year-old Babrak to fill his father's place on the leadership council. This was not just a sentimental action. Babrak had three things that qualified him to fill his father's shoes— intelligence, a passionate desire for revenge, and, despite being part of the terrorism organization only a short eight years, a hands-on kill number second only to that of al-'Aqran himself.

Finally, al-'Aqran's assessment brought him to Asaf, just as that man scooted his chair to the table next to his leader. "What is the latest on our assets in the United States, Hamad?"

Al-'Aqran saw Asaf shoot a quick look to Talib, who, as the communications man, should have received this question. Out of the corner of his eye al-'Aqran saw Talib give a slight nod. *Good. At least one man puts the Cause before his own ambitions,* he thought.

"Tahir has informed me that the chosen four have been activated and have been given their instructions," Asaf answered.

"And the Yamani girl is among those readied?"

"As you ordered, *sayyid.*"

"Good . . . good," al-'Aqran said, more to himself than to anyone at the table.

"Are you sure this Naheed Yamani is the right person for the job?" Hejazi's voice interrupted his thoughts. "She seems to me to be nothing more than a spoiled little rich girl who, when the going gets tough, will go running home to the protection of her grandfather. We can't afford another failure like the debacle of your protégé, Hakeem Qasim."

All eyes turned to al-'Aqran to see how he would respond to this challenge.

At that moment, a thin, veiled woman walked up carrying a tray containing six small cups of Turkish coffee. The aroma hit al-'Aqran as his cup was gently placed before him, and it helped to ease his growing anger. Dark brown foam formed a soft, gritty barrier to the rich liquid underneath. In his subconscious, a clock began counting down the five minutes it would take for the dregs to settle. One more deep inhalation, and peace returned to his mind.

Hejazi had ignored his cup and was looking defiantly at al-'Aqran. The older man just smiled to himself. *His play has begun. A little more rope,* he thought. *Just a little more rope, and this son of a goat herder will hang himself.*

Without acknowledging Hejazi's remarks, al-'Aqran turned back to Asaf. "And our plans to bring Allah's revenge upon Covington?"

"Also in process, *sayyid.* Right now he is surrounded by many people. We have initiated a plan to isolate him and then draw him out. If we cannot get to him, we will find a way to have him come to us."

A picture of Hakeem Qasim as a boy flashed in al-'Aqran's mind. The child's body and soul had been damaged by the American missile that had slaughtered his parents. Al-'Aqran had taken this shattered boy and recreated Hakeem into a young man of courage and purpose. He had instilled the concepts of honor and revenge into his mind and had taught him the skills he would need to accomplish those goals. During those times of training together, the older man had almost come to think of Hakeem as a son. He had so much pride and hope in the young man.

But you still sent him to his death, did you not? he heard from the left side of his mind. *Oh, but what a glorious death it was to have been!* the right side answered back.

"May I ask you something, *sayyid?*" The tone of Hejazi's question instantly turned up the heat again in al-'Aqran's body.

"No, you may not," the old man snapped.

Hejazi pressed on anyway. "A thousand pardons, but I must ask it anyway. Is this vendetta against Covington really for Allah, or is it for you?"

"As far as you are concerned, there is no difference between the two!"

"Please, *sayyid*! Words like that are close to blasphemy! I understand your hatred against this man, but please do not equate your will with that of our beneficent creator!" Then a condescending smile spread across his face. "Please do not be angry if I find it necessary to press this point. I am simply concerned for you and for our organization. I know you spent a horrible time in the hands of Satan's minions, and may Allah greatly reward you for what you suffered. I can hardly imagine anyone coming back to leadership so quickly, especially someone of your . . . experience. Maybe some rest is what is needed for you. Then, after a time, you could return to us and lead us with a clearer mind and a more direct purpose."

Al-'Aqran could see in Hejazi's smile that the man thought he was establishing the upper hand. *Fool! Time to start tying the noose.*

"While I appreciate your concern, my *Egyptian* friend, you must know that through Allah's grace my mind is clear and my purpose is set. But since you have convinced yourself, at least in your small, addled brain, that you have the clearer head, what would *you* have us do? Covington has brought a great dishonor against the Cause! Would you see us turn a blind eye to that?"

Al-'Aqran saw Hejazi cast a glance at his eye patch and then, realizing he had been noticed, quickly look down at the table.

When al-'Aqran spoke again, his volume matched his intensity. "Answer me! What would you have us do, you weak man?"

Hejazi's head came up, and al-'Aqran could see him muster the last of his courage. "I did not come here to insult you . . . or to be insulted!"

"Your very presence here insults me!" Al-'Aqran could feel his face reddening, an angry sweat breaking out across his hairline.

"Nevertheless, you ask what I would do?" Hejazi said, his own voice rising. "I would stick to our original plan of mobilizing our assets! The first phase of our strategy against the Americans is about to launch; the second phase—which, as the lesser prophet Jeremiah spoke, will have voices mourning in Ramah—is well in process.

"What would I *not* do? I would not let personal feelings put our whole organization at risk! I would not let a desire for revenge potentially unravel our well-woven tapestry for the destruction of the West. Hakeem Qasim failed—maybe it was Allah's will or maybe he was just too weak! But that is in the past, and now we must look to the future!"

Al-'Aqran's hand slammed down on the table, rattling the coffee cups and spilling the one that sat before him. Hushimi quickly pulled out a handkerchief to mop up the liquid, but al-'Aqran swept his hand away. "Do you not understand? There is no difference between the past and the future! Honor is honor! And there is no time limit on honor! How can we look forward when the past is still mocking us?"

"It is not mocking us! It is not mocking the Cause! It is mocking Hakeem, and it is mocking you!"

"I am the Cause! I am the Cause," al-'Aqran shouted, his fist accenting each word on the table. "If I am mocked, the Cause is mocked! If I am insulted, the Cause is insulted! Do you still not understand, you ignorant son of a sow?"

Hejazi shot up out of his chair. "I will not be insulted! You have obviously been more affected by your time with the Americans than you think! The Cause is not one man!" Hejazi swept his arms around to the other men. "We, together, are the Cause! By saying otherwise, you insult not just me but everyone at this table! We have given up everything to come and serve Allah's purpose, but you so easily dismiss that sacrifice with your words! I'm sorry to say it, but I think it is time for a change in leadership. Your own words have condemned you."

Looking at each man around the table, Hejazi continued, "I ask that each of you stand with me, signifying your agreement that, for the good of the Cause, we must put the past behind and focus on our future of bringing the Great Satan to its knees!"

Rather than reply to this challenge, al-'Aqran smiled and leaned back in his chair. *It is done. The fool has overplayed his hand. He has officially hung himself. Now let him dangle from the end of his own rope.*

Perspiration poured down Hejazi's full face as he turned to one man after another. Hushimi and Talib bored holes into the tabletop with their eyes. Asaf and Zahir, however, stared defiantly at Hejazi as they held their seats. *Those two are my warriors,* thought al-'Aqran.

After a tension-filled minute had passed, the defeated man sighed deeply and silently took his seat. Hejazi said nothing more, but his hard look at the downturned heads of Hushimi and Talib bespoke a betrayal.

When he felt the point had been clearly made, al-'Aqran finally broke the silence, his voice calm and friendly. "My dear Kamal, how is your son, Atef? You must be so proud to have such a legacy to carry on the Hejazi name. Isn't he at . . . what university is he at again, Babrak?"

Still keeping his eyes locked on Hejazi, the young man answered, "He is taking his medical studies at October 6 University, southwest of Cairo, and stays in room 435 of the school's dormitory."

Al-'Aqran watched as the color drained out of Hejazi's face. "A doctor for a son—what a marvelous thing."

"A-Atef . . . ," Hejazi stammered, "Atef has nothing to do with this, *sayyid.*"

"I agree that he does not now," al-'Aqran answered. "However, if I ever hear of you questioning any of my decisions again, it likely will necessitate our dear friend Babrak personally—how should I say it—checking in on the progress of your son's studies. Do you understand?"

Hejazi was visibly shaking but managed to slowly nod his head.

"And now, you are excused from this room and from this council. Hamad will contact you later as to if and how your services might be needed."

Al-'Aqran watched as Hejazi stood, head bowed, and made a quick exit. As soon as the door latched, al-'Aqran swept his empty cup off the table and sent it crashing against the wall. Pushing the table away from him, he got up and limped through the thin cotton curtains behind him and onto the balcony.

Below, the masses of people were filing by, filling the sidewalks and spilling out onto the street. The noise of car horns, street vendors, and a thousand private conversations danced around him. He watched until he saw Hejazi walk out of the building and join the human river. His eyes didn't leave the disgraced man until he had crested the hill two blocks up.

Al-'Aqran turned now to his right and gazed out at the blue waters of the Bosporus Strait. A massive cruise liner was making its way under the Fatih Sultan Mehmet Bridge, while far below its decks water taxis and fishing boats carried out their commerce.

An organization is only as strong as its weakest link, he remembered reading a long time back. *Well, that one weak link has been removed. It is time now for the rest of the chain to begin swinging.*

**THURSDAY, MAY 14, 3:45 P.M. MDT
DENVER, COLORADO**

"I spy with my little eye something . . . white!"

Scott Ross laughed, "Yeah, I guess it is a little sterile in here. I keep expecting Nurse Ratched to come down the hallway with my medication."

The corridor that Scott, Riley, and Skeeter were walking down was absolutely without color—from the gleaming tiles to the painted bricks to the can lights mounted on the wall. *A person could suffer from snow blindness walking through here*, Riley thought as his Merrells squeaked their way across the thickly waxed floor.

The only things that broke up the homage to sensory deprivation were the secure entry system and black nameplate next to the occasional door. The plate mounted on the wall where the three friends now stopped read *Front Range Response Team*.

Scott placed his hand on Riley's arm. "Although I know I don't need to say this, I still need to say this. Nothing you see in this room leaves this room."

"No problem. It saves me the trouble of having to swallow the microfilm from my secret spy camera," Riley responded. When Scott stopped laughing, he continued, "I understand, buddy. But you better watch Skeeter—he's the one that's always shooting his mouth off. Right, Skeet?"

"Mmmm," Skeeter replied.

"I'll start worrying about the big guy after he learns to speak in complete sentences," Scott said, smiling, as he turned toward the retinal scanner. After hearing a beep of recognition, he punched in a six-digit code. The lock audibly disengaged, and Scott pulled the door open.

Riley's eyes were met with a veritable visual feast for surveillance technology junkies. *How many millions of dollars did it take to deck out this room?* he wondered. As he took in the scene, he spotted Khadi staring over Tara's shoulder at a computer monitor. A glimpse of her profile reminded Riley that she was the most beautiful woman he had ever seen. The insecure teenage kid in him again wondered what in the world she was doing giving him the time of day.

As if feeling Riley's gaze on her, Khadi suddenly looked up and saw him. Her face lit up, but she held up a finger indicating that she still needed a minute.

Riley gave a quick wave letting her know to take her time, then turned to Scott. "So, are you going to give us the grand tour?"

"Of course. We've still got about fifteen minutes before Jim's schedule will open up for our meeting."

"Skeeter!" a voice called out from across the room. Riley, Skeeter, and Scott looked over in time to see Virgil Hernandez doing a Starsky & Hutch slide over the well-polished wooden conference table and landing between two chairs.

Giving Riley a quick "Hey," Hernandez put his arm around Skeeter and started leading him over to his workstation. "Dude, I've been digging on that whole 'was the Third Punic War a just war' thing you turned me on to. That's a hairy question."

"Yeah, boy," Skeeter agreed as he walked away with Hernandez. "Polybius's hypothesis was that Rome usually acted out of fear—you know, like more of a hyperpreventative philosophy—instead of a traditional just war model of . . ."

Riley turned to Scott as Skeeter's voice faded out, and they both started cracking up. "That one sentence contained more words than I've heard Skeet say in the past three months," Riley said, raising an eyebrow. "'Hyperpreventative philosophy'? Someone's got way too much time on his hands!"

For the next fifteen minutes, Scott showed Riley around the new facility. It wasn't until Riley greeted the third analyst that he noticed something had changed in the way they treated him. In contrast to when he'd worked with CTD a few months ago, now as he went up to the analysts at their workstations, they quickly checked what was on their monitors (Gooey had actually turned his off) and casually placed their arms across any papers that might be scattered in front of them. *Interesting development,* Riley thought.

But even as he was checking out all the new state-of-the-art equipment and talking with the analyst team, his eyes kept going back to where Khadi stood in conference with Tara. He was relieved—and maybe a little disappointed—to see that he was not a distraction to her. Ever since her initial acknowledgment, she hadn't even looked his way.

"Must be something pretty major they're talking about," Riley said to Scott.

Scott smiled. "Why? Because Khadi hasn't given you the time of day since you came in?"

"She waved to me," Riley answered, more defensively than he had intended.

"An outstretched finger is not a wave, my friend," Scott continued to dig.

Riley started to reply, but Scott cut him off. "Sorry, Mr. Covington, but it is time for your meeting to begin. Khadi, Tara," he summoned over his shoulder, then pointed at his watch. They each gave a quick nod and began gathering the papers around them.

Scott then called out, "Skeeter, you'll want to be part of this too."

Giving Hernandez a pat on the shoulder, the big man joined up with Scott and Riley.

/////////////////////////

The one room Riley had not seen yet was Jim Hicks's office, and that was right where Scott led him. Scott gave a quick knock on the glass door, then opened it without waiting for a reply.

Hicks stood up as Riley entered the room and leaned over his desk with his hand outstretched. "Riley! How're you doing?"

Riley grabbed Hicks's hand and gave it a warm shake. Although their relationship had started out extremely rocky, the past months had created a deep respect between the two men. "Doing all right, thanks. You?"

"Can't complain; can't complain. Skeet?"

"Fine, sir," Skeeter replied in his Mississippi drawl as Hicks's hand disappeared in his own.

"Excellent. Please, guys, sit down," Hicks said, motioning to the small conference table in his office. He turned to Scott. "Khadi and Tara?"

"On their way."

"Good." Hicks took a seat at the head of the table. "So, how's football?"

"Football's football. You love it; you hate it."

"Hey, Riley," Scott interrupted, "while we're waiting on the females, tell Jim about that medical workout thing you did—you know, the one in the bubble."

"Nah," Riley demurred.

"Come on, Riley, let's hear it," Hicks encouraged him.

"You sure you're interested?"

"If I don't hear it from you, I'll hear it from Scott—and far less accurately, I'm sure. Better to get it from the source."

"Okay," Riley began. "So a few weeks ago, I'm in that big white bubble off of Peoria and Arapahoe in Englewood—you know the one I'm talking about?"

Hicks nodded while Scott already began snickering.

"Wait for it," Riley admonished Scott. "Anyway, I guess the Mustangs were thinking I've gotten banged up in who knows what kind of ways over the past few months, and they want to see what kind of shape I'm in. The doc they sent puts me through all sorts of run drills and pattern drills. I check out okay. Then he wants to see how I handle contact.

"He tells me to wait on the field, and he walks over and picks up a pad. Now, he's a pretty big guy, but I'm still thinking, 'This guy's no professional. This is not going to be pretty.' So he walks up to me and says, 'Okay, I want you to go all out. But since I've got to be watching you, I'm not going to go up against you; she is.' And he points to this girl on the sidelines.

"She comes running out, and she's like five feet eight and 245 pounds. I turn to the doc and say, 'I'm not going up against her!' And the girl says, 'What's the matter? You scared?' I say, 'Yeah, scared I'm going to kill you!'"

Hicks was laughing. "Let me guess—wrong thing to say?"

"Oh yeah! The girl goes ballistic! She throws down the pad and yells, 'Come on! I don't need no pad! I'm a two-time judo champion! I'll have you crawling! You'll be begging for mercy!'"

Just then, Khadi and Tara walked in. Khadi started shaking her head. "Ah, the infamous judo-chick story."

"May I continue?" Riley asked Khadi.

"Please," Khadi encouraged him, then leaned over to Tara to fill her in on the backstory.

"So, I'm looking to Skeeter over on the sidelines for some help, and Mr. I've-Got-Your-Back calls out, 'If she ain't packing a weapon, I can't do nothing.' Now, I don't know how much you know about football contact, but most of it is in the . . ." Riley started grabbing around the front of his own shirt as he searched for the right word.

That made Scott and Hicks laugh even more. "I think *chest* is an acceptable term to use in mixed company," Scott assured Riley.

"Okay, so most of the contact is in the *chest*." On the last word Riley unconsciously lowered his voice, which caused everyone to lose it—even Skeeter. Riley's face turned a dark shade of red. "You guys going to let me tell this story or not?"

"Of course," Scott answered, "as long as you quit using such offensive language."

"So, *anyway*," Riley said, trying to regain control of the room, "she's all up in my face while I'm trying to tell the doc I'm not doing this. She's saying stuff like, 'What's the matter? You afraid of a little female contact, choirboy?' and 'Come on, it's not like you're married or anything!' I tell her, 'That's true, but you're sort of missing the point!' I finally just start walking off the field, and the doc stops me and tells the gal to pick up the pad.

"I knew I wasn't going to get out of there without doing this contact drill, so I figured, let's just get this over with. So, we start going down the field—me taking it a little easy, pushing into her and her falling back. That didn't last long. Jim, seriously, this chick wanted to kill me! She was hitting high! She was dropping low! Forget the Cause! Forget any terrorist psychos! This girl was and is enemy number one." Riley sat back in his seat while everyone laughed.

"Wait! Don't stop now, *choirboy*," Scott encouraged Riley. "Tell him the end!"

Riley's face started to redden again as he leaned forward again. "Okay, so we get to the end of the field then come back up. When we finally cross the fifty, I'm fed up. I give her one final push and she goes flying back onto the ground. I'm thinking, 'Great, I just broke her,' so I rush over to help her up. But before I can get to her, she jumps up, gets this big ol' smile on her face, and says, 'Nice work, Covington.' Then, as she runs past me, she slaps me on my . . ." Riley's voice trailed off again, and he nodded his head backward.

"I think the word *buttocks* also meets with governmental standards," Scott finished. "Oh, boy! Of all people for that to happen to."

"No matter how funny it sounds, it looked even better," Skeeter said with a big grin on his face as he moved his hands around in front of himself, imitating Riley trying to figure out where he was going to grab the girl.

They all had one more laugh at Riley's expense, and then Hicks brought the meeting to order.

"Riley, this isn't going to take too long. I brought you in here basically to tell you one thing. You have got a target the size of Montana on your back right now."

Out of the corner of his eye, Riley saw Skeeter unconsciously shift his hand closer to the Heckler & Koch concealed under his light jacket.

"You know, this isn't exactly news. Costa Rica made that fact pretty clear." Riley saw Hicks bristle at the reminder of those events, but he pushed on anyway. "I've got Skeeter, who won't even let me take a shower without standing there holding the towel. We take all the necessary precautionary measures. I'm not sure what else I can do except to go into hiding."

Hicks just stared at Riley, and no one else at the table said a word.

"Wait, you're serious? You want me to go into hiding? You've got to be kidding me! There's no way I'm running away to go hide in a cave—leave that to the al-Qaeda vermin! I mean, come on, you're acting like this is the eighties and I'm Salman Rushdie!"

"You're right," Hicks said, keeping his calm, "but if you remember, Rushdie only had one psycho who died trying to kill him. So far, your failed assassin body count is up to five."

Khadi now spoke up. "Riley, you need to listen to Jim. He's not telling you to go into hiding right now. He's just saying that you need to be ready to dive for cover at the drop of a hat and stay there if need be. None of us would even be suggesting this, except that the information we've been getting is . . . well, it's just a very dangerous world for you right now."

"We've always known that what little's left of the Cause would be gunning for me for a while. We're taking precautions against it. Now you're getting *information* that says this isn't enough anymore? Can one of you please share with me what this information is that's so terrible I should scurry into a hole like a scared rabbit?"

"No, we can't, actually," said Hicks. "Since you've been decommissioned, this stuff is beyond your clearance. And I just want to make it clear," he continued to the rest of the table, "that I will not tolerate any of this information being *accidentally* left out on a desk for Riley to *accidentally* see. Understood?"

Khadi snapped back at Hicks, "Listen, Jim, if you think that I am unprofessional enough to compromise information just because Riley and I—"

"I wasn't talking about you, Khadi; was I, Scott?"

Both Scott's and Khadi's faces reddened.

"Understood, boss," Scott replied quietly.

Riley sunk back into his chair. Suddenly, the way the analysts outside had covered up their work during his office tour made a lot more sense. Riley was angry, but not at Hicks. Rules and codes were covenants that he lived by. Even though he didn't like it, he understood where Hicks was coming from.

"Can you give me anything that could help me to make my decision?" he asked Hicks.

"Sure, let me give you all I can. Right now you've got three strikes against you. Strike one, early this morning our time, the Cause—of which, by the way, we're learning there's more than just a little left—got some Muslim cleric to declare a *fatwa* against you for blasphemy against Islam."

"Blasphemy against Islam? When have I ever—?"

Hicks held up his hand to stop Riley. "That's not really the point, is it? The fact is that it has been declared, and they've come up with their reasons. That means you're going to have a bunch of radical Islamists from all camps promised a golden ticket to heaven if they take you out."

"By the way, Riley," Tara interjected, "this is probably going to hit the major news outlets in the next few hours, so be prepared to be barraged by the media. You'll also want to think through what the ramifications might be with the Mustangs."

"Good point," Hicks continued. "Thanks, Tara. Now for strike two. For those for whom the golden ticket is not enough, the Cause has also put out a $5 million bounty on you."

"The most Rushdie ever had was $3 million," Scott said. "But before you let that go to your head, remember that was back in 1989. If you adjust that three mil for inflation, he's got about a hundred grand on you. Sorry."

"Scott, just once in one of these meetings I'd like you to ask yourself, 'Is what I have to say going to help the situation or hinder it?'" Tara challenged.

Scott was about to reply, but Hicks took back control. "Listen, if I let you two start going at it, we'll never get out of here, so zip it—the both of you! Now, strike three is the Cause itself. We've intercepted enough COMINT to know that you are number two on their to-do list."

"Number two, huh? What's number one?" Riley asked.

Hicks smiled. "Sorry, Riley. Can't tell you that. But I hope you can see why we're so concerned right now."

Riley sat back in his chair. *How have things come to this? How, in five months' time, have I moved from being first-string linebacker to*

Islamic Enemy Number Two? He sighed heavily. "You know, I didn't ask for any of this."

"Actually, you did, sir," Skeeter said, and all eyes turned toward him. "When you said you weren't going to let those terrorists win. When you put your life on the line instead of sitting back all comfortable and letting everyone else do the dirty work. Yeah, you were asking for it all right . . . and that's why I'm with you asking for it, too."

Skeeter's words hung in the air.

"Dude's getting downright verbose," Scott said when he couldn't stand the silence any longer.

"So what do I do?" Riley asked, ignoring Scott's comment.

"For now, just keep doing what you're doing," answered Hicks. "We're going to be getting Skeet more help, so he doesn't need to worry as much about his perimeter—just about you. Also, we're going to be setting your parents and your grandfather up with some protection."

Riley breathed a sigh of relief. "Thanks. I was just going to ask you about that." The thought of his family getting hurt because of a vendetta against him gripped his stomach and brought a burning to his throat.

"If you've got no other questions . . ." Hicks stood before Riley had a chance to ask any, indicating the meeting was at an end. He reached out and grabbed Riley's hand. "Basically, you just need to be careful. Don't do anything stupid that puts you or your security detail at extra risk. Riley, I know you're a praying man. The best thing you can do right now is just start praying that we can finish off the Cause once and for all. If we don't and they get their way, then all indications are that your life will just be one of many that ends by their hands."

FRIDAY, MAY 15, 5:45 P.M. EDT
PHILADELPHIA, PENNSYLVANIA

Isaac Khan boarded the subway from the Washington Square West neighborhood of Philadelphia.
Pushing through the people standing around the
doors, he dropped himself onto a rare rush-hour
seat. He hefted the backpack up onto his lap,
causing the passenger in the next seat to glare at
him—a look Isaac returned until the man turned
away.

The train rattled and bumped, but the people
on board were eerily quiet. Typically, the noise in
the car would increase greatly over the next two
hours as the commuters were replaced with those
heading out for a night on the town.

Isaac knew that today, however, would be
anything but typical.

One stop later, the train eased to a halt at 8th
Street. Feigning a hip injury, Isaac limped out the
door and made his way to a bench. He dropped
himself down with a grunt and set his large backpack on his right.

Leaning back, he pulled his bright orange
Philadelphia Flyers cap over his eyes and listened
to the bustle all around as people transferred from
the upper SEPTA subway line to this lower PATCO

Speedline to make their way back home to the New Jersey suburbs of Camden, Haddonfield, and Cherry Hill Township. Others moved the opposite direction, up the stairs to catch the Broad Street Line to take them north to Olney and Fern Rock or south to catch the Philadelphia Phillies night game against the New York Mets.

After a few minutes, Isaac, with his head still back, let his hand slip down the rear of the backpack. His blood began racing as he reached the small hole in the rear padding. His fingers found a key, which he turned and then pulled out. Immediately he began counting in his head. However, his heart was beating so fast and so much adrenaline was pulsing through his body that he twice lost count somewhere after thirty. Finally, leaving the backpack on the bench, he stood up and began quickly moving toward the stairway—his hip injury miraculously healed.

Isaac merged with the crowd on the stairs. Businessmen pushed up against him; women brazenly brushed against him; young punks cut in front of him without so much as an "excuse me." Frustration filled his mind with the realization that these were the people who were going to get away. How he wished that all of these arrogant, obnoxious people would feel Allah's wrath today.

Cresting the top of the stairs, he had just joined the mass moving toward the northbound tracks when the blast hit.

It was strong enough to cause movement under his feet, but where he really felt it was in his ears. The explosion itself was deafening as it echoed through the station, but then came the most frightening sound of all—the metallic spray of thousands of screws ricocheting off of cement and tile.

The panic was instantaneous. People began running and screaming. An enormous cloud of smoke and dust rushed up the stairs and spread throughout the first floor. Isaac sucked in a lungful of the gritty vapor and immediately began coughing.

Bodies fell to the ground around him as the strong pushed the weak from their escape path. There was a mad scramble for the narrow stairs that would take the crowd up to street level and freedom. Isaac quickly merged in with the mob, at one point ducking his head down and throwing his dust-covered Flyers cap to the ground.

For a moment, Isaac thought he wasn't going to make it up the stairs. The funnel of fleeing people crushed the air out of him. It felt like trying to pass too thick a rag through too small a gun barrel. A woman next to him was screaming hysterically, and Isaac marveled that she had the breath to do it.

When he finally broke free into the fading afternoon sun, the fresh breeze felt like Allah's blessing upon him. Elation rushed through his body. He wanted to scream! He wanted to dance! Finally, after all these years, he was the hammer in the hand of God. Isaac could almost hear the words "Well done, my child!"

Leaving his handiwork behind, Isaac began walking back to Washington Square West, struggling to control his pace. A rush lightened his head every time another siren raced past. Although part of him wanted to stay and watch the rescue attempts, he knew that would be foolish—and foolishness was one thing that Allah would not abide, especially not from one of his chosen servants.

Besides, Isaac desperately wanted to get back to New York, where he knew that safely tucked away in his apartment, under his bed, two more backpacks awaited him.

FRIDAY, MAY 15, 5:30 P.M. CDT
SOUTH BEND, INDIANA

Mohsin Ghani used the end of his $130 Burberry woven silk tie to wipe the sweat and tears from his eyes. Although the basilica was temperature controlled, it felt to him like it was located two planets closer to the sun. Mohsin had been using a tie-matching handkerchief as his face towel, but that was now sitting next to him on the pew, crumpled in a damp ball. A three-quarters-empty water bottle sat beside it.

Mohsin could not believe the situation he was in. It was absolutely surreal. Just over a decade ago he had walked through the Basilica of the Sacred Heart when he visited the University of Notre Dame. Back then, he was an excited college senior searching for the right graduate school. Now, he had returned to blow the building up.

What are you doing here? Mohsin's head spun, and for a moment he felt like he was going to faint. He took a deep swallow from the water bottle.

Get it together, he chastised himself. *It's not like you have a choice.*

Just reach into the backpack, turn the key, and walk out. You'll be well gone before the . . . before the . . .

Another sob escaped him, causing a well-dressed woman in the next pew to turn slightly and offer him a tissue. Mohsin muttered a thank-you and loudly blew his nose.

The twentysomething next to him gave him a good-natured elbow and said, "Lighten up, buddy; this is a wedding, not a funeral."

When Mohsin didn't acknowledge his remark, the young man turned to his friend on the other side and said something that soon had both of them quietly snickering.

Anger flared in Mohsin's heart. *You see? These are the kind of arrogant people who deserve what they are going to get! I'm trying to find a way to save their lives, and here they are mocking me. So do it! Just do it! Turn the key, excuse yourself, and drive back to Chicago. You can leave the TV off! You never even have to hear about it! Besides, these people are nothing to you—less than nothing!*

Mohsin's attention was suddenly drawn to the front of the church by a young lady singing the title track to his favorite Norah Jones CD. Many an evening Mohsin had spent stretched out on his couch with a glass of pinot grigio, dreaming about "coming away" with Norah and kissing her on a mountaintop. *Merciful Allah, what am I doing here? How can I do this?*

Heaving a big sigh, Mohsin continued his prayer. *I am so weak. Please give me the strength to accept the things I cannot change and to carry out the task you have placed before me.*

Carefully, his hand found the cutout in the rear of the backpack. The key was warm to the touch. He let his thumb and forefinger rub its top and bottom. *Just one quick twist and it's done! Just one quick twist!* Mohsin's fingers clamped down on the small copper key. *How much can I push it before it accidentally turns?* He began softly applying clockwise pressure. *Maybe a little more and it will turn by mistake. I don't want it to, but* insha'Allah*, maybe God has willed it.*

The key budged. Mohsin gasped and pulled his hand away. "I can't," he said out loud.

"Then don't," said the guy next to him, causing his friend to laugh out loud and the well-dressed woman in front to shush all three.

I can't! I won't! They'll just have to understand that I'm the wrong person for this job. I'm not telling them they're right; I'm not telling them they're wrong. I'm just saying that they need to find someone else to do it.

With Mohsin's decision came an overwhelming sense of peace to his heart. He suddenly felt light, like he was in a dream. For the first time he really noticed his surroundings. The columns supporting the roof of the neo-Gothic church were topped with incredibly ornate, gilded caps. Surrounding the basilica were windows of intricate, colorful stained glass. *Just think: you just saved all this. You, Mohsin Ghani, made a decision, and as a result, all this beauty lives on.*

Up front, below the enormous golden main altar, the bride stood radiant in her mermaid-cut gown—the white of her bare shoulders showing clearly through her sheer mantilla veil. She was staring into the face of her soon-to-be-husband with so much love, so much excitement, so much passion.

Today, you had the power of life and death. You could have chosen to end the lives of this beautiful young woman and all who love her. Instead, you, Mohsin Ghani, benevolently chose to bestow the gift of life.

Mohsin slid down in the pew and tilted his head back until he felt the coolness of the old wood. Above him he discovered the murals that were spread across the arched ceiling sixty feet above where he sat. Most of the people depicted he didn't recognize. But then he found Moses—the great prophet of Judaism, Christianity, and Islam—his namesake.

Am I not like Moses? Moses had the power of life and death over his people. Several times God wanted to wipe out the entire nation, but Moses intervened. In the same way, haven't I intervened for these people, and hasn't God granted them life?

Continuing to ride the endorphin rush, Mohsin was drawn deeply into the mural. He closed his eyes, envisioning himself leading a mighty nation through the wilderness—Mohsin, the Great Prophet.

His imagination so carried him away that he didn't notice the pronouncement of the new couple; nor did he see their recession down the aisle. He didn't hear the parting insult of the young man who sat next to him. Instead, he just sat there, the mighty servant of God, until a priest touched him gently on the shoulder and said, "Son, it's time for you to go now."

Instinctively, Mohsin's hand grabbed for the backpack. "What?"

"You need to go, my son. There's another wedding starting soon."

"Oh, of course. I'm sorry."

Sliding the backpack over his sweat-soaked suit coat, Mohsin began to walk out. It was then that the deep sense of peace was forced out of him by an overwhelming feeling of dread. His knees buckled as he walked, and he caught himself on the font at the entrance to the basilica. They—whoever "they" were—would not let this slide. The men behind all this would soon come looking for answers. As he leaned on the marble, the tears began flowing again.

Get yourself together! Just make it home, and you can figure things out there. There has to be a way to make them understand that I'm not the right person for this job. They'll have to see all the ways I can help them other than doing this. That's what I'll do—I'll just explain it to them.

The water in the font looked cool and clean, and Mohsin dipped his hands in and splashed water on his face. He reached for his handkerchief, then realized he had left it on the pew. He used his sleeve to dab the water from his eyes, then walked out the door, feeling the cool breeze on his wet face.

I'll just explain it to them. They'll have to understand, Mohsin kept telling himself. But way deep down, in that part of his mind that always told the truth no matter how much he wished to ignore it, Mohsin knew as he crossed the grass to get back to his car that he was no better than a dead man walking.

The thick smoke swirled around Riley's head and stung his eyes. "You know, it's a scientifically proven fact," he said to Keith Simmons, who was looking way too comfortable sipping an Arnold Palmer in an Adirondack chair, "that no matter where you stand around a charcoal grill, that's the direction the wind is going to blow."

"Can't argue with physics," Simmons replied. "What I can't figure out is why you have that little jobber burning when you've already got your big old Nuclear Chef 2000 gas grill going. You could cook a water buffalo on that thing!"

Riley dabbed his forehead with a hand towel he had hanging over his shoulder. Although it had been two hours since he and Simmons had finished their workout, the unseasonably warm afternoon sun combined with the heat of the grills made Riley feel like his face would never be completely dry again. "Ah, my blissfully ignorant young protégé. First of all, this isn't just any gas grill; it is an infrared grill specially designed for the finest of steak-grilling perfection. However, for our corn, we want a little extra flavor. Thus, the Weber and our mesquite charcoal."

"Tell you what, Emeril, you cook the food, and I'll eat it. Any details beyond that, you can tell them to Skeeter here. Right, Skeet?" Simmons said, reaching to the next chair over and clapping Skeeter on the arm.

"Mmmm," Skeeter replied, never taking his eyes off the tree line spread across the back of Riley's property.

"See, I told you he'd warm up to me," Simmons said.

"Trust me, where Skeeter comes from, that's called a conversation." Sparks flew as Riley dumped the white-dusted coals from the smoker onto the grill. He quickly arranged the briquettes with a pair of tongs, feeling the heat curl the hairs on the back of his fingers. After dropping the top grate onto the barbecue, he said, "I'll be right back. I'm going to go snag the food."

"Go for it," Simmons replied before turning to Skeeter and saying, "I ever tell you about the time I was playing beach volleyball back in college? I was on spring break down in South Padre—"

The story cut off as Riley closed the patio door. *No big loss; I've heard that one so many times before. Guy jumps up for the spike . . . guy lands wrong on the sand . . . guy's toe pops off at the joint. Story still gives me the heebie-jeebies thinking about it.*

The coolness inside the house gave Riley a quick chill after standing in the heat for so long. As he crossed to the refrigerator, he could see the red message light blinking on his phone. *Can't imagine anyone I really want to talk to right now,* he thought. *Although that does remind me . . .*

He reached over to where he had dumped out his pockets on the kitchen counter and picked up his cell phone. Sure enough, he had forgotten to turn it back on after practice.

The last thing anyone wanted to have happen at a team meeting was for their cell phone to go off, especially Riley since it had been his first day back at minicamp and Coach Burton hadn't seemed all that happy to see him. The $1,500 fine would have been mild compared to the tongue-lashing he would have received. In fact, Coach hated cell phones so much that players and coaches alike knew without a doubt that if their phone went off, they were one step closer to being out the door permanently. Riley could remember one time when an assistant coach's cell phone had started ringing during a full team meeting. The man had gotten so panicked when he couldn't figure out how to silence the ringer that he had finally thrown the phone across the room, shattering it against the wall.

While the phone powered up, Riley pulled the steaks out of the refrigerator—three sixteen-ounce ribeyes, marinated to perfection. A beep from his cell phone told him he had messages there, too. *I'll deal with those later,* he thought as he slid the phone into his shorts pocket. He swung the patio door open and was greeted with the two outdoor constants—heat and Simmons's voice. Stacking the butter baste on top of the plate of corn, he walked out to the grills, nearly stumbling as he shut the door with his foot.

"Okay, Simm, come on up and learn from the master," Riley interrupted.

"I told you—as long as it ends up on my plate, I don't care how it gets there."

"Sure you care. You just don't know that you do. Come on."

"Better go," Skeeter encouraged him, "else we're never going to eat."

Simmons reluctantly pushed himself up from his chair. "What happened to the good old days when I could go to someone's house and just be served without actually having to participate? Okay, so show me the . . . Hold up, what is that?" he asked, pointing at a bowl of yellow liquid.

"That, my dear uninterested friend, is a baste for our corn. Take a whiff," Riley said, holding the bowl up to Simmons's face. "You've got melted butter, freshly cracked pepper, and a truckload of garlic."

"Oh yeah. Consider my interest piqued. And what've you got on those steaks?"

Riley put down the bowl and lifted the Pyrex dish holding the steaks. "It's called Montreal seasoning. This marinade and Mario Lemieux are the best things that ever came out of that city."

"The only good things," Skeeter muttered under his breath.

"Now, now, Skeet," Riley chided him, "while most of the civilized world may agree with you, you must remember that there are certain things that we shouldn't say . . . at least not out loud."

Simmons took a deep whiff of the steaks. "Man, that smells incredible too."

"Ask him what's in it," Skeeter said, still watching the trees.

"What?" asked Simmons.

"He didn't say anything."

"Ask him what's in the seasoning," Skeeter repeated.

"Who invited you into this conversation anyway?" Riley complained. "Go guard something."

"So, Chef Pach," Simmons said with a smile, "what's in the seasoning?"

Riley sighed. "Okay, if you have to know, I have no clue what's in the seasoning. It comes in a packet. You happy, smiley-boy?" he said to a grinning Skeeter.

"Ecstatic."

"Dude, don't hate on my man Skeeter," Simmons said, walking over and putting a hand on Skeeter's shoulder. "I like it when he opens up."

"Yeah, well maybe it's about time he closes back down," Riley said, dropping the steaks onto the grill. The ensuing sizzle all but drowned out the last two words of his sentence.

As he reached over to start basting the corn before dropping it onto the Weber, he saw Skeeter whispering something in Simmons's ear. *Oh no. What now?*

"Hey, Pach," came Simmons's voice as Riley placed the first ear onto the grill, "aren't you going to ask me how I want my steak done?"

Riley looked over and saw the two men laughing. Skeeter said, "There's only one way a steak is cooked around here—the Riley way."

"Why? Don't you know how to cook steaks any other way?" Simmons asked.

But before Riley could defend himself, Skeeter answered for him, "Sure, he knows how. He just figures, 'Why would anybody want it cooked any different from how I like it?'"

"Well, why would they?" Riley said with a smile. He set the rest of the corn on the grill, and then turned back to crosshatch the steaks. The smells in his backyard were just reaching the heavenly stage.

A ring came from his front pocket, and Riley pulled out his cell phone. The caller ID said *Scott Cell*, so he hit Talk. "Hey, Scott."

"Pach! Where've you been, man? I've been leaving messages all over." Riley could hear concern in Scott's voice. *That's never good.*

"Sorry, my bad. I've got a buddy over, and we're cooking some steaks. What's up?"

"As you can imagine, things are going crazy here. I just wanted to see how you were handling all this."

Great, thought Riley, *another one of Scott's cryptic calls.* "Scott, I have absolutely no clue what you're talking about . . . again. Handling all what?"

"All what? Philadelphia! Haven't you been watching the news?"

A sick feeling spread through Riley. "Scott, we came right from practice to my backyard. I haven't heard a thing."

Riley heard popping starting from the corn on the grill and quickly began turning the ears over while Scott said, "We've been hit again. A bomb in a subway station in Philly."

"Oh no. Is it bad?"

"Rush hour combined with an explosive device containing thousands of screws. You do the math."

"How did . . . hang on a sec. Skeet, can you come take over?" While Riley headed toward the quiet of the pool area, the big man walked over. As they passed, Riley said to him, "We've been hit again—a bomb in a subway in Philly."

Immediately, Skeeter grabbed Riley and pushed him toward the house. "Finish your call inside! Keith, get over here and watch the food."

Simmons was about to protest until he saw Skeeter drawing his gun. "You got it, man!"

Riley knew better than to argue with Skeeter. After he closed the patio door, he said into the phone, "Scott, you still there?"

"Yeah, what's going on?"

"Skeeter."

"Enough said."

Riley looked out the window and saw Simmons standing in front of the grill, looking at him helplessly. Riley motioned for him to flip the steaks over. Simmons gave a thumbs up and set to work.

Beyond Simmons, Riley could see Skeeter kneeling in a defensive posture, scanning the tree line with the barrel of his gun looking like a third eye.

"Okay, tell me what happened."

"There's not much to tell yet. We still don't even know if it was a suicide bomb. I'll tell you what I *can* tell you when I get more intel. Right now, I just wanted to make sure you were okay."

"We're fine." Riley rapped on the glass door and pointed at the corn. Simmons began turning them again. "I can't believe they've started again."

"Pach, don't go jumping to any conclusions. We don't even know who 'they' are yet. There are a lot of other bad guys in this world. We don't need to automatically assume it's the Cause."

"Yeah, you're right." But the sick feeling in Riley's stomach told him that Scott wasn't right. *No, this is the Cause. You guys said it yourselves: we hurt them, but we didn't kill them.* "You'll keep me up-to-date."

"That's what I promised you. Hang in, bud. I'll call back later."

"Thanks, Scott." Riley pressed End, then sat down at the kitchen table. He put his head in his hands and prayed, *Lord, please don't let this start again. I just . . . I don't want to go through this again. I can't go through it again.* The dead face of his friend Sal Ricci flashed in his mind. His chest felt like a hand had gripped his heart. *But if You do let it start, please protect those around me.*

Suddenly, the door opened behind Riley. He jumped up, slamming his knee into the table leg. "Oh, stinkdog!" he yelled, grabbing his wounded joint as he turned around.

Simmons was there laughing. "Buddy, you've got to learn some better cussword substitutes. I was just wondering if I should take the food off. It's looking pretty done."

Riley had totally forgotten about the barbecue. "Yeah, please. Thanks."

"You okay, man? And what's up with Rambo out there?"

"I'm fine. Just bring the food inside, if you would, and I'll tell you about it when you get in. I don't think Skeeter's going to be eating with us."

As Riley watched Simmons pull the steaks off the grill, he tried to think through how to break the news to his teammate. Simmons still carried a long scar on his leg from the December attack on Platte River Stadium. Riley knew that his emotional scar was a lot bigger.

What a shame, Riley thought as Simmons carried the food toward the door. *Even with all this great food, I think Simm's about to become the third person to completely lose his appetite.*

FRIDAY, MAY 15, 7:30 P.M. PDT
HOLLYWOOD, CALIFORNIA

Hundreds of flashes lit up the warm California night. The premier of Larry Matthew's latest directorial work was certainly a cause to be celebrated, and all the beautiful people of Hollywood had come out to do just that. Long cars, short dresses, and big jewels were evident all around. The red carpet was stretched out, and the rope barriers on either side could barely contain the entertainment reporters and paparazzi who were all shouting out, "Taylor! Taylor!" trying to get the attention of the costar of the film as he made his way to the entrance.

In the middle of this media circus, Naheed Yamani held her camera up and let its shutter click off a series of pictures. When the furor died down, she gave a squeeze to the excessively hairy arm of the man standing next to her. "I'm so glad you're here to help me, Wes! I don't know what I'd be doing if I hadn't found you."

Wes, who had the appearance of a man for whom female attention was not commonplace, got a big smile on his face. "You just lift your camera when I lift mine and point it in the same direction. We'll get you through this."

Naheed rapidly clapped her hands as she

bounced up and down. "Thank you, thank you, thank you! If I don't get these pictures, my boss will kill me, and I absolutely need this job. Oh look, here comes another one!"

A black Lincoln stretch limousine pulled up to the curb. Wes and a hundred other photographers got their cameras at the ready, elbowing each other to get the right position. Naheed followed suit. As the next batch of beautiful people stepped out of the car and made their way down the carpet, the cameras all started clicking and whirring, and shouts of "Ashley! Ashley!" filled the air.

While everyone's attention was on the young celebrity couple, Naheed took the opportunity to look around at the security. No police or rent-a-cops seemed to be near her position in the middle of the media mob. Her placement seemed perfect.

"You can put your camera down now," Wes said with a grin. "Besides, you forgot to press that little button on top that we talked about."

Naheed looked at her camera like she had just now discovered it in her hands. "Oh! You're right! I don't know what happened! I just froze!" Tears began forming in her eyes.

Suddenly, the crowd swelled up again. "Lana! Lana!" Lana paused on the carpet as if she were actually astonished to hear her name. She let the look of surprise slide into her well-rehearsed, million-dollar smile. After giving a final wave, she continued into the theater.

"I stink at this! I'm so busted," Naheed said as she grabbed Wes's arm again and pressed her whole body up against his side.

Wes took a moment to experience each and every one of her curves, then answered, "Don't cry. C'mon, I told you I'd get your back. I'll tell you what, when I process my pics, I'll shoot some off to you. They won't be the same ones I'm using, but I can guarantee you they'll still be great."

Now the crocodile tears really flowed. "You're an angel! You're my big ol' angel sent straight from heaven," Naheed cried, pressing even tighter against him. Wes quickly handed her his handkerchief, the texture of which almost made her lose her lunch. "Thank you so, so, so, so much! But I'll only let you do that on one condition."

"Of course you can credit yourself for the pics."

Naheed laughed and slapped his arm. "Not that, silly. *You* need to promise *me* that I can take you out for a drink when this is all done."

Wes gave as big a bow as the cramped conditions allowed him and spoke using his renaissance faire voice. "Well, if that's the cost these days for chivalry, m'lady, then I will gladly pay the price."

Naheed replied with a curtsy. "My hero." Wes's big smile revealed teeth that made Naheed think of her great-uncle Abadi, whose rancid kisses all the girls hid to avoid.

After a moment, she said, "Oh goodness, I've been crying! I must look a mess!"

"You look beautiful," Wes replied, instantly turning red.

Naheed gave him another playful slap on the arm. "Oh you! Flattery will get you everywhere! Actually, I really need to find a bathroom to freshen myself up."

"Why do you need a bathroom? Here," he said, turning his camera toward her, "you can look right into the reflection of my lens and—"

"Wes Freeman," Naheed said, feigning indignation, "didn't your mother ever teach you to never ask a girl why she needs to run to the restroom?"

Naheed squatted down and opened her backpack. Inside she found her small clutch purse. Right before pulling it out, however, she reached under the handbag and twisted a key. After pulling the key out and sliding it into the front zip pouch of her purse, Naheed stood back up and said, "You don't mind if I leave my stuff here, do you? My boss gave me so much junk to bring, it weighs a ton!"

"Well, I'd hate for anything to happen to it while—"

"What could happen to it while the gallant Sir Wes is in charge? Ple-e-e-ase?"

Naheed could see Wes melting under her touch. "Sure. Let's just put it right up against my legs so that I can feel it's there." He slid the bag up against himself. "Holy smoke, you aren't kidding! What do you have in this thing?"

"For me to know, and for you later to find out! But no peeky. Promise?"

"Promise."

"Good, a girl's got to have a few secrets," Naheed said with a wink. She stood up on her toes and gave Wes a kiss on the cheek, then said with all the earnestness she could muster, "Wes Freeman, I'm glad I met you."

"I'm glad too. Now go, so you can hurry back."

Naheed began weaving her way through the crowd. She could feel Wes's eyes on her back, so she turned around and gave him a coquettish wave. Wes responded with another half bow.

What an idiot, Naheed thought as she turned around. *Talk about someone who deserves to die just for being so stupid!*

The three blocks to the car seemed like an eternity to Naheed. She had forgotten to look at her watch when she activated the device, so she had no clue when it was going to go off. Although she didn't feel bad about placing the bomb, she wasn't sure if she actually wanted to hear it.

She had just started her engine when the blast reached her ears. She looked in her rearview mirror and saw the rising cloud of smoke. *You've done it, girl! Welcome to the wonderful world of terrorism!* She tried to smile, but something in her heart was tearing.

Okay, you knew this part might be tough. Just don't think about it. Just don't think about it.

Do you realize how many people you just killed?

Just don't think about it!

People a couple hundred meters away with screws imbedded in their bodies.

Just don't think about it!

How many kids? How many kids are screaming in pain right now, or will be screaming when they find out their mommy or daddy's just been blown to pieces?

JUST DON'T THINK ABOUT IT!

Naheed snatched her iPod out of her purse, slipped in the ear-buds, and spun the volume up to full. The music drowned out her thoughts during the drive to LAX, the dropping off of the rental car, the ditching of the blonde wig, the retrieval of her own car from long-term parking, and most of the drive back north to San Francisco. By the time the battery on her nano finally gave out south of Tracy, she had sung and danced the night's events into a well-hidden and seldom-accessed drawer in her mental filing cabinet.

A quarter mile up the road, Abdullah Muhammad could see the soft yellow porch lights of the farmhouse. In the fields surrounding his car, fireflies blinked on and off and crickets chirped in the balmy late spring air. As Abdullah dragged on his Newport, his mind processed his next steps. *First thing, shoot the dog. All these places have dogs, and all these hicks have guns.*

The menthol smoke streamed up through the crack in the driver's side window and was quickly wisped away by the gentle night breeze. The thought of breaking into the house made Abdullah hesitate for a moment. In his mind he heard Denver Police dispatch announcing a 459 in progress. A humorless chuckle escaped his lips. *I guess I can't worry about a simple B&E when I already have a quadruple homicide among the evening's earlier activities.*

That first operation had been a crucial transition in his life. It was the moment he had metamorphosed from law enforcer to lawbreaker; from protector to killer.

Abdullah's badge had gained him entrance into the house on Sibbitt Road in Hyannis, Nebraska. His nerves caused him to shake outside the door, but once he crossed the threshold, he switched to automatic pilot. All the fears and doubts evaporated the second his silenced Walther P99 ended the life of the father in the entry hall. Abdullah could still see the look of surprise on his face, just before new holes opened up on his chest and on his upper left cheek.

When the mother poked her head out of the kitchen to find out "what all the hubbub was about," a 9 mm slug dropped her, too. A second one at close range finished the job. All in all, that first part had been almost too easy—anticlimactic in a way.

However, he knew that the most difficult part still awaited him. Abdullah tried to separate himself from his actions as he climbed the stairs. He wanted to cut and run, but either adrenaline or an overwhelming sense of duty kept him moving forward.

The little girl's room had a sign that read, KEEP OUT: TRESPASSERS WILL BE TICKLED! Slowly, he turned the handle, praying to Allah that the child would not wake. The last thing he wanted was to actually see his victim's face. A powdery citrus scent met him as he opened the door. The room was very frilly and very pink. The walls were plastered with 4-H ribbons, pictures of the girl's friends, and posters from the latest High School Musical movie.

For the first and only time, Abdullah felt a twinge of guilt about what he was doing. But he quickly dealt with that by pulling the P99's trigger twice. The girl's body twitched only once, then lay still. The movement had been so quick, so subtle. Abdullah stood in the doorway, waiting to see if she would move again—almost wishing she would move again, wondering if he could bring himself to fire another round if she did move again. *Can't get stuck here,* he thought as he forced himself to leave the room. *Gotta keep moving.*

Abdullah then went to the next room and pumped the same number of rounds into the young boy—this time without stopping to look around. The less thinking he did, the better. He just let the hatred he had for America and its arrogant culture be his driving force. *These kids might be innocent now, but just give them twenty years.*

On his way out, he didn't forget to leave the envelope on the father's body—careful to avoid the blood that continued to spread on the man's shirt.

Now you've got one more house to visit; then you can call it a night, Abdullah thought as he took one last pull on his cigarette. Rather than flicking the butt out the window like he usually did, he stubbed it out in the ashtray—no sense giving the detectives a free DNA sample. He turned the ignition key and his car quietly purred to life. Keeping the lights off, he engaged the transmission and slowly made his way up the county road.

The brake lights glowed red as he eased the car past the mailbox and turned to the right. The driveway was paved, so he went ahead and pulled in. Three-quarters of a mile off of K-27 at this time of night, there was not much chance anyone would drive by and see his car here. As he drove up behind the family's Suburban, he let his side window slide down and held his pistol through the open space. Sure enough, a yellow Labrador retriever came running toward the car. The dog had time to let out one bark before a silenced shot put it down.

Abdullah held his breath as he watched the house for lights and listened for any sign of movement. It took a minute to satisfy himself that Fido had failed in his final mission. Before opening the door, Abdullah took a moment to perform *du'a*—a prayer of supplication for forgiveness and strength. "Allah, you have chosen me for this task. I do not relish it. In fact, I am appalled at what I have been asked to do. But still I will do it—for you, and for you alone. Forgive me for the violence I am about to commit. Bless me as I follow your will."

Abdullah sighed heavily, and then reached to the passenger seat, where he had laid the Walther. He picked up the gun, then looked back at the second item that was lying on the leather. Unfortunately, this family was not going to meet as clean or quick an ending as the first. *Give me strength, Allah. Give me strength.*

Moments later, Abdullah was walking up the flagstone path to the front door. Stepping onto the porch, a terrible thrill went through his body as he saw his reflection in the glass storm door. A black nylon mask covered his face. In his left hand the Walther was pointed straight ahead. In his right, a machete angled down to the ground.

Good thing you said your prayers, he thought. *You're in for a long night.*

SATURDAY, MAY 16, 8:45 A.M. MDT
FRONT RANGE RESPONSE TEAM
    HEADQUARTERS
DENVER, COLORADO

"If I wanted to know what everyone else knows, I would have recruited out of Quantico or Langley! But I didn't! I recruited you! So quit feeding me information that everyone else knows, and give me something new!"

Scott Ross watched as Jim Hicks stormed back into his office and slammed the door behind him, shaking all three of the glass walls. Adrenaline rushed through his body as he struggled to control his own temper. Any other supervisor, any other time of his life, Scott would have let his inner passive-aggressive spend the next five minutes plotting the best way to sabotage the casters on his boss's roller chair. However, Hicks had proven to Scott many times in the past months that he was a man to be respected.

Scott turned back to the conference table. Despite the heavy air-conditioning in the room, there was a lot of heat coming from where his team sat—most of whom were plotting their own methods of creative revenge. He took a long pull on his Yoo-hoo & Diet Mountain Dew Code Red, feeling the cool carbonation hit the back of his throat and slide on down.

Let it go; set the example. It's time to grow up. He could see the anticipation in the eyes of the analysts, waiting for him to throw out one of his classic Scott-isms. *Sorry, guys, not this time.*

"Jim's right, gang! Let's hit it!"

A look of disappointment spread across the faces of his team. Evie tentatively raised her hand.

"Yes, Evie," Scott reluctantly said, knowing that whatever she had to say would not be helpful in the least.

Wearing her most innocent puppy-dog look, she asked, "Does this mean we aren't going to have an opportunity to assuage our wounded feelings by exacting revenge against Mr. Hicks through cutting gibes and biting sarcasm?"

Scott tried to fight back a smile. *Come on, set the example. Set . . . the . . . example! Yeah, right! Who am I kidding? Besides, I think growing up is best done with baby steps.* "I'm sorry to say that's true, Evie. Besides, with Mr. Congeniality so audibly back in his office, such comments, although well deserved, would technically be behind his back, thus having the very real potential of infracting the Office Sniping Code of Ethics. So, let's leave Mr. Feed-Me-Something-New alone. Now, is there any other business we must address before we get down to it?"

Not one to be left out of a meaningless banter session, Virgil Hernandez answered, "Well, now that you mention it, Scott, I was thinking it would really be cool to get one of those Dippin' Dots vending machines—you know, that super-frozen ice cream stuff—and, like, any money we make off of it we could put toward an end-of-the-year Christmas party."

"Dude, I love Dippin' Dots!" Gooey said, looking interested in the conversation for the first time since their meeting began. Evie and Williamson joined in with their support for the idea.

"It's against code to have vending machines in this building's work rooms," Tara quickly pointed out.

"Scott," Khadi said with a look of impatience. She moved her hand in a circle indicating that she would very much like to get the show on the road.

"Right," Scott replied, taking control of the meeting again. "Virgil and Joey, you form an off-hours vending machine task force. If you get one, bring it in at night and make sure you hide it well. Remember, it's only a code violation if you get caught." Scott ignored the exasperated sigh from Tara and pressed on. "Now, how about a little business? Is Mr. Attitude really right that we don't have anything new on Philly or SoCal?"

"I'm afraid he is," Khadi answered. "Right now we're depending on other sources for our intel, and it's slow in coming."

"Is that because they don't have any new intel or because they aren't giving it?" Scott asked.

Hernandez, suddenly very agitated, answered, "I can guarantee you they've got more than they're giving us. They're just not in any rush."

"It's just more of that interagency politics we're always dealing with," Khadi added.

"Can you hack in and get whatever they have?" Scott asked Hernandez.

"Not without permission," Tara quickly pointed out.

Scott pressed a button on the phone in front of him. Hicks's voice came over the speaker. "What?"

"Can we have permission?"

"To do what?"

"You don't want to know."

"Granted." The line went dead.

"Looks like you've got your permission," Scott said to Hernandez. To the rest of them, he said, "Go do your thing for the next two hours. Right now we've got nothing. When we come back together, that nothing better have become something."

SATURDAY, MAY 16, 5:45 P.M. EEST
ISTANBUL, TURKEY

"The third bomb! Why have we not heard of the third bomb?" A vein in al-'Aqran's forehead throbbed as he pointed an accusing finger at Tahir Talib. "If I discover that this Ghani did not properly receive his instructions . . ." Al-'Aqran dropped back into his chair, letting the implied threat hang in the room.

The Cause's leadership council was again sitting around the small apartment's kitchen table. Talib was visibly shaking, which was just how al-'Aqran wanted him. The man's voice took on a pleading tone. "I swear upon the holy book, *sayyid*, all instructions were communicated, and the devices were delivered. I—I can't explain what has happened."

Al-'Aqran stewed for a few minutes while the rest of the team sat around him not daring to speak. A standing fan loudly oscillated past him, circulating the hot air in the room and cooling the sweat that was on his face. CNN International ran on a television to his right, but he had mentally tuned it out. All the pertinent information about the attacks on Philadelphia, Pennsylvania, and that cesspool, Hollywood, California, had been given. He didn't expect the small-town operations to make international news until someone made the connection with the overall attack. *But not word one has been mentioned about the university. What happened to the university?* Then a thought struck him.

"The notes! The notes left in the houses! We announced the university attack in them, did we not?"

Talib looked to his comrades for support, and finding none, he answered, "Well, not in so many words, but we did reference—"

Al-'Aqran exploded, throwing a small dish with the remains of a biscuit at Talib, just missing his head. The dish crashed instead against an ancient Westinghouse refrigerator. "Not in so many words? What does that mean? We talked about their universities, true? And now we have nothing to back that up! We look like fools!"

"*Sayyid*, look at the news," Talib pleaded, pointing toward the television. Sweat was pouring off his face, and the damp stains under his arms had just merged with the ones on his chest and back. "Look at the destruction in the subway. Look at how their decadent entertainment industry has gone into mourning. I would hardly say we look like fools."

"Are you stupid? Answer me! Are you stupid? You must be, because you obviously do not get it! Even young Babrak knows what

I'm saying! Explain it to him, Babrak, because apparently he can't understand my voice."

Babrak Zahir, who until then had been calmly twirling a pen through his fingers, said, "If you reference an attack and it takes place, it is a show of strength. If you reference an attack and it does not take place, it is a sign of weakness—a lack of infrastructure or courage. Is that simple enough, my dear Tahir?"

Talib's face quickly turned red with anger. "I understand the ramifications. I don't need them explained to me by some freshly weaned whelp of a—"

"Ah, but apparently you do," al-'Aqran interrupted with a slam of his hand on the table. "Apparently you do! And you may want to watch what you say to young Babrak. This freshly weaned whelp has grown quite a set of teeth."

Talib's complexion turned from red to white, and al-'Aqran noticed the waver in his voice. "I meant no disrespect to either of you. I'm just at a loss. Truly, *sayyid*, everything was set for the attack at Notre Dame University. I don't know what has happened, but I will find out and deal with it."

"With the strongest possible measures?"

"With the strongest possible measures."

Still not trusting Talib, and also wanting to humiliate him a little more, al-'Aqran turned to his right-hand man and said, "Hamad, you will work with Tahir to discover the source of this problem and remedy it."

"Of course," answered Hamad Asaf.

"Very well, you may all go except for Babrak. I must speak to you." Al-'Aqran noticed the fear in Talib's eyes at Babrak being held back. *Good. The man deserves to be in fear of his life. Incompetent fool!*

When everyone had left the room, al-'Aqran motioned for Babrak to join him in the small living room. The older man turned off the television and twisted the fan so that it was facing the new setting. He eased himself into his usual blue fabric wing chair. Above the chair was a stylized drawing of a nineteenth-century pilgrim going on a *hajj*. A stiff beige couch supported by peeling chrome-plated legs stretched along the wall to his right. Across that whitewashed wall was a long, framed banner with the Arabic words of the *shahadah—I testify that there is no god but Allah, and Muhammad is his prophet.*

Al-'Aqran was gratified to see Babrak continue standing until he nodded him to a place on the couch. *This young man knows something about respect.*

"Tahir is a good man; we both know that," al-'Aqran began, "but he has made a costly mistake. I want you to remain cold to him for the next several days. Put some fear into him, but do not touch him. Do you understand?"

"Yes, *sayyid.*"

"Good. Now what has been done about our Egyptian friend?"

"Kamal Hejazi met his fate and is now in the Bosporus. As for his son, he suddenly removed himself from his studies at October 6 University, and no one has heard from him since—nor will they."

"Excellent. Learn from this, my young friend. Never leave a cancer in the body. It will only spread."

"Yes, *sayyid.*"

"I am proud of you, Babrak. You give much honor to the name of your father. Now go. And please greet your mother for me."

Al-'Aqran watched as Babrak walked to the door and left the apartment. *He has courage and ruthlessness, but does he have conviction? The first two will turn you into a killer. The third is what transforms you into a leader. I guess only time will tell with this one.*

SATURDAY, MAY 16, 9:00 A.M. MDT
INVERNESS TRAINING CENTER
ENGLEWOOD, COLORADO

A strange mood hovered around minicamp this morning. The typical playful excitement was nowhere to be found. Although nobody spoke of the attacks of the previous night, they seemed to be in the forefront of everyone's minds. The moment the reports had begun to air on the news, many of the players and coaches had flashed back to that devastating Monday night game five months ago.

Now, in the linebackers' room, fear, anger, and grief all mixed together into a cloud that hung over the players. Emotions were high, and tempers were short.

Linebacker coach Rex Texeira was covering the front whiteboard with a diagram of a coverage scheme in which Riley would have the option of holding back in short yardage or driving in toward the quarterback. "What's going to be your trigger, Pach?" he asked.

Unfortunately, Riley's body and his mind were in two different places.

"Covington, you with us?" Texeira tried again.

Keith Simmons leaned forward across the thin table that held his bulky playbook and clapped Riley on the back of the shoulder. "Pach, man, Coach's talking to you."

Riley's mind quickly snapped back to the present. "What? Oh, hey, Coach, my bad. What'd you ask?"

Frustration was evident in Coach Texeira's voice as he began to explain the play again. As soon as Riley saw that it was a play he had already committed to memory, he found his mind trying to fade out again. His feelings were too strong to be worrying about whether the three slot opened up or not.

He started looking around the room, trying to keep himself in the here and now. There were fourteen long, thin tables lined up in three rows. Each table had one black office chair stationed at it. Each veteran had his favorite place to sit, and woe to the rookie who sat in a veteran's seat.

The room was surrounded by whiteboards, all except for the rear wall, which housed a projector for showing film on the drop-down screen at the front of the room. The rear wall also held a small video camera. That little camera, known to the players as "big brother," linked into Head Coach Burton's office so that at any time he could look in on what was going on in the individual position meetings.

The boards on either side of the room were mostly clean except for a number of large magnets labeled to represent the offensive and defensive positions and a list written in thick black erasable ink. This was the linebackers' fines list: about twenty-five infractions, each paired with a dollar amount ranging from $25 to $150, written out in descending order. At the top of the list were basic issues, such as *Late - $150*, *Sleeping - $100*, and *Holding Back - $100*. As the list progressed, however, the terms became more obscure: *Stupid - $75*, *Drama - $50*, *Dogging - $50*, and the all-too-descriptive *BRAAAP! - $25*.

"Now, I'll try it again," came Texeira's voice cutting through Riley's room inventory. "What's going to be your trigger, Pach?"

"QB drops, receivers gun, and I can pop three," Riley answered, trying to mask his absolute lack of interest.

"Exactly. Welcome back," Texeira said sarcastically.

Yeah, you can keep your "Welcome back," because I'm not staying long, Riley thought as the screams and panic of that night not many months ago poured back into his brain.

The numbers and letters cycled through at a blinding pace. Gooey could have set the program to not show the password combinations as they were tried and rejected, but really, what would be the fun of that? It had taken him long enough to build the firewall-busting program; the least he could do was watch it fly.

He glanced to his left to see if Joey Williamson was sufficiently impressed with the program and was frustrated to see him riffling through some recently printed flash-traffic.

"Not a firewall alive that can withstand this onslaught," Gooey said proudly, nodding toward the computer screen.

"Mmm, cool," Williamson replied without looking up.

"And while this computer is looking for a way through the front door of the LAPD server, I'm over on this one digging me an SSH tunnel through the rear."

"Wow," an unenthusiastic Williamson muttered.

"'Wow'?" a frustrated Gooey said as he snatched the papers from his coworker's hands. "Is that the best you can do? 'Wow'?"

Williamson snatched them back. "What do you want me to say? All hail Gooey the Great! Thou art majestic and all-powerful in thine hacker-ocity!"

"Forget it," Gooey said, turning back to his screens. "You wouldn't know good hacker-ocity if it came up and . . . Boo-yah! We're in!"

Williamson dropped the flash-traffic on the desk and leaned in. On the "back door" screen was a map of the main LAPD server.

"Gooey the Great does it again!"

"And don't you forget it, son," Gooey gloated as he began his search for uploaded videos of the attack in Hollywood.

Within three minutes, files were pouring through the hole Gooey had punched in the firewall. In the time it took Williamson and Gooey to go to the office refrigerator, mix Red Bulls with canned Starbucks Doubleshots, and pound the drinks down, every digitized scrap of information the LAPD had on the tragic event had been transferred to the FRRT server. Fully caffeinated and sugared, the analysts sat back down to begin sifting through their newly acquired treasure.

As they cycled through video after video—some from news crews and entertainment shows, others from ATMs and various other passive surveillance cameras—they searched for anything that might give a clue to the identity of the terrorist or terrorists responsible for the deaths of so many people.

Soon, Gooey's frustration level rose. He sat back in his chair. "We don't even know what we're looking for!"

"Go back to the crane shot," Williamson said. "Something's bothering me about that one—like we're missing something there. Anyway, it'll help us reestablish our bearings."

Gooey did some quick mouse and keyboard maneuverings, and a video with a view from high above the red carpet appeared.

"Good," Williamson continued. "Now back it up to ten minutes prior to the blast and dial the speed back from triple time to time and a half."

Both men leaned in close to the monitor. The video showed what one would expect to see at a movie premiere—limos pulling in; limos pulling out; paparazzi taking pictures; stars waving to the ever-growing crowds of people.

"Wait! Back up the video again," Williamson said suddenly. "Look at the top of the screen. Check out Miss Babelicious walking out of the media pit."

"Woof," Gooey responded appreciatively.

"Down, Goo-dog; that's not what I meant. Back up the video. . . . Now, see, she's coming out of the pit—so where's her camera? Where's any equipment?"

"Maybe she's the on-air personality. No equipment needed for that, and she certainly seems to have the necessary 'talents,'" Gooey said, bouncing his eyebrows up and down.

Not taking Gooey's bait, Williamson went on, "Look at her clothes. TV chicks don't wear jeans to a premiere. Besides that, she's leaving before the main stars arrived. What kind of entertainment babe does that?"

"Dude, it's such a long shot."

"It's better than anything else we got."

"True that," Gooey said, warming up to the possibilities of this lead. "Tell you what, why don't you slide on back to your workstation. Let's split the videos and see if we can find her on any other camera. Who knows, maybe we'll get lucky. Tell you the truth, I'm kind of anxious to see if we can put a face to that walk," Gooey finished with a sly wink.

Riley sat on the low, carpeted bench and leaned back into his locker. The fingers of his right hand picked at the grain of the maple that made up all the lockers and trimmed the whole room. He had blown it this morning, and he knew it.

After the position meeting, the linebackers had hit the field to run some basic plays. Riley could see that first-round draft pick Afshin Ziafat was struggling with the Mustangs' defensive system. However, the compassion he typically felt for the rookies seemed to be nowhere in sight for this newbie. Through head shakes and audible sounds of disgust, Riley let Ziafat clearly know how little he thought of his game.

What was worse, when he could see that he was getting under Ziafat's skin, it only made him want to do it all the more. Finally everything broke after one play in which Ziafat ducked inside when he should have gone outside. His path took him right into Riley.

Riley saw him coming and with one well-placed forearm stood Ziafat straight up. "Son, have you ever even played this game before?"

It was very apparent that Ziafat had had enough. He went chest-to-chest with Riley and shouted, "You got a problem with me, Covington?"

Riley was more than prepared to dish it back. "Yeah, I got a problem with you! My problem is that you don't answer direct questions! I asked you if you've ever played this game before?"

Ziafat looked like he was ready to give back a little of what Riley was giving him, but then his features softened. "Listen, Riley, I know this is a tough day for everyone. I can't imagine—"

Suddenly Riley's hands drove into Ziafat's chest protector. Ziafat flew backward to the ground. Riley stood over him with his finger pointing at Ziafat's face. "You're right! You can't imagine! In fact, you have no idea! So just start playing your game and stay out of my way!"

Riley turned and walked away before Ziafat had a chance to respond. Behind him, he heard linebacker coach Rex Texeira call an end to their drill. That had been twenty minutes ago. Since that time, everyone had wisely given Riley some space.

That was a stupid thing to do, Riley berated himself. *Face it: you weren't climbing on the kid because of his game. You were on him because of his name! Welcome to the land of bigotry, buddy! How does it feel? The one thing you swore you would never be . . . well, here you are.*

Riley walked to the glass-front drink refrigerator and pulled out a twelve-ounce bottle of Gatorade. He twisted off the cap on the way back to his locker and thought for the thousandth time, *They can pay us millions of dollars a year, but they can't afford to get us full-size bottles.*

He sat back into his locker and downed the drink in one long swig. *Lord, help me get control of myself—especially where Ziafat is concerned. Forgive me for my attitude and for going at him when he didn't deserve it. Forgive me for my prejudice. Give me love in my heart, 'cause right now, it ain't there.*

Riley tossed his empty bottle across the room and into the garbage can. "Nice shot," a voice said.

Turning his head, Riley saw Ziafat standing at his locker. Riley nodded. "Had a little practice."

Ziafat took a few tentative steps toward Riley. He looked like he had something to say, so Riley waited him out. Finally, Ziafat said, "Are we cool, Riley? I mean, I know I was messing up out there, but this seems like it's more than just my game."

What did Pastor Tim say that one time? Riley asked himself.

Sometimes you've just got to say words of love and hope your heart will follow. "Call me Pach. And, yeah, we're cool. I'm just working some things out. Got a lot of stuff that's still a little fresh with me."

Riley could see the relief on the kid's face, which did seem to lighten his own mood a bit. "Excellent, man. Thanks. I just really want to learn from you and Simmons—you know, bring my game to the next level. I remember taping your games back when you were at the Academy. You had some mad skills. I'd sit with a remote in my hand and watch . . ."

Ziafat's voice went on, but Riley was no longer paying attention to it. Creeping up behind Ziafat were six players—two defensive linemen, three offensive linemen, and a fullback. All eyes in the locker room were on these men.

When they were a few feet behind Ziafat, they pounced. All six players drove the rookie to the ground and held him there while he struggled and squirmed. Chris Gorkowski ran up with a full box of athletic tape in one hand and a jar of Vaseline in the other.

The players began grabbing tape out of the box and wrapping it around Ziafat. Cheers and taunts sounded through the locker room. Soon Ziafat looked like a giant white cigar with a head sticking out the top and a couple of shoes at the bottom. Riley noticed that even though he was yelling threats at the players, Ziafat was laughing the whole time. They stood him up, and Gorkowski stepped in and coated the tape with a thick layer of Vaseline.

Riley just shook his head. Trying to get athletic tape off is a pain; trying to pull up a corner when it's covered with Vaseline is nearly impossible. As Gorkowski was finishing, Ziafat turned to Riley and said with a smile, "Sucks to be a rookie."

"No doubt."

No sooner were the words out of Riley's mouth then Ziafat was hoisted up on the shoulders of the offensive linemen and taken into the training room. Riley listened until he heard the splash of something very large being dumped into the ice tub and the accompanying cheer. *Hopefully they dropped him in feetfirst,* Riley thought, knowing Ziafat would be stuck in the tub until some trainer had pity on him and helped pull him out. Then he would spend the next hour or two trying to get the tape off.

Keith Simmons came to his locker, three down from Riley's. He was laughing as he sat down.

"Mr. Simmons, did you have anything to do with that?"

"Me? Why, Mr. Covington, you know it is my express goal to make every rookie feel right at home here with the Colorado Mustangs."

Riley stood up and started getting undressed for the showers. "Yeah, you're a regular welcome wagon."

"Just doing my part. Besides, with how low everyone was feeling today, I figured we needed something to lighten the mood."

Riley chuckled and turned to Simmons. "You're probably right. Did you notice his reaction, though? He wasn't screaming and cussing like most guys do. He was just laughing and taking it."

"Yeah, it kind of takes the fun out of it. You know who he reminded me of?"

"Who?"

"You."

"Me?" Riley asked, surprised.

"Definitely you. When you got taped, you were laughing and making fun of the offensive linemen. You kept daring Gorkowski to use more and more Vaseline. Finally I got so frustrated at your attitude that I strapped a piece of tape across your mouth."

Riley laughed. "I had forgotten about that. My lips were chapped for a week. Some things you just try to block out."

"Yeah, well, I think you and the rook might have more in common than you think."

We might have, Riley thought as he moved toward the showers. Riley felt a moment of guilt when the hot water shot out of the nozzle and hit his body, knowing what the ice bath must be doing to Ziafat . . . but it was just a moment. *Sucks to be a rookie. No doubt.*

EIGHTEEN

There was excitement as the team gathered back together around the table. At one end, Gooey was in conference with Joey Williamson. A large flat-screen monitor had already been raised out of its cabinet, and a small portable control board sat in front of Gooey.

Scott could sense the feeling in the room—like racehorses ready to break out of the gate. *Good; that means they're not coming back empty-handed.* After taking a long pull on his mug, he called to Khadi, who was still at her workstation with her phone headset on. "Give me one more minute," she replied, then went back to her conversation.

Khadi'll have to play catch-up. It's time to get this ball rolling. Turning to Virgil Hernandez, Scott asked, "So, how'd you do hacking into the intel?"

"The world was our oyster," Hernandez said with a twinkle in his eye. "Expect irate calls from the FBI, CIA, headquarters of Homeland, and various and sundry other law enforcement agencies."

"They'll get over it. So what'd you come up with?"

"Hold on," Khadi interrupted. She was just taking her seat and seemed very excited. "I just got off the phone with Jennifer Buehler over at the New England Response Team."

She paused, apparently waiting for the typical response from the analysts when their New England counterparts were mentioned. Sure enough, a chorus of robotic-sounding voices sang out, "NERT! NERT! NERT!"

Khadi continued, "Jen's just sent me their footage from the subway attack. Gooey, pull the file up off my e-mail. I already know you've hacked my password."

"Sure thing," Gooey sheepishly replied.

"Busted," Williamson said under his breath.

The flat screen flashed to life showing Khadi's computer desktop. Gooey went to her e-mail and quickly typed in her password, causing snickers from the other analysts. Pulling up the file, Gooey made the video go full screen. It was a wide shot of the lower level of the 8th Street subway station in Philadelphia. A train was just pulling up.

Khadi picked up the narrative. "This train stops, and the crowd disembarks. Gooey, put a highlight on the orange hat—no, the limping guy—yeah, that's him. He shuffles over to the bench and sets his backpack next to himself. Okay, you can double-time the video . . . until . . . now! Watch his hand. It slips down his backpack, and then he pockets something that he pulled from the back of it. Go ahead and double-time it again. . . . There! He gets up and heads for the stairs—notice no more limp and no backpack. Go forward again. Minute and a half later . . . boom!"

"What happens to our suspect?" Tara Walsh asked.

"I think Jen's team spliced the video together. Go forward, Gooey. . . . Yeah, here we go. He comes up the stairs and starts heading toward the train. Boom! He joins the panicking people heading for the exit. Tag him again with a highlight, because he's going to try to lose us. He's in the crowd, when—there!—he dumps the hat. He moves up the stairs, but unfortunately, he vanishes after that. NERT's still processing through other bank and surveillance cameras trying to pick him up again after he gets out of the station."

"Khadi, call NERT back, thank them profusely for the video, then ask them to send the raw footage from every camera in the area," said Scott. "I don't want to rely on their analysts. Gooey, go back to the best frame we have of his face."

"We don't have much," Gooey answered, quickly backing through the video. He found a frame, and then began pounding some keys trying to clean up the picture.

"Lighten up on the board," Hernandez chastised him. "That's government property."

Ignoring him, Gooey said, "Here we go. That's about as pretty as I can get it."

"Tara, tell me what you see," Scott said.

"Extremely hard to tell. His features possibly put him as Middle Eastern—"

"No surprise there," Scott interrupted.

"No, but what's got me a little confused is what seems to be his age. I wouldn't be surprised if he turned out to be in his fifties to sixties."

"Interesting. Not your typical young punk with a bomb belt. Gooey, when we finish here, I want cleaning up this picture to be your highest priority. Then shoot it off to every police and intelligence agency on God's green earth."

"Scott, I think NERT's doing that already," Khadi pointed out.

"Let them do it. Gooey'll triple the resolution, then give them something they can actually work with."

"Point well taken," Khadi acquiesced.

Scott turned to Hernandez. "Okay, your turn. What'd you find?"

"Well, the FBI was working with LAPD, piecing together footage of the Hollywood attack. Gooey and Williamson found it on the LAPD server and kinda borrowed it. Goo-man?"

Gooey punched a few more keys, and the scene on the monitor changed to an overhead view of the red carpet walk in Hollywood.

Hernandez continued, "Now, the blast originated in the media pool. They're so packed together, it's almost impossible to see any bags or equipment. So instead, we focused on who was coming and who was going."

Williamson jumped in. "Goo and I were specifically watching

the camera pit. You'll notice, not many people leaving. The few who do are all carrying equipment, or at least a camera bag. That is, until Legs Houlihan."

"Who?" Khadi asked.

"Just a nickname," Williamson apologized. Gooey stopped the video and zoomed in on the back of a young woman. Scott whistled until a glare from Tara stopped him mid-blow.

Williamson continued, "Now, check her out. All she's taking out of the camera pit is her little purse thingy. Six minutes later, the bomb blows."

"A girl with a 'purse thingy' is not much to go on," Tara pointed out.

"True," Scott said, "but it's better than anything else we've got. Awesome work, you guys! Evie, you start working on this girl's pic, then run it past Goo before you send it out."

"Got it!"

Suddenly, Hicks burst out of his office and began running down the steps to the table. "We've got a note! Gooey, move over; I've got to bring up my e-mail."

"It's okay, boss; I'll get it."

"How . . . ? Never mind; we'll talk later."

"Where'd they find it?" Scott asked as he stood up to give Hicks his seat.

"A sheriff in Wallace County, Kansas, picked it up at a triple murder."

"Say what? A murder?"

"Yeah. They say it was a nasty one. Mom, Dad, and a twelve-year-old son. Hacked up pretty badly." A collective groan sounded around the table.

"Are they sure this is connected?" Tara asked. "If it is, this is a different M.O. than any terrorist attack we've seen before."

"Apparently the note spells it out. How you coming on *my* e-mail, Gooey?"

"Got it."

The flat screen now flashed from a still of Hollywood to a hand-written sheet of paper. Each person read the note quietly to themselves.

In the name of Allah the Judge,

Let it be known that the punishment of Allah has visited America. The Great Satan has felt the mighty hand of a greater God. For America's self-indulgence, for her imperialism, for her support of the Zionist occupation, for her occupation of Iraq, for her exportation of cultural filth, for all these things, Allah has meted out justice upon the once-mighty Western whore.

Let it be known that no child of Satan is safe from the hand of Allah. We have demonstrated our ability to strike you in your subways, in your universities, at the celebrations of your decadent media that spreads through the world like an immoral plague, and in your very homes. No place is safe—not your big cities, not your small villages. Wherever you are, the Cause will be there too.

Let it be known that this is a first strike. Allah's wrath will not end until America has been brought back down to the mud out of which she rose.

Allahu Akbar! In the name of Allah and his prophet Muhammad! The Cause will strike again! Allahu Akbar!

"At least we definitely know who we're dealing with," Scott said. "What I'm trying to figure out is the 'universities' comment."

"That threw me, too," Hicks said.

"I think we've got to get the FBI checking any suspicious activity on any campus. That's too big for us," Tara said.

Hicks nodded. "Good call. That's an intel nightmare. You make the contact."

"Will do."

"Scott, I need to talk with you in my office, and then you and I are going to check out the Kansas scene where the note was found. Everyone else, from now on you live here. By policy, I can't ask you for more than twelve hours a day. You know what I think of policy. Your whole purpose in life right now is to figure out where the leaders of the Cause are and what they're doing still alive. Remember, any time off you take could translate into bodies."

"No pressure," Gooey said as he moved toward his workstation.

As they all stood up, Evie said, "Guess that kills my weekend plans."

"What were your weekend plans?" asked Khadi.

"To get a life outside of my job."

Khadi smiled. "It's time you learn now, sweetheart. If you want a life, you're in the wrong business."

Scott laughed at Khadi's comment. *This is definitely not the job path for someone who wants to settle down with a wife, 2.5 kids, and a golden retriever—not necessarily in that order.* He grabbed his mug and followed Hicks up to his office, then dropped into his usual chair, kicking his Birkenstocks up onto the wide desk.

"What's up, mein commandant?"

"First of all, I want you to get those guys down there to quit hacking everyone's passwords."

Scott leaned back in his chair and put a reflective tone to his voice, "Ahh, Jim, Jim, Jim. You may as well ask me to make the fish to stop swimming, the birds to stop flying, the dogs to stop sniffing each other's—"

"Listen, just make them stop. It creeps me out thinking that everything I write is open to their prying little eyes. Second, with al-'Aqran securely tucked away in a CIA black prison, I want to know who's running the Cause."

"That's a good question," Scott answered, sitting up straight. "We know they have leadership in the Middle East, but we don't know much about who or where. Al-'Aqran's number two man, Mohammad Zahir, was taken out when we rescued Riley in Italy. His son, Babrak, is a seriously bad character, but he's almost certainly too young to have a real leadership position. The only other guy we really know of is Hamad bin Salih Asaf. He's a networking guy. It's very possible that he might have stepped up."

Hicks sat for a moment, thinking. Then he picked up the phone. "I'm going to give Charlie Anderson a call at CIA and ask him to run it up the line to squeeze al-'Aqran a little more for some answers."

"I think I'll probably have better results asking the kids to stop stealing your password," Scott said, raising an eyebrow.

His prediction turned out to be accurate. He shook his head as he listened.

"Hey, Charlie, this is Jim Hicks. . . . Yeah, thanks, it's a pretty good gig. Listen, I know you're busy, but I wanted to ask you a favor. I'm sure you're up on the note found with the family in Kansas. . . . Yeah, it's bad stuff—totally new paradigm. What I wanted you to do is have your boys put some pressure on al-'Aqran—remember, the leader of the Cause that we handed over to you guys. . . . I know you can't say anything about him. I'm just saying if you *did* happen to have him in one of your little secret hideaways, it would be a huge help to try to draw the Cause's leadership structure out of the man . . . I'm not asking you to promise me anything, Charlie! I'm just saying . . . Listen, just call me if they find out anything. Can you at least promise me that? . . . Didn't think so. Thanks, Charlie. As always, it's been a joy talking to you."

Scott shook his head as Jim slammed down the phone. "Let me guess," Scott said. "'We can neither confirm nor deny our custody of said bad guy.'"

"Exactly. I'm thinking, 'I put the guy into CIA's custody myself, and now you can't even tell me you have him?' This interagency, my-turf-your-turf secrecy crap is going to be the end of our intelligence as we know it. Even the bad guys know enough to run their information through the Hezbollah clearinghouse. If our agencies won't talk to each other, how in the world can we expect . . . ?"

Here it comes—the interagency turf tirade. Set the mental alarm clock for fifteen minutes. Settling back comfortably in his chair while Hicks continued to yell, Scott took a long pull on his Yoo-hoo and Code Red mix, hoping the caffeine would put at least some sparkle of interest in his eyes. *Don't let him ask a question. Please don't let him ask a question,* Scott thought as he gently drifted off to his quiet, soothing little happy place—a deserted little island populated by himself, Tara Walsh, an endless supply of piña colada mix, and nothing else.

MONDAY, MAY 18, 2:30 A.M. CDT

CHICAGO, ILLINOIS

The Superior 110 building rose a gallant twenty-seven stories above West Superior Street in downtown Chicago. The luxury-living high-rise boasted a panoramic view of Old Town, Michigan Avenue, the Gold Coast, the Loop, and River North. A twenty-four-hour doorman greeted and checked everyone who entered, and each lavish living space was decked out with a high-tech alarm system and a closed-circuit camera. Everything in the building was designed for safety and security.

But all that was of little comfort to Mohsin Ghani when he woke up with a gun pressed firmly against his forehead.

Mohsin blinked twice, hoping he was dreaming, but the cold steel on his warm flesh made it very clear that this was all too real. "W-who are you?"

The large shadow that hovered over him brought a finger to his mouth. "Shhh, don't speak."

Considering Mohsin was just this side of speechless anyway, it was an easy request for him to fulfill. But although his mouth was still, his mind started racing. *You knew they were going to come for you! You just didn't know it would be like this!*

Mohsin's breathing rate started increasing, and claustrophobia set in. The sheets and comforter that he had pulled tight around himself only a few hours ago now felt like a straitjacket. *It's okay, it's okay. Calm down! Just do what he says. He could have killed you already, and he hasn't. You've thought this all through. Let them see what you can do in your position. If that fails, offer this man money!*

"What d-d-do you—?"

The barrel of the pistol pressed harder, pushing Mohsin's head deeper into his down pillow. "I said don't speak," the voice growled.

Mohsin tried to nod his head, but the pressure of the gun didn't allow him any movement. He began sucking deeply for air. He closed his eyes tight, trying to ride out the sensation.

Finally, the gun pulled back. Mohsin could feel his skin separate from the weapon. He reached up and rubbed his forehead, feeling for blood on the perfect O that had been embossed onto his flesh.

"Slowly get out of bed and walk to the den," the intruder said.

Mohsin did as he was told. As he walked past the man, he could tell that the gunman was at least six inches taller than his own five-foot-eight-inch frame, and his tight black T-shirt took away any doubt that overpowering him was out of the question. *This isn't a time for brawn anyway; it's a time for brains, and you've got plenty. Just use them!*

The two men walked out the bedroom door, took a left through the kitchen, and came to the den.

"Sit there," the man said, pointing to a leather club chair. "Slide the ottoman out of the way."

Just take it easy and do what he says. The more time it takes, the better chance you have. "May I speak yet?"

The man didn't answer. Instead he reached next to Mohsin and turned on a standing lamp. He then pulled a cord on a lamp across the small den from Mohsin and sat down in a couch next to it. Crossing his legs, he stretched his arm along the crushed velvet back and laid the gun in his lap.

"I'm not going to have any trouble with you, am I?" the man said calmly.

"No! Of course not. What am I going to do? Throw a lamp at you?" Mohsin chuckled nervously.

"No, I guess not. Let me introduce myself to you. My name is Abdullah Muhammad."

"I'm Mohsin Ghani. I'm very pleased—"

"I know who you are, Mr. Ghani."

"Of course you do. Sorry," Mohsin said with a weak smile. "Please feel free to call me Mohsin."

Abdullah's look made it fairly clear that he would not take him up on the offer. "I've been sent here to find out what happened the other day."

The coolness of the night was moving from the hardwood floors up through Mohsin's body. He tried to control his shivers. *He's talking to you. This is good. Now make your story believable!* Mohsin drew a deep breath. "I wanted to do it. I had it all planned out. I drove to South Bend. I was even at the chapel during the wedding, just like I was supposed to be."

"South Bend? Were you at Notre Dame?"

"Of course. Isn't that where you sent me?" Then a thought struck Mohsin. "You aren't my contact, are you?"

"No. I'm a soldier like you are. But unlike you, I did my duty with honor."

"You—you were one of the bombers? Where were you? Philadelphia?"

"No."

"California?"

"No."

"But . . . oh no." A sick feeling swept through Mohsin. He had watched the news with horror at the brutal homicide scene unfolding in Kansas. Then, earlier today, a second family had been found shot in cold blood in their home in Nebraska. "Which . . . ?"

"Both," Abdullah said. He uncrossed his leg and leaned forward. "You can see, Mr. Ghani, I am not a man to be trifled with or tested. So, if you will please proceed with your answer to my question . . ." Abdullah leaned back and resumed his former position.

Mohsin desperately had to use the bathroom, but he knew that would be out of the question. However, that need, combined with the cold and his fear, now had him shaking all over. He tried to control his voice, but it still came out wavering.

"I was in the chapel. I had the backpack. I tried to do it, but I just couldn't!"

"Couldn't, or wouldn't?"

"Both! There was just no way! I'm not some cold-blooded mur—" Mohsin saw the corner of Abdullah's mouth turn up ever so slightly. "No offense, but I just couldn't do it."

"No offense taken. Some of us are just weaker than others. Now, I have just one more question for you before I go."

"Before you . . . yes, of course. Ask it. Please! Anything you want to know." For the first time, Mohsin saw potential light at the end of the tunnel.

"What, Mr. Ghani, do you think should be the punishment for a soldier who doesn't do his duty?"

Fear caused Mohsin's bladder to let loose. "Oh! I'm so sorry about that!" He tried to stand up out of the wetness.

"Sit down!" Abdullah roared.

Mohsin dropped back down to the already cooling puddle.

A mocking smile appeared on Abdullah's face, increasing Mohsin's shame. "It's okay, Mr. Ghani. There's no need to be sorry. It's *your* furniture. Now, my question, please."

"Give me another chance! Please! I have connections. Lawyers, politicians, bankers. I can get you into places that you've only dreamed of gaining access to."

"We don't need your access, Mr. Ghani," Abdullah said calmly.

"How about money? I know it costs a lot to fight a righteous war like this. I have over $300,000 in the bank, and with my salary I can give at least $200,000 more every year. Or . . . or maybe you and I can even arrange a deal?"

A dark look filled Abdullah's eyes. "We don't need your money, Mr. Ghani. And if you try to bribe me again, I'll shoot you where you sit."

"I'm sorry, I'm sorry, I'm sorry! Maybe you could give me one more chance. I'll do it this time. I swear I will—on my parent's graves, on their honor! I still even have the backpacks in my bedroom closet. I hate these American pigs and all they stand for. Give me one more chance to deal them a mortal blow. In the name of Allah, I will fight!" Mohsin emphasized his final words by pounding his hands on the arms of the chair.

Abdullah began slowly nodding his head. "A very interesting offer. Now, as for me, I believe once a coward, always a coward. But luckily for you, I am not the one who makes these decisions."

Hope began to fill Mohsin's chest. *I just need to make it through tonight. If I can simply buy some time, then I can disappear.* "Who does make the decisions? Is there a way I can talk to him?"

"As a matter of fact, there is." Mohsin watched as Abdullah pulled a cell phone out of his pants pocket. "My phone can take thirty seconds of video. That's how long you have to plead your case. Then I will send the video to the decision-maker, and we will see what he says. Is that fair?"

"Yes, sir! That's more than fair!" Mohsin knew he had a reputation as a fast-talker. There was no better deal that he could have been given than to plead his case.

"Then I'll tell you what, Mr. Ghani. I want you to put your head back, close your eyes, and think about what you are going to say. I'm sure you're aware that those thirty seconds are pretty important to you. You're going to want to make good use of them."

"Yes. Thank you!" Things just kept looking better and better. Now Mohsin had time to put together the best plea possible.

Mohsin leaned his head back and felt the cold leather against his sweaty head. The stink of urine filled his nostrils, but he tried to drive it from his mind. *Come on, think! Say something about how much you hate America. Do a* mea culpa *about the last time.*

A faint metal-on-metal sound caught Mohsin's ear. He started to bring his head back up but stopped himself short. *What's the matter with you? Do not look! He told you to keep your eyes closed, and that's what you're going to do. So, say you're sorry, then say how much you hate America, invoke the name of Allah—maybe mention Allah's mercy and beneficence. Then finish off with—*

"Time's up, Mr. Ghani."

As soon as Mohsin brought his head up, he saw what had made the metallic sound. Abdullah had screwed a silencer to the end of his pistol. Mohsin began shaking again.

"Don't worry. It's just a little precaution," Abdullah said with a smile. "Just in case things don't go your way."

"S-s-sure. Makes sense." Everything Mohsin had prepared in his quiet interlude had now fled his mind. In its place was only pure fear.

"Now, I'm going to press this button. When I do, I want you to say your name, wait two seconds, then proceed with your statement. Do you understand?"

"I understand. Say my name, wait two seconds, then make my statement."

"Exactly. And don't mess it up, Mr. Ghani. I'm only giving you one try at this. Are you ready?"

Mohsin nodded.

"Ready, and go."

Mohsin saw Abdullah start the recording.

"My name is Mohsin Ghani," he said, and then paused. After counting *one* in his head, his eyes widened as he saw Abdullah pick the gun up off his lap. Everything seemed to suddenly slip into slow motion as he watched the silencer level at his face. With perfect clarity, he saw Abdullah's finger pull back on the trigger, saw movement in the gun's bore, and then Mohsin Ghani saw no more.

TUESDAY, MAY 19, 3:30 P.M. MDT
PARKER, COLORADO

The afternoon thunderstorm arrived just minutes
before Riley pulled into the Caribou Coffee parking lot. It looked like a typical Denver summer
storm—mostly bark with very little bite, lasting
just long enough to back up street drains and ruin
the shine on freshly washed cars.

Riley looked to his right. "A downpour like
this could last five minutes or fifteen. You want
to go for it?"

"I'm game," Afshin Ziafat said with a smile.

"How about you, Skeeter?" Riley asked, turning to the backseat.

"I've been wet before," Skeeter replied.

Riley threw open his door and ran across the
water cascading over the asphalt. The fifteen yards
from their parking place to the front door was
enough to soak all three men and to fill Riley's
left Merrell from a misjudged gutter puddle. Riley
and Ziafat were laughing as they walked into the
coffeehouse.

The interior was designed to have a Colorado
cabin feel. Large logs crossed the ceiling, and the
store centered itself on a floor-to-ceiling stone

fireplace. Rustic wooden tables and chairs were mixed with smaller intimate seating areas with deep, comfortable chairs and small, bear-shaped ottomans. The cozy, woodsy ambience made Starbucks seem antiseptic by comparison.

Instantly Riley spotted Khadi lounging in a sitting area where two overstuffed chairs flanked either side of a small coffee table, and he wondered again if this was such a good idea. After Ziafat's attempts to reach out to him, Riley had felt some serious conviction about his attitude toward the rookie. He knew that Ziafat had nothing to do with what had happened at the end of last season. Riley was blowing him off purely because of his name and his faith—an attitude that stood little chance of passing the WWJD test.

So, when practice ended yesterday, Riley held Ziafat back on the field. Ziafat, evidently still a little tentative after his recent taping incident, kept looking around.

"Don't worry, you're clear," Riley had said. "Hey, I was wondering, would you join me for coffee tomorrow? There's someone I'd like you to meet."

Ziafat had jumped at the chance, and that invitation had led to this meeting. Riley saw Khadi smile when she spotted him. But the smile faltered just a bit when she saw that he was not alone. A sinking feeling crept into Riley's gut. *You forgot to tell her that Afshin was coming, didn't you, you idiot?* The three men reached Khadi just as she rose from one of the chairs.

"Hey, Khadi," Riley greeted her, giving her a quick hug.

"Hi, Riley," Khadi replied, then reached toward Skeeter and wrapped her arms around the big man. When she pulled back, she said, "You're soaked. Haven't you ever heard of an umbrella, you big oaf?"

"Saw one in a catalog once," Skeeter replied. "Didn't think much of it." He left her laughing and went to sit at a table facing the front door.

Riley put his hand on Khadi's back and said, "Khadi Faroughi, this is Afshin Ziafat. Afshin, Khadi."

"It's a pleasure to meet you, Khadi."

"It's a pleasure meeting you, too. And a little bit of a surprise," Khadi said, turning her gaze to Riley.

"Okay, I'm a bonehead. I forgot to call. Sorry," Riley said, realizing that he'd been doing a lot of apologizing lately.

"If it's a problem, I can go," Ziafat offered, leaning toward the door.

"No, please. I'm sorry. I've been a little stressed lately. I'm not reacting well to change," Khadi said with a little laugh. "Please, sit down."

Both Riley and Ziafat pulled wooden chairs from nearby tables. "One of you better sit in the soft chair, or I'm going to feel like a queen holding court," Khadi said.

After thirty seconds of a "No, you," "No, you" routine, Riley finally convinced Ziafat to sit across from Khadi.

"Thanks," Ziafat said, dropping his large frame into the low chair.

"So, how've Riley and the team been treating you?" Khadi asked.

"Oh, I think they're coming around," Ziafat answered with a raised eyebrow toward Riley.

"Being a rookie is never fun," Riley said, noisily scooting his chair a little closer. "Afshin's been handling it better than most."

"I'm trying. Khadi, can I ask you a question?" He suddenly seemed to get a little tongue-tied trying to formulate his question. "Are you the one that I read about who was in the middle of all the stuff with Riley?"

For a moment Khadi hesitated; then she answered with a slight nod.

Ziafat's face lit up. "Wow, what an honor to meet you! I have got so much respect for you! All my family loves you, and my youngest sister wants to go into the FBI because of you. In the Persian community, it's not often we have someone we can cheer for in the war against terrorism."

Although Khadi had received honors from many women's, Persian, and intelligence organizations, it was still obvious that she wasn't used to the recognition. She tried to control a quick blush. "Thanks, Afshin. That really means a lot. That crazy man back in Iran does so much to destroy people's images of us. It was nice to shove one back in the terrorists' faces. May I ask you a question now? *Kojha bozorg shodee?*"

Ziafat's face brightened, and he laughed. *"Kheilee jaha boodeem, valee beeshtaresh dar Houston boodeem. Shoma chee?"*

"Arlington, Virginia. Pedaram doctor bood oonja." Suddenly Khadi looked at Riley. "I'm sorry, we're being rude. I just so rarely get to speak Farsi to anyone face-to-face."

"Don't be silly," Riley said with a wave of his hand. "That's one of the reasons I wanted to introduce you to each other. I had heard Afshin speaking Farsi on his cell phone, and I knew you missed the language. Please, go ahead. I'll get our drinks."

"No, Riley, let me get them," Ziafat said, getting up.

"Sit down, rookie, and tell me what you want," Riley said, already up and taking his first steps away.

"Okay, okay, thanks. Mind if I have a spiced chai?"

"You got it. And I don't need to ask what you want," Riley said to Khadi. "Coffee, black. The thicker the better."

Khadi responded with a smile and a wink. *"Avaleen nasleh Irani-Amricayee hastee?"* she asked Ziafat.

Riley felt pretty good about himself as he made his way to the counter. He ordered the drinks, then watched Khadi and Ziafat while he waited. They definitely seemed to be hitting it off. *It's good to hear Khadi laugh again. It's been a while since I've seen her really happy.*

Khadi caught Riley's eyes fixated on them. Embarrassed, he quickly turned and started fiddling with some little tins of mints. He then began examining a fancy espresso machine but had a hard time concentrating through Khadi's laughter.

Forcing himself to block out their conversation, Riley found his thoughts drifting to his time here with Whitney Walker. Now there was a laugh—her whole face lit up, and her eyes seemed to glow a beautiful green.

What am I doing? Daydreaming about another girl while Khadi's twenty feet away? Again, a feeling in the pit of his stomach told him that he should tell Khadi about his meeting. *Yeah, but is it really worth the headache? Besides, I haven't spoken to Whitney since that day. If there was anything there, it's dead now.*

The drinks were called. Riley put them in order, then slid two fingers through the four mug handles. He stopped first at Skeeter and placed a decaf in front of him.

"Hmm," grunted Skeeter in appreciation.

As he approached the others, the conversation abruptly stopped but they both kept smirks on their faces.

Riley pretended not to notice as he passed out the cups. "A black coffee and a spiced chai." He sat down and said, "Please, keep going. I'm fine."

"Thanks, Riley." Khadi reached across to touch Ziafat's forearm while she continued her story.

A strange sensation swept through Riley at their physical contact—one he didn't remember feeling since high school when he caught his prom date dancing with the quarterback. *Quit being an idiot,* Riley scolded himself. *They've just met. Besides, you have no claim on her.*

But as much as he told himself that, the more they talked and laughed, the more of an outsider Riley felt. Eventually he sat back in his seat and brooded, declining the offers they gave to include him in the conversation.

After a few minutes, Riley noticed that the conversation between Ziafat and Khadi had started to take on a bit of a heated tone. It was almost as if Khadi were on the attack, with Ziafat trying to back off from something he had said.

Finally, Khadi stood up and angrily turned to Riley. "It was a nice attempt, Riley. Probably right out of the Christian evangelism handbook. Bring a great-looking young man who speaks the girl's language. He'll tell her some stories, then talk about all that Jesus has done for him. She's bound to fall all over herself renouncing her former Muslim ways!"

Riley was still trying to catch up in the conversation from when she had called Ziafat great-looking. "What are you—?"

"Tell you what. You boys stay here and have your little tent revival. I've got to get back to work. It was a pleasure meeting you, Afshin. I'm glad Jesus has done so much to change your life."

Khadi stormed out the door, letting her hand slide across Skeeter's shoulders as she passed as a way of saying good-bye.

Riley turned to Ziafat and said, "You're not a Muslim?" at the same time that Ziafat said, "She's not a Christian?"

"I've never been a Muslim. I grew up a Christian. Didn't you read my bio?"

Riley was already on his feet and heading toward the door. "What possible reason would I have for reading a rookie's bio?" he replied, slamming the crash bar and running outside. Skeeter went right out after him.

Khadi was about to get into her car. The storm had stopped, and now the afternoon sun was visibly evaporating the water off the asphalt. The low vapor swirled around Riley's feet as he ran.

"Khadi, wait!"

Khadi closed her car door and turned to Riley. There were tears in her eyes. "What is it?"

"I didn't know. I swear to you, I had no clue he was a Christian. I was just trying to do something nice for you."

Khadi leaned up against the side of her BMW 328. She pulled a tissue out of her purse and dabbed her eyes. "I know, Riley. You're always trying to do something nice. You just don't always think it through when you do."

"Maybe I should have read his bio. I could have told him not to mention religion. I just didn't think about it."

"Riley, it's not about bios or religion or anything. And I'm sorry I overreacted back there. It's just that I wanted some time with you—alone. Well, as alone as we can be with that big lunk of a shadow with you all the time," Khadi said, throwing a thumb toward Skeeter, who was busy scanning the parking lot.

Riley had a helpless, deer-in-the-headlights look. "I'm sorry, Khadi. I didn't know."

"Of course you didn't know. There was no way for you to know. I just hoped you would have figured it out."

Riley's mind raced for some sort of appropriate retort but came up blank. So instead, he silently stared at the bronze wildlife sculpture at the museum across the street, waiting for a comment to be made that he could actually respond to.

Khadi continued, "I know I'm not being fair. It's just . . . Jim has us pretty much living at the office. I'm under so much stress, and I get so little time off. I had just hoped to be able to talk with you, maybe vent with you. Laugh with you a little."

Things were finally starting to make sense to Riley. He wanted to *do* something for her, but she just wanted to *be* with him. *Stinking Mars and Venus stuff again,* he thought. "I'm so sorry, Khadi. I should have read the signs."

Khadi gave a sad laugh. "Remember when you told me you could never be an analyst? It's true. I shouldn't have expected you to read any signs."

They stood quietly for a minute. Then Khadi said, "I need to go."

"When are you off next? Any chance of giving an unfeeling, insensitive lout like me a second chance?" Riley asked, trying to end the conversation on a lighter note.

Khadi looked at the ground and slowly shook her head. "That's just the thing, Riley. I don't know when I'm going to get more time off. And truthfully? My life is full of so much stress right now. This . . . this . . . 'relationship' we have is just adding to it. I think we probably need some time apart so we can think it through."

Riley was stunned. "But—"

"No buts right now. Please. Just know that I think you are an incredible man, Riley Covington." The softness in her face floored him, but before he could react, she had dropped into the driver's seat and was throwing the Beamer into reverse. A light flick of her fingers, and she was gone.

Riley stood there in a state of shock. *What just happened? How did . . . ? I mean, we were . . . What in the world just happened?*

A large hand fell on Riley's shoulder. Skeeter said, "Sorry, Pach. I know you're hurting, but you got to move inside. Can't stand out here in the open no more."

"What did I do, Skeeter? Better yet, what do I do now?"

Skeeter sighed, and then shook his head. "Can't help you there, man. I just got to get you back inside."

Riley nodded and followed his friend and protector back into the coffeehouse, wondering what possibly could go wrong next.

WEDNESDAY, MAY 20, 6:30 A.M. MDT
PARKER, COLORADO

Slowly, the plunger slid down the inside of the carafe, pushing all the grounds to the bottom. Left above the wire mesh was rich, dark coffee with all of the oils still in it, not sucked out as they typically are by a paper filter. Riley inhaled deeply and let the aroma fill his senses.

"Skeeter," Riley said to his friend, who was leaning on the other side of the kitchen's granite-top island, "this may be the cup of coffee you tell your children and grandchildren about."

Skeeter, looking unimpressed, said, "Not going to know unless you pour it, am I?"

"Point well taken." Riley tipped the French press toward Skeeter's insulated tumbler and filled it to the top. Then he poured some into his own ceramic mug. Riley's thin sweats didn't do much to protect him against the cool morning air. But that just made the feel of hot cup against cold hands that much more pleasurable.

Screwing the lid onto his tumbler, Skeeter said, "Gonna go talk to Scott's boys out front, then walk the perimeter of the property. Thanks for the coffee."

"No prob. Tell the guys thanks." In mornings

past, Riley had tried to send coffee to the security detail in front of his house. They always turned him down, preferring to drink out of their government-issued thermoses. *Don't know what they're missing.*

Riley watched Skeeter walk out dressed in his usual all black. His HK45 was tucked tightly against his side in a shoulder holster, and Riley could see the bulge around his ankle where his Glock 29 was tucked away. *Most people never see their guardian angels,* Riley thought. *There goes mine walking out the door. Thanks again, Lord, for sending Skeet my way.*

It had been a long night. Riley had replayed the scene with Khadi over and over in his mind. A few times he had almost called her. But she said she wanted space, and calling her right now would be invading that space. Around two o'clock this morning, he had finally resolved to try her on Friday. That would give her three days to think, and him three days to try to figure out what in the world he was going to say to her.

A quick glance at the clock on the oven told Riley that he still had ten minutes before he was scheduled to iChat with his folks. He took his mug and sat down with the *Rocky Mountain News* at the kitchen table. Kicking his feet up on the chair next to him, he separated the newspaper. Out of habit he turned to the Sports section first and quickly scanned the football columns. The stories themselves didn't interest him that much. He mostly wanted to check whether any of his free-agent friends had signed.

Not seeing anything of interest, he tossed that section aside and went back to the front page. Not surprisingly, there had been no new breaks in the weekend's attacks. Riley had been trying to fish information out of Scott and Khadi but had yet to get a decent bite. It was definitely hard being on the outside of the information stream. Even Skeeter knew more than he did. But Riley knew it would have to be some pretty extraordinary circumstances for his friends to compromise their clearances.

"NEBRASKA FAMILY LAID TO REST" read a top-of-the-fold headline. Riley blew on his coffee, took a sip, and then scanned the story.

Munroe family of Hyannis, Nebraska . . . All four members killed

*Friday night as part of a coordinated terrorist attack. . . . Note left behind
in which the Cause took credit. . . . Responsible for the bombing at Platte
River Stadium last December. . . . Attack thwarted by Colorado Mustang Riley Covington. . . . Small town of just under three hundred people
quadrupled in size as people flooded in to pay their respects and express
their sorrow. . . . Governor Atlee broke down as he spoke. . . . Secretary of
State Watts, Undersecretary of Homeland Security Blackmon, and Sena-
tors Boyles and Hollenback were in attendance. . . . Small group protesting
America's involvement in Iraq . . .*

Riley laid the paper down and closed his eyes. Anger surged in
him again, and he opened his eyes to find himself white-knuckling
his mug. He took a quick sip, then pushed it away.

Ever since the incident at Saturday's minicamp, he had been trying his best to put on a good face for everyone. Inside, however, he
was feeling very different. Beneath the smiling face there was rage,
frustration, sorrow, fear, and a growing desire for revenge.

*Why did it have to be the Cause, Lord? If it had been any other group,
I might have been able to let it go. But not them!*

Riley reached for his cup and took another swallow of coffee to
try to keep his emotions down. He sighed deeply, then folded the
paper and slid it to the other end of the table. Reading it was doing
him no good.

Another look at the oven told him it was still five minutes until
the iChat, but he figured he'd try his parents anyway. Knowing his
dad, he'd probably had it up and ready fifteen minutes ago.

Riley pulled his MacBook out of the computer case sitting next
to the table and lifted the screen. When he opened up the iChat
program, an icon indicated that his parents were already online.
He clicked it, then waited for an answer. A moment later, a futuris-
tic sound effect indicated that a new window was opening on his
screen, and there was his dad's face.

"Morning, Riles."

"Morning, Pop." Riley's dad appeared ready for a day of work on
the farm. He looked just like an older and darker version of Riley,
and his voice had the same deep tones. Dad was wearing a Colorado
Mustangs cap and holding a Colorado Mustangs coffee mug, both
of which looked like they'd seen better days.

"Mom said she'd be here soon. She's still getting herself together this morning."

"Does she not understand that I'm the only one looking at this?"

Dad laughed. "Sure, but you know how she is with cameras. I think she figures that somehow every other picture of her will get lost or destroyed, and the only image her great-grandchildren will have of her is this old lady with no makeup and her hair tied up in a scarf."

"This isn't even being recorded," Riley said, shaking his head. His mother had always been big on posterity; never mind that her only son was yet to even marry.

"I'll let you explain that to her. So, how're things? You look like you've been thinking a lot."

Riley often wondered what it was like for kids who could pull the wool over their parents' eyes—the kids who could get away with saying 'fine' when asked how things were. He'd never had that luxury. Riley's folks—especially his dad—read him like a book.

"I've been trying to keep a stiff upper lip, but haven't been succeeding much."

"Ah, the old 'keep a smile on your face and your emotions stuffed down deep and no one will ever know the difference' routine. You were never very good at that."

"Gee, thanks."

"Consider that a compliment, Riles. It's much better to live a what-you-see-is-what-you-get kind of life than it is to have people always wondering if you're really telling them the truth."

Riley just nodded. Listening to his dad's voice and seeing the familiar surroundings of the family kitchen on his computer screen was already helping to lighten his mood.

"So, you want to talk about it?" Dad offered.

Riley thought for a few seconds, then answered, "I don't think so, Pop. Not yet. Just keep praying that God keeps my mind pure. Some of the ideas for revenge that pop in there are pretty detailed and pretty graphic."

Dad leaned back in his chair, causing the picture to pixilate briefly. "I know what you mean, Son. Once you've seen the type of things you've seen, it's hard to keep them out. When you do want to talk more, you know where I am."

"Thanks. You know I'll take you up on it when I'm ready. So, how are the goats?"

Eight years back, Riley's parents had decided to convert their small acreage to an organic goat farm. Since then, they'd started building a bit of a reputation for their dairy goat products, particularly their cheeses.

"They're as obnoxious as always. Last week a couple of them got out and found our newspaper recycle bin. They ate half the papers in there before I finally rounded them up."

Riley had despised the goats ever since one of them had snuck up behind him and bit him on the backside. It had been three days before he could sit without pain. "Remember, if you get tired of them, I still have a recipe for *mbuzi* stew that I picked up on that missions trip to Uganda. Then you could get your milk from—oh, I don't know—a cow maybe! You know, like God originally intended!" Riley still couldn't understand why they had gone with goats. He'd been trying for years to get his parents to get rid of them and start a real dairy farm.

They both laughed. Then his dad leaned in close to the computer screen and said quietly, "That reminds me. Your mom is going to send you some cheese—a new *chèvre* recipe that she's trying out."

"Why does she do that? She knows I can't stand the stuff. I just end up giving it all away."

"I've never understood what your issue is with goat cheese," Dad said a little defensively, taking a long drink out of his coffee mug.

Riley shook his head. "I don't know. It just makes everything taste so . . . so . . . Greek."

Dad almost lost his coffee on the computer. "Okay, I wasn't expecting that answer. That's about the most ridiculous reason for not liking goat cheese I've heard. I think I'll have Mom post that on our Web site."

"Swell."

"Just do me a favor and pretend you like it—for your mom's sake. Besides, this is *chèvre*; maybe it'll make everything taste all French instead."

"And that's supposed to be better?"

Just then Mom appeared on the screen back by the sink. She was silhouetted by a window that looked into the backyard and toward the barn. "Jerry, is our son complaining about our livelihood again?"

"Come on, Mom. It's not like that," Riley protested.

Mom poured herself a cup of coffee and sat next to her husband. She looked like she was ready to go to Sunday morning church. "Listen, sweetheart, just because some poor disillusioned woman raised you on Kraft Singles and Velveeta doesn't mean that you can't broaden your horizons now that you're out from under her rooftop."

"Hey, I object. You were a good cook growing up."

"Of course I was—as long as the recipe had the words *cheesy*, *bake*, or *casserole* in it. It's no better than if you were raised at a church potluck."

"Oh, please," Riley laughed. "You were an awesome cook. Look at me; I turned out okay."

"Yes you did, Riley. You turned out wonderfully. I'll take that as one point on my side."

"Tell you what," Dad jumped in. "I'm going to leave you two to your mutual admiration society. I've got work to do. Take care of yourself, Riles. Remember, I'm always only a phone call away."

"Thanks, Pop. Good talking to you." Riley watched as his dad walked off the screen. A moment later he heard the rear door open and close.

"Your dad's really concerned about you," Mom said, turning the computer so that she was lined up directly with the built-in camera. "It's been a while since I've seen him as agitated as when he read that the Cause was responsible for those horrible attacks."

Riley wanted to kick himself when he realized that he had been so wrapped up in his own feelings that he hadn't asked his dad how he was handling the situation.

Mom continued, "I know what you're thinking, and don't beat yourself up. Dad would have just told you that everything was okay. He doesn't want to worry you."

"Are you okay with everything?"

"I tell you what, sweetheart. I just spend a lot of time praying—for you, for the team, for Scott and Khadi and the rest of the gang. God taught me a long time ago that even though I may be totally helpless, He's not. He just keeps reminding me that whatever happens, He's in control. The only time things start going haywire is when I try to take it back."

"I hear you, Mom. I think that's been my problem. I release everything to God; then I take it back. Then I release it; then I take it back. It's like I've got my trust in God on a yo-yo."

Mom chuckled softly. "I know, dear. And don't go thinking that I have it all together myself. Prayer is the only thing that keeps me from being a nervous wreck, especially when it comes to your safety. Well, prayer and Skeeter Dawkins. Which reminds me, is he around so I can say hi to him?"

"No, he's out walking the property."

"Well, tell him I asked for him. Say, does he like my cheese? If he does, I can send—"

Suddenly Riley's speakers distorted and the picture on his screen momentarily froze.

"Mom? Mom, you there?" Then the signal caught up and Riley was able to see back into the kitchen. What he saw made his blood freeze.

The view from the computer had shifted to the right. There was glass from the window scattered over the kitchen counter, and water was spraying up from the sink's faucet. The cabinets were all opened, and their contents were spilled onto the counter and the floor. But what frightened Riley the most was that his mother was nowhere to be seen.

"Mom!" Riley yelled at the computer. "Mom!" He snatched up his cell phone and dialed Skeeter's number. Skeeter answered it on the first ring.

"Skeet, get back here now! Something's happened at my parents' house."

"I'm there," Skeeter replied.

Riley was breathing fast, and his mind was racing. *Lord, what's happened? What should I do?* He picked up his phone to call Scott, and then put it back down. "Mom! Mom, are you there?"

"Riley . . ." a faint voice came over the computer's speakers.

"Mom! Are you okay?"

"Riley . . . explosion . . . your dad . . . help . . ."

Skeeter burst through the front door and ran to Riley. "What—?"

"Shhh! Mom, can you hear me? Mom! Are you there?"

But there was no response. To his left, Riley heard Skeeter on the phone saying, "Scott, something's happened at the Covingtons' in Wyoming! Figure it out and call me!" He slammed closed his phone. "Pach, what happened?"

But Riley didn't answer. He couldn't answer. Instead, he just stared at the computer screen looking for any signs of movement. Finally, after a few minutes of stillness, he dropped his head into his hands and prayed.

WEDNESDAY, MAY 20, 7:00 A.M. MDT
PARKER, COLORADO

Riley's first impulse was to race to Wheatland, but Skeeter restrained him. There were too many unknowns, too many possible scenarios. The best thing to do right now was to sit tight and wait for word.

More than ten minutes passed before there was any movement on the computer screen. When it finally came, there was a lot of it. Police and paramedics suddenly rushed left to right across Riley's computer.

"Hey! Hey, someone tell me what's going on!" Riley yelled. Then he recognized one of the first responders from a charity event he had hosted. "Sheriff Cooper! Sheriff Cooper, talk to me!"

The kitchen table was hit by someone or something and pushed backward. This shifted Riley's view to the refrigerator, which had been covered with pictures of friends and family and newspaper articles about himself. Now the door was completely bare. Riley strained to listen to what was being said.

A woman crossed the screen rolling a gurney. The table was pushed back again, apparently to make room. This time, however, the movement was too abrupt for the computer. The picture on Riley's screen suddenly made a ninety-degree turn toward the ground, then froze. A bubble popped up on Riley's computer indicating, "Mom&Dad has left the iChat."

"Wait! Wait!" Riley's fist drove hard into the kitchen table. He tried reconnecting, but there was no response.

Soon afterward, Grandpa made a quick call saying he was making the seventy-mile drive from Cheyenne to Wheatland. An hour passed after that call. Riley paced, he sat, he prayed, he paced some more.

"Skeeter, what's Scott saying?"

Skeeter, who had positioned himself by the front window, shook his head. "Said there was an explosion. Said he'd call me back when he's got more."

So many thoughts were going through Riley's mind. The prospect of life without his parents was an eventuality that had never even occurred to him. Riley's family had always been small. His grandmother on his dad's side had died right after Riley had been born. His dad had had only one brother, the man whom Riley had been named after. He had been a marine who was killed while guarding the final evacuation from Saigon in 1975.

Riley had never been very close with his mom's side of the family. No real reason; it just kind of happened that way. He saw his Grandma and Grandpa Hopkins every couple of years. His mom had two sisters and one brother, but it seemed the only time he heard from his aunts and uncles or cousins was when they wanted an autographed ball or some tickets to a Mustangs game.

The waiting was killing Riley. His thoughts began flying all over the place. *That leaves me and Grandpa, which means that I'm about ten to fifteen years away from being alone in this world. And Mom so desperately wanted to see her grandkids. Why couldn't you have found someone to at least give her that pleasure? And realize that this has all happened because of you—because of your great desire to go out and play soldier?*

Stop it! Don't go there yet!

What's taking Grandpa so long?

All mom wanted were a couple of grandkids so she could make little blankets and Halloween costumes.

"Skeeter, try Scott again!"

"Will do."

How come I'm not in the car right now driving up?

Because, like Skeeter said, I'd be playing right into their hands. But what good am I here?

Answer the phone, Scott!

Lord, please help me to know what to do.

This cannot be happening. Help them, Lord. Protect them. Heal them.

Watch over the responders; don't let this be a trap.

It's been an hour. Where's Grandpa? What did he say his record was for that seventy-mile trip? Was it fifty-two minutes?

What am I going to do about all those goats?

Finally a familiar ring tone sounded on Riley's cell phone. Even without looking at the caller ID, he knew it read "Grandpa Covington." *Lord, let it be good news.* He sat down at the table. "Hello?"

There was a pause, then he heard Grandpa Covington's voice. Rather than its usual soothing bass, it seemed tight and strained. "Riles, son, you need to know first of all that your mom is all right. She's got a concussion, but the doctors say she'll be fine."

"And my dad?" Riley asked hopefully.

Grandpa sighed heavily; then with a barely controlled voice he said, "Your daddy's gone, Riley. They killed him. They killed my son."

Riley felt dizzy. He wanted more information—needed more information—but couldn't think of the questions to ask. "Why? How?"

"Someone rigged the barn door. When Jerry opened it, a bomb went off. The security detail was with him when it happened. One of them's dead and the other is pretty near."

Riley felt another punch to his gut. Not just his dad, but two more lives snuffed out on his account. Two more families destroyed because someone wanted revenge on him.

"Grandpa, I'm . . . Grandpa, I'm so sorry. They did this to get to me. I wish . . . I'm just so sorry." Riley was doing everything he could to keep himself together, but he was failing.

Suddenly, Grandpa's voice changed, and anger filled his words.

"Don't do that, Riley! Don't you dare take this on your shoulders! My son was an honorable man, and he died an honorable death living the life that God called him to. Don't you take that from him. Somebody is responsible for this, but that somebody isn't you. Do you understand?"

"Yes, Grandpa," Riley said quietly.

"I said, do you understand?"

"Yes, sir!" Riley responded, more out of reflex at hearing a commanding military voice than out of any conviction.

"Good. Your Grandma and Grandpa Hopkins are on their way here. Should be another few hours. I'm going to stay with your mom until then. Then I'll be coming down your way."

"Grandpa, shouldn't you stay up there with Mom?" Riley protested. "Besides, it seems like I'm not the safest person to be around right now."

"Listen, son, I need to see you. Whether you need it or not, *I* need it."

Plans for revenge had already begun forming in Riley's mind. The last thing he wanted was for his grandpa to come down and talk him out of it. "Listen, Grandpa, I don't even know where I'll be in three or four hours. I've got a call in to Scott Ross right now."

Grandpa's deep bass was back, but there was no soothing in it. "No, you listen, Riley. You're the only blood I've got left. We need to talk. I'm asking you to be there when I arrive."

Riley sighed. How could he say no? "Of course, Grandpa. I'll be here. I just can't promise how long."

"Fair enough. I love you, Riley. We'll get through this."

Riley hung up the phone. He felt dazed, like when he took a full-frontal collision from a fullback. *Dad's dead?* It seemed so surreal.

Dad, who had survived two tours in Vietnam, who had made it through a horrific head-on accident with just a punctured lung and two broken legs, who had bested his high blood pressure by switching to goat cheese.

Dad, who was a husband, a father, a navy man, a patriot, a church deacon, a farmer.

Dad was dead—taken out by someone simply as a way of drawing out his son.

Dad was a casualty of war—collateral damage.

Riley felt Skeeter's hand on his shoulder. "I heard, man. I'm so sorry."

"Yeah. Thanks, Skeet." Riley stood and walked to the kitchen, where he leaned forward against the granite-top island. "I . . . I feel like I should be crying. But I can't. It just doesn't seem real."

"Ain't no way to *be* feeling, except how you *are* feeling."

Riley nodded.

"Talked with Scott. He'll get here soon as he can."

"Thanks." Then a thought struck him. "Is . . . ?"

"No, man. I told him to come alone."

"Good. I appreciate it." As much as he would have liked to see Khadi right now, after their last meeting her presence would only serve to confuse things more.

Skeeter went back to his position by the door, leaving Riley to think. For some reason a picture of learning to ride a bike flashed in his memory. It played like a movie in his mind, maybe because so many times he had seen the video his mom had taken that day.

There he was, pedaling along with his dad holding on to the seat. It was a Saturday, and Riley could remember how strange it had been seeing his school parking lot so empty. Riley and Dad would make a pass across the parking lot, then turn and go back the other way. Bit by bit, he was starting to get the feel of balancing the bike.

Riley could still remember the feeling. As long as Dad was holding the seat, he knew he was safe. So Riley pumped the pedals moving faster and faster. But this time, when he looked back to see if his dad was keeping pace, there was no one there. His dad was standing way back in the parking lot with his thumbs up in the air. Riley panicked and almost lost control. But then he suddenly realized that not only *could* he do it on his own, he *was* doing it on his own.

Dad's not going to be there to hold on to the seat anymore. But you know you can still make it. Thank You. Thank You, Lord, for the time You gave me with Dad. Please help me as from here on out I learn to ride on my own.

Riley went back to the table, put his head on his arms, and tried to shut down his brain.

Evening brought no relief from the busyness of Istanbul's streets. Al-'Aqran limped past the open stalls and small storefronts, his old walking stick taking some of the pressure off his knees. Hamad Asaf, speaking on his cell phone, slowed his usual pace in order to remain alongside his leader. As they traveled the narrow road, each open door brought a different sound—a stereo system, pans clattering on a stove, men arguing in Turkish, women haggling over fabric—that blended with the many smells: baking *simit* and *lavash*, *kebabs* and *shawarma*, cloves and saffron, coffee and spiced chai.

As the two men weaved through the mass of people, al-'Aqran reflected that the flow of pedestrians in these tight streets must be as mysterious and bewildering to a stranger as experiencing the automobile traffic patterns of a foreign country. A Westerner would always be easy to spot as he bumped into one person after another. But al-'Aqran and Asaf easily found their way through the hundreds of passersby.

Asaf hung up the phone. "It is done," he said to his leader.

"Both the mother and the father?"

"Just the father," Asaf responded with an apology in his voice. "The mother is injured."

"Hmmm." Al-'Aqran walked a few more paces, thinking. Finally, he said, "It is enough. A man would be a fool to go to war for his mother. But for his father? Honor demands a response. Is there any movement from Covington?"

"No, *sayyid*, not yet."

The old man nodded. "It will come."

Al-'Aqran turned into a teahouse and sat at a table near the door. He was not thirsty, but he was finding these walks back from the *'Asr* prayer at the mosque harder and harder to take. Tea was as good an excuse as any to give his joints time to rest.

He ordered for himself and for Asaf. "And what of the pig-eater in Chicago?"

Asaf retrieved his phone, pressed a number of buttons, then passed the phone to al-'Aqran. A still picture showed on the small screen. A man was sitting in an expensive-looking chair. There was obvious fear on his face.

"Press the button marked 'OK'," Asaf told him.

When al-'Aqran did so, a video began. The man said, "My name is Mohsin Ghani." Then his eyes widened and a red hole appeared to the left of the bridge of his nose just before the back of his head exploded out. The video ended.

Asaf took back his phone and said, "Our man retrieved the three backpacks from the apartment. One of them he used at the home of Covington's father. The other two he is holding for a future need."

"And tell me—" Al-'Aqran stopped himself as the black tea was delivered to the table. When the waiter retreated, the old man wrapped his hands around the tulip-shaped glass until he could feel the burn slowly penetrating his thickly calloused hands. "And tell me of the preparations for the next phase, once these initial waves are completed."

"The warriors are waiting to be awakened. We know whom we will use and where they will attack. Logistically, phase two will be much easier than phase one. Easy-to-conceal automatic weapons will be used, and the security is very low. The martyrs will be carrying many rounds of ammunition, and obviously, the targets will be congregated together."

"Very good, old friend," said al-'Aqran, grasping Asaf by the forearm. "You have done excellent work. Have Tahir let our people know that it is time to launch the next step of our initial phase."

"Yes, *sayyid*."

The chair creaked as al-'Aqran leaned back. Other than one coward, everything was going according to plan. Soon America would hear from the Cause again, and what little confidence they had left in their security would come crashing to the ground.

Riley watched as Skeeter turned the doorknob with his left hand while holding his HK45 with his right. When the door opened, Scott Ross walked in, and Skeeter quickly closed the door after him. Scott wore his usual Birkenstocks and torn jeans, and today he rounded out the ensemble with a Molly Hatchet *Flirtin' with Disaster* 1979 tour T-shirt.

"Hey, Skeeter," Scott said somberly.

"Scott," Skeeter answered, returning to his post by the front window.

This meeting had been heavy on Riley's mind. If he had any chance of hunting down the people who had done this to his dad, he had to get back in with the Counterterrorism Division. And if there was one person who could finagle him back in at CTD, it was Scott Ross.

Riley rose from the kitchen table and met Scott halfway through the great room.

"Serious apologies for taking so long to get here."

"I just appreciate you coming," Riley said as he embraced his friend.

"I'm so sorry, Pach," Scott responded with a

crack in his voice. They separated, but Scott still held Riley by the shoulders. "From everything you've told me about your father, he was a good man."

"That he was."

Riley sat down in his overstuffed leather chair. Scott dropped himself in his usual place on the matching couch and crossed one leg on top of the other.

"It's bizarre, man," Riley said. "Sometimes it feels real; other times it's like living out a movie script."

Without looking up, Scott replied, "I can't imagine."

The two men sat in silence for a minute. Scott was fidgeting with the strap on his sandal. Riley knew that was usually a sign that he had something on his mind.

"Was that Meg Ricci I saw pulling out?" Scott finally asked.

Riley nodded. "Yeah, she came by to see if there was anything she could do."

What Riley didn't say was that it had been a very strange visit. Meg had come across as part friend, part psychiatrist, part mother, and part wife. Riley tried to make it clear without offending her that he wanted nothing to do with any except the first of that list. Unfortunately, she seemed to miss every sign he tried to send her. The hug at the end of her visit, along with a surprising kiss, had left Riley feeling very uneasy, particularly since it had all taken place under Skeeter's watchful eye.

"That's nice," Scott said as he moved to the edge of the couch next to Riley. When Riley didn't respond, he continued, "I read the doctor's chart on your mom. It sounds like she's going to be okay."

Riley was momentarily surprised that Scott had seen his mother's medical report; then he remembered whom he was talking to. "I've just heard concussion. Anything else I need to know?"

"No, she was lucky that the barn was set so far back from the house. The house itself kept its structural integrity. The blast wave just blew out windows and shredded the siding with shrapnel." Scott stopped a moment, then said, "I'm sorry, Pach. That was a pretty callous way of putting things."

Riley waved his hand. "No, Scott. I need to know. You're fine. Go on."

Scott rubbed the back of his neck while he talked, and Riley could see that he was having a hard time making eye contact. "Well, your mom went down with the blast and smacked her head hard on the kitchen counter. She also received some cuts from the falling plates and glasses. Your dad . . . If it's any consolation, he never knew what hit him."

A vision of his father's body bursting into thousands of pieces flashed into Riley's mind. He quickly pushed it away. "No, it's not much consolation, but it's something. What I want to know is how did they get the bomb in place? What happened to our security?"

A small bronze bear cub was sitting on one side of Riley's coffee table. Scott picked it up and began rolling it from one hand to the other. "There was security, but they weren't ours. I'm guessing these guys probably made regular rounds—too regular. It was all just a matter of timing. The perp came through the back property. He could have set the thing and been gone in under five minutes."

"Were the night guys the ones killed?"

Scott shook his head. "No. They had gone off about two hours before the explosion. These guys were the day shift."

Riley nodded, and tears formed in his eyes. He forced them back down. "Somewhere along the line I want the names of the detail who were killed. I want to do something for the families. I just don't think I can deal with it quite yet."

Riley saw a soft smile appear on Scott's face. "Yeah, I figured as much. I've got all their information written down. I'll just leave it with Skeet when I go."

"Thanks, buddy. Hey, if it's all right, I've got something I need to talk to you about."

Scott put the bear back on the table and sat back. Riley could see something in Scott's eyes. It was the kind of look a person gets when they've had way too much to eat and know they're in for a rough night ahead—a dread mixed with extreme discomfort.

"Go ahead, Pach. I'm listening."

"I need your help, Scott. I need you to start whatever process it's going to take to get me back in with CTD."

Scott's surprisingly silent response took Riley off guard. He expected Scott to say that he already had things in motion—that as soon as he had finished meeting with his grandpa, Riley could go down and get fully briefed. But Scott just sat there completely still. Riley could tell that his mind was racing.

"Scott, did you hear me? I need for you to get things going again. I know you guys are going after the Cause. I've got to be part of that. You need me to be part of that."

Riley saw Scott's eyes reddening as he searched for what to say. Finally, he leaned forward and burst out, "Pach, dude, it just ain't going to happen."

Riley was stunned. He almost started laughing, thinking it was another of Scott's ill-timed and ill-conceived jokes. "What do you mean, it's not going to happen? It's just like last time. You call me in, the paperwork gets done, and then we go out and take them down."

"Not this time, Riley. You're too close. You're too . . . unstable right now."

Desperate, Riley said, "Then give me a couple days to stabilize, Scott. Come on, you're my best friend! You can't do this to me!"

Scott's voice had taken on its own pleading tone. "Can't you see? It's because I'm your best friend that I'm doing this."

Riley leaped out of his seat. He couldn't believe his ears. He began pacing in front of the fireplace. Then a thought struck him. "Are you doing this, or is it Jim? Jim's dogging me again, isn't he? Come on, man, you've got to fight for me! Make Jim understand that I'll never put my own feelings over the mission! You know that!"

"It wasn't just Jim," Scott said quietly. "We all made the call."

Riley stopped his pacing, and stared at Scott. "'We all,' meaning who?"

"Jim, me, Tara . . ."

"And Khadi."

"Yeah, and Khadi." Scott stood and moved toward Riley. "My friend, you need to trust us. Let us fight your battles for you. You know me. I swear I will do everything humanly possible to bring these guys down. We just need you to stay out right now."

How could my friends have turned on me like this? He wanted to hit something—to hurt someone. Scott was temptingly close, so Riley walked toward the kitchen. *This is just so insane!*

Suddenly, he spun around. "So, what do all my *friends* expect me to do? Forget about the Cause and play the happy football player?"

Scott dropped down on the back of Riley's leather chair. "That's another thing, Pach. After we all talked, Jim called up the Mustangs and told them to put you on injured reserve for the year. They're going to give some story about a blown Achilles."

It was very good that Scott was no longer in swinging distance. Out of the corner of his eye, Riley saw Skeeter move a little closer to Scott so that he could intervene in case things turned physical. *Yeah, you better move in, Skeet,* Riley thought as he glared at Scott.

Scott shifted uncomfortably under his gaze. "Pach, think about it, and you'll see we're right. You're too hot right now. You'd be putting the whole team at risk—not to mention the fans."

Riley tried to find something to say in reply, but deep down he knew they were right. Just that quickly, his rage turned to sorrow, and he felt the darkness descending on him again. It was the same darkness he had felt not too many months ago after calling Meg Ricci to tell her that her husband had been killed in the Platte River Stadium attack.

Deflated and defeated, Riley asked, "Is there anything else that your little cabal decided for my life?"

"Just one more thing," Scott said softly, but he seemed reluctant to say what.

"Come on. Out with it. Am I going into hiding in Montana? Or maybe the witness protection program? Yeah, maybe I'm getting a new identity. That would be swell." Riley could see his sarcasm was cutting Scott, but he didn't care.

"Nothing like that. It's just we don't think it's a good idea for you to attend your dad's funeral."

"Is that 'we don't think it's a good idea' or 'you're not going'? Sorry, you've got to make things clear to a dumb, loose-cannon jock like me."

"Come on, Pach, this isn't easy for—"

"Answer the question!"

"We'll set up a simulcast for you if you want. You can even say something at the service by video feed. But, no, you won't be going."

Riley went to the large, two-sided fireplace and placed his hands on the huge stones that made up the mantelpiece. Facing away from Scott, he said, "This morning, I lost my father. And now I've lost my career. I've lost my opportunity to avenge my father's death. And I've lost my chance to celebrate his life. I've got you guys to thank for three out of the four."

"Pach, it's not like that." Riley could hear the hurt in Scott's voice. "You know we're doing this because we love you."

Silently, Riley stared at the mantle.

"Come on, man, don't do this."

"Hey, Scott—" Skeeter's deep voice carried across the room—"he needs some space."

"Sure, you're right." Scott walked up to Riley and said, "You need anything, Pach, you just call, okay?"

When Riley didn't respond, Scott headed toward the door. Riley could hear Skeeter and Scott whispering, then the sound of one person slapping the other on the back. The door opened. The door closed.

Riley turned and saw Skeeter looking at him.

"You know he's right, Pach."

With venom in his voice, Riley said, "Shut up, Skeeter. Don't make me hear it from you, too."

"Let me finish," Skeeter continued in his usual matter-of-fact baritone. "You know that he's right. But that don't mean it's the end of the story."

"I'm listening."

Skeeter shrugged. "All I'm saying is sometimes when you're losing, the best thing you can do is change the rules of the game."

Confused, Riley shook his head. "I have no idea what you're talking about."

"Good. Then think about it. Maybe it'll give you something to occupy your brain for a while other than self-pity." Skeeter turned back toward the window indicating that his part in the conversation was over.

Riley tried to rekindle his anger with Skeeter, but Skeeter was one of those men who spoke so few words that whenever he made the effort to say something, it was usually worth thinking about. Besides,

Riley's mind was so filled with feelings of sorrow, guilt, betrayal, and desire for revenge that there was no room to be angry at his friend.

Sitting back down in his chair, Riley let the darkness flood over him. He gave in to thoughts of vengeance. His mind began visualizing the ways he could kill those who had killed his father.

But just as he began sinking into the depths, Skeeter's voice pulled him back out. "Gonna have to dream of killing them all later, Pach. Grandpa Covington's here."

WEDNESDAY, MAY 20, 3:00 P.M. MDT
PARKER, COLORADO

A red dot danced on the small patch of white between the blesbok's horns. The dot steadied, and a metallic click echoed through the large room. "That is an amazing piece of work," Grandpa Covington said as he handed the assault weapon back to Riley. "How'd you come across it?"

Many tears had been shed when Grandpa first arrived—tears from an overwhelming sorrow at the loss of a father and a son; tears from an intense gratitude to God for the assurance that Jerry Covington was with Him; tears from a comforting peace that slowly took root as the result of grandfather and grandson being together.

When they were finally cried out, the two men sat down in the great room. Riley had been ready to start talking, but Grandpa said, "We've got plenty of time for that. First things first. If I remember right, last time I came to visit you, you met me at the door holding an M4. Now that you're truly in imminent danger, I don't see you carrying anything."

"Gramps," Riley answered in a way designed not to hurt his grandpa's feelings, "I don't know if you saw them or not—maybe they were making rounds—but I've got a four-man security detail outside, and Skeeter's in with me. I should be okay."

"I'm old, son, but I'm not blind. I saw them out there. And by the way, apparently your security detail has been upped, because now you have six including the two who were watching me from the house across the street."

"It has?" Grandpa was a former air force pilot whose great eyesight and keen awareness of his surroundings had allowed him to chalk up seven MiG kills to his credit in the Korean War. Still, those two extra "security agents" could have just been the neighbors. "Hey, Skeeter, how many people we have out there?"

Without turning from the window, Skeeter held up all the fingers on his right hand and the thumb from his left.

"Fair enough," Riley said to Grandpa. "So I've got six outside and Skeeter in here. There are motion sensors all through the back property. I'll be okay."

"Apparently it hasn't sunk into your brain yet," Grandpa replied, leaning forward and tapping Riley on the side of his head—one of the few things Grandpa did that drove Riley absolutely crazy. Riley could hear the beginnings of frustration in Grandpa's voice. "You are in a war. You've got folks who want to take you out so badly that they just killed your father. Think about it—when you were in Afghanistan, were you ever without a weapon near you?"

"No."

"Why not?"

Riley despised answering obvious questions. But out of respect for Grandpa, he said, "I was in a war zone, and you never know what's going to happen in a war zone."

"Bingo! I'm sure Scott's got a good detail for you out front, and there's no one I'd want by my side more than Skeeter. But the fact remains that they are still human, and humans can go down with one shot. You agree, Skeeter?"

"Yes, sir," said Skeeter, who was apparently listening to every word from his place by the window.

Grandpa turned back to Riley. "So, let's get you soldiered up. Then we can talk."

Riley didn't answer for a minute. He hated the idea of having to walk around his home armed. This house was his sanctuary. It was his place of safety where he could relax and let his guard down. But there was no arguing with Grandpa's logic. People were out to kill him, and when the next attempt came, he didn't want to get caught empty-handed.

There was a fine line between house and bunker. Riley felt that he was about to cross that line.

Riley reluctantly stood and said, "Let's go. Skeet, we're heading down to the vaults. We'll be back up in a while."

Skeeter gave a thumb-up in reply, and Riley and Grandpa moved to the basement. The bottom of the stairs opened into a large entertainment room. In the center of the room was an open minitheater with an enormous screen and recliner seating.

To the left of the theater was a game area containing a pool table, a shuffle board table, and a recently delivered Riley Covington's Football Force pinball machine—a bad-taste venture from EA Sports that Riley just couldn't bring himself to plug in. To the right was a kitchenette with bar seating, sink, soda machine, convection oven, and mini popcorn maker. On either side of the long bar were archways. Riley led Grandpa through the right archway and into the Dead Room.

The Dead Room was the name Scott Ross had given to the den, where Riley's hunting trophies covered the walls. Domestic animals such as elk, moose, and deer mixed with the more exotic eland, kudu, and blue wildebeest in this static menagerie. Dozens of glass eyes watched Grandpa and Riley pass through to a hidden doorway tucked behind a full-standing gemsbok. Riley pushed the door open, and the two men entered.

Two large green vaults stood in this tight room. After punching in a four-digit number on the left vault's keypad, Riley passed his thumb across the fingerprint recognition device. Three loud clicks told him that he was free to pull open the double doors.

The second vault held Riley's few antique guns and his hunting rifles. This one, however, contained what might be considered an enthusiast's weapons. In here were a wide assortment of handguns, an M4, an AK-74, and several other assault weapons—mostly gifts from buddies in the various branches of military and special ops.

It was out of this vault that Riley had pulled the personal defense weapon that Grandpa had just used to place an imaginary bullet into the blesbok's forehead. Grandpa handed the rifle back to Riley, and they both sat down on couches in the Dead Room.

"It's called a Micro Tavor. It's become the standard assault weapon for Israeli special ops."

Grandpa nodded appreciatively. "How'd you come by it?"

"You remember when I told you about my buddy, Munir Saygeh? The IDF guy who was in my AFSOC training?"

"Right. The one who was the military governor of Jericho when it was passed over to the Palestinians. I thought he was just a tour guide now."

Riley's eyebrows rose. "Sure, and Skeeter's just my butler. Anyway, when he heard about all that happened last January, he wanted to send one of these MTAR 21s my way. I got Scott in on it, and he, in his usual Scott way, cleared it through the proper channels."

"It's a beautiful weapon. I'm amazed at how light it is."

Riley hefted it up in his hands and tucked it into his shoulder. "Yeah, six and a half pounds, and only twenty-three inches long. And since it's got an integral silencer, suppression doesn't lengthen the barrel at all."

"How does the short barrel do at distances?"

"This thing has the power of an M16 and the accuracy of a sniper rifle. Laser and MARS red-dot sight are built in and turn on automatically when the safety is off. It fires great, too. The short stock tucks right back into the shoulder."

Grandpa whistled his admiration for the weapon, then said, "Riley, I want you to promise me something. I want you to promise me that this MTAR isn't going to leave your side until this whole thing comes to a resolution. There are people who are not going to rest until you're dead. So when you shower, I want this leaning outside the glass. When you sleep, it's sharing the pillow next to you. Will you do that for me?"

Riley laid the weapon across his lap. "Sure, Grandpa. You've got me convinced."

The relief of not having to argue the point showed in Grandpa's eyes. "Good. Now, I'm assuming the Mustangs are going to let you out of the rest of minicamp based on what's happened. If not, you can probably have Jim Hicks . . ." Grandpa stopped when Riley leaned back on his couch. The darkness had come back, and Riley felt as if he had suddenly aged ten years.

"I think it's time we *really* talked," Riley said quietly.

WEDNESDAY, MAY 20, 3:30 P.M. MDT
PARKER, COLORADO

Grandpa slid himself back on his couch, which sat across from Riley. A long, low table supporting a mounted pheasant stretched between them. Grandpa leaned his arm on the back of the couch and said, "Go ahead, son; I'm listening."

Riley took several deep breaths in order to get control of his emotions. The hot coals of his rage were smoldering. If he had any hope of a productive, intelligent conversation, he knew he had to keep that fire under control.

"I spoke with Scott just before you got here."

Grandpa sighed disapprovingly. "I figured you would. You going back in with CTD?"

"No, Gramps," Riley said angrily. "You'll be happy to know they turned me down flat. Said I was too close—too unstable."

"Were they right?"

"What do you mean, were they right?" If Grandpa kept talking like this, Riley's coals of rage would soon be a blazing inferno.

"Think about it. Including Skeeter, you've got seven security agents in and around your house. There are people out to kill you. You're in your basement holding an Israeli assault weapon like it's a throw pillow. And your dad . . ." Grandpa's voice caught. He paused a moment, then exhaled sharply through his nose. "Well, all that to say, how stable could you be right now?"

That was not the supportive answer Riley was looking for. "Listen, I've been in stressful situations before. I mean, good night! Think about what my last half year has been like!"

"Yes, but they never touched your family until now, did they?"

Riley didn't answer. His right index finger moved slowly back and forth over the serial number plate embedded in the left side of the MTAR 21's stock. In Riley's mind, instability meant a lack of self-control, and *self*-control seemed to be the only kind of control he still had over his life.

"Listen, Grandpa, I agree that I'm overly emotional—I mean, who wouldn't be? My dad's been dead less than twelve hours. But I'm not going to go fly off the handle and do something that puts other people at risk. Unstable? No. Maybe you could convince me of *volatile*. But not unstable."

Grandpa nodded agreement. "Volatile it is. But it still doesn't change the situation."

"No, it doesn't," Riley said, finally starting to calm down. "I just need you to understand where I'm at. I'm still a long ways from the deep end, and in no danger of falling off."

"I'm tracking with you. So, no CTD. Now, tell me about the Mustangs. I could see by your reaction when I mentioned them that something's going on."

A disgusted chuckle escaped Riley before he said, "Apparently I've blown my Achilles. They're talking about IR-ing me for the year when training camp comes around."

Grandpa leaned forward on the couch. "I'm sorry, Riley. Was that the Mustangs' idea?"

"CTD's. Needless to say, Scott's not my favorite person right now. Oh, and one more little tidbit just to round things out: I've been banned from Dad's funeral."

Grandpa eased himself back and stared at the ceiling. Riley waited for a response, but the old man remained silent. He hated it when his grandpa was quiet like this, because it usually meant he was trying to find a diplomatic way to tell Riley he was wrong. To save him the trouble, Riley shouted, "Go ahead and say it, Grandpa! Scott's right and I'm wrong!"

Grandpa locked eyes with Riley and said, "Okay, Scott's right and you're wrong."

Riley dropped the assault rifle on the couch and began pacing. A battle was raging in his mind. *You know Grandpa's right. You know Scott's right. You just don't want to be wrong! You just don't want to be out of control of your own life! What would you have decided differently if you'd been given the time to think it through? Nothing! Well, nothing except for joining back with CTD. That's the killer decision there! That takes away all my options.*

He stopped in front of a Texas Dall sheep and let his hand follow the curve of its horn out to the tip a few times. Still not looking at Grandpa, Riley asked, "So, what are you saying? Am I just supposed to sit here with a target on my back until eventually some *hajji* scores a bull's-eye?"

The rhetorical question hung in the air for a minute until Grandpa said, "Why don't you come sit back down? Let's talk this through."

Riley stood there a few more moments, then made his way back to the couch.

As he did, Grandpa added, "And, no, that's not what I'm saying."

Riley dropped hard onto the couch. The emotions of the day were beginning to take their toll on him physically. "I'm sorry, Grandpa. I don't know what I'm feeling. I don't know what I'm saying. All I do know is that there are people out there who killed my dad—*your son*—and they need to pay."

Grandpa looked at Riley with a sad smile on his face. "Finally something we agree on."

Riley nodded and pulled the assault weapon next to him. His hand began absentmindedly investigating it the way a person unconsciously explores the features of a lapdog they are petting.

Grandpa finally broke the silence. "Tell me why you want to be involved in tracking these people down. Who are you wanting to help?"

"I'm not sure I get your question."

"Okay, let me put it another way. Are you wanting to do this for God?"

"Well, no."

"Why not?"

"Because God can take care of Himself." Riley had been down this road with Grandpa before and wasn't sure he wanted to do it again.

"Go on. What do you know to be true about God?"

Riley exhaled heavily. "God's in control. He's got a plan. He loves me. He can turn any bad thing into good. Yada yada."

"Okay. So you're not wanting to hunt these people down for God—"

"Not solely for God."

"Okay, not solely for God," Grandpa amended his original statement. "Then who else?"

Angrily, Riley said, "How about Dad? Don't you think I owe it to him to bring down the people who did this to him?"

"What? You mean like avenge his honor? Sounds like what you told me the rationale was for a certain stadium bombing."

"Oh, come on, Grandpa! That's below the belt!"

"Okay then," Grandpa continued with remarkable calmness. "What do you know to be true about your dad?"

"He's dead!" Riley blurted out.

"Is he?"

Riley paused to cool down. He was finally starting to see where Grandpa was going with this. "Okay, physically, yes—which is too bad for us. Spiritually, no—which is wonderful for him."

"Exactly," Grandpa agreed. Then Riley saw the calm exterior begin to crack. "Son, I'm dying inside thinking of what Jerry experienced when that bomb went off. And I'm hurting desperately over what this means for your mom—and for you. But for Jerry himself, I'm not shedding any tears. Jesus was and is his Savior. Your daddy loved God and served Him every day of his life. And he is experiencing things right now that we can only imagine."

Riley felt the same emotion building in him that he heard in Grandpa's voice. "I hear you, Gramps. Like the apostle Paul said, we don't grieve like other people who have no hope. We don't need to fear death, because we know it's only a beginning, not an end."

"And why is that, Riley?"

"Because our hope, our faith, is in the real Jesus—the one who sacrificed Himself on the cross, rose from the dead, and promised us an eternity with Him if we receive Him as our Lord and Savior. Dad believed that, and I believe it, so I know that I'll see Dad again."

"So, does your dad need your help?"

"Guess not." Riley remembered a time at the Air Force Academy when he had walked a Christian friend of his through that same reminder when that young man's father had unexpectedly died in a collision with a drunk driver. *Never thought I'd have to go back through it for myself.*

"So, why do you want to do this, Riley? Why fight this war?"

Riley stared at the black-tipped orange feathers that smoothed their way down the chest of the pheasant on the table between the two men. *Why do I want to join this fight? If it's not a holy fight for God or an honor fight for family, what's left? Am I really just doing this for me? Am I that self-absorbed? Lord, give me a reason to battle or take the desire away from me.*

Riley looked up at Grandpa and saw that he had his eyes closed. His lips, though, were gently moving. The knowledge that he wasn't the only one praying encouraged him to continue the thought process.

Come on, God. Am I really supposed to turn the other cheek on this? If I do, aren't I a walking dead man—probably Skeeter, too? And then who else is going to die besides us? Because these people have proven that they will not stop. Who else besides us?

And suddenly, the fog cleared, and Riley had his purpose.

"It's for them."

Grandpa's eyes opened after a moment, as if he was concluding a conversation before turning his attention to Riley. "It's for whom?"

"For them. For everyone else. For you and for Mom. For Skeeter and Scott and Khadi and Jim and all the others who are on their hit list."

"What about you? Isn't this also for you?"

Riley shrugged his shoulders. "It'd be a lie to say that if I killed the people today who are responsible for Dad's death, I wouldn't feel a sense of satisfaction. I've still got a darkness hanging over me that's going to take a long time to shake. God and I are going to have to work through that together.

"However, I can honestly say that my main motivation is not revenge. And it's not self-preservation either. Jesus took away that fear of dying. In fact, on days like today it doesn't sound like a half-bad thing."

"Okay, let me ask you this: You've got agencies all around that can hunt these terrorists down. Why *you*?"

Silence filled the room as Riley processed this question. Finally, he said, "Grandpa, I've been put in a unique situation, not of my own choosing. These people are going to kill me, and then kill again. And every day I can keep them focused on me is one more day they won't be going after someone else. And every one of them that I stop is one more whose killing days are over."

Riley could see tears brimming in Grandpa's eyes. "Riley, I have to say that I hate everything you've just said. I hate it because of what it means for you—how it puts you in harm's way. I hate it because every word you said is true. You have been placed in the middle of an impossible situation. People are coming for you, and they won't stop until they get you. And I hate that sitting back and doing nothing simply isn't an option."

A sad smile spread across Riley's face. "Trust me, you won't see me dancing up and down. I'd much rather go back to my safe, easy life. Unfortunately, it looks like safe and easy have both been removed from the table as options."

Grandpa leaned forward. "Well, you've answered the 'why' question. That's the most important one. Once the 'why' is answered, then the 'what' and the 'how' come a lot easier. And to answer those two questions, I think we probably need Skeeter with us."

Riley stood up. "I agree. Let me go—"

"Wait, son," Grandpa said, holding up a hand. "Let's talk about this after dinner tonight. We both need to pray this through, and this old man needs to try to get a little rest."

"Of course. I'm sorry, I wasn't thinking," Riley said, rushing over to help Grandpa up off the couch. "You head upstairs and crash. I've got a little more work to do down in the vault."

Grandpa let Riley pull him up and then embraced his grandson. As he held him, he said, "Your dad was so proud of you, Riley. Proud of all you've done, but even more proud of who you are."

Riley's throat constricted, and he felt tears welling up, but he fought the urge to cry. *Hold it together. There's too much to do. You've got plenty of time for grief later.*

"Thanks, Grandpa," he managed to croak out. "Thanks for everything."

When Grandpa stepped back, it looked as if he was fighting the same urge as Riley. Without saying anything more, he turned and went through the archway toward the stairs.

When he heard Grandpa reach the top of the stairs, Riley went back to the vault. He began stacking boxes of ammunition, magazines for the automatic weapons, and clips for the handguns. Carrying the stacks out to the Dead Room, he carefully slid the pheasant off the table with his foot, letting it drop onto the thick carpet. Gently, he set everything down onto the table. And when he picked up his first clip and a box of 9 mm hollow-point rounds, he began Riley Covington's transition from defensive player of the year to a deadly offensive weapon.

WEDNESDAY, MAY 20, 8:00 P.M. EDT
NEW YORK CITY

The antacid tablets fizzed in the water. Isaac Khan held his hand over the rim of the glass and felt them effervesce onto his skin. The sensation felt good—fresh. And freshness was something that his life was definitely lacking after five days holed up in his small, simple studio apartment.

Currently, his life was similar to that of a detective on stakeout—extreme boredom mixed with moments of intense adrenaline. Every time he heard someone outside in the hallway he found his heart beating faster and his hand reaching for his gun.

Last night, Isaac had nearly ruined everything. Around 11:00 p.m., a knock had roused him from a half slumber. He quickly stood up from the kitchen table, accidentally knocking his chair over in the process. Grabbing his gun, he ran to the door and looked through the peephole. The guy on the other side had been saying something, but Isaac wasn't able to clearly make out the words until he was at the door.

"Pizza," the man had said.

Quietly, Isaac had lifted the barrel of the gun until it was pressed three inches of wood away from the visitor's heart. He examined the stairway behind for any movement and took full advantage of the fish-eye peephole lens to scan the hallway. *This has to be a ruse,* he told himself. *It is simply too coincidental.*

"Come on, dude! I know you're in there! I heard you!"

Frantically, Isaac had weighed his options. He could try to climb down the fire escape, but they would surely have that covered. He could detonate the bombs, but he didn't have permission to do that.

"Dude, I've got two other pizzas and only ten more minutes to deliver them!"

Then a door had opened across the hall, and Isaac's dilemma was solved. The deliveryman had given the neighbors their pizza, then flipped the bird to Isaac's door before disappearing down the stairs.

Isaac had fallen onto his bed and thanked Allah for the restraint that he was sure came from God alone. Allah still had plans for him, and Isaac was grateful that he had not interfered with those plans in any way.

Beep, beep sounded from Isaac's digital watch, telling him that it was the top of the hour. He swigged down the glass of milky antacid water and picked up the television remote. CNN Headline News would be giving their hourly report. Isaac watched it faithfully to see if any new information had been discovered about him or his fellow conspirators.

The first time he had seen a picture of himself on the TV, Isaac had gone into full panic mode. There he was, in full color, walking in the Philadelphia subway station wearing a bright orange hat and carrying a backpack. The picture itself—one that most of America was now very familiar with—was a grainy still lifted from a video. Based on size and build, the person in the picture could have been one of ten million men of similar proportions in the country. The few features that one could discern would maybe cut that number in half. Isaac, however, could clearly see himself in the picture and suddenly he felt like every friend or acquaintance of the last ten years must recognize him too.

So he took to waiting at the table, the .45 caliber pistol that had been given to him along with the backpacks sitting in front of him.

Isaac waited for the accusing call from a coworker. He waited for the police to burst through the door. But there was nothing; only Isaac, CNN, and the cockroaches.

Finally, Isaac had come to the conclusion that no one could recognize him, and that the only reason he could see himself in the picture was because he knew it was he. Everyone else in America just saw an anonymous orange-capped figure. In fact, what they saw was no different than what he saw in the still shot of the woman bomber from California—a faceless, nameless blob.

That realization had given him a greater feeling of peace in his apartment. However, he still didn't want to wander outside, although he continued his daily commute to the mini-mart located on the street level of his building. If those stopped, it wouldn't be long before Mr. and Mrs. Lee sent someone up to check on him. The Lees were good people—immigrants, like himself—always kind to him. He hoped they avoided riding subways.

Headline News wasn't saying anything new, so Isaac turned it off before he had to endure another story about a baby polar bear or a music star who couldn't remember to put on her underwear before she left the house. Both were equally inane and irrelevant to Isaac. Both equally summed up the trivial and shallow nature of American culture.

Oh, how he hated this country! Isaac was ready to strike again. In fact, he was desperate to strike again. The exhilaration of being a tool in the hand of his God was like nothing he had ever experienced before. He had felt such power, such purpose.

America spent its time straining to hear the quiet voice of Shaitan, the Great Whisperer, seeking to do his bidding and serve his purpose. At first Isaac had just thought it was the government, but now he knew it was the masses, too. Last Friday, Isaac had walked up to the people of America—to the listeners of the evil whisperer—and shouted the name of Allah! And his most perfect, beneficent name was still ringing in their ears.

As he gloated in his victory, a call came through on his cell phone. Immediately, his breathing rate increased, yet he still paused a moment. *Have I been finally found out? Or will this be my next set of instructions? Great Allah, let me be your hammer once again!*

Isaac answered the phone. "Yes?"

A voice heavy with a Middle Eastern accent said, "Map two. Friday. 7:30 p.m." Then silence.

Isaac looked at the phone's display and saw that the call had ended three seconds after it had started. Even though he had committed the maps to memory, he still rushed the few steps to where he had the backpacks hidden under his bed. Wedged between the two packs were the maps. Quickly, Isaac retrieved the envelope and sat back at the table.

Holding it in his hands, he ran his finger over the word *Warrior* that had been written on the front, feeling every bit of the power that word held. Isaac untucked the flap and pulled the three pages out. As he turned to the second map, elation filled his soul. *Oh, Allah, please help me to carry out your plan. These people, more than any others, deserve to feel your wrath. May the weeping of this nation be my song of praise to you!*

Isaac returned the maps to the envelope and replaced them in their hideaway. Stretching out on his bed, he fell into the first sound sleep he'd had for days, content in his calling and in the knowledge that God was watching over him.

WEDNESDAY, MAY 20, 7:30 P.M. MDT
FRONT RANGE RESPONSE TEAM HEADQUARTERS
DENVER, COLORADO

"I've got her!" Gooey cried out from his corner of the FRRT Room of Understanding.

"You've got who?" Scott asked from across the room, knowing that the answer could be anything from a mouse that had been nibbling away at his bag of Cheetos to a video of the Queen of England at a beach party dancing the Frug with the Duke of Somerset.

"Her! Legs Houlihan!"

Scott immediately dropped the file he was reading and joined the rush of bodies heading toward Gooey's workstation. "Legs Houlihan" was the nickname the analysts had given to the long-legged perpetrator of the Hollywood bombing. Scott elbowed Evie Cline aside, ignoring the protest that would ultimately end up costing her $2 at the profanity jar.

Leaning over Gooey's shoulder, Scott said, "Let's see her."

"Just a second," Gooey said. Once everyone was assembled, he began, "So, I went through all the standard security cameras from the various buildings, and—"

"Goo, can we for once see the picture without hearing a story with it?" Scott said impatiently.

Gooey shook his head. "Trust me, you'll want to hear this; it's a good one. I moved on to ATMs—"

"Gooey! Picture, not story!"

"But—," Gooey pleaded.

"Now!" Scott demanded.

Gooey turned and glared at him, then spurted out, "Illegalgamblinghousesecuritycamera!"

Scott, half frustrated and half intrigued, sighed and said, "Okay, out with it."

Gooey's big smile showed his variously gapped teeth. "You guys know my sister is with LAPD, right?"

"You have a sister?" asked Joey Williamson.

"A female Gooey. Ewww," said Evie.

"So, anyway, I give her a call," Gooey proceeded, ignoring their comments with aplomb. "I have her racking her brains trying to think of another camera we've missed. Then she remembered this punk clothing store that has illegal gambling in the back. PD knows about it, but they let them keep it open because they run undercover ops out of it. This place is apparently big on security, so they have these mega-expensive cameras hidden outside the door and on the street.

"When Homeland put out the call for all video in the area, these guys are obviously not going to go announcing they've got tapes. So, I ask Bunny—"

"Bunny?" coughed Virgil Hernandez after losing his mouthful of bottled water.

"—to pay them a visit. She gets the video, no questions asked, which is actually on disc. Uploads it to me. And this is what I found."

Gooey pressed enter on his keyboard and his thirty-inch flat panel display filled with the image of a stunningly beautiful blonde woman in the process of walking down the sidewalk.

A low whistle emanated from Williamson, who then said, "I told you she'd be a looker."

"Careful what you say, Joey," said Hernandez. "I think the current politically correct term is 'hottie'."

"Both of you, shut it," said Scott. Although he, too, was struck by her beauty, he didn't want to let that cloud his judgment. "Don't forget what she's accused of doing. Goo, you're sure this is the same woman who ducked out the back of the media crowd?"

"No doubt," Gooey answered, and with a few more keystrokes, he split the screen with the current picture on the right and a still of the woman leaving the site of the movie premier on the left. "These two pictures were taken two blocks and three and a half minutes apart."

"Tighten up on her face," Khadi commanded. Gooey complied.

"Look at her features," Khadi continued, using her finger to trace the woman's cheekbones and lips. "She's definitely Arab. I'd say Saudi or one of the Gulf states. Gooey, can you run the video of her walking?"

"Coming right up." The screen changed and the cars in the background began moving. The woman appeared in the screen, walked five steps, and then disappeared under the camera's view.

"That's what I thought. Run it back one more time. Now watch her posture—straight up and down. This girl was not raised in a slum."

"Good call, Khadi," Scott said. He paused for a moment to quickly think through a plan of attack. "Okay, here's what we do. Goo, clean up that picture best you can. Also, if Khadi's right about her being Arab, then this girl potentially has dark hair, and I'm guessing that the blonde muskrat she has on her head probably ended up as roadkill on the side of the highway somewhere. So, put together a spread with her having blonde hair and black hair. Then send it and the video around to all of us.

"We'll want to get this to all other agencies and the media, but not quite yet. If she sees herself, we'll lose her. Before we do that, Virgil and Evie, I want you to do a facial analysis and run her through every database we can get our hands on."

"Start with Middle Eastern work and visitor visas," Tara added.

"Excellent," said Scott. "This girl doesn't look like she came in trekking across the Coahuila countryside. I'm going to give you twenty-four hours to ID this chick. After that, we're going to have to let it out. Goo, send the pics to me first. I'm going to go brief Jim."

Everyone quickly moved back to their workstations. Scott knew this group prided itself on being better than anyone else—on being able to find what no one else could find. The threat of bringing other agencies in was the best motivator he could have given. As he ascended the steps to Jim's office, watching the flurry of activity below, he prayed they had enough time to find this woman before she struck again.

WEDNESDAY, MAY 20, 7:00 P.M. PDT
SAN FRANCISCO, CALIFORNIA

Naheed Yamani was in an extremely bad mood, and the wind that was noisily whipping the flags above her head wasn't helping.

She was angry with herself for not realizing that her new LaROK French army jacket would do nothing to keep out the cool, damp San Francisco air. She was angry with her friend June Waller for leaving fifteen "Are you all right? Is everything okay with us?" messages on her cell phone, when all Naheed wanted was for her to go away.

But most of all she was angry with her contact for insisting on a face-to-face meeting, then making her wait for a half hour in Union Square with only the Macy's storefront to look at. *I should have said no,* Naheed chastised herself. *This is way out of standard operating procedure. I should have insisted we keep to our regular system.* But she hadn't, and now she was here . . . waiting.

Wrapping her arms around herself, she hunched over to protect her body from the wind and stared at the ground. *This is ridiculous! I'll give him five more minutes; then I'm out of here.*

She closed her eyes and listened to the sounds around her—to her right, the metallic roll and clanging bell of a cable car passing; behind her, a homeless man cursing a tourist who had refused him money; next to her, a pigeon cooing down by her foot. She opened her eyes and saw that the bird was closer than she was comfortable with, so she gave the colorful male a quick kick.

Suddenly, another foot appeared next to her on the bench, and a voice said, "You're just way too pretty to be sitting here all alone."

Naheed looked up. *This is definitely not my contact.* A handsome, dark-haired young man wearing a UC Berkeley T-shirt was grinning at her and leaning a little too far into her personal space. About twenty-five feet back, she could see two of his buddies watching and laughing.

Naheed just stared at him.

Apparently he was a guy whose good looks usually paid better dividends around the sorority houses, because he seemed genuinely surprised that she wasn't falling all over herself in his presence. Slightly flustered, he said, "Don't worry, gorgeous, I leave a lot of girls speechless. How about I buy you a drink and we'll see if we can loosen you up a bit?" His grin turned into a wide, toothy smile.

Still without saying anything, Naheed adjusted her gaze from "go away I'm not interested" to "I've killed once and I'm not averse to doing it again."

The artificially whitened smile quickly evaporated. Slowly backing away, the guy said, "Hey, miss, I'm sorry. I didn't mean anything by it. I was just joking with you."

Naheed watched as he quickly turned and rejoined his friends. One of them must have made a smart remark, because the guy pushed him hard, then stomped off. The other two followed.

"Who is your friend?" said a heavily accented voice to Naheed's right. Turning, she saw a Middle Eastern man whose age could have been anywhere from forty to sixty—the baseball cap, sunglasses, and scars made it difficult to tell.

"Where have you been?" Naheed countered.

"That is none of your business, girl," the man said with his eyebrows raised.

"And my friend is none of yours," Naheed snapped back. "Now tell me why you broke protocol and insisted on this meeting."

The man nodded. "They told me about you. Let us see if we can start again. My deepest apologies for being late."

Naheed, feeling good that she had so quickly gained the upper hand, said, "You are forgiven."

"Thank you," the man said with a small bow. He stepped in front of Naheed, then took the place next to her on the bench. "Please allow me to introduce myself. My name is Jibril."

"Right—you're Jibril . . . the messenger angel. If your name's Jibril, then I'm Azra'il," Naheed replied, tired already of this man's games and his forward demeanor.

Jibril laughed—a confident laugh that bespoke experience and control. Naheed began wondering if she really did have the upper hand. *"Na'am*, I may not really be named after the great revealer of the Koran, peace be upon him, but you—you truly are the beautiful angel of death.

"You asked why I broke 'protocol,' as you call it. I wanted to meet you to thank you in person for the work you have done on behalf of the Cause."

"So, you've thanked me. I'm cold and hungry. May I go?"

Again Jibril laughed. "Why are you in such a rush? We have things to speak of. Then maybe I can take you to a place where we can both warm up and have a good meal." He stretched his arm along the back of the bench, lightly touching Naheed's back. She bristled at the contact and leaned forward, causing Jibril to chuckle, but without the same good humor as before. "Sit back and pretend that we like each other. We do not want to attract attention. We are just a man and woman enjoying each other's company."

Who does this guy think he is? "We look more like a father and the daughter of his waning years," Naheed responded, reluctantly returning her back to the bench.

A hard thumb suddenly dug under Naheed's shoulder blade, causing her to flinch, but she bit her lip before she could cry out. Water formed in her eyes.

Jibril leaned close to her ear. She could smell curry and stale coffee on his breath. "I have lived too long and seen too much to be disrespected by a little girl like you. You are just a cog in a wheel; a first step of many steps to come. This is not all about you, so stop acting like I should care about your feelings. Do you understand me, child?"

Naheed rapidly nodded her head. The thumb pushed deeper, then pulled back, resting on a place alongside her spine. Naheed's shoulder spasmed twice, then settled.

Okay, just get through this, Naheed thought. *Try to show respect, and then get out as soon as you can.* "What do you want from me, *sayyid*?"

"Oh, the formality. Please, call me Jibril. And it is not I who want anything from you. Remember," he said with a twinkle in his eye, "Jibril is just a messenger. What is important is what our leader wants from you."

"You mean the one-eyed man?" burst out from Naheed's lips before she could stop it. She had often had nightmares about the old man who had visited her at her training camp graduation.

A dark look flashed across Jibril's face—fear mixed with anger. But just as quickly, his smooth, in-control demeanor returned.

Very interesting, thought Naheed. *I think I may have hit closer to the truth than I expected.* She mentally filed it away for future exploration.

"You are not here to ask questions, young Azra'il. You are here to listen. At four o'clock Friday afternoon, you are to drive to Pier 39. In your trunk you will find a backpack, same as the one before. You are to carry it to the *kurradj*—"

"The *kurradj*? You mean the carousel."

"*Na'am*, the carousel. There you are to arm the device, and then walk away. Simple as that." Now an intensity entered Jibril's voice that Naheed hadn't heard before. "However, if you sense any trouble along the way, you *will* use the emergency detonator. Do not let yourself or the device fall into the hands of the evil ones. Do you understand?"

Naheed gave a bitter laugh. "Why do I sense that you are more concerned about the device than about me?"

Jibril spread his hand across her back, leaving his palm resting on the clasp of her bra. The physical contact made Naheed cringe inside.

"We are all expendable—even the angel of death," he said with a laugh. "Now, our interview is concluded. Would you care to join me for a meal?"

The only thing Naheed wanted was for this man to leave and for herself to take a long, hot, cleansing shower. "Thank you, *sayyid*, but I must decline. I haven't felt well since this morning."

"Of course, womanly things. We will plan to dine next time. In the meantime, may the peace of Allah be upon you," Jibril said as he rose to go.

"And upon you," Naheed mumbled, thankful to see this man leave.

However, just as he was nearly standing, he dropped back down. Putting one hand on Naheed's cold-numbed knee and cradling her chin with the other, Jibril said, "Maybe next time we meet, things will not be so tense. We can gather as two friends—fellow warriors in the same struggle. I would like to get to know you better, Naheed Azra'il."

When Naheed didn't respond, Jibril smiled, gave her knee a painful squeeze, and left.

Thankful to be free of him, Naheed stood and hurriedly made her way back to her car parked around the corner at the Ellis-O'Farrell Garage. As she went, she couldn't shake the feeling of Jibril's calloused fingers on her face nor the look of death in his eyes. *He is the one who should be named Azra'il! What has he seen—what has he done in his life?* She shuddered.

Arriving at her MINI Cooper, she dropped into the seat and started the car but couldn't bring herself to put the car in gear. The trembling was making her too unsteady to drive. She reached over and turned the heat on full blast, knowing full well that the temperature was only a small part of the reason she couldn't stop shaking.

Another bomb, and this one at a carousel on a Friday afternoon when it's sure to be packed with kids! Is this really what I signed up for? I thought I'd be assassinating leaders or sabotaging military installations. But blowing up kids on a Friday afternoon?

The hot air soaking into her body helped soften her nerves. *You always said you'd do this only as long as you wanted. When it didn't feel right anymore, you'd have Grandpa help make you disappear back home. So think—do you still really want to do this?*

Naheed was starting to get hot now, so she turned down the heater. The car slipped easily into gear. *Just one more,* she told herself as she drove. *Just one more to prove myself, then I'll insist on something different. If they say no, then I'll be done. But if they say yes, then the real adventure will finally begin.*

THURSDAY, MAY 21, 8:15 A.M. MDT
PARKER, COLORADO

"Covington Dad Killed in Bomb Blast" was printed across the top of the still-folded *Denver Post*. Below the headline was the top half of a picture that allowed Riley to see the devastation to his parents' barn. He had been leaning against the island in his kitchen staring at that photo for ten minutes now, but he couldn't bring himself to unfold the paper. *How could somebody do this? What must have happened to Dad when that went off?*

Finally, when he could take it no more, Riley stepped around the side of the island and pressed his foot down on the lever that opened the trash can. The lid went up, the paper swept in, the lid went down. One problem solved. But Riley knew that was the smallest of the problems he would be facing today.

When Riley had asked Skeeter yesterday evening to join Grandpa and himself for a planning session, Skeeter had wanted to take the night to process through Riley's request. Riley had put up a brief argument, but, because he was so emotionally drained, he'd given up much sooner than normally he would.

Grandpa and Riley had eaten a quiet homemade dinner delivered by Pastor Tim Clayton's wife, Ashlee, then retired to the great room. There they told funny stories about Jerry Covington for a few hours until they were too sad to talk anymore. Giving each other a final long hug, the two grieving men retired to their bedrooms, where both had lain awake for most of the night wrestling with their own despondencies.

Now, despite being as physically and emotionally wiped out as he'd ever been, Riley was still feeling the itch—the itch to do something. He had never been one to whom waiting came naturally. There were people out there who had hurt not just his family but also hundreds more families in recent attacks. Now they were coming after him. Inactivity was simply not an option.

Riley pulled three small pans off a hanging rack and dropped them onto his range. Turning three of the six dials to medium, he called out, "Ten minutes until breakfast!"

Grandpa's voice echoed from upstairs. "I'll be there!"

Skeeter didn't respond from his place by the front door. Riley wondered if he had moved at all last night.

Extra-virgin olive oil circled each pan exactly one and a half times; then, while that heated up, Riley began cracking eggs into a large bowl. Last night, after heading upstairs, he'd had a chance to talk with his mom for a short time. That had been a very difficult conversation, full of sorrow and apologies on his side, and grace and mercy on hers. One thing she had said still stuck with him: "With all you military men in my family, I've always had to hold on to you with a loose grip. I put my faith in God, and He always protected you. Now, if I've always trusted God in the good times, how could I not trust Him in the bad times, too?"

Lord, give me that kind of faith, Riley prayed as he twisted the top off a can of spinach. *You've given me so many good times; don't let me bail on You just because things get tough.*

He opened the refrigerator to pull out the cheese for the omelets. As he reached for a nice Swiss that he had picked up the other day, his eye caught a block of Covington Farms goat cheese. With a sigh, he made his choice and finished off the omelets.

Grandpa came down in time to butter up some toast and press the coffee. When the plates were all down, Skeeter joined the men at the table.

"Would you mind blessing the food, Gramps?"

"Of course. Precious Lord, thank You for your constant provision and Your unending grace. Guide us now as we seek Your next steps. Amen."

Skeeter raised an eyebrow to Riley when he took the first bite of the omelet. Grandpa tasted it and grimaced. "Goat cheese, huh?"

"I thought it might be a good tribute," Riley said quietly.

"No, it was a good thought, Riley. It's just . . . honestly, I could never stand the stuff. I pleaded with Jerry and Winnie to open a real dairy," Grandpa said with a laugh.

Riley took a bite of his omelet and pushed his plate away. "Tribute or no tribute, I just can't eat this," he said, straining to swallow.

Skeeter, with a mouth full of eggs, waved his hand toward himself and said, "Mmmph." The plates made their way down to his end of the table.

Riley went back to the kitchen and got a couple of bowls, some cereal, and some milk, while Skeeter continued his work on nine eggs' worth of omelet.

"So, what's our plan?" Riley asked, sitting back down at the table.

"Let's first figure out what we know," said the elder statesman of the group, pouring himself a bowl of Cheerios. "First, and most basic, there are people who want to kill you."

"And they're probably not going to stop until the Cause has its head chopped off," Riley added.

"True," said Skeeter, "but that ain't our job. That's for CTD and Scott and Jim at the Response Team. This can't turn into no Riley Covington, International Man of Mystery thing."

"No, I hear you, Skeet. Let the big boys deal with the big boys."

Grandpa put down his spoon and said, "I think we can also safely assume that they don't think they can hit you at your house with all your security. That's why they tried to draw you out with what they did yesterday."

"Which is the whole catch-22 of this situation. If I stay here, I'm safe, but everyone else who is close to me is at risk. If I go out, I'm at risk, but everyone else is safe. It's a lousy choice, but not much of a decision." Riley sipped his coffee, then leaned his chair back on two legs.

"I think there is one more thing we can put on our list," Grandpa said. "I talked to my people, and I've been assured that the Cause has a limited supply of trained and ready soldiers. So every hit against them is a hard hit."

Riley and Skeeter looked at each other, then both started chuckling.

"What's so funny?"

"I'm sorry. It just struck me kind of funny that you talked to 'your people.' I didn't know you even had people."

A tired smile crept across the old man's face. "Listen, at your age, son, all your friends are scrambling around trying to be stars. At my age, my friends wear their stars on their shoulders. A few phone calls to the right people, and it's amazing what you can discover."

Quickly sobering up, Riley said, "No, you're right. I'm sorry. These must be the mood swings of instability."

"You're not unstable, remember? You're just volatile."

Riley nodded. *Back to business,* he thought. *How do I draw these people away from the ones I love?* "In football, sometimes an offense is surprised by a defensive formation. They know that if they don't change things up, they're going to get stomped. So, they call an audible. They quickly change the play at the line of scrimmage in order to try to regain the upper hand."

"We're listening," Grandpa said.

"I was just thinking. They're expecting me to either run up to Wyoming to see Mom or to stay here in hiding, in which case they'll go after someone else. What if we were to call an audible and shake things up for them?"

"What did you have in mind?" Grandpa asked.

"How about if Skeet and I leave here and go into hiding some-place else?"

"That's no different than you staying here," said Skeeter, putting his fork down for the first time in five minutes.

"It is if we do a lousy job of it."

Grandpa shook his head. "Okay, you've officially lost me."

"Just walk with me on this. I'm still trying to formulate it myself.

Keith Simmons has a cabin up in the mountains—Silverthorne or Dillon or one of those places. What if Skeet and I hole up at his place, then let it get out that we're there? I mean, we don't, like, pass out flyers and stuff, but maybe we get Keith and Afshin to accidentally let it slip in the locker room that we've gone to the mountains. If it gets to some of the rookies or bubble players who are trying to ingratiate themselves to the media, it will definitely get out. Maybe I could call up Whitney Walker, also, and either 'accidentally' mention it to her or even come right out and ask her to include something about it in a story."

Skeeter was nodding. "I'm tracking. Security here is operating under the assumption that somehow we are being watched. Another thing we could do is to have Keith come by and deliver the keys."

"Wait a minute! Wait a minute," Grandpa shouted. "Before you go working out all the ways that you are going to get them to where you're hiding out, you'd better figure out what you're going to do when you get there."

Riley shrugged his shoulders. "Wait for them."

"That's your plan? Wait for them?"

"Best I've got so far."

They all three sat silently. Finally Riley spoke quietly but earnestly. "Listen, Gramps. I'm betting that the place is surrounded by trees, so there will be plenty of places to stage a defense. Also, it's isolated, so if anything happens, Skeeter and I are the only ones at risk. You said it yourself—any hit against them is a hard hit. I think this scenario gives us the best chance of delivering that hard hit."

Grandpa sighed heavily. "Well, if you're going to do this, you could certainly stand to use a third gun."

"No, and please don't make me argue the point with you. I need you to take care of Mom. Also, we may need you to do a few things back here or maybe call on your people again," Riley finished with a forced grin.

"You mean I can be old Alfred to your Batman?" Grandpa said with a sad chuckle.

"Exactly. But I guess that does make Skeeter here the Boy Wonder." They all laughed softly.

Riley continued, "So, we've got a plan. Gramps, I did some work in the vaults last night. Would you double-check what I've done and see if I've missed anything? Skeeter, why don't you see what information you can dig out of Scott about who's after us. Don't let him know yet what we're doing, because I don't want him involved in this. I'll start making some phone calls to Keith and Afshin and maybe Whitney. Let's look to leave first thing tomorrow morning."

As they stood up to go, Grandpa caught Riley's arm in an unusually tight grip. "Hold back a second. Do you remember the story of Esther in the Bible?"

"Yeah, she was chosen as queen of Persia and saved all the Jews."

"Exactly. I was just thinking about a conversation that Esther had with her cousin Mordecai. She knew she had to see the king, but doing so could cost her her life. Mordecai sent her a message saying, 'God's going to save his people one way or another. But maybe you've come to your position for such a time as this.'"

"Yeah, I remember that. Amazing story."

"But do you remember her response, Riley? She says, 'Get the people praying. I'm going to do what I have to do. I'm going to go see the king. And if I perish, I perish.' That's total commitment to doing the right thing. That's what I've just heard from you. Jesus put it as, 'Greater love has no one than this, that he lay down his life for his friends.'

"Riley, I'll be your Mordecai. I'll get the people praying, and I'll do whatever I can for you back here. As hard as it is to think about, I couldn't be more proud of the fact that you are willing to show your 'greater love.'

"Now, I'm going to let go of your arm, but don't say anything back to me, because if you do I'll lose it and I'm just plain tired of crying." Grandpa gave Riley's arm a final squeeze, then went to the basement.

Riley watched him go with a sad smile on his face. *Laying down your life for your friends. Lord, that's why I'm doing this. This isn't for me. Honestly, I'm leaving it to You to pay back those who killed Dad. Please, Lord, just let me be part of stopping these people before they take more innocent lives. If I can give my life so that others won't feel the pain that I'm going through, then so be it.*

After pausing for a moment to collect his emotions, Riley cleared his throat low and deep and picked up his phone to start making calls.

THURSDAY, MAY 21, 4:15 P.M. MDT
FRONT RANGE RESPONSE TEAM
   HEADQUARTERS
DENVER, COLORADO

"Gooey, you been in my Yoo-hoos again?" Scott called as he pulled his head out of the FRRT refrigerator.

There was no response, but even from across the room Scott could hear the sound of bottles clinking as Gooey shoved his metal wastebasket deeper under his workstation.

"Gooey, have you been in my Yoo-hoos?"

"Sorry, dude. I can't hear you. I'm too busy working."

"We've got a match!" Evie Cline called out, bringing to a halt any more discussion of Yoo-hoos. It had been almost twenty-one hours since she and Virgil Hernandez had last left their workstations.

While everyone rushed to Evie's workstation, Scott excitedly called Jim Hicks, "You'll want to come down for this, boss. We've got the girl."

Without waiting for an answer, Scott dropped the phone and moved toward the crowd. Through the chatter, he could hear Hicks's door fly open and feet pounding down the metal stairs.

"Cline!" Hicks called out. "Send it to the big screen!"

"Sure thing," Evie answered.

Immediately, everyone left Evie's desk and grabbed a chair around the conference table. A large video monitor began its ascent from a long black cabinet. It flashed on, and a beautiful female face greeted everyone.

"Talk," commanded Hicks.

"Her name is Naheed Yamani. Age twenty-four. Saudi. Been in the country for six years. We had a hard time finding her, because she didn't come in through the standard channels."

Hernandez now jumped in. "That's right. Her grandfather is Prince Yaman ibn Abdul ibn Aziz al-Saud. Definitely not one of the key power-broker al-Sauds, but still wealthy and connected enough to get what he wants. Apparently he pulled some diplomatic strings to get her here and set her up in a Nob Hill address in San Francisco."

"You're sure this is our girl?" Hicks asked. "Nothing about her matches our typical profile."

Evie split the screen with the picture Gooey had enhanced from the Hollywood attack. "I think there's little doubt," she said.

Hicks nodded his agreement. "Okay, Tara, I want you to contact the West Coast Response Team. I want a two-man crew to do a silent recon into this gal's residence. I want them to take her down if she's there or wait for her if she's not. Gooey, you coordinate with Tara and WCRT to give us a video feed of the operation.

"Khadi, you find out all you can about this Prince Yaman character. See if there is anything we can dredge up to put some pressure on him to give up his granddaughter. Everyone else, go back to what you were doing."

Jim turned to go but quickly stopped himself. "I do want to emphasize, though, that we do not want this picture to get out—not yet. We do not want Yamani to go underground, because chances are, if she does, she'll end up hidden away in her grandfather's palace, far out of our reach. We understood?"

A chorus of "Yeah, boss" sounded around the table.

"Good. Scott, come up to my office with me. My brain hurts, and I need you to do some thinking for me."

"Sure thing, Jim," Scott answered with a frown. He knew that this usually meant Hicks was in desperate need of a quick shot from his secret bottle, and since he had promised himself never to drink alone again, he liked to have Scott sitting across his desk from him while he did it.

Another phone call from Meg Ricci, Riley thought as he silenced his ringer. *How many calls does it take to make the transition from concerned friend to stalker?* But then, feeling bad for his attitude, he said out loud, "Cut her a break. She's just being nice."

"Simmons is here," Skeeter called from the front window.

Riley ran to the other window and peeked through the curtain. Sure enough, here came Keith Simmons. He was wearing his after-workout sweats and carried an envelope with directions and keys to the cabin prominently in his right hand. *Good man,* thought Riley.

Skeeter opened the door and took the envelope from Simmons while they were still in the doorway.

"Nice job, linebacker," said Skeeter.

"Right back at you, bug man."

But then, when he saw Riley, all the humor drained out of his demeanor. "Pach, man, I'm so sorry about your dad," he said, giving Riley a hug. "It's just so messed up!"

Riley returned the hug, then said, "Yeah, it is messed up. It still hardly feels real."

"I know what you mean. It was like that for me when Grammy died."

Simmons had been brought up by his grandmother. Riley could still remember how completely devastated Keith was when she had unexpectedly died of a heart attack two years ago.

Simmons continued, "Hate to say it, bro, but it don't ever really hurt less. You just learn better how to live with the pain."

An awkward silence followed until Simmons asked, "Hey, is your gramps around? I'd like to meet him."

"He is, but he's taking a nap upstairs. Why don't you hang around until he gets up?" Riley started moving toward the great room, but Simmons stopped him.

"I appreciate it, but I just wanted to drop that junk off to you. You got too much stuff to do to worry about entertaining me."

Thinking again about what could happen at Simmons's cabin, Riley asked, "You sure you're okay with me doing this, Simm? It could get ugly up there."

"You mean things might get broken? Please, what do I care?" Simmons said with a shrug. "It's just a building. Besides, if you get the place all tore up, I know where you live."

Riley smiled. "I don't know how to thank you enough, my friend."

"Don't think about it. Hey, Pach, before I leave, would you mind if I, like, you know, prayed for you?"

The tears that, of late, were always just below Riley's surface welled up again in his eyes. "Dude, it'd be an honor."

Simmons put his hand on Riley's shoulder. "God, it's Keith again. You know I'm not used to this, so please forgive me if I mess it up or sound stupid. You know Riley—of course You know Riley; You knew him before You knew me—so, anyway, Riley here is going to go fight some really bad guys. Guys who hate him, and who, best I can tell, hate You, too. So please protect him. Help him to kill a whole bunch of them—I mean, if it's okay to pray that he kills people; if not, then scratch that last part. Just watch over him, okay, Lord? Bring him back safe. Oh, and Skeeter, too. I pray the bad guys fall over dead just by looking at how scary he is. Thanks, God, for listening. Amen."

Riley wrapped his arms around the big man. "Thanks, buddy; that was awesome."

Simmons got a big smile on his face. "Yeah, it wasn't bad, was it? So, Pach, you take care of yourself. And don't give a second thought about the cabin—I built it once, I can build it again. You got it?"

"I got it. Thanks."

Riley watched as Simmons went back to the door. He stopped to say a few things to Skeeter, then laughed and slapped him on the back. And then he was gone.

The whole team was gathered around the table, watching the big screen. The screen was split in two and showed the same scene from two different perspectives. Two CTD operatives walked down a short hallway, and the views the FRRT was watching were from small cameras mounted on their protective eyewear.

Because they were trying to keep a low profile, the two men were dressed in casual clothing, and their weapons were tucked away. Along with their regular firearms, each agent carried a Taser X26; they had specific instructions to take Naheed Yamani alive.

As they arrived at the door, Scott and the analyst team could hear one operative telling the other, "Okay, let's do this."

The left operative knocked on the door. They waited. The tension was high in the Room of Understanding. The analysts were anxious to see what was on the other side of the door. Scott, Khadi, and Hicks felt a different sort of anxiety, since each of them had numerous times been in the same dangerous place as these two operatives. Anything could happen—bullets could fly, the door could be rigged with explosives, someone could come up from behind or from across the hall.

The operative knocked again. After waiting a moment, one of them said, "Forget this, we're going in."

The shot on the left screen tilted down, and the viewers watched as experienced hands slipped the lock. He looked up at his partner and said, "We go in on three. One, two, three!"

THURSDAY, MAY 21, 6:45 P.M. PDT
SAN FRANCISCO, CALIFORNIA

The last day had been rough for Naheed Yamani. One moment, she thought she had steeled herself to go through with the bombing. The next moment, she was ready to pick up the phone to call her grandfather. And through all the vacillations, one constant remained—the feel of Jibril's hand on her face.

If you run, do you really think a man like that would just let you go? Do you really think that, even if you could get out of the country, he wouldn't find a way to hunt you down and kill you?

Naheed slid deeper into the bathtub until her head was under the hot water. This was her sixth bath in the last twenty-four hours. For some reason it was the one place she felt at least some semblance of peace.

A sound reached her under the water, like a distant hammering. She quickly sat up to listen but didn't hear any more. Her body floated back down to the water.

Then the sound came again, and there was no doubting what it was now. Someone was at the door.

Naheed stood up and wrapped herself in a thick, white terry cloth robe. As she walked out of the bathroom, she heard something that froze her in her tracks—the lock on the door was being disengaged. Like a deer in headlights, she watched as the door opened.

Naheed heard a gasp from the person walking in. It was a Hispanic woman pushing a small cart. It was hard to tell which of the two was more startled. The woman said, "*Lo siento.* I knock. Nobody answer. Room service, madam. So sorry."

Smiling, Naheed said, "No, you didn't do anything wrong. I forgot I had ordered it. I apologize."

"Oh, no, madam. You sign please?"

"Of course." Naheed signed the bill, leaving a large tip.

The woman nodded her gratitude and left the room.

Naheed carried the food from the tray and set it on a table next to the window. As she ate, she watched the airplanes take off and land and thought about the possibilities of escape. That was one of the best things about her handlers moving her to the Airport Marriott—she was that much closer to getting on a plane if she felt the need to run.

7:55 P.M. MDT
FRONT RANGE RESPONSE TEAM HEADQUARTERS
DENVER, COLORADO

The loft was empty. The team had watched as the operatives scoured the place. There was no doubt that Yamani had been there recently, but just how recently was hard to tell. Hicks instructed the agents to remain there in case the girl showed up, then shut off the feed.

"So, when do we release her picture?" asked Tara.

Hicks was silent for a moment, then said, "Let's wait until morning. It's too late for her to do any mischief tonight, and I don't want her seeing herself on the evening news and bolting. Hopefully she'll show up at her loft. If she doesn't, then we'll blitz the media with her picture.

"Tara, let WCRT know our plans. I want them coordinating the coverage of the airports in case we have to go the news release route. Also, let them know that Khadi, Scott, and I are on our way out there. I want to be on-site when they bring her in. If WCRT has problems with any of that, have them take it up with your old boss Stanley Porter. That should shut them up."

"You got it, boss," Tara said as she quickly jotted down notes.

Turning to the analyst team, Hicks said, "You guys all did great work tracking down this Yamani woman. But don't let it go to your heads. We've still got another bomber out there to ID, and we still don't know squat about who killed those two families. So pat yourselves on the back, then get over it and get back to work. Scott, Khadi, we leave in fifteen minutes."

Scott smiled at his team as Hicks returned to his office. Once the door was closed, he said, "Wow! That, my dear friends, is a great motivator." Then, giving his best Jim Hicks impersonation, he said, "You guys are almost, kind of good. But don't be thinking that I really think that, because even though I do, I don't. So don't let that go to your heads because—"

Suddenly Hicks's door swung back open. "Scott, are you impersonating me again?"

"No, sir," Scott said innocently to the snickers of his team, "just doing damage control."

"Well, knock it off, and let your merry little band get back to work!" Hicks slammed his door closed again.

Williamson raised his hand. "What if we really did have a merry little band? We could play weekend shows in LoDo and call ourselves something like Pickety Nosegeeks."

"Or how about Ana and the Lysts?" suggested Evie.

"Roadkill Monkey," offered Gooey.

"How about the Let's Get Back to Work Players?" said Tara as she stood to go.

"No, that doesn't quite have the edge of Roadkill Monkey," replied Scott. "Oh, you mean how about we all just get back to work. I get it. Good one, Tara." Then, looking back at his analyst team, he said, "And, you guys? Good work! Take a moment to celebrate. As opposed to Mr. Grumpy-pants, I don't care how long you take patting yourselves on the back."

Even though the drive up to Silverthorne would
be less than ninety minutes, Riley wanted to get
an early start. The more time he and Skeeter had
to scout the cabin's location and set up defenses, the better he would feel about his basic plan,
which thus far consisted of:

Step One—Go up to Keith Simmons's cabin.

*Step Two—Shoot the bad guys before they
shoot you.*

Might be worth fleshing out step two a bit, he
told himself. The rear of the Yukon looked like it
belonged to an international gunrunner. All told,
there were four assault rifles, two sniper rifles, six
handguns, various and sundry small explosive
devices, and as Scott Ross would say, ammunition out the yin-yang.

Which reminded Riley that he needed to give
Scott a call. This conversation would not be a fun
one, but it was only right to let FRRT know what
he and Skeeter were up to.

"Hey, Skeet, can you put that call in to Scott
now?" Riley wanted to use Skeeter's phone since
it had encryption capabilities.

Skeeter put down the heavy tarp he was carrying to the truck and pulled out his phone. After a few moments of going through the encryption process, he handed it to Riley.

"Scott?"

"Hey, Riley. How're you doing, man?" Scott's voice sounded tired and a little hesitant.

"Hanging in. First off, my friend, I owe you an apology. You were just doing what you thought was best for me. I didn't treat you right." While he talked, Riley walked over to his leather chair in the great room and settled in.

Scott's voice seemed to lighten just a touch. "Don't sweat it. It's forgotten. How's your mom?"

"She's okay. It's killing me not to see her, but I know it's best."

Riley took a deep breath, preparing himself for the next part of the conversation. But before he could say anything, Scott jumped in. "So, what's up, Riley? Calling to say you're going rogue?"

Riley was momentarily speechless. Then he asked, "Did Skeet talk to you?"

Scott gave a soft laugh. "Impressive. You put the words *Skeet* and *talk* in the same sentence. Dude, remember, who am I?"

"You're the evil genius," Riley answered with a small smile.

"Exactly. I've been waiting for this call. I just didn't expect it quite so soon."

"So, what do you think?"

Scott didn't answer right away, and when he did, his voice was as serious as Riley had ever heard it. "I think there's a strong likelihood that you and Skeeter are going to get yourselves killed." There was another long pause. "But I know that for you, there's really no other option. You've always seemed to lack that basic self-preservation gene. That's why we followed you in Special Forces in Afghanistan. That's why at the beginning of this year we followed you in Italy and California. We knew that when it came down to it, you'd take the bullet for us. So we were always ready to take the bullet for you. And, Riley, that's what makes this time so hard, because I can't be there to take your bullet."

"Thanks, Scott. I—"

"That's not to say that I like what you're doing, or that I think it's the right thing. I'm just saying that I understand."

Riley squeezed his eyes tight and rubbed the back of his head. "Fair enough. This wasn't really an ask permission kind of call anyway."

"It never is with you, Pach. It never is. So, can you tell me where you're going?"

"I don't think so."

"You know that if I had five minutes to think about it, I'd figure it out anyway."

"I'm sure you would."

"Listen, you need any questions answered, you just call me, okay?"

Surprised, Riley asked, "What if Jim finds out?"

"Jim? You leave him to me. What's he going to do? Fire me?"

Riley smiled when he heard Hicks's voice in the background yell, "Yes!"

"Listen, Scott, I told you this because I thought you all had a right to know, and because, in case anything happens, I didn't want to leave our friendship on a bad note. You know you're like a brother to me."

"Thanks, Pach. I needed to hear that. Now, I've got things to do, so I'm going to go before I start getting all moist-like. Take care, buddy, and call if you need the cavalry."

"You got it, Scott. Hey, and will you tell Khadi that . . . just tell her what's happening—tell her that I wanted her to know what's happening?"

"Will do."

"Thanks, Scott. Later."

FRIDAY, MAY 22, 6:40 A.M. PDT
SAN FRANCISCO, CALIFORNIA

"Later," said Scott as he hung up the phone.

Hicks was watching him from across the conference room in the West Coast Response Team headquarters. Khadi had her head down in her hands. Three minutes passed before anyone spoke.

Finally, Jim could stand it no longer. "Scott, I've trusted your judgment in the past, and it's worked out. That is the *only* reason I'm not putting Riley under protective custody right now. 'Cause if the Lone Ranger and Tonto go off and get themselves killed, it'll be both our jobs."

Khadi raised her head and glared at Hicks with red eyes.

"Sorry, Khadi. You know how I feel about Riley and Skeeter. Ever since Costa Rica, I promised myself I'd never let things get out of my control like that again. And now, here I am stuck in California while people are gunning for those two back in Colorado. It's just a lousy situation."

"We know what you're saying, Jim," Scott assured him.

"And if he calls for help?" Khadi asked.

Hicks stared at them for a moment. "Give him what he needs. Just don't tell me about it."

By a visible force of will, Khadi kept the tears from escaping. "Thanks, Jim, but—"

Suddenly, the door burst open and Niko Garisyan blew into the room. Garisyan was the head of the West Coast Response Team and had a reputation for having a personality similar to Jim Hicks in a really bad mood.

"So, we've got nothing on that Yamani woman. You going to finally release the picture? Because, I swear, if she hits us again while we're sitting on her photo, I will personally make sure you stand trial. You understand?"

"My, aren't we all full of vim and vigor this morning?" Hicks said with a smile on his face. Scott couldn't help but smile too. He knew that Hicks cut the man a little slack, because even though Garisyan was a pain in the backside, he was very good at what he did. Hicks had also told him that the WCRT director was none too happy to have someone else come into his office and take charge. Scott couldn't imagine if the roles were reversed. Hicks would be a terror to be around. But that's just how things were, and Garisyan would have to deal with it.

"So, there wasn't any street activity? No visits or phone calls made?" Hicks asked.

Garisyan rolled his eyes. "What? You think I'm new at this? If there was any activity, I would have told you about it. So, do we release the photo?"

Hicks looked briefly at Scott and Khadi. "You got all the airports covered in case she makes a break for it?"

Garisyan gave a sigh like he was disgusted at even being asked such a question.

"Okay then, Niko. I grant you permission to release the photo."

Without saying anything, Garisyan turned toward the door. Before he made it out, Hicks said, "Hey, Niko, we're getting a little hungry. Any chance of you fetching us a few Danishes while you're out?"

The slamming door drowned out Garisyan's two-word response.

FRIDAY, MAY 22, 8:15 A.M. MDT
PARKER, COLORADO

It felt good to be on the road. The parting with Grandpa had been rough, but both men had successfully kept it together. A few hugs and a double slap on the hood of the Yukon as Riley pulled out, and they were gone. *Lord, if I live to be that old, let me be just like that man,* Riley had prayed.

After turning onto the freeway, Riley turned to Skeeter. "You ready for this?"

"I was born ready," the big man replied with a grin.

"Nah, you were born ugly, and you've just never outgrown it." They both let out a little nervous laughter.

The plan was to head downtown, do a little "wrong way on a one way street" action to make sure they weren't being followed, then head up to Simmons's cabin. But on the way, Riley had a call to make.

"Hello?" said Whitney Walker, in an I'm-a-very-busy-person-don't-waste-my-time-you-better-make-this-interruption-worthwhile tone of voice.

"Whitney, this is Riley Covington."

Instantly, Whitney's voice changed completely. "Riley! I'm so sorry about your father. How's your mother?"

"Thanks. Mom's doing all right."

"And how are you doing? Do you want to meet and talk?" Then it seemed like she realized how she sounded. "I mean, off the record, of course."

Riley shook his head. *Once a reporter, always a reporter.* "Actually, I've got something for you on the record. You just can't name me as the source."

"Okay, I'm listening." There was a little hesitancy in her voice.

She's in a quasi-reporter mode, Riley thought. *Respond to her that way. Here goes.* "I want you to report that an anonymous source told you that Riley Covington has left Parker to go into hiding. After the death of his father, he was too afraid to stay in his house, so he has left the city for the mountains."

"Why does this sound like a planted story?"

Riley could hear resistance. He knew Whitney was too sharp for him to try to finesse things, so he opted for the truth. "Because it is. Listen, Whitney, I can't tell you much." Out of the corner of his eye, he saw Skeeter give him a look of warning. Riley nodded at him. "All I can tell you is that my dad is dead, and that more people will die if I don't do something. So I'm doing something, and I need your help for it to work."

"Is what you're saying in the story true?"

"Mostly. Well, the first half at least."

"That's what I figured."

"I really need for you to get this out, starting with the Web this afternoon, then the newscast tonight. If you do this, I promise you I'll give you an exclusive interview when this is all done."

Whitney's voice took a hard edge. "Don't insult me, Riley. If I'm doing this, it's for you, not for a story. Believe it or not, sometimes reporters do stuff just because it's the right thing to do."

"Fair enough. I'm sorry. So, will you do it?"

"I'll do it. The Web this afternoon and the newscast tonight."

Riley breathed a sigh of relief. "Thanks, Whitney. You don't know how important this is."

"You just take care of yourself."

"You got it."

Riley ended the call. *Between Keith and Afshin getting the word around camp and Whitney getting the word out directly in the media, I can't imagine the hajjis won't see it,* he thought. *Then, with Keith dropping off the key, hopefully they'll be smart enough to put two and two together to track us down. Now all Skeeter and I have to do is to figure out what in the world we're going to do once they find us.*

FRIDAY, MAY 22, 8:30 A.M. MDT
INVERNESS TRAINING CENTER
ENGLEWOOD, COLORADO

Keith Simmons watched the perspiration form on the forehead of Clayton Cox. *It's good he's sweating,* he thought. *Dude deserves to sweat!* Simmons's face was only inches from the other man, and although Cox's stale coffee breath made him want to gag, he refused to back away. *Maybe a little intimidation is what it takes to remind this idiot that he's working for me!*

Finally, Simmons pulled back a bit. However, he still remained on the edge of his chair in the Colorado Mustangs cafeteria. "You're a lucky man, Clayton. If this were last year, my reaction would have been quite a bit different. But I'm a new man now," Simmons stated proudly.

Relief seemed to spread across Cox's face. "Yeah, I've noticed. Congratulations on your new—"

Simmons's hand came down hard on the table. "But that don't mean I'm a pushover. You're my agent! You're supposed to be working hard for me! The front office has been promising a new contract for over twelve months now. I see guys getting re-signed all over the place, and what are you doing? You're playing around in Cancun."

"Now, wait just a minute, Keith," an offended Cox answered.

"No, you wait just a minute! When is the last time you talked to them?" Simmons knew he was working himself back up into a frenzy, but he couldn't help himself. "Answer me that, *Clayton!* When was the last time you talked to the Mustangs about *me?*"

"Keith, you have to look at it from their perspective as well," Cox answered, skillfully dodging the question. "What incentive do they have to give you an extension and be on the hook for a more than $10 million signing bonus? If I were them, I'd do the same thing. I'd watch you closely all the way through the minicamps, the organized team activities, and the off-season workouts. I'd watch your physical strength and your mental and emotional commitment to the team. If you still looked like the Keith Simmons of old, *then* I'd start the negotiating."

Simmons dropped back into his chair. This was not what he wanted to hear. The sooner he could get a contract, the sooner his future could be stabilized, and the sooner he'd get that huge up-front check—really, the only guaranteed money he'd have. Without that signing bonus, who knew what could happen between now and then—a workout injury, a car accident, even tripping and falling at home could keep him from getting his contract. *Sometimes you feel like rolling yourself up in Bubble Wrap just to keep from getting injured. Shouldn't Cox know how tough this waiting is?*

"Why do I feel like I'm negotiating with them on one side and now with you on the other? Is that what I'm doing? Aren't you supposed to be on my side? Or have you forgotten that 400k of my $10 million signing bonus goes into your bank account? I know you've got like thirty other players you're looking out for, but are any of them going to bring you that kind of green?"

Cox looked hurt, but Simmons knew that his agent was just trying to formulate another line for him. *Next will come the flattery, then the promises.*

Sure enough, Cox said, "Listen, Keith, you know the money isn't as important to me as making sure you and your family are financially set for life."

Simmons stifled a disbelieving laugh.

"All I'm saying, my friend, is that it's not a question of *if*, but *when*. I mean, get real! You're Keith Simmons! The Mustangs would be fools not to sign you. But if for some reason they get a serious case of the stupids, you know there'll be a long line of teams waiting to pay the big money for one of the best linebackers in the league."

Simmons cracked a smile. *Dude's slick,* he thought. "Go on."

"You just set your jaw on doing what you always do. You don't have to do anything more than that. I promise you that if they see the Keith Simmons who's been tearing up opposing offenses for all these years, your big day will come very soon. After that, Keith Simmons won't ever have to wonder about finances again. Keith Simmons's kids will grow up in the best neighborhoods and end up in the best colleges. And not only them, but you'll end up leaving a financial legacy for your grandkids and your great-grandkids and your great-great-grandkids." A big smile spread across Cox's face. "You just do your part, *mi compadre*, and I guarantee you I'll do my end of the deal."

Silence hung in the air for a moment. Finally, Simmons's mouth opened into a smile wide enough to match his agent's. He grabbed the Cinnabon that had been cooling on the table in front of him and took a huge bite. Through a mouthful of sugar and dough, Simmons said, "Don't stop now, man. This is just getting good!"

FRIDAY, MAY 22, 9:00 A.M. PDT
SAN FRANCISCO, CALIFORNIA

The cell phone rocked Naheed out of a deep slumber. She had been dreaming, but she lost the dream as soon as she awoke. All that lingered in her mind were scattered images of darkness, violence, and Jibril.

Still groggy, she reached for her phone and read the caller ID. Sarah Michaels—the name she had assigned her contact number for the Cause.

"Hello?" she said, the taste of last night's bottle of wine thick in her mouth.

"Azra'il, still sleeping so late on the day you go to collect more souls? If I didn't know better, I'd think your heart was not in your work."

An unpleasant feeling swirled inside her— excitement mixed with loathing. "What do you want, Jibril?" This was not the way she wanted to begin any day, let alone a day like this.

"Taking that tone with me is not a good way to start our conversation, little girl. Would you like to try that again?"

Naheed took a deep breath. *You've just got to get through this day. That's it, just one more day.* "Good morning, Jibril."

"That's much better. Now, I'm going to ask

you to do something, but first I want to remind you that you are committed to following through with today's activities. If you do not, I don't care where you are or whom you're hiding behind, I will hunt you down and kill you slowly. Do we understand each other?"

"Yes, it's understood. Now say what you have to say, then leave me alone."

"Turn the television on to CNN."

A sick feeling spread in Naheed's stomach. "Why?"

When Jibril didn't answer, Naheed turned on the television. She used the channel guide on the back of the remote to find CNN. Full screen on the television, Naheed saw her driver's license photo. The words below read, "Naheed Yamani—Alleged Hollywood Bomber."

Panic was not an experience that Naheed was used to. She prided herself in being able to keep calm in most situations. But seeing her picture on the television made her completely lose control. *I've got to get out,* she told herself. *But how? I can't fly, because they'll have my picture. I can't drive, because no matter where I stop everyone will recognize me. Can I call Grandfather? Is it too late for that?* While her mind was racing, a voice kept sounding in her ear—"Naheed, Naheed." Then she realized that she was still holding the phone.

"What?" she yelled.

"Naheed, calm down! Get control of yourself," Jibril commanded.

Naheed took two deep breaths, then repeated, "What?"

"I know you are frightened. But realize that nothing has really changed."

"What? Are you serious? Everyone in America has seen my face!"

"What I mean, young sister, is that you still have a job to do. You will do that job. If someone sees you, you will ensure in the manner we discussed yesterday that you are not caught. If you are able to complete the mission, I will call you with a rendezvous point, and we will get you out of the country."

Out of the country? This is something new. "But why can't you get me out of the country now?"

"Because you have not completed your mission yet."

"But it's very probable that I will die completing the mission."

"*Insha'Allah*, it is in the hands of Allah. Now, I suggest you leave your hotel immediately. We have delivered to you another car—a gold Buick Century with dealer plates. You will find the keys under the front seat and the package in the trunk. Find yourself a parking garage, and wait out the time there."

Naheed was pleading now. "Please, Jibril, is there no other way?"

"There is no other way, child. Courage, Naheed! Remember why you signed up to fight all those years ago. Don't let the ease of their lives or the decadence of their culture rob you of who you truly are. Remember your roots, young warrior; remember your honor and the honor of your family—the family of al-Saud. Now go, and may Allah go with you."

The line went dead. Naheed cursed and threw the bedside lamp across the room. "You want to know why I joined up all those years ago?" she cried out to the ceiling. "For the adventure! For the glory! Not so I could die blowing up a bunch of kids at a merry-go-round! Is this really what you want, God?"

Vaulting off the bed, she dumped her suitcase and threw it against the wall. The alarm clock, television remote, and hotel phone soon followed. Naheed began pulling the drawers out of the desk and side tables and dropping them to the floor. Phone books ripped and flew.

When she came across the Gideon Bible, she stopped. "Is this what we're fighting against?" she called to the ceiling. "Is this it? If so, then I'll fight for you! Here, watch me fight for you!" She began tearing handfuls of pages from the Bible and throwing them on the floor. Stomping on the fallen pages, she cried out, "Do you see? Do you see me fighting? Is this what you want?"

Finally, she dropped herself on the bed. Rolling over and burying her face in the pillows, she cried out, "I'll do it! I'll do it, I'll do it, I'll do it!" Naheed lay there breathing hard into the pillow until Jibril's warning about getting out came to her mind. Instantly, she realized all the noise she had made with her tantrum.

She jumped out of bed and quickly got herself dressed, then put on her blonde wig, sunglasses, and wide sun hat and ran out the door, leaving all her other belongings behind.

She took the stairway down to avoid an elevator confrontation, then hurried with her head down through the lobby. When she was just about to the front doors, she heard, "Miss! Miss!"

Naheed's heart dropped, and she felt vertigo setting in. She leaned her hand against the concierge's desk as she slowly turned around. "Yes?"

It was a woman behind the front desk. "Will you be checking out?"

"Uh, not yet. Late checkout, please, for room 324." She turned and pushed through the revolving door that seemed to slowly, slowly release her to the outside and freedom.

A quick glance and she spotted the car just five spaces from the front entrance. Naheed drove the few short miles to the long-term parking at San Francisco International Airport and began the period of waiting for her destiny to arrive.

FRIDAY, MAY 22, 11:00 A.M. MDT
INVERNESS TRAINING CENTER
ENGLEWOOD, COLORADO

What had started out as a great morning with his agent promising him money, fame, and happiness had turned into one of the worst practices of Keith Simmons's career. He blew coverages. He dropped easy pickoffs. He got his clock cleaned by a straight-arm block courtesy of center Chris Gorkowski. Now he was tired and sore.

Despite all that, he still had a big grin on his face as he tore the tape off his ankles and wrists. Riley was counting on him to get the word out about his "running away"—*yeah, like Pach would run away from a bunch of . . . What'd he call them? Hobbies, hoshies, hotties?* "No, definitely not hotties," he said with a laugh.

Unfortunately for Simmons, he had an extremely one-track mind, and football was not where that track was running today. His bad practice could be attributed to one thing—he had been trying to come up with a plan. Finally, at the end of the day's sessions, the pieces seemed to fall together, and the plan emerged. He held Afshin Ziafat back to bring him in on it.

Now, in the locker room, he looked over at Ziafat, who just

happened to be looking back at him. Ziafat gave him a wink and a thumbs-up. *Z might turn out to be not a half-bad kid after all.* Simmons nodded toward his left, then stripped down and headed to the showers. Ziafat followed him in.

Just be yourself, Simmons kept telling himself. *Don't let 'em see anything different.* "Hey, Gorkowski!" he shouted to the big center, who was bent over in front of his locker, picking up his towel for the showers. "This is one sight I did *not* need to see! Pass the crackers, boys. I think we found us some cheese!"

Gorkowski aimed a wicked snap of the towel at Simmons, who dodged it with a remarkably graceful pirouette. Simmons laughed. "Now, now, don't go getting all out of sorts. I just calls 'em how I sees 'em."

He twisted the shower knob just as Ziafat came up to the nozzle next to him. "Look at these low-flow showerheads," Simmons said loudly to the rookie linebacker, hoping to attract the attention of the others around them. "Another one of those brilliant cost-cutting measures by the pinhead bean counters in the front office.

"Now, you see, Z, there was a time—last year to be precise—when, if you turned this here knob, the water would come out all *shoosh,* and you could get yourself clean! Now when you turn it on, it comes out *fffft.* I mean what's up with that? I can just picture it, some middle management brainiac says, 'Hey, we can save five dollars a day if we make the showers go *fffft* instead of *shoosh!*' And his little cubby mate says, 'You rock, Dexter! Besides, they're stupid football players. They won't know the difference between *fffft* and *shoosh.* Let's go tell Mr. Salley!' And they skip off hand-in-hand to Mr. Salley's office. That, my dear friends, is how we got low-flow showerheads," Simmons concluded, noticing that his story had drawn the desired crowd of eavesdroppers.

"Probably the same Einsteins who decided it was costing too much to give us potato chips with our lunch," Ziafat said, once he finally stopped laughing, following along with Simmons's plan.

"Yeah, that'll save them another ten bucks a day—almost enough to bring on another punter. It's all making sense now," Simmons said to laughter. "Hey, Snap, what'd Pach used to call the front-office bean counters?"

"Idiot savants without a talent," Gorkowski responded, laughing along with everyone else.

Taking his cue, Ziafat asked, "Hey, Simm, speaking of Pach, how's he doing? Didn't you go see him or something?"

Yeah, I'll take this rookie any day, Simmons thought. Everyone was suddenly quiet, anxious to hear how their teammate was doing. Lowering his voice, which meant turning his vocal megaphone down from an eight to a five, Simmons said, "Yeah, but I'm not supposed to let anyone know. Dude's really struggling about his dad."

Gorkowski spoke up, pounding his hand with his fist, "If I ever find the sons—"

"Yeah, you and me both, Snap," Simmons said quickly, wanting to keep control of the conversation. "So, it was kind of weird when I was there. I'm standing around and I notice Pach had a bunch of stuff packed, and then I hear his buddy, Skeeter—you've all seen Skeeter: the Incredible Bulk? So Skeeter's on his phone saying something about the mountains. I'm guessing Pach's probably bolting out of here and hiding out up in the high country."

"Couldn't blame him if he did," said Ziafat. "Can you imagine having somebody wanting to kill you so badly?"

"Isn't that how it is when we play the Bay Area Bandits?" one of the rookie offensive linemen joked.

Gorkowski threw his wet towel at the man, hitting him in the face. "This ain't funny, you little mama's boy football player wannabe! This is Riley Covington's life we're talking about! You say one more thing without asking permission, and I'll take you to the ice bath and hold you under for an hour! Now go get me another towel!" The rookie faded to the back of the crowd and then ran to the stack of fresh towels. "Sorry about that, Simm. You were saying?"

"Well, actually Z was talking about people wanting to kill Pach. Which reminds me, I don't think Riley would want his business getting around. You know the media would make a huge darling out of anyone who let this slip," Simmons said, laying out the bait and hopefully setting the hook in some rookie's cheek.

"Let it be known," Gorkowski began, causing Simmons's heart to sink, "that anyone who leaks any of this to the media will have to answer to me! And I can promise you that before I have you booted from this team, I will personally introduce you to your own private hell! Understood?" Gorkowski pointed to Simmons and gave him a wink.

Simmons turned his head and rolled his eyes. *Okay, Lord, I did my part best I could. Please don't let a well-meaning oaf like Snap mess it all up.* He took a quick look at Ziafat, who had a big smile on his face.

"You done good," Ziafat mouthed.

Simmons nodded. *I hope he's right, Lord. I do hope he's right.*

Farragut, Isaac Khan read to himself. Looking up at the statue that stood in the middle of the park, he couldn't help but admire the man. Farragut stood strong and rigid, holding what appeared to be a telescope. Isaac slowly walked around the monument, looking for any other inscribed words or plaques that might tell more about this man, but there were none.

What a waste, to have done enough to have a statue erected and a park named in your honor, but there is nothing here to tell about your exploits or heroic deeds. Back home in Pakistan, when they erect the statue in my honor, they will make sure that children for generations to come know the name of Ishaq Mustaf Khan and what he did for the great name of Allah!

Briefly he closed his eyes and pictured a child with his father standing at the foot of a bronze statue such as this. The little boy stared up while the father pointed and spoke in his son's ear, "This is *Sayyid* Khan—a true warrior for the faith." *Oh, Allah, thank you for bringing honor back to my humble household.*

Leaving the monument, Isaac found a metal bench where he could wait out his time. He still had fifteen minutes to get to the Metrorail stop, and he could easily see the sign from here.

He was surprised at how few people were around. When he'd come to scout the location earlier this afternoon, the place had been packed––people eating and relaxing under the trees, throwing baseballs and Frisbees. He'd even seen a television news crew conducting interviews with passersby. Now the place seemed like a ghost town, and he felt a little exposed sitting by himself in the middle of this park.

As he sat and waited, the question of timing again came to his mind. *There were so many more people traveling earlier in the day! Why do they have me wait until the evening? The devastation could have been so much greater! Do they not understand?*

Then a smile spread across Isaac's face, and he shook his head slowly from side to side. *Old man, you are thinking far above yourself. They have thought this through. Maybe they know when someone specific will be traveling, or maybe they are coordinating with another attack. Is it your place to question?* He drew the backpack tighter to his side. *It will all be over soon. The arrogant people of America will again have to deal with the hand of Allah. That is what ultimately matters.* He looked at his watch again and waited.

FRIDAY, MAY 22, 4:10 P.M. PDT
SAN FRANCISCO, CALIFORNIA

The bar rose at the Pier 39 parking garage, and Naheed drove in. She crumpled the parking ticket she had just pulled and threw it on the floor of the car, knowing that the chances of her making it back here without being spotted were slim to none. *But still . . .* After she finally found a space and pulled in, Naheed reached over and picked the ticket back up. Smoothing it against the center of the steering wheel, she said, "You will be my symbol of hope. Maybe you will help me find my way back." Gently, she slipped the ticket into the front pocket of her jeans.

In six minutes she would begin her walk down the pier. That would give her seven minutes to reach the carousel and activate the device, then six minutes to make her way back to the car. The thought of making that trip churned her insides. "It's impossible—absolutely and completely impossible!"

She tilted the rearview mirror and examined herself. *Tell me how you are going to get all the way there without being recognized, let alone make it back. Why didn't you grab your bag with your disguises when you ran out this morning? Except for the wig, you are the exact picture they showed on the television, and you can bet they've already put out pictures of you with blonde hair.*

She took off her wig and twisted her hair into a thick bun. Then, picking the wide sun hat up from the passenger seat, she placed it on her head, making sure that all her hair was tucked under, and she looked at herself from various angles. "At least that's something."

The dashboard clock told her she had only three minutes left. *The last one was so much easier. I was completely anonymous, and the people who died were not truly worth mourning. But this . . .*

Oh, Allah, I declare that you are one, and that Muhammad is your Prophet. Grant me success on your mission. Smile upon me as I do your will. Let me live to see my family again. However, if I am discovered, give me the strength to meet you this day. I do this for you, and for you alone.

But even as Naheed said those final words, Jibril's face appeared behind her closed eyes, and doubts crept in. *Who are you really doing this for? Would you be here if Jibril hadn't threatened you? Don't you think Allah knows the duplicity of your motives?*

"Stop it! Just stop it!" she said as she flung the door open, making hard contact with a white LX 470 next to her. Naheed held her breath, waiting for the Lexus's alarm to go off. When it remained silent, she stepped out of the Buick and opened the trunk. A large black backpack sat in the center of the compartment. Naheed rolled her eyes. *Could they have made it more obvious?*

After adjusting her hat and sunglasses one last time, Naheed hefted the bag out of the trunk and slipped it over her right shoulder. She felt in the shoulder strap for the emergency detonation buttons—the top one activated the device, and the bottom would detonate.

The top button pushed in easily with a small click. Naheed hefted the bulk of the bag one more time, centering it better on her back, then left the garage.

Isaac stepped from the center island of the Farragut North station onto a train bound for Metro Center. Since the ride would be only two minutes, he didn't bother to sit down. He felt very conspicuous carrying the backpack and wearing a Washington Capitals cap—*Why didn't you devise a more creative disguise?*—but the other passengers seemed too wrapped up in their own business to pay him any attention.

He felt a distinct sense of déjà vu as he looked at the people around him. The noisy teenagers trying to be noticed, the young couples heading out for a night on the town, the businessmen trying to get home while dinner was still warm, the many workers heading for their night shifts. Most likely all these people would survive this night. But there were many more just like them who were traveling at this very moment to Metro Center who could not possibly expect what would be awaiting them when they arrived.

They are like sheep belonging to an evil shepherd. They are too stupid to know what is really going on. They just live their lives day by day while their shepherd steals and kills the flocks of others. These sheep may hear rumors of what their shepherd does, but do they care? No, as long as they are being fed and watered, they are content to let the shepherd do whatever he wants. Sorry, sheep, Isaac thought with a smile, *but tonight there is a wolf among your flock.*

The train slowed, then came to a stop. When the doors opened, Isaac disembarked to a long side platform. After taking a few steps, he stopped to look around for the escalator and his route of escape, but when he finally spotted it, he cursed himself. The escalator was going down.

He had so carefully planned out his route—how could he have failed to check whether the red line ran on the upper or lower level? *Stupid!* Taking a deep breath to control himself, he thought, *Okay, not a major problem. Just take the escalator down and find a place on the lower level. It will look like you are transferring to another line.*

But Isaac knew the danger of being out in the open much longer in the central hub of the Metrorail system. In just one quick pass he spotted eight uniformed members of the Metro Transit Police Department.

Make me invisible, O God. With his right hand, he pressed the top button embedded in the backpack's strap. One more quick prayer, and Isaac began the walk to the escalators.

4:23 P.M. PDT

It seemed everyone was staring at Naheed as she walked down the boardwalk. It started with the young guys near the entrance playing empty white plastic buckets like drums for change and soon spread to the popcorn vendor and the guy selling maps and the little sticky-faced kids holding on to their dripping ice-cream cones. But when she turned around, certain she would see a band of vigilantes ready to pounce on her, there was just an oblivious crowd of people enjoying their afternoon at the bay.

Calm yourself. You're almost there. She slowed her pace from the speed-walk her panic had induced. Looking ahead, she could see the carousel partially obscured by a second-floor bridge. *Two more minutes and you're there.*

She had walked down one more set of stairs when a sound reached her. There was so much noise around; it was hard to distinguish one sound from another. But she could have sworn she heard a scream. Trying not to show anything on her face, she slowly looked left, then right. And then she saw them. Thirty feet away, a woman holding a toddler was frantically talking to a security guard. As she spoke, she pointed right at Naheed.

Naheed picked up her pace until she was almost running. She saw the security guard yelling into his walkie-talkie as he began to move toward her. People near the guard overheard his call for help, and panic began to spread. More people started screaming and moving in her direction, as they frantically tried to get off the pier.

Acting purely on instinct, Naheed turned and joined the growing tidal wave. She threw off her sun hat. To her left and right she could see more security guards looking into the crowd from their places along the storefronts.

As she neared the entrance to the boardwalk, three, then four, then five police cars pulled up. Their doors flew open, and the officers raced toward the crowd.

Naheed locked eyes with a security guard ahead on her left. Immediately he broke from his position and raced toward the policemen. *It's over,* a voice screamed in her head. *Press the button! Press the button!*

As she ran, she placed her thumb on top of the bulge in the strap. *Do it! You're dead anyway! Just do it!*

But as much as she willed herself, she couldn't overcome her instinct for self-preservation. Her thumb moved off the button.

The security guard had found a policeman and was pointing at Naheed. She looked left, then right, for an avenue of escape. *Can I go back?* she asked. But as she whirled to look behind her, a man flew into her with such force that the wind was knocked from her.

She fell backward, and her head slammed onto the wooden pier. The man dropped heavily on top of her. Stars floated in front of Naheed's eyes, and the ringing in her head drowned out the words her assailant was yelling at her. His knee was pressed hard into her chest, making it difficult for her to draw a breath, and he was stretching her hands over her head. She blacked out.

When she came to, Naheed was surrounded by police. She had been flipped over so that she was lying facedown. Handcuffs encased her wrists. *Your life is over,* she thought. *You should have pressed the button, you fool.*

Hands forced their way under her arms, and she was hauled to her feet. Off to her right she could see the backpack with a group of officers surrounding it. Just beyond them stood a middle-aged man wearing shorts and a torn San Francisco wharf T-shirt. There was blood running down his leg, and a policeman was questioning him. He was staring right at her, and in that instant she knew that he was the one who had brought her down.

The walk to the police car was complete mayhem. All around her, tourists had their digital cameras, video cameras, and cell phones out, taking pictures of her. People screamed and cursed at her. Someone threw a plastic cup of Coke, hitting her in the side of the face and drenching the officers on either side of her. Immediately, two of the surrounding policemen pushed into the crowd to find the culprit.

When she finally arrived at the police cruiser, someone placed a hand on her head and pushed her into the backseat. A female officer followed her in. When a second officer started up the car, the one next to Naheed said, "Okay, Matt, I'm going to Mirandize her." Then, turning to Naheed, she said, "You have the right to remain silent. Anything you say can and will be used against you in a court of law. You have the right to an attorney. If you cannot afford an attorney, one will be appointed for you. Do you understand these rights?"

"Yes," mumbled Naheed.

"Do you want to speak with me?"

"No." But then a thought occurred to her. What was it she always told her friend June? *Remember who has the power.* A small glimmer of hope appeared in Naheed's mind. *You may seem helpless now, but remember—information is power. And information is the one thing you've got left. They've made people disappear before in Guantánamo and other places. Play your cards right, and you just might be able to disappear back to Grandfather's household.*

Turning to the officer next to her, with an arrogant look in her eye, Naheed said, "Actually, I may want to talk. But not to you. Bring me someone with authority. We'll see what happens then."

7:25 P.M. EDT

At the bottom of the escalator was an island platform with tracks running to the left and the right. Isaac walked to a subway map and saw the faded remains of a vulgarity outlined on the plastic covering. *Just one more example of the disrespect these people have for others,* he thought with disgust. As he pretended to be examining the map, he used his peripheral vision to scan his surroundings. There were a number of transit cops down here, too, but not like up above.

Walking down a little ways, he found an empty bench and sat down. His hand found a sticky place on the seat, and Isaac quickly wiped it hard across his pants. The plan was to wait for the next train to arrive, activate the bomb, then join the people leaving the train—twenty steps to the escalator, maybe forty more steps to the next escalator, then freedom. As he waited, he closed his eyes and pictured again the statue that would one day be erected in his hometown of Bela.

"Are you okay, sir?"

Startled, Isaac opened his eyes to find a transit policeman standing next to him. "Uh, yes, officer. I was just daydreaming," he said, forcing a smile onto his face.

The officer returned the smile. "Yes, I find myself doing that too, sometimes. May I ask where you're heading tonight?"

"Is there something I've done wrong?"

The transit cop chuckled. "No. It's just with what happened in Philadelphia, we're trying to be extra careful. So, where *are* you heading tonight?"

Isaac racked his brain trying to come up with a destination. "The monument," he finally blurted out.

"The Washington Monument? Well you're in the right spot but on the wrong side. You'll want to take a train from the other side of the island to Federal Center."

Isaac congratulated himself at having guessed right. "Thank you, officer," he said as he stood to change sides of the platform.

"Do you mind if I look in your backpack, sir? You know, just being careful," the officer said as he slid himself between Isaac and his bag.

A thin smile forced itself on Isaac's face. "Is that really necessary, officer? I'm just an old man doing some sightseeing."

"I realize that, sir, and I apologize. It'll only take a moment." As he said this, a train ground to a halt next to the two men.

"Really, officer, if you'll please just let me take my bag and go," Isaac said, hearing the growing fear in his own voice. He could see a tightening on the other man's face.

One of the officer's hands slowly moved to his gun, while the other pressed a button on a microphone that was clipped to his shoulder. "This is Lytle. I've got a suspect with a suspicious bag. Request backup." From behind Officer Lytle, Isaac could see two officers begin running their way. "Now, sir, if you'll just give me permission to check your bag, this will all be over within a minute, and you'll be on your way."

Sweat broke out on Isaac's forehead. There was no way to get to the bag except by going through the policeman, and within seconds more cops would arrive. Isaac had to act quickly.

Reaching his hand into his jacket, he said, "Officer, if I can just show you my—"

"Take your hand out of your jacket," Lytle commanded, drawing his gun at the same time Isaac drew his. Both men fired.

Officer Lytle fell back into the screaming crowd unloading from the train. Isaac dropped to his knees, pain flaring through his chest. He tried to take a breath but received little for his efforts. Ahead he could see the other two cops closing in on him, both with guns drawn.

With all the strength he had left, Isaac launched himself forward and fell across the black backpack. Isaac's hand scrambled underneath the bag, searching for the detonation trigger. One of the officers was within ten feet. *Give me success, Allah. Please grant your servant success.*

The transit cop dove through the air, but he never landed. Isaac's hand had found the button, and with one push he sent himself and 113 other souls to their final judgment.

FRIDAY, MAY 22, 7:00 P.M. PDT
SAN FRANCISCO, CALIFORNIA

How did you let yourself get into this situation?
Naheed asked herself. *All your friends from back
home are married and living in nice houses—children
running around their feet. But would you settle for
that? No! You had to have adventure. You had to seek
glory. The little domestic lives of your friends were not
enough. Remember how you used to shake your head
so condescendingly every time you heard about one of
them settling down to family life? "How nice," you'd
say with a smirk on your face. "How ordinary." Well,
tonight, they're tucked away in their "nice" little homes
sleeping next to their "ordinary" little husbands, and
you're here with your life ruined!*

Naheed cursed herself as she looked around
the room she had been placed in over an hour
ago. It was all white except for the stainless steel
of the table in front of her and the three surrounding chairs—one of which she was handcuffed to.
Above her, a fluorescent tube light in the ceiling
kept changing the shadows of the room as it slowly flickered its way to its death—and with each
flicker, Naheed felt the already firm band of her
headache clench even tighter.

As she waited—for what, she didn't know—her

mind drifted to a late-night spy movie she had watched a few weeks ago. In it the espionage suspect was being held in a room very similar to the one she was in now, except that the furniture was wooden. When the goons came in to torture him, he saw that his end was near, so he bit down on a cyanide capsule that he had hidden in his mouth and died a gruesome but quick death. *What I wouldn't give to have that option open to me,* Naheed thought, unconsciously running her tongue between her cheek and gums.

Another blast of pain grew like a mushroom cloud expanding in her head. The cloud solidified into sharp masses stabbing the inside of her skull, and she closed her eyes tightly in a vain attempt to counteract the pressure. The place on her chest where the Great American Hero had dropped his knee hurt with every breath she took. But that pain was tolerable. It was the headache that left her feeling weak and nauseous.

Forcing her eyes back open, she stared defiantly at one of the three cameras that were keeping constant watch on her. *Who's back there? What are they waiting for?*

Trying to keep herself alert, Naheed began looking for patterns in the holes punched through the acoustic tiling that covered the walls of the room. The strain on her eyes, though, caused another wave of pain to rush like a tsunami through her head. Her teeth clenched as she rode the wave out.

As she forced herself to hold back the tears and look strong, the door to the room opened and three people walked in. The first was an older man who looked like every movie stereotype of a marine drill sergeant. He was about five-seven and had his head shaved down to the scalp. When he sat across from her, Naheed noticed that he had the hairiest arms she had ever seen. He was wearing a red tropical print shirt that he left hanging outside his pants.

The second person reminded her of the burnouts that used to hang out around San Francisco's Tenderloin district down at the bottom of Nob Hill. Tall and chunky, he had a blond goatee that grew at least four inches below his chin. As opposed to the California dapper of the first man, this one was wearing a black Deep Purple Machine Head Tour 1972 T-shirt, tattered jeans, and sandals.

The third person Naheed recognized. "Khadi Faroughi," she said with a wicked smile. "I've read about you in the newspapers. I know people who would very much like to meet you to ask you about your betrayal of Islam."

Naheed was gratified to see the look of surprise on Khadi's face at being recognized. *Gain the upper hand!* But then the woman quickly composed herself and said calmly as she walked to the third chair, "Miss Yamani, I already met your people six months ago. Actually, I only *saw* them through the lens of my sniper scope as their heads popped."

Naheed heard a stifled laugh from the larger of the two men. *Come on, take control of the situation. Try to keep them off their guard.* "You may have seen a few, but there are many more of us. I'm sure someday you'll meet them face-to-face when you least expect it."

Khadi began thumbing through the files she had carried in without bothering to reply.

Looking Naheed straight in the eyes, the older of the men asked, "Are you going to be good?"

Naheed stared back at him.

"Scott, uncuff her," the older man said.

The burnout walked behind her and released her hands. Naheed kept her poker face, but inside she was smiling. *Obviously they want what I have to give. Now, carefully, play it out to your advantage.* The older man was still watching her, not saying anything. Naheed decided to wait him out.

Finally, he leaned forward and rested his arms on the table. "Miss Yamani, my name is Mr. Hicks. This is Agent Ross and apparently you've already recognized Agent Faroughi. I'm sure you know that you are in a bad situation. Maybe I can make it better, maybe I can't. Someone told me you wanted to talk, so here I am. Talk."

Naheed could hear in the gravelly monotone of Hicks's voice that he wasn't going to be a pushover. *Careful. Play this right. Obviously if Faroughi is with them, these are experienced players.* She tried to keep a calm exterior, but inside some serious doubts were raising their ugly heads. *The only power you have is information, and when that's gone, you're helpless. So give just a little bit at a time, and you can keep control.*

"Shouldn't we agree to some terms before I begin sharing with you what I know?" Naheed said, angry with herself for the slight waver in her voice.

"Terms?" Hicks said with a smile. Then he turned to Khadi and said, "Agent Faroughi, Miss Yamani would like to hear my terms."

Still without looking up, Khadi responded, "She doesn't want to hear your terms."

"You don't want to hear my terms," the older man said, turning back to Naheed.

Don't let them intimidate you! Look at all the cameras in this room. What can they do to you? "I'm afraid I must insist on knowing what I can expect in exchange for the information that I have." Out of the corner of her eye, Naheed saw Khadi look at her, shake her head, then turn back down to her files. Behind her, she could hear the other agent begin cracking his knuckles—*pop . . . pop . . . pop.*

Hicks's face reddened a bit, but his voice remained level. "Miss Yamani, I cannot promise you anything if you tell me what you know. However, I can promise you plenty if you do not. You may have noticed that once you entered this building, the uniforms disappeared. We are a counterterrorism agency. As such, we have a little more latitude in how we . . . How should I say it? In how we convince suspects to cooperate with us."

From behind her, the larger man, Scott, said, "What happens in the interrogation room stays in the interrogation room."

"Well put, Agent Ross," said Mr. Hicks.

Naheed's heart was beating very rapidly now, and what had started out as internal shaking was starting to make itself known on the outside.

Leaning back in his chair until it tilted on two legs, Hicks continued, "Let me tell you the way this usually works, since you are so interested in knowing what you can expect. Most often I am the one directly involved in the active persuasion of the suspect. Agent Faroughi stays near in case the uncomfortable circumstances cause a person to unconsciously revert back to a native tongue—in your case, Arabic. Am I right?" Without waiting for an answer, he finished, "Agent Ross behind you is a little squeamish about these things, so he will probably leave the room."

"The sight of blood makes me feel all woozy inside," Naheed heard from behind her.

Naheed felt powerless to stop her eyes from darting around the room, futilely looking for some avenue of escape. *Active persuasion? Blood? How can this be happening? Is he really threatening you with torture—in America? He's got to be bluffing! Call him on it! Keep the upper hand!* "Listen," she said, mustering up all the bravado she had left, "do you think I just came to this country yesterday? Do you think I didn't see the scandals of Gitmo, the waterboarding debates? What do you think the ACLU would say if I turned up bruised and blood-ied? What do you think the *L.A. Times* would write? I have rights. I am innocent until proven guilty. You can threaten me all you like, but I'm not talking until I get some promises. And I'm certainly not talking to some old, bald-headed psychopath who's got nothing to say to me except empty threats!"

Suddenly, a finger flicked hard on the knot at the back of her head. Pain shot through her body and the room did a little spin. Through her haze she heard a voice behind her say, "Don't be rude to Mr. Hicks."

Looking back at Hicks's unchanged face through watery eyes, Naheed heard him say, "You're making the assumption that the ACLU or the *L.A. Times* will see you again. Or that *anyone* will see you again. You should not make assumptions in areas you know so little about. It only makes you come across as a naive little girl. So, you've heard my terms, Miss Yamani. Do we talk, or does Agent Ross leave the room?"

He has got to be bluffing! But what if he's not? You know the moment he hurts you, you'll tell him everything. You'll fold like a leaf, you coward!

As she wrestled with her weaknesses, a fresh flood of pain burst forth from the depths of her brain and filled her head. Naheed low-ered her chin to her chest and held her breath as the wave swept through her whole body. When the misery began to subside, reality sunk in. *How can you keep control of the situation when you can barely even think? The only hope you have is information! Just give him a little bit at a time. As long as you know something he doesn't, you're useful to him. Try to win him over with your helpfulness and your helplessness. Turn on the waterworks and make him feel sorry for you.*

"Jibril," Naheed said, bursting into tears. Off to her right, she saw Khadi's head pop up.

"Jibril—Allah's messenger," said Scott.

"Who's Jibril?" asked Hicks.

Between sobs, she managed to say, "My contact, but I don't think Jibril is his real name."

"What does he look like?"

"He's tall, middle-aged, scars on his face. He has a strong Iraqi accent. I can't tell you much more—I only met him once."

"When was that?" Hicks asked, passing her a handkerchief from his pocket.

Inside, Naheed began smiling. *He's beginning to soften already.* "It was two days ago, at Union Square across from Macy's."

"What did you talk about?"

"I told him that I wanted out. I begged him to let me go home to Saudi Arabia. He got very angry. He threatened me. He said that if I didn't plant the bomb on Pier 39, he would kill me, and then he would torture and kill my parents and my brothers and sisters. It was the same thing he had said when he forced me to leave the bomb in Hollywood." More tears spilled from her eyes. "I swear, Mr. Hicks, I never wanted to hurt anyone. You have to believe me. I was just so scared."

She was relieved to see her big play working. Hicks was nodding, and she could hear compassion in his voice when he answered, "I can understand your fear, Naheed. If this 'Jibril' is the man who forced you to do these things, then we definitely want to make him suffer the consequences. You said you only met with him once. How did he usually make contact?"

"There were only a few contacts. Twice by coded text message, and three times by cell phone."

"Cell phone?" said the man behind her. "Come on, isn't that a little risky?"

Continuing to focus on Hicks, Naheed said, "Jibril was always good at making our conversations sound innocent—nothing to raise any alarms."

"Do you know the number he contacted you from?"

"No, but it's saved on my cell phone under the name Sarah Michaels."

"And your phone would be . . . ?" Khadi asked.

"In a Buick Century, gold, first level of the Pier 39 parking garage. I don't know who it's registered to."

Hicks looked up at one of the cameras and nodded. Then looking back at her, he said, "This is good, Naheed. I appreciate your cooperation. Are you thirsty? Can I get you something to drink?"

Hope began to fill Naheed's heart as she shook her head. *Maybe I can make it out of this after all. He seems to be softening up to the helpless little girl. Just be careful and don't press your luck.*

"Okay, now getting back to the day in Union Station—"

"Union Square."

"Right, Union Square," Hicks said with an impatient wave of his hand. "Obviously I'm not from around here. So, you met there. Did you walk? Did you sit?"

Play him, play him. You've just about got him hooked. Naheed made herself shiver, as if the mere remembrance of that day were almost too much for her. "We sat and talked. He became very angry. I was glad we were out in the open, because I don't know what he would have done to me if we had been alone. I pleaded for him to not make me do any more of his horrible acts and just let me go home. He said that after Pier 39 he would arrange for me to get back to Saudi Arabia, and he promised they would leave me and my family alone forever."

"They? Jibril and who else?"

"The one-eyed man."

Naheed saw Khadi's head pop back up and Hicks's eyes widen. *Idiot,* she thought. *You've said too much!*

"Did this one-eyed man have a name?" Hicks asked, suddenly very impatient.

"No, I've never heard it. He was no one really. So, when Jibril promised—"

"Wait," Hicks interrupted. "Go back to the one-eyed man. Have you ever met him before?"

Naheed tried to dismiss him with a wave of her hand. "Really, he's no one. I remember meeting him only one time when I finished my training."

"But you said 'they' would leave you alone. That makes me think that you have reason to believe that he might still be involved in the Cause?"

"I don't know, Mr. Hicks. Like I said—"

The sound of Hicks's chair sliding across the floor cut through the room as he thrust himself forward. Forget the compassion, forget the softness, forget the games. No longer was there any doubt who was in charge. Even as his hand slammed down on the table, he yelled, "Think! Is this one-eyed man the head of the Cause?"

Truly frightened, Naheed answered, "I don't know! I mean, Jibril never came right out and said it, but his reaction when I asked made me think that maybe he was."

"That's not good enough! I need more! Do you know where this one-eyed man is now?"

"I know nothing about him except what I've told you."

"You better think hard one more time," Hicks said, leaning across the table and grabbing hold of one of her wrists, "because, if I find out you've been lying to me, we're going straight to plan B! Now, do you know where this one-eyed man is?"

"I don't know! I swear it, I don't know!" Tears were streaming down Naheed's cheeks as she attempted to pull her arm out of the man's iron grip.

Naheed saw Hicks look at the man behind her. Then, deliberately releasing her wrist finger by finger, he nodded his head slightly and calmly said, "You've done well, Naheed. I'll be back in a little bit and we'll talk more. In the meantime, I'm afraid Agent Ross is going to have to secure you to your chair again."

Her arms were pulled roughly back behind her. She felt cold metal encompass her wrists and heard the rapid clicking of the cuffs being locked down.

The three agents exited the room quickly, leaving Naheed alone with her thoughts. She sniffed hard to control the flow from her nose but could do nothing about the tears. *Oh, what have you done, you stupid fool? You've shown how weak you are, and now they know how to get what they want from you. Why did you say so much? Why didn't you hold on to the one-eyed man story? They would have paid dearly for that information. Face it, little girl, you thought you had the upper hand, but you were beat by the master.*

FRIDAY, MAY 22, 7:30 P.M. PDT
SAN FRANCISCO, CALIFORNIA

Even though Scott's legs were a good six inches longer than Hicks's, he still had a hard time keeping up with his boss. Trying to keep pace with Scott was Khadi, who was almost in a full sprint. As they ran, the thick cloud of Hicks's profanity-laced mutterings surrounded the two analysts as it blew back and assaulted them. It was not unlike the agony of being trapped behind a cattle truck on a narrow country road.

"Where are you going?" yelled Niko Garisyan as he popped his head out of the room where he had been monitoring the interrogation.

"Your office! I've got to make a call," Hicks shouted back.

"Sure, be my guest," Garisyan said sarcastically.

"You can bet I will," Scott heard Hicks mumble.

"Hey, Hicks!"

Hicks stopped and spun around to face Garisyan. Scott could see that the red he had spotted on his friend's clean-shaven neck carried around to his face. A vein in his forehead was visibly throbbing.

When Garisyan saw Hicks's look, he dialed his tone way back. "What do you want me to do with the girl?"

Hicks turned back around and continued down the hall, calling over his shoulder, "I'm done with her! Interrogate her some more, then ship her off to Langley or Guantánamo or some prison where she can accidentally get mixed in with the general population and get a shank in her gut! I really don't give a rip!"

When he reached the office, Hicks swung open the door and sat in Garisyan's chair. Scott and Khadi sat across from him. "Close the door," Hicks growled. "I don't want anyone eavesdropping."

Scott got up and did as Hicks had asked. When he came back, Hicks had his head in his hands.

"Okay, tell me why I have this sick feeling in my stomach telling me that al-'Aqran is our one-eyed man? Even though I know he's supposed to be safely tucked away in a black-site prison, somehow he's wrapped up in this."

Khadi leaned forward in her chair. "I've got the same feeling. His involvement could answer something that's been bugging me for a couple of weeks now. You know how much I've studied the Cause over the years. There is no one I know of in their organization who could have stepped up in leadership this quickly and pulled off what we've seen—especially with the Washington, D.C., bombing today and this near miss."

"Maybe there was more reason for your CIA buddy's evasiveness the other day than just the typical Langley secrecy," Scott added.

"I swear, if I find out they've been holding out on us . . ." Hicks reached for the phone. He punched in some numbers, waited a moment, and then said, "Is this a secure line? . . . This is Jim Hicks, director of CTD's FRRT. Put me through to Charlie Anderson. . . . Yes, I understand he's busy with the subway bombing. Why do you think I'm calling him at the office instead of at home? Now, please put him on the line. . . . Listen, lady, I'm not sure where you're getting the idea you have a choice in the matter! Go tell Anderson that Jim Hicks is on the phone—now!"

Hicks closed his eyes and rubbed his forehead. Scott could see that it was taking every ounce of strength he had not to totally lose control.

Hicks suddenly straightened up. "Anderson, you short-sighted, territorial weasel! What's going on with al-'Aqran? . . . Listen, you can cut the shadowy spy crap! I've got the Hollywood bomber here, and she just told me that a one-eyed man is running the show at the Cause! Now, either they just recruited Sammy Davis Jr. from the dead or there's something going on with al-'Aqran, so spill it!"

Scott watched as Hicks listened. The older man suddenly dropped back in his chair and put his hand over his eyes. "Unbelievable! How . . . ?" Taking his hand away, Hicks saw Scott and Khadi looking at him. He tore a sheet out of a report that was sitting on Garisyan's desk, wrote something on it, then slid the paper over toward Scott. *HE BROKE OUT* was written in large, angry letters.

Hicks began waving for the paper to come back to him. When he got it, he wrote three more words, then gave it back. *CHECHEN LECHA ABDALAYEV* had now been added to the sheet.

"I know that name," Khadi whispered to Scott. "He's the head of the Chechen Freedom Militia. They're a mercenary group who used to fight to further their cause, but when the money ran low, so did their altruism. Now they just hire themselves out to the highest bidder."

Hicks's voice cut through. "So, do you have any idea where he's at now, or did your super sleuths lose him after he crossed into Ukraine?"

Scott was no longer listening. One of the things that made Scott so good at what he did was that he never forgot anything, and he was a master at tying together seemingly random pieces of information. "It's like doing connect the dots, only without the numbers," he had once said.

And now Scott's mind was racing. He had heard of Abdalayev too, and not that long ago. His mind began processing through all the communications intelligence he had digested over the past weeks. *Come on, think. It wasn't an action report. It wasn't status. Movement! It was a movement report!* Scott visualized the flash report, absorbing all the pertinent information before returning it to the overfilled filing cabinets of his brain.

Scott quickly scribbled, "Abdalayev in Prague—possibly making deal for services" and shoved it over to Hicks, who read it with a nod.

"What's Abdalayev doing in Prague?" Khadi asked quietly.

"From what I remember, the speculation is that he's meeting with representatives of the government-in-exile of the Abkhazia Autonomous Republic."

"Remind me of the background of that situation."

"The Abkhaz people seceded from the country of Georgia, did a little ethnic cleansing of the Georgian population, and set up camp—all with the help of the Russians. The government that had been in power fled to Western Europe. Since that time, this exiled government has been working hard to get their ducks in a row to try to get their stomping grounds back. Unfortunately, just when it was looking like that might happen, the Russians started aiding the rebel warlords again, stopping any progress.

"Then Russia did that whole invasion of Georgia thing over the other breakaway republic, South Ossetia. Once all the dust settled there, it left the Abkhaz government-in-exile realizing that the Georgian leadership wasn't going to be able to help them at all. They're on their own. The thought on Abdalayev was that he and his little merry band of cutthroats were going to be hired by the exiled government to, well, cut some warlord throats."

Khadi was about to ask another question but quieted as soon as Hicks started speaking again.

"So, the summary of your answer is, 'Yes, we did lose him.' Amazing! Three cheers for the greatest spy agency in the history of Western civilization. . . . No, you *do* have to listen to this, Anderson! We handed you the guy, and you lost him! Now he's blowing Americans up again. . . . Yes, that *is* my interpretation, and it's a pretty accurate one. Now, what about Abdalayev being in Prague? Are you guys going to pick him up for interrogation? . . . Never mind how I know, just answer the question."

Silence filled the room as Hicks listened and Scott and Khadi watched. The knuckles on Hicks's hand whitened as he held the phone. Like the terrestrial rumblings before a volcanic eruption, Scott recognized the signs that Hicks was about to blow. He just had time to thank God that he wasn't on the other end of the line, and then Mount St. Helens lost its top.

"So, that's how it is, huh? In your great cumulative wisdom, you all made a decision, and that's how it's going to be? Well, I hate to burst your bubble, you and your little skirt-wearing debutantes, but I've got a different plan! You boys may be too worried about the political fallout to do anything. I, on the other hand, have no such scruples. So get your little CIA boys to clear the path for my team and me, because we've got a date to meet Mr. Abdalayev. . . . No, actually you will. And do you know why? Because if you don't, I'm blowing the lid off this to the press. How do you think it'll play when the American public finds out that some prisoner got a little too tired of being tortured in some secret prison, so he broke out of the CIA's slippery grasp and began bombing the crap out of the country? . . . No, you better believe I will, because unlike you, I'm more concerned about protecting our citizens than I am about covering my own backside *or* whether or not I'm stepping on any other country's toes.

"We'll go in fast. We'll go in discreet. But you better believe we are going in. I'll call you back in an hour with details. In the meantime, you've got some people to talk to!"

Hicks slammed down the phone, stared at it, then snatched it off the desk, yanked the cords out of the back, and threw it against the wall. Scott and Khadi knew Hicks well enough to wait him out.

After five breaths in through the nose and out through the mouth, Hicks said, "Abdalayev broke al-'Aqran out of a black-site prison in Poland almost two months ago. The Langley boys know he crossed the border into Ukraine, but they don't know what happened after that. They think he's gone to sand country or to one of the 'Stans."

"Wow, they really went out on a limb with that prediction," Scott observed. "What about Abdalayev?"

"They knew Abdalayev had surfaced in the Czech Republic, but they said the CIA can't do anything to him because the Czechs are giving him safe travel and we've got to honor that."

"Safe travel? Why are the Czechs protecting him?" Khadi asked angrily.

Scott answered for Hicks. "Two reasons. First, because Abdalayev is from Chechnya. And as you know, the Chechens and the Russians are about equal on the who-hates-who-more scale with the

Palestinians and the Israelis. Second, by helping out the Abkhazian government-in-exile, Abdalayev is going against the Russian-supported warlords who have control of the autonomous republic. In both cases, the Czechs see him sticking it to the Russians."

Khadi was nodding. "The enemy of my enemy is my friend."

"Exactly. The Czechs haven't come close to forgetting the 1968 Prague Spring when Soviet tanks went rolling into Old Town Square. And with Mr. I-Can't-Be-President-Anymore-So-Make-Me-Prime-Minister playing puppet-master in Russia, a lot of folks have concerns about the tanks coming back someday. The more effort the Russians have to expend in Chechnya and Abkhazia, the less they have available to put elsewhere."

Scott's history lesson had allowed Hicks time to calm down. "That's about the gist of it. Anderson tells me that Abdalayev is untouchable. I politely disagreed.

"So, here's what I want to see happen. Scott, you call our ops boys, catch them up, and tell them to be ready to fly out 0600 tomorrow—CIA's got a strip where we can put the jet down. Khadi, call Tara and have her get the analysts digging up everything they can about Abdalayev—how he travels, who he's meeting, where he's staying, what firepower he carries, all that stuff."

"You got it, Jim," Scott said, pulling his phone out of his pocket. "You going to get back to Anderson to work out the logistics with the CIA?"

Hicks sighed. "Later. First, I'm going to get on with Director Porter and tell him about how my plans will most likely destroy my career and his as well."

FRIDAY, MAY 22, 11:30 P.M. MDT
SILVERTHORNE, COLORADO

Covington Runs for the Hills
by Whitney Walker
FOX 31 SPORTS

DENVER—For a man who is already a riddle wrapped in a mystery inside an enigma, the bizarre tale of Riley Covington just keeps getting, well, bizarrer. After suffering an Achilles injury—an incident which seems more likely to have originated in Roy Burton's fertile imagination than from Covington "missing a stair" at home—anonymous sources tell us that our own homegrown superhero has fled town to go into hiding in the mountains. "If [the authorities] can't even protect my family, how can they possibly protect me?" Covington allegedly said.

Meanwhile, sympathy and sorrow continue to be the order of the day at makeshift memorials both at the home of Riley Covington's parents and at the end of his own street in Parker. Cards and flowers cover the corner.

"It's just so, so wrong. Who does something like that?" one weeping fan said holding a candle.

"It just shows that none of us are safe anymore," said a mother who had driven from Pueblo so that her two children could leave homemade cards for Covington. "Riley has been such a role model for my boys that we felt we had to support him in his time of need."

Supporting our hero in his time of need—that was a common theme heard throughout the Denver metro area. Wherever you've gone, Riley Covington, this town wishes you well.

"Thanks, Whitney, I owe you one," Riley said to himself. The reporter had certainly done her job—maybe a little too well. As Riley scanned the comments posted by readers after the online article, he knew she had dug herself a pretty deep hole. Fans were calling for her head because she had done exactly what Riley had asked her to do—get the word out that he was heading for the mountains. *Gonna have to make sure I make that right.*

Hearing about the memorials put a slight crack in Riley's defenses. For the past twelve hours, he had been working hard at locking all his emotions behind a strong wall. A couple times he'd even gone a full half hour without thinking of his dad. Feelings were simply not something he had the luxury of dealing with at the present moment. People's sympathy—while he appreciated it for what it was—did not help the matter at all.

Focus, buddy. Before shutting down the computer, he quickly checked the *Denver Post* and *Rocky Mountain News* Web sites. Both had their own versions of the story, which they had either ripped off from Whitney or gathered from their own Mustangs sources.

Riley got up from the desk in the bedroom and felt his way through the pitch-black room to the front door, where Skeeter had situated himself. Skeeter had shunned the deep leather armchairs that sat just behind him in the small den in favor of a wooden chair from the dining room. Simmons's "cabin" was less an actual cabin than it was a mini mansion placed in a woodsy setting. A steep path led from the driveway to an elegant wood and glass front door. The structure itself was two stories with a finished basement. It was beautifully decorated in mountain chic—lots of logs, leather, and antlers. *Why couldn't this be an old, run-down, one-room log cabin? Then I wouldn't feel so bad if the place gets blasted into tiny pieces.*

Skeeter turned as Riley placed his hand on Skeeter's shoulder. "You doing okay?"

"Mmmm," Skeeter grunted with a nod, turning back to the outside. As his eyes began to adjust, Riley could see the night-vision goggles that the big man was wearing.

The goggles were just one part of a "care package" that Scott had asked the ops guys at FRRT to put together for them. Although Riley and Skeeter had been halfway to the Eisenhower Tunnel when they got Scott's call, they'd gladly turned around to pick up their little box of goodies. Thanks to Scott, they now had two pairs of night-vision goggles and a series of ten trip flares that surrounded the perimeter of the property. As far as weaponry, Scott had equipped them with both fragmentation and stun grenades, neither of which Riley hoped they'd have to use. If they did, it would mean that things had deteriorated far beyond what he had hoped.

"You feeling good about the defenses?"

"Best we could do with what we've got," Skeeter replied.

Riley stood next to his friend and listened to the stillness of the night. All was quiet except for the incessant barking of a neighbor's dog. The dumb thing had been barking when they arrived. It had barked while they set up the trip flares. It barked now that they were back in the cabin. Earlier, Skeeter had hiked over to see the dog. He reported back that it was a large Rottweiler that just seemed mad at the world.

"Whitney got the article out saying we're in the mountains. You thinking it'll be enough?"

"We'll see."

Riley nodded. "Yeah, I guess we will."

Silence again. Riley's eyes continued to allow him more details of the man next to him.

"Skeet, can I ask you a question?"

"Mmmm."

"Don't take this the wrong way, but why're you here? You are good enough to have any gig you want. Jim even offered for you to head up his whole ops team, didn't he? That'd be a perfect situation for you. Or you could be bodyguarding for the rich and famous— pretty little starlets who don't have people trying to kill them. Instead, here you are hiding out in the mountains with *hajji*-enemy number one."

Silence descended back into the room. Skeeter shifted, the dog barked, Riley waited. In the midst of the quiet, Skeeter spoke. "My mama was a great woman. Never was a person alive who loved with more sacrifice and devotion. My daddy ran off when I was three. From that time on, Mama worked to make me something. She never took another man; she never even dated. I was her life.

"We never had much, and Mama felt that by her going to the doctor she would be taking food out of my mouth. So by the time she finally had to go, the cancer had spread through most of her body. I guess the blessing was that there was no long, drawn-out death.

"I was thirteen when she passed." Skeeter paused. "I can still remember one of the last things she said to me. She said, 'Skeeter, you want to know how to make your life mean something? You find one thing you believe in, and then you give yourself to it—I'm talking everything you got.' Then she took my hand and said, 'You're my one thing, boy. And it's because of you that my life has meant something.'

"I struggled for a lot of years after her passing. But then I met you in Afghanistan. I saw your principles. I saw your commitment. I realized you reminded me a lot of my mama. Before I knew it, I realized that I had found my one thing I believe in."

Riley stood silently, waiting to see if there was more. But Skeeter was done. A wave of melancholy swept through Riley—an emotion that had its genesis in the personal knowledge that he was not near the man Skeeter and others had built him up to be. *In fact, if they knew what I was really like, way down deep, they'd be out of my life in a heartbeat.*

"Why don't you get some shut-eye? I'll take first watch," Riley said as he picked up his night-vision goggles from a side table. "I'll wake you at three."

"You won't need to wake me," Skeeter replied, making his way only as far as the couch in the family room, avoiding the comfort of the bedrooms.

Riley knew it was true. No matter how soundly Skeeter slept, he would be awake and relieving Riley by 2:45 a.m. at the latest.

"Don't want to see you before three, Skeet. I'll send you back to bed."

"Mmmm."

Riley exhaled deeply as he adjusted his goggles. He shook his arms out, then leaned his head first left then right until he heard the pops. *Time to empty the mind and focus.* Picking up his Micro Tavor, he checked his clip, flipped off the safety, and sat down to begin what he prayed would be three hours of absolute nothingness.

SATURDAY, MAY 23, 4:00 P.M. GMT
OVER THE ATLANTIC OCEAN

Where does all that hate come from? Scott asked himself as he set his copy of Vikram Chandra's *Sacred Games* on the seat next to him. He stared out the window at the seemingly endless blanket of clouds far below him. The story was a fictional account of religious riots in Bombay, India, long before the city went through its name and culture transformation to become modernistic Mumbai. Hindus were killing Muslims, and Muslims were killing Hindus.

And it's not just there. In the Balkans, you have Orthodox Christians and Muslims killing each other; in the Middle East, it's Jews and Muslims; in Nigeria, it's Muslims and Christians; in Sri Lanka, it's Hindus and Buddhists.

Growing up in a pluralistic, religious melting pot like America, we don't understand that kind of deep-seated hatred. And that's to our disadvantage, because we end up giving too much benefit of the doubt to those who just want to kill us because we are us.

Scott leaned his head back and closed his eyes.

Lecha Abdalayev kills for money—that's a concept we can at least sort of grasp in our capitalistic culture. So what are the ramifications of his motivation? First, his men are not zealots. One who is not a zealot is more easily broken. Second, it is possible that even Abdalayev may have his price—although judging by his dossier, that's a much longer shot.

A shout and a cheer broke Scott's concentration. He popped his head over the back of his seat to a poker game that had been going on for two hours now. A huge pot had just been taken, and everyone was either congratulating Kim Li or razzing Ted Hummel.

As he scanned the laughing faces, a good feeling spread through Scott's body. Most of the team from the operations following the Platte River Stadium bombing had accepted Jim Hicks's invitation to relocate to Denver to become part of the Front Range Response Team. Only Kyle Arsdale had declined the offer in favor of becoming a cop in his hometown of Albuquerque. Over the past few months, Matt Logan, Kim "Tommy" Li, Jay Kruse, Carlos Guitiérrez, Ted Hummel, Steve Kasay, Chris Johnson, and Gilly Posada had become like family to him—the brothers an only child like him had always longed for.

"Hey, Scott, you want in?" asked Guitiérrez as he shuffled the cards.

"Nah, I'll just watch. I don't have the jing to play with you high rollers."

The group laughed as six hands were dealt out. Scott was bored, but he wasn't in the mood for a game. He was looking for someone to gab with.

He looked past the game and saw Posada in the back row of the C-37A Gulfstream V, reading through Abdalayev's file. Next to him sat a stack of at least six more thick files.

Across the row from Posada was Chris Johnson. Since coming to Denver, Johnson had begun taking courses at the University of Denver's Graduate School of International Studies in hopes of getting his masters in international security. As a result, he rarely was without a book in front of his face—today's fare was *Globalization and War.*

Across the aisle from Scott was Hicks. He had his MacBook out and was examining a map of Prague. *Perfect,* Scott thought with a smile. He leaned across and pointed to an area by the Vltava River. "Hey, I heard there's a place down here by the Charles Bridge that serves a mean stroganoff—you know, the kind with a real sour cream and wine sauce."

"I'll see if I can work it into our agenda," Hicks said without looking up.

"Really?"

"No."

"Come on, what's the fun of going to a country to shoot people if you don't take time to experience the culture? I was thinking we'd go into town, snatch Abdalayev, throw him in the trunk of the car, and then stop by someplace for a big dish of stroganoff or some roast pork and dumplings. We could even grab a box of *kolache* for the trip back."

Hicks shook his head and closed his computer. "Okay, Scott. I know you well enough to realize that you aren't going to let me get any work done. What's up?"

"Nothing really. Just thinking of the motivations behind Abdalayev and people like him. You think you'll be able to turn him?"

"I doubt it. Abdalayev may not be a fanatic, but he's got a lot of hard history behind him. He'll take his silence as a point of honor."

"So what's your plan?"

Hicks put his computer in the seat next to him and stowed his tray into the armrest to give himself room to stretch out. "I'm hoping we can get some of his team. If so, we've got a better shot of getting some information about al-'Aqran. The problem is, we're not even sure whether anyone's with him."

"I'm just hoping that my Russian is good enough for me to talk with these guys. I know my Arabic's not, and I never saw the need to study Chechen. Woulda been nice to have Khadi along." As he talked, Scott stood up to stretch his legs. It had been five hours since they had taken off, and it would be another five before they landed.

"I know it. But we had room for ten, so it was either you or her."

Scott leaned forward into Hicks's row and said quietly, "Tell me the truth, Jim; did you bring me for my skills or for my looks? If it was for my skills, I'll respect your decision. If it was for my looks, then I'll just feel used."

Hicks gave Scott his "shut up, you sick freak" look, then reached to the other seat for his computer. But before he could open it up, Scott began talking again. Hicks set the computer back down.

"Only reason I'd want to still be back there is for Riley and Skeeter. I can't remember the last time I felt so helpless in a situation."

Hicks heaved a sigh. "I've been thinking about them too. I have to tell you, Scott, I still don't know if I agree with you about letting them go rogue. We could have them in a nice, secure building right now."

"Yeah, but like Riley said, other people might be dying instead to draw him out. Besides, could you imagine dealing with them? They'd be a nightmare. And you know they'd find a way out."

Jim chuckled. "They probably would. And then we wouldn't know anything about where they were. No, I guess I don't know what else we could have done differently. Hopefully, if they get in enough trouble, they'll be smart enough to call FRRT so Khadi can send in some backup."

"It's funny. When I told her she was going to be staying behind, reminding her about Riley was the only way I could keep her from running up to your office and chucking a chair through your door."

Hicks rolled his eyes. "Believe me, she was still ticked—and she let me know it."

"Don't sweat it. She's had plenty of time to think it through. I'm sure she's over it by now."

SATURDAY, MAY 23, 10:15 A.M. MDT
DENVER, COLORADO

Let's see, we have a female who has lived in Europe and has excellent language skills and extensive urban ops experience. Then we have a male whose greatest asset seems to be his ability to belch the entire chorus to Michael Jackson's "Billie Jean." So, whom do they choose? Oh yeah, I forgot to mention, Belchy the Clown is best buddies with the boss.

Khadi knew she wasn't being fair. Scott and Hicks would go do their thing, and when they came back everything would be fine between them and her. But for now, it still hurt to be the one left behind.

"Hey, Khadi, I'm sending you something," Evie Cline's voice

called out through the Room of Understanding. "Didn't know if you'd seen it yet."

An envelope popped up on Khadi's computer screen. She double-clicked it, and the message opened. In the right corner of the mast-head was a peace symbol wearing round John Lennon glasses. Below, Khadi read the words *All we are saying . . .* and again wondered what Evie was doing in a job like this.

Turning her attention to the message, Khadi saw that Evie had sent her a link. She clicked it, bringing up the Fox 31 News Web site and a story headlined "Covington Runs for the Hills." Immediately her hackles were raised, and by the time she had finished the article, she was out for blood.

A reporter running a story about Riley's "recuperation trip to Costa Rica" had almost gotten them all killed just over a month ago. *Don't these idiots know that the bad guys read the paper too?*

Seeing that Whitney Walker had written the story, Khadi did a quick search in a database and found her private cell number. She endured four rings, then a pert, happy little message. Khadi's message was not quite so happy.

"Whitney Walker, this is Khadi Faroughi with the Counterterrorism Division of Homeland Security. You have exactly thirty minutes to return this call before I send someone out to pick you up and drop you into an interrogation room." She left the callback number, then hung up the phone and resisted the urge to slam it on her desk.

Bringing back up Evie's e-mail, Khadi hit Reply and typed, "Find out what you can about this bimbo and get back to me." By the time she hit Send, her telephone was ringing. Khadi looked at the number—*Ah, apparently Miss Walker screens her calls.*

"This is Faroughi."

"Miss Faroughi, this is Whitney Walker. What gives you the right to leave threatening messages on my phone? I've a good mind to go to your superior!"

Suspecting that Whitney's indignation was mostly bluster, Khadi tried to keep the upper hand by remaining calm. "While I can't speak to the quality of your mind, I can tell you that my superior would agree with me. Besides, I wasn't threatening you; I was just explaining procedure."

When Whitney responded, Khadi could hear hesitancy in the midst of her outrage. "You have no right to insult me, Miss Faroughi! I am just responding to your request for a phone call. Now what is it you want? I have things to do."

Khadi tried to keep control by counting backward from ten, but, by the time she reached seven, she launched. "You think that was insulting? You haven't even heard the beginning of insulting! I want to know what kind of brainless idiot posts a story that gives the whereabouts of a person who has gone into hiding? You think terrorists don't read the Internet or watch the news? In your great quest to break a story, you very well may have led the people who have been hunting Riley Covington right to his doorstep!"

"Wait a second. I thought I recognized your name. You're Khadi. Riley told me about you."

The use of Riley's first name startled Khadi. "How do you know Riley?" she managed to say.

Whitney's voice was much more gentle now. "We've gotten together for coffee a couple of times—just business, of course."

Of course, thought Khadi, who had seen Whitney's picture on the Fox Web site and had read her bio. "If you really are friends with Riley, that's all the more reason why this story makes no sense."

"I . . . I . . . Khadi, I don't know what to do. Riley swore me to secrecy. Not only that, but I could lose my job—although that's looking very possible right now anyway. You're not the only one upset about the story."

Feelings of competition and of alliance were wrestling for supremacy in Khadi's heart. *Put the jealousy stuff out of your mind right now,* she chastised herself. *This is about Riley, not you!*

"Whitney . . . can I call you Whitney?"

"Of course." There was relief in Whitney's voice at Khadi's new tone.

"Whitney, I would never ask you to break a confidence or divulge a source. However, it feels like you have something you think you should tell me. You need to know that whatever you do tell me, I will do my best to keep it under the strictest guard. You have my promise."

Khadi could hear the other woman breathing. Finally Whitney

said, "Riley asked me to put out that story. He told me he and Scooter were going into the mountains, and he wanted the people who were after him to find them there."

The mispronunciation of Skeeter's name told Khadi that Whitney and Riley weren't too close . . . yet. However, she still felt a twinge of jealousy that Riley would entrust his plan to this woman and not to her. *You were the one who needed some time apart, remember? Deal with regrets later.* "Did he tell you where he was going in the mountains?"

"No. But I'm sure you could figure it out. Riley spoke very highly of you when we were together."

The phrases "spoke very highly of you" and "when we were together" battled in Khadi's heart. "Is there anything else you can tell me?"

"No. I'm sorry, but that's all he said."

"Whitney, I owe you an apology," Khadi said after a pause. "I thought you were using Riley to further your career, but it turns out you were just sacrificing for a friend."

Whitney laughed softly. "It's fine. I have to admit, it feels good to know there is at least one other person who knows why I posted the story. Everyone else thinks I need to either be jailed or loaded on the first plane out of town."

"Well, if things get too bad for you, give me a call. We've got some pretty good resources around here. I'm sure we can find a way to make things better."

"Thanks, Khadi. Riley was right. You do seem to be a pretty terrific woman."

Khadi smiled. "No, thank you. I needed to hear that. I look forward to meeting you sometime."

"Me too. Bye for now."

Khadi hung up the phone, rested her elbows on her desk, and put a fingernail in her mouth. Just as she was about to bite, she remembered that she had given up that habit two years ago. Instead she grabbed a pack of Trident out of her purse and popped a piece into her mouth.

As she chewed away the nervous energy, her mind drifted. *What's Riley doing right now? I wonder if he's thinking about me, or if he even thinks about me at all anymore. And why am I sitting here acting like a stupid little seventh grader with a crush?*

Shaking her head, she pulled her computer keyboard toward her and began the process of finding Riley's hideaway.

TUESDAY, MAY 26, 9:00 P.M. CEST
PRAGUE, CZECH REPUBLIC

Death stood still, his stark bones only partially protected against the elements by the blue cloak draped over his shoulder. In his left hand he held an hourglass. In his right, a bell. Nobody moved as they waited to see what Death would do.

Suddenly, Death raised his right arm and the bell rang out once, twice, three times. The crowd around Scott began to ooh and aah as the bell continued ringing the time and the doors above Death and his three companions—Vanity, the Miser, and the Turk—opened and each of the twelve apostles took his turn blessing the crowd and the city from his place on the amazingly intricate medieval animated astronomical clock.

Eventually, the rooster crowed, the doors closed, and the onlookers dispersed as the chimes sounded out nine o'clock.

Scott faded away with the crowd and returned to his previous perch on the steps of the statue of Jan Hus. Five other members of the ops team were positioned in alley entrances and church doorways at various points around Old Town Square. But Scott's Bohemian look fit in well enough with the ever-present European traveling hostel crowd to allow him to hide out in the open.

The night was perfect—mid-fifties with a fine mist creating arcs around the square's lights. Scott pulled his trench coat tighter around himself, though not tight enough to reveal the outline of the Magpul Masada assault weapon that was pressed against his right side.

This weapon still amazed him. It was lighter than an M16, with a folding stock that made it perfect for concealment. But what really set this weapon apart was its barrel—free-floating for increased accuracy and completely interchangeable. Right now, all the team's Masadas were fitted with AK-47 barrels, which meant that should gunplay erupt, the shell casings would initially lead the Czech authorities in directions other than American special ops.

There was much less hustle and bustle than usual tonight, but there were still plenty of people braving the elements—mostly couples walking arm in arm, being extra careful not to slip on the wet cobblestones. One area remained particularly busy—a constant flow of people went in and out of the restaurants that made up the far side of the square.

Scott's stomach grumbled at him as he watched the Italian restaurant where Lecha Abdalayev and two of his men were having dinner with four members of the Abkhazian government-in-exile. In the window, he saw a pretty young woman using a fork and spoon to twirl pasta heavily coated with some sort of white sauce. *Maybe Abdalayev will bring out a doggy bag.*

Abdalayev's free passage from the Czech authorities was turning out to be both a blessing and a curse. On the plus side, Scott and Hicks knew where their quarry was at all times. On the minus, the man was never isolated enough for the team to safely take him.

The last two nights watching the Chechen had been completely futile, but tonight Scott felt the first rays of hope. Because Abdalayev had chosen to have dinner in the middle of Old Town Square, he had a bit of a walk to get to his car. Also, this was the first night dark enough to allow the team free movement.

The front door of the restaurant opened, and Abdalayev's two companions walked out. They stopped under the awning and lit cigarettes. As they joked back and forth, Scott could see their eyes scanning the square.

"Velvet One, this is Velvet Two. The goons are out. Get ready for movement."

Scott had chosen the call signs for the operation in honor of the Velvet Revolution of 1989, when the Czechoslovakian people had overthrown their communist government without firing a shot. *Gotta give folks like that some serious props.*

"Copy, Velvet Two. Movement imminent," Scott heard Hicks say through his earpiece.

Casually, Scott got up from the stairs and stretched. After taking one last look at the huge statue of the great religious reformer, he slowly walked off in the direction of Abdalayev's car. The dampness that had soaked through his clothes sent chills into his skin as he moved through the square.

"Velvet One, Velvet Six. Party Boy is moving, but Party Host is still on the dance floor." Abdalayev had left the restaurant, but apparently the Abkhazians were still with him.

Not good, Scott thought as he continued walking, giving a wide berth to a group of teens that had circled up with a hacky sack.

"This is Velvet One. If Party Host continues with Party Boy, we're still a go. But Party Host only gets buzzed, not wasted. Repeat, Party Host gets buzzed. Only Party Boy gets wasted. Copy?"

"Velvet Two copies," Scott said, then listened as the rest of the team spoke their affirmations. Hicks had been very clear that although Abdalayev's men could be dealt with as needed, none of the Abkhazians should be killed. They could be hit with the Tasers, but nothing more unless they fired on the team. This had the potential of making things very complicated in the midst of battle, trying to figure out whom to shoot and whom to taze.

Scott ducked into a narrow alley between a flower shop and an art gallery. Abdalayev's car was just around the corner. In his mind Scott pictured everyone's position—Jim was stretched out under some newspapers on a park bench across the street from the car; Posada and Kruse would be coming up the street from the opposite direction; Kasay was tailing Abdalayev, watching him from a distance. The rest of the guys were split into two vans, one here and one waiting on the opposite side of the square in case things went all catawampus.

"Velvet One, Velvet Six," came Kasay's voice. "Party Host is breaking off. Repeat, Party Host is breaking off."

"Copy, Velvet Six. Okay, boys, it's party time."

Scott's heart started racing as the pre-action adrenaline hit his bloodstream full force. He was about to move into the dark depths of the alley when the sound of coarse voices and boots scraping across the cobblestones came right up next to him. *Oh, great, the mist must have muffled their approach.* Instinctively, Scott thrust his hips forward and pretended to urinate against the wall.

The three men spotted Scott as they passed the alley. Turning toward them, Scott locked eyes with Abdalayev. He shrugged his shoulders sheepishly. One of the men said something in their harsh language, and all three laughed. They continued on.

"Velvet Two here. Party Boy's rounding the corner." The relief was evident in Scott's voice. He slid out of the alley and moved up behind the men. As he rounded the corner, shots began to ring out. Two double taps each from Posada and Kruse dropped Abdalayev's driver, who had been waiting for his boss with the car door open.

Instantly, the mercenary's two companions had their pistols out and began returning fire. Abdalayev turned to escape back the way he had come, but Scott came behind him ready to drop him with the Taser. Both men tumbled to the ground. Scott got a handful of the Chechen's shirt, but a fist to his ribs allowed the other man to break his grasp, scramble up, and run.

Jumping to his feet, Scott gave pursuit.

Ahead he saw muzzle flashes and heard more shots. One man dropped, but the other man kept running. *Kasay!* "Velvet One, Velvet Six is down in the square! Repeat, Velvet Six is down in the square," Scott yelled. As he raced past, he could hear Kasay groaning.

Scott was gaining on Abdalayev. Although he wasn't in the best shape, his legs were longer and younger. To his right, toward the restaurants, he could hear people shouting. *Stay where you are, folks! Don't get caught up in this!*

At the far end of the square, the two men passed through an archway and came alongside the massive, Gothic Týn Cathedral. Scott dove for Abdalayev and caught him around the waist. Both men went down hard, their weapons clattering away. Scott pulled himself up Abdalayev's back and began driving his fist into the side of the man's head. But the seasoned veteran had been involved in too many fights to let himself get taken that easily.

Surprising Scott with his strength, Abdalayev rolled himself over. Scott felt a blow to his side that took his breath away. Before he knew what happened, he was flung onto his back, and the Chechen mercenary was on top of him. A fist connected twice with the side of his head. Scott's vision grayed. Something flashed in the lights from the side of the cathedral, and far back in Scott's foggy brain he recognized it as a knife. *So this is the end,* he thought peacefully.

Suddenly, a body flew into Abdalayev. Scott rolled onto his side and saw Hicks drive his rifle butt into the Chechen's face. All the while, Hicks was trying to keep the onlookers back by yelling, *"Policie! Policie!"*—the one Czech word that Scott had taught the team.

A loopy smile spread across Scott's face. *Wow, it's SuperJim,* he thought as the gray faded toward black, *come to save the day. . . .*

TUESDAY, MAY 26, 1:45 P.M. MDT

SILVERTHORNE, COLORADO

Riley trudged through the calf-high grass and thanked God again for his Doc Martens boots. He and Skeeter had too many other things to be on guard for to take the time to examine each other's bodies for ticks.

He had woken up in a foul mood this morning. Today was his dad's funeral. Even now as he walked through the beautiful high country, the bitterness of missing it burned in his throat. *What's Mom feeling? Does she really understand why I'm not there?* Riley missed her desperately. He knew he could never be fully at peace until he heard her say that everything would be all right.

Added to that, June 1 would have been his dad's birthday, and this was about the time he usually started scrambling to find a present. Last year, Riley had driven up to Wheatland to give him his gift in person—a Lincoln clay pigeon trap, fully automatic, with a 320-target capacity. He could still hear his dad's laughter each time the trap adjusted its position. Grandpa had been there too, and the three of them had lost count of how many targets they'd burned through that afternoon. He did know it had taken them a full ten minutes to shovel up the shells.

Riley stopped and squatted low. The day was warm even at this elevation, and Riley took off his cap to wipe his face with his sleeve. Everything was quiet except for the wind blowing through the tops of the sixty-foot lodge pole pines and that stupid dog's barking. Carefully, Riley moved ahead, one slow step after another.

Then he spotted it—a thin wire three inches below the top of the grass. Riley walked to the tree where it was tied off, then followed the wire twenty feet to the M49A1 trip flare. The thing looked like it had been around since the Vietnam era, but beggars couldn't be choosers, and Riley was grateful for what Scott had given them.

Riley slowly backed away from the device, then began the short hike to the next one. On the other side of the property, Skeeter was doing the same thing. It had been four days since they had set the flares, and it was a wonder that some elk or moose or overgrown deer mouse hadn't triggered one of them. *What does that say about the chances of a bad guy triggering one? We've got to look at these as nothing more than lottery tickets—if they hit, great! But we certainly shouldn't be counting on them.*

The breeze cooled his face, and Riley stopped for a moment to relish the feeling. *What would I say if I were at Dad's funeral? That he was a good man? That he taught me everything I know? That I only speak in clichés?*

Think, what would I say? That Dad was a godly man, and through his example he showed me what it means to live a godly life and what it means to truly be a man. Chills rose on Riley's skin, telling him that he had nailed it. *Going to have to tell that to Mom,* he thought, continuing on.

As Riley walked, he felt his cell phone vibrating in his pocket. It was Meg Ricci again. She had been calling at least five times every day, and her messages were becoming more and more frantic. Exasperated, Riley finally took her call.

"Meg, you've got to stop calling."

Riley could hear the relief as the words gushed out. "Riley, it's you! Finally! Are you okay? I was so worried about you. How's your mom? When are you coming back?"

"Meg, listen to me. You have got to stop calling me. I'm in the middle of something really important here."

"Are you in the mountains? I read you were in the mountains. Where are you? Can I help you at all?"

"I can't tell you where I'm at. I really can't tell you anything."

"Of course, of course. That's fine. You and your top secret stuff." Riley thought he could hear irritation in her words. "I've just been so worried about you, and it seems like Alessandra is asking every hour for Uncle Riley. Are you all right up there? Is Skeeter with you?"

"Meg, please, listen. I'm in the middle of what is probably a life-and-death situation. Your calls are not helping matters. Please stop calling. I promise you that when this is all over, you and Aly and I will all go out to dinner or something."

Riley could hear the hurt in Meg's voice when she answered, "Sure, of course. We'll do dinner. I didn't mean to be a pain, Riley. I was just worried about you."

Riley rolled his eyes. "You weren't a pain. You were just being a good friend. I'm just in a weird spot right now."

"No, sure. You just do what you need to do. I'll be waiting for your call. Sorry to have troubled you."

"Meg, that's not what I meant. You didn't do anything . . ." Riley realized that he was talking to dead air. "That's why men become hermits," he said as he thrust his phone back into his pocket. Shaking his head, he continued his search for the next wire.

TUESDAY, MAY 26, 10:15 P.M. CEST
ŽIŽKOV
PRAGUE, CZECH REPUBLIC

Scott felt as if his head were on the rack of a ball return at a bowling alley, and every thirty seconds or so someone bowled another frame. He took a long swig of some brown carbonated drink that Kim Li had given him, then placed his forehead back on the cool Formica table. The only solace he took was that thanks to Hicks's creative use of his gun butt, Abdalayev was probably feeling the same way.

At least everyone lived. That was the best thing Scott could say for the way the operation had gone down. Actually, it was probably more accurate to say that at least everyone from Team Velvet lived. Abdalayev's driver and one of the men with him currently didn't meet the minimum heart rate level needed to sustain life. *I'm sure somebody somewhere will shed a tear for them, but I can't imagine who.*

Scott wasn't the only one hurting in the CIA safe house situated in the largely Romany, or gypsy, district of Žižkov. Steve Kasay was feeling it after taking three rounds to his protective vest, and Jay Kruse had needed to have Carlos Guitiérrez do some fancy needlework on him after getting grazed on the thigh.

But at least they had their man, along with one bonus goon. The two men were awaiting their fates in adjoining bedrooms.

"How you feeling, tough guy?" Scott looked up to see Hicks standing next to him with a smile on his face.

"Like God confused my head with a Wiffle ball."

Hicks laughed. "So, what I want to know is where'd you get that speed? I looked over and all of a sudden you were flying out of there like you had just heard there was a free all-you-can-eat at Wahoo's Fish Tacos."

"Dude, I've got skills you can't even imagine." Pain quickly turned Scott's smile into a grimace. "I'm just glad you showed up when you did."

"Yeah, well . . ."

"Do you know in some Eastern cultures when you save someone's life you must accept that person as your loyal companion for the rest of your days?"

Hicks scowled. "It's a good thing we're not in an Eastern culture, or I'd pull my gun out and finish the job Abdalayev couldn't."

Scott turned his face back to the table. "Right now, my friend, I'd welcome it. So when are we going to talk to Party Boy?"

"Soon as I hear back from Tara on his buddy's identity. I want to know whether he's worth using or if he's just throwaway."

Hicks left to check on the prisoners, and when he did, some of the other guys moved in. Matt Logan congratulated "Jackie Joyner-Ross" on his athletic prowess. Kasay leaned in very close to his ear and said loudly, "We like your version of the rope-a-dope, too! Very Ali-esque!" Kasay's voice sent a painful rumble through the jungle of Scott's muddled brain.

Before Kasay could pull back, Scott's fist launched out, landing solidly on the other man's bruised chest. Kasay cried out in pain.

The guys watching burst out laughing. This was part of the post-op adrenaline cooldown. All that energy was still rushing through their veins, but the only ones they had to take it out on were each other.

"Scott, come here." Scott turned to see Hicks waving him over. Easing himself out of the chair, he crossed the room.

"What's up?"

"Just heard from Tara. That other guy in there is Doku Bakhmadov. It's believed he's number three in the Chechen Freedom Militia."

"In other words, he's probably a guy who knows stuff. Which means—"

"Which means we don't have to put all of our eggs in Abdalayev's basket." Looking over Scott's shoulder, Hicks said, "Hummel, Logan, Li, go help Johnson carry bad guy two into Party Boy's room."

"Yes, sir," the three men said in unison.

"Let's go," Hicks said to Scott, and together they entered the second bedroom. "Stand down," Hicks commanded Gilly Posada, who had been guarding the Chechen with a rifle pointed at his heart.

"Yes, sir," Posada said, moving back but still keeping his weapon at the ready.

There was commotion at the doorway as the four men carried the other prisoner into the room still tied to his chair and cursing. As soon as he saw his commander, though, he shut up.

"Move him right behind Party Boy," Hicks ordered. The men set the chair down on the dusty wood floor three feet behind Abdalayev.

The leader of the militia had seen his better days. His left eye was swollen, and blood from a gash in his forehead had traveled down his face and matted his long beard. When he noticed Scott, he asked in Russian, "How's your head, boy?"

"Looks like it's better than yours, old man," Scott answered back in the same language.

A faint smile of surprise showed on Abdalayev's face. Then, switching to English, he said to Hicks, "So, what brings you to me?"

"Al-'Aqran," Hicks replied.

"Ahh, I should have known," Abdalayev said with a nod. "He's been busy, has he not? He was an angry, bitter old man. Not at all pleasant company."

"Well, then, you shouldn't feel that badly about telling us where you took him."

Abdalayev slowly shook his head. "Tsk-tsk-tsk. Commander . . ."

"Hicks."

"Commander Hicks, you know that is something I cannot do. Even mercenaries need to have their ethics."

This time it was Hicks's turn to shake his head. "Is that your final answer?"

"I'm afraid it must be," Abdalayev said with a resigned smile.

"Too bad," Hicks said as he pulled out his pistol and shot Abdalayev in the head. Blood and brain matter flew onto the militia's number-three man. Bakhmadov cried out. Hicks placed his boot on Abdalayev's chest and tipped his chair back until it fell into the other man's lap.

Keeping his gun leveled at Bakhmadov, he said, "Do you speak English?"

The man looked at Hicks with huge, panicked eyes.

"I said, do you speak English?" Hicks asked again, drawing back the hammer on his gun.

"Little. *Nemnogo.* Little," Bakhmadov blurted out.

"Scott, translate to Russian."

Scott nodded and leaned in close to the man's ear. The smell of fresh blood and flesh churned his stomach.

"You are not the one we are looking for, so I don't care at all what happens to you. Thus, you have two choices: you will either live or you will die." Scott gave a simultaneous translation. "If you choose life, you will walk out of here a free man. If you choose death, I will put away my gun, pull out my knife, and begin working on you until you change your mind. Do you understand your choices?"

Bakhmadov nodded his head vigorously.

"Do you choose life?"

Again an emphatic affirmation.

"Good choice," Hicks said as he holstered his gun. He reached down and pulled his knife out of its boot sheath.

Bakhmadov said something to Scott. "He wants to know if we can move Abdalayev off his lap as a sign of good faith." Scott was really hoping that Hicks would say yes. Abdalayev's sightless, staring eyes gave him the creeps.

"Tell him that the fact that he is still alive is all the good faith he is going to get." Hicks leaned in toward the blood-spattered face of Bakhmadov. "Now, do you have any more questions for me?"

Bakhmadov shook his head. "*Nyet.*"

"Good. Now I'm only going to ask each question once. Give me a wrong answer and I remove a part of your face." To emphasize, Hicks used his knife to flick a little notch in the upper cartilage of the man's ear. "Understand?"

"*Da!*"

"Very good. Now, where did your boss take al-'Aqran?"

Bakhmadov looked at the knife that Hicks now slowly twisted in front of his face and said, "Istanbul. It is where the Cause has made its home."

"Very good, Doku. May I call you Doku?"

The man nodded. Sweat was pouring down his face in red rivers.

"Who hired you, Doku?"

"A Saudi named Hamad Asaf. He works for al-'Aqran."

"Where did you meet to arrange the deal?"

"Beirut. The meeting was arranged through Hezbollah."

Scott's mind started racing, putting together all the connections. But he pulled his focus back when he heard the dangerously passive-aggressive tone of Hicks's voice.

"Hmm, that's very interesting. So, Doku, you know there have been some bad things happening in my country, do you not?"

Bakhmadov nodded his head rapidly. "*Da!*"

"And you've known all along who's responsible for it, correct?"

"*Da,*" the Chechen answered softly.

"You can understand why that would make me very unhappy with you, can you not?" Hicks asked as he slowly scraped the edge of his knife across Bakhmadov's left cheek.

The other man winced. "I am so very sorry, sir."

"I suppose you are," Hicks said, reaching back to wipe the remnants of beard, flesh, and blood from his knife onto Abdalayev's shirt. "So, that's why you're going to tell me if you've heard of anything else that your friends in the Cause have planned."

Bakhmadov winced as Hicks laid the edge of the blade against his right cheek. "Please, sir, the only thing I heard Commander Abdalayev talk about in regards to the Cause was Beslan!"

The word *Beslan* echoed through the room. Immediately, the tip of Hicks's knife was at the mercenary's throat. "What about Beslan? You better tell me everything you know, or I swear I'll slice you apart piece by piece!"

Bakhmadov cried out in fear and pain. "Please! Please! I'll tell you what I know! It isn't going to be like Beslan with the torture of the children. The Cause doesn't have that type of army in your country. Instead, it will be martyrs going into grammar schools and killing as many children as they can!"

"When?" Hicks screamed out. "When?"

"I don't know! I swear to you I don't know!" Bakhmadov's blood was beginning to stream down Hicks's knife.

Hicks spun around and walked to the door. He stood facing it, then suddenly cried out and plunged his knife deep into the wood. For two minutes, Scott stood and watched his friend staring at the door. Finally, Hicks worked his knife out, then walked back to Bakhmadov. There was terror in the other man's eyes.

When Hicks spoke, his voice was again calm. "Now here's the most important question, and I want you to think very, very hard. Do you have any idea where in Istanbul al-'Aqran might be staying?"

"I do not know. I swear to you, sir! I would tell you if I knew! Commander Abdalayev met Hamad Asaf outside the city and made the transfer there! I promise you, it is the truth!"

Hicks slowly brought the knife up to Bakhmadov's face, then tapped his nose twice with the flat of the blade. "You know what, Doku? I believe you. My friend here is going to ask you some more questions. I want you to be as cooperative with him as you were with me, okay?"

Bakhmadov nodded. "Yes, sir."

Hicks leaned in close, and Scott could smell the faint odor of alcohol seeping out of his sweaty pores. He whispered, "Get what you can from him, then call in the CIA and turn this piece of trash over to them."

"Yes, sir," Scott said as Hicks left the room. There was little doubt in Scott's mind that he was making a beeline to the bottle of Jack Daniel's he had stashed away with his gear. Hicks was a troubled soul, and Scott knew that times like this were the reason why.

Unfortunately, there's nothing I can do to help him with his demons right now, Scott thought as he turned back to Bakhmadov. "Now, where were we?"

WEDNESDAY, MAY 27, 10:15 A.M. MDT

SILVERTHORNE, COLORADO

The Micro Tavor assault rifle lay in pieces in front of him, and Riley attacked each element in turn with oil and a brush. Skeeter had been outside for the last half hour examining their defenses. With him were the only two weapons that were not next to Riley waiting to be cleaned.

Right now they're in the linebackers' meeting, Riley thought, visualizing the white room with its narrow tables and big black faux leather chairs. *Simm is probably mouthing off to some rookie about a missed coverage during drills. And Coach Texeira is standing up front helplessly trying to get a word in edgewise.*

Riley laughed quietly at the thought, but just as quickly, the smile left him. *I should be there. Simm is great, but the leadership of the linebacker corps belongs to me. That's another thing they've stolen.*

One of the negatives of spending so much time waiting was all the thinking. And all that thinking was beginning to turn Riley bitter—bitter at the Cause for putting him in this situation, for taking his dad from him, and for keeping him from his mom. But he was also bitter at Scott for actually being able to go out and hunt the bad guys, bitter

at Meg for constantly bugging him and reading more into their relationship than was really there, bitter at Keith Simmons for taking his
leadership role on the Mustangs, bitter at the Mustangs for giving
him a fake injury and sending him packing, bitter at Khadi for . . .
well, for whatever it was that Khadi had done wrong.

Riley put down the barrel of the weapon, picked up the MEPRO
21 red dot sight, and began the polishing process. *I wonder how
Afshin is doing. I hope he and Simm are doing some sort of Bible study
together.* A twinge of jealousy gripped Riley's insides, and he couldn't
help thinking, *Although I should rightfully be the one teaching Simm
about his new faith.* But he knew that was whacked-out thinking, and
he quickly left changing that attitude on God's lap.

A sound caught Riley's ear—a vehicle was coming! Riley rapidly
reassembled the rifle as he had practiced so many times before and
ran to the front window. He saw Skeeter running toward the door.
Riley reached over and opened it for him.

"Stand down! It's okay," Skeeter said, his hand pushing Riley's
barrel toward the floor.

This put Riley more off guard than hearing the vehicle's approach.
"What do you mean it's okay? Who is it? Why didn't I know about
it?" Then a thought struck Riley. "No, Skeeter, don't tell me . . ."

But when the dark blue Suburban turned into the steep driveway,
Riley could see the driver plain as day. Angry now, he wheeled on
Skeeter. "Man, this is so messed up! What do you think you're doing?
Or is that the problem? You finally decided to try thinking and this
is what happened?"

Skeeter looked at Riley with anger in his eyes. "Pach, disagree,
man, but don't disrespect."

That let some of the air out of Riley's emotions. "Yeah, okay,
you're right; that was wrong for me to say. But still, this is just so
messed up!"

So many thoughts and feelings were racing through Riley as he
watched the SUV stop and Khadi slide down off the front seat. She
walked around to the back and lifted the rear gate.

"Well, if you ain't gonna help the lady . . . ," Skeeter said and
walked out the door.

Skeeter gave Khadi a hug, but while she was in his big embrace,

Riley saw her shoot a quick glance toward the door. Anger, excitement, hurt, and hope all swirled through his brain. *Why didn't they tell me? That's the most aggravating part! I feel like they just ran a double reverse on me, and I'm left standing here looking like a fool! Besides, what's she doing here? She's liable to get herself killed.* Then another thought struck him. *Right, and she knows that, and still she came . . . for you, buddy. You know it was for you.*

Riley stood in the doorway watching until the vehicle was unloaded. Khadi came toward the door with an overnight bag over her shoulder. Skeeter was behind her, carrying two assault weapons and a large green duffel bag. As Khadi stopped at the front step and looked up at Riley, an awkward silence ensued with both Riley and Khadi caught up in their own thoughts.

Finally, Riley said, "Oh, hey, let me get your bag for you." He leaned down and slid the bag off Khadi's shoulder. She willingly let him take it. "Come on in," he said as he walked back inside. Khadi and Skeeter followed.

"Nice place," Khadi said, looking around. "Either Keith Simmons has some good taste or some good decorators."

"You know about Keith, huh? I suppose Skeeter told you," Riley said, surprised at his accusatory tone.

"Skeeter didn't tell me anything," Khadi replied defensively.

"Oh, he didn't? Then how did you find us?"

"Come on, Riley, you guys did everything except lay out bread crumbs leading to this place. I just can't believe the Cause hasn't found you yet."

Riley nodded. *Of course Khadi didn't need any help tracking you down. But still . . .* "Then how did Skeeter know you were coming?"

"Well, if we're going to play twenty questions, I called him and told him," Khadi said. "I didn't want you guys firing on me. Skeeter tried to talk me out of it, but I told him I was coming anyway. Then I made him promise not to tell you."

"Why?"

"Why? Because of this right here! Because of the angry phone call I knew I'd get! Because I knew that if you told me you didn't want me here, then there was no way I could bring myself to come!" Khadi paused and took a deep breath. "Because it's easier to apologize than it is to ask permission, okay? So, I'm sorry, Riley. I just . . . I just had to be here."

Looking at her with her head down, Riley wanted nothing more than to wrap his arms around her and tell her that he was thrilled to have her near him, that everything was going to turn out all right. *But everything's not all right, and you can't let yourself fall into that emotional trap again.*

"I *am* glad you're here, Khadi. We don't know how many may be coming at us, and it's always good to have an extra gun."

Khadi looked up at him with a hurt expression that stabbed at his heart. "Another gun . . . right."

"Listen, why don't you stow your stuff in one of the upstairs bedrooms. Then you can come back down and I'll run you through the defenses we've set up."

"Sure, Riley," Khadi said, snatching her bag off the floor. As Khadi ran up the stairs, Riley thought, *This ain't camp, and there's no time here for summer crushes. I don't know what she was expecting when she came up here, but if it was anything other than a military operation, she's sorely mistaken.*

WEDNESDAY, MAY 27, 11:00 A.M. MDT
FRONT RANGE RESPONSE TEAM HEADQUARTERS
DENVER, COLORADO

"Hee-yuk, hee-yuk, hee-yuk. Have a scrum-diddly-deeelicious birthday! Hee-yuk, hee-yuk, hee-yuk. Have a scrum-diddly-deeelicious birthday!"

Tara shook her head. She had only stepped out to the bathroom for three minutes. These guys must have been waiting for their opportunity all morning.

She knew just what they'd done, because they'd done the same thing last week. That time the loop had been Carly Simon singing the chorus of "You're So Vain" over and over. Evie had explained to her later that the guys had pulled the voice module out of a talking Hallmark card, rigged it so that it played over and over, and then hidden it somewhere in Tara's work area. Tara could picture the card this new one had come out of—Goofy sitting in the middle of a huge cake that he had somehow managed to fall into.

"Thank you, guys," Tara called out to the team. "Now, for the love of all things holy, would someone please shut Goofy up?"

Evie stood up from her chair, did some quick work with a lighter, and then brought a chocolate cupcake over with one lit candle in the middle. The whole gang joined in to sing "Happy Birthday." Tara blew out the candle, Evie peeled the clear tape away from under Tara's keyboard and retrieved Goofy's voice, and everyone went back to work.

As Tara got ready to eat her cupcake, she noticed a finger-width swipe taken out of the side of the frosting and knew without a doubt that if she did an analysis she'd find it thick with Gooey's DNA. Unfortunately, the thought of Gooey's DNA on her cupcake made her a little queasy, and she slid the paper plate to the corner of her desk.

This was the last place she wanted to be celebrating her thirtieth. For Tara, special days were all about family, and her mom had been planning on flying her home. Her brothers and sister were going to get together and have a regular Walsh family shindig. Obviously, that never happened.

Tara was touched that the team had remembered—or, probably more accurately, that Evie had remembered and that the guys had gone along with it. They had all been working extremely hard these last weeks—and nonstop ever since they'd gotten the call from Hicks last night.

"Have the team stop all their Washington, D.C., subway stuff," Hicks had said. "I want everyone to focus on all known members and associates of the Cause, starting from the top down. We need a huge break if we're going to find them in Istanbul.

"Also, I want you to reconstruct a trip Hamad Asaf took to Beirut sometime in February or March, along with any ties he might have to Hezbollah. Finally, I want you to look for a chink in the Cause's armor—a nasty habit someone in leadership might have, a disgruntled ex-member, anything you can find that could give us an edge."

The Room of Understanding had been a flurry of activity since then. Tara knew the ops team was on its way to Istanbul. She hoped she had something to give them when they got there.

"Tara, Tara, Tara!" called out Joey Williamson. "I've got a definite maybe here!"

Tara rushed to Williamson's workstation, the other analysts following. On his screen was a Web news page with the masthead of *Al-Ahram Weekly Online*. "Okay, I'm working on Kamal Hejazi—the Egyptian dude. Can't find anything new on him. So I start looking for stuff on his family, and I come up with this." He pointed to a short headline that said, "Medical Student Disappears."

Williamson continued, "Seems this kid is studying to be a doctor at October 6 University—"

"That's the name of the place? What's that all about?" asked Virgil Hernandez.

"Apparently, they named it that since it's located in 6th of October City."

"Gee, that clears it up."

"You're welcome. So this kid is there doing his student thing, then a couple of weeks ago he just disappears. The kicker is, look at the kid's name—Atef Hejazi."

"And . . . ," said Evie.

"And when you look at his private transcript from the university, it shows that his parents are Kamal and . . . and whoever. They don't really care too much about the mother's name."

"Hejazi's a fairly common name," said Tara. "It's not like Smith or Jones, but there are a lot of Hejazis around."

Williamson gave her a "duh" look. "That's why I'm calling it a definite maybe. Besides, I'm not done. Look here: it says that the mother flew back into the country to follow the investigation. What two questions does that bring up?"

Hernandez answered, "What country did she fly in from, and where's Dad?"

"Bingo!"

Tara felt a flush of excitement. She was semi-sold. "Good work, Joey. Let me contact our assets in Cairo and have them find out if this is really the right woman. If so, you just may have found their weak link." As Tara rushed back to her desk she couldn't help thinking that this might turn into a good birthday after all.

THURSDAY, MAY 28, 6:45 P.M. MDT
SILVERTHORNE, COLORADO

Riley leaned over Khadi's shoulder. It was all he could do to put the scent of her hair—a fragrance reminiscent of sipping piña coladas on a Hawaiian beach—out of his mind and focus on the monitor.

Khadi was saying, "You can see here our four quadrants—two at the rear of the cabin and one on each side. Right now it's just set up for standard view, but if you flick this switch here, the cameras switch to night vision."

The blind spots behind and on either side of the cabin had been the biggest concerns for Riley and Skeeter. They had the trip flares set up, as well as motion detectors. But without a visual, they were still flying blind. Skeeter had had the good sense to mention that concern to Khadi before she came up. And Khadi had had the good sense to bring up a duffel bag with a monitor, four cameras, and a lot of cable.

It had taken since yesterday afternoon to finally work all the bugs out of the system, but now the team was able to see all around the cabin. "Excellent, Khadi. Thanks."

Khadi turned to Riley. The proximity of their

faces made it hard for him to hear her words. "So, does that mean you're glad I came?"

There was an earnestness in her eyes that made Riley settle himself back into his chair. He and Khadi had been avoiding any real conversation since she had gotten here. The full impact of missing his dad's funeral on Tuesday had really hit him hard yesterday. That, combined with the ambiguous nature of their relationship, had left both Riley and Khadi walking on eggshells. *Looks like one of those shells is about to crack.* "You know I was glad to see you."

Khadi's humorless chuckle made it clear that she knew no such thing. "You picked a heck of a way to show it."

"Come on, Khadi, you know it's . . . complicated. Any minute now we could be attacked by people wanting to kill me." Glancing at her shoulder, where he knew below the thin, black, cotton T-shirt was an ugly scar less than six months old, he said, "I've already seen you become collateral damage once for helping me out. I'd never forgive myself if that happened again. And then there's that other stuff. . . ." Riley could tell by the way she looked to the floor that she knew exactly what he meant.

"Right, the 'other stuff,'" she said quietly. "You know, if there was one thing I wish I could take back, it would be that 'other stuff.'"

"Yeah, but it's not that easy. Besides, it's more than just what happened at the coffeehouse. It's the whole situation. You deserve more than to spend your life holding on to a relationship that we both know can never be. You know that I am so convinced of my Christianity that I will never change. And you . . ."

Now Khadi looked up and said with simulated bravado, "And I . . . I am a Muslim. It is what I was born; it is what I live; it is what I will die." Khadi shook her head and softened her voice. "I know all that, Riley." Reaching over to take Riley's hand in hers, she continued, "I also know that since I've met you, my life has changed. I'm different—better. I've never met another man like you, a man for whom I'd willingly lay down my life. I guess what I'm saying is that I can't imagine going through life without you being part of it. And . . . I just need to know if you feel the same way."

Riley's heart started racing, and a light sweat broke out on his forehead. He had never had a woman talk to him like this before. *What do I say to her? She is the perfect woman, except . . .*

Is that 'except' really enough to keep us apart? Can I really go on denying my feelings for her? Lord, do You really want us apart? I mean, it's possible that I could be reading Your Word completely wrong, isn't it? Or am I now just trying to find a way to justify what my heart's telling me to do? I just have a hard time believing that You would have brought this incredible woman into my life, only to force me to keep her at arm's length.

Look at her, Riley. This strong woman is placing her life in your hands. What are you going to say to her? Whatever it is, you better make it good, because whatever you decide will probably determine your relationship from here on out.

Riley reached out and lifted Khadi's face. Her damp brown eyes were filled with hope and fear. At that moment, Riley couldn't imagine not staring into those eyes for the rest of his life. He placed his hand on her cheek and said, "Khadi, you know I'm not good at expressing my feelings." He let out a long sigh. "But if anything happens to me up here, you need to know that I . . . I . . . I don't hear the dog."

"What?" Khadi looked totally confused as Riley quickly stood up.

"I don't hear the dog! Come on," he yelled as he grabbed his Tavor and ran toward the front door and Skeeter. "Skeet, what's up with the dog?"

"The thing stopped barking about a minute ago—real abrupt-like."

"The dog is a little under a quarter mile straight out the door, so that puts at least part of the assault team to our front," Khadi said, finally catching up.

As if to confirm Khadi's point, one, two, three trip flares suddenly launched fifty yards from the front of the cabin and shot into the sky.

"Skeeter, go back and make sure the rear of the cabin is locked up. Khadi, see if you can pick up anything on the monitors. Go!"

While Skeeter and Khadi ran off, Riley threw the chair away

from the front window, squatted down, and tried to pick up any movement outside.

6:58 P.M. MDT

Abdullah Muhammad almost lost his step when the ground abruptly slanted. However, he had been over the path he was running so many times now that he was able to catch himself and continue forward.

The last thing he had needed was that dog breaking free and getting mixed up in everything. Putting a silenced round from his sniper rifle into the Rottweiler—that obnoxious creature that had been the bane of his existence for the last four days—had been one of the most satisfying moments since this whole crazy second life had begun. However, he fully expected that satisfaction to be eclipsed in the next ten minutes when he saw Riley Covington stretched out on the ground.

Coming upon a tree to which he had tied a red ribbon, Abdullah cut left. He kept running. Everything was about timing now.

The Cause had been able to give him all the money and weapons he needed. What they couldn't supply him with were more people. "You have shown yourself to be a creative and resourceful warrior. You can figure out how to kidnap one man," they had told him. *Stupid fools! What I needed was cannon fodder to draw fire while I snatched up the football hero.*

Instead, Abdullah had spent three days plotting and planning—trying to find just the right moment to kill the big bodyguard and capture Riley. Unfortunately, the right opportunity had never come, and now the woman was with them. *Well, if capturing Riley for your little propaganda videos was Plan A, unfortunately for you, I have moved on to Plan B—kill them all!*

There was a Plan C, but Abdullah hoped he didn't need to go there. Too much risk and not enough control made that a less desirable option in his mind. *So make this happen! You've been watching; you know their defenses! There may be three of them, but you've got the upper hand! The timing is perfect—twilight, when the shadows are long, making your camouflage most effective and their night vision useless. And*

the plan is perfect—pick them off one by one. This is your day; take it!
Another red ribbon told Abdullah he was fifty yards from the back
of the house. He carefully stepped over the wire for the trip flare and
crouched down. Slowly, he made his approach.

As he neared the tree line, he looked at his watch. *3-2-1-NOW!*
On the opposite side of the property from where he waited, an alarm
clock told a small motor to begin whirring. The motor was nailed
to a tree and had a narrow metal rod sticking out from it. The rod
began to spin, taking up the slack on three thin wires. As the wires
grew taut, they pulled the trip lines that they had been attached to,
sending three flares up into the evening sky.

As soon as they launched, Abdullah ran forward toward the back
of the cabin. He had one chance to get this right. As he reached the
rear deck, he pulled the pin on an incendiary grenade and threw it
through the kitchen window. He bolted back to the tree line, then
made his way around to the front—to the perfect hiding place from
which he could drop the inhabitants of the house one at a time as
they escaped the soon-to-be-burning cabin.

7:03 P.M. MDT

Riley heard breaking glass from the rear of the cabin. Skeeter yelled,
"Willy Pete!" Then he cried out in pain. Instantly, Riley was up and
running toward the kitchen.

"Khadi, cover the front!"

"Willy Pete? Who's Willy Pete?" Khadi asked as the two passed.

Riley kept moving but called out, "It's a white phosphorus grenade! It means that this cabin is going to be in flames in about ten
minutes at the most!" Riley was all too familiar with white phosphorus, an agent useful because of its incredible ability to burn, from
his time in the military. He knew the moment the WP contacted air,
the chemicals would burn at 5000 degrees Fahrenheit, igniting and
melting through anything it came into contact with.

Riley was almost at the kitchen when Skeeter came running out.
He was holding his smoking left arm out in front of him. "Pach!"
he called.

Instinctively, Riley pulled his long knife out of its belt sheath.

He grabbed Skeeter's arm and slammed it down on the dining table. In the middle of the man's dark forearm Riley spotted what he was afraid he'd find—a glowing dime-sized hole with smoke spiraling out of it. "Hold on," he said to Skeeter as he took his knife and sliced a three-inch chunk of flesh out of his friend's arm.

"Argh!" Skeeter swung with his other hand, shattering the back of a dining chair.

Riley closely examined where he had pulled the deep plug out of Skeeter's skin, looking for smoke. He knew that if any of the WP was still in there, it would continue burning all the way through the bone.

Satisfied, he said, "Sorry, bro," as he snatched a cream-colored fabric placemat off the table and tied it around Skeeter's arm. The blood immediately soaked through.

Riley could smell the hot, dense smoke of the WP that was starting to fill the cabin, but the cloud was beginning to take on a new odor—burning wood. He didn't dare go look at what was happening in the kitchen—one look at the bright glare of the shell could permanently damage his retinas. The only escape was out the front of the cabin. He took hold of his friend's sweating face and said, "Focus, man! You in the game?"

Skeeter's eyes suddenly narrowed, and Riley could see the anger in them.

Riley gave him a slap on the cheek and said, "Let's do this!" The two men ran together to the front of the house.

Abdullah used a rope to pull himself into the tree. Once up, he settled into a crook between two large branches. His sniper rifle was strapped to his back. He pulled it off and pressed his eye to the scope.

Scanning the cabin, he could see smoke beginning to pour from the rear windows to his left. However, there was still no sign of movement to the front. *They'll come; just be patient. They don't have another option.*

Suddenly, the front door swung open. Abdullah's trigger finger twitched, but he stopped himself from pulling back. Then the windows from the rooms on either side of the door shattered. The front door was right in the middle of the crosshairs on Abdullah's sight. *What are you doing, Covington? Come on, let me see your face. I've got a little present for you—your girlfriend and your houseboy, too. You know you've got to come out, so just—*

A shape flashed across his sight. He pulled the trigger but saw only wood from the doorframe splinter. Immediately, gunfire fanned from the two windows, but Abdullah didn't worry about it. He knew he was too high and at too extreme an angle to get hit by the cover fire.

Looking up from his sight, he saw Riley running full speed up the steep incline of the driveway. Cursing, Abdullah spun the rifle to the right and began firing. Riley dove to the ground, rolled, and then popped back up and continued his flight. Abdullah could see his shots kicking up asphalt and dirt as Riley juked and dodged his way to the dirt road and into the woods beyond.

No! It wasn't supposed to happen this way! Abdullah thought as he slid down the rope and onto the ground. His M16A4 was propped against a tree. He grabbed it and began running along a path parallel to Riley's, still keeping himself well inside the woods. *Well, not to worry. This is how I wanted it from the beginning. It's one-on-one now, Covington, and you are overmatched!*

7:10 P.M. MDT

The last time Riley could remember running this fast was after an interception against the Bay Area Bandits. Unfortunately, the enemy now was much more dangerous than some adrenaline-hyped fullback. *Where's the bullet going to hit? Will it be a body shot, so I can feel my insides scrambling? Or maybe a leg, dropping me so someone can come up and finish me off at close range?*

While those thoughts were going through his brain, the same words were coming out of his mouth over and over again: "Lord, help me! Lord, help me! Lord, help me! Lord, help me!"

Khadi and Skeeter had fought his plan. "It's a suicide mission and you know it!" Khadi had argued.

"Man, you don't even know where the *hajjis* are. You could be running right into them," Skeeter pointed out.

"That's if you even make it that far! Right now, every gun is pointed right at this door. They're just waiting for us to come out."

"That's what's going to make this work," Riley said, sounding confident, but only half-believing his words. But the phrase "Greater love has no one than this, that he lay down his life for his friends" kept running through his mind, and he knew he had no choice. *Lord, take me if You have to,* he had prayed, *just let me save my friends.* "They're expecting us to come straight out, guns blazing! But if you guys give cover fire while I go out full-bore on a diagonal, I just might make it to the woods."

"'Just might' is not good enough," Khadi had said.

"It's the best we have. Listen, Khadi, in ten minutes this whole cabin will be burning. I'm not thrilled about this. But I'm the one they want. If they see me go, hopefully they'll come after me. That gives you two a fighting chance of getting out of this. If we just do what they're expecting, I think we're all dead." Turning to Skeeter, Riley said, "You understand me, don't you?"

Skeeter nodded his agreement, but there was still rage in his eyes. "Yeah, I hear you."

Riley turned back to Khadi. "I've made my decision. It's how it's going to be." Then he put his hand around the back of Khadi's neck. "I'm going to make it, Khadi. I have to; we've got a conversation we need to finish."

Thirty seconds later, Riley was running out the front door into the great unknown. *What was I thinking?* he asked himself now as he jumped a fallen tree. Once he made it into the woods, he realized he had no idea where he was going; all he knew was that he was trying to get there fast.

Truth be known, he hadn't really expected to make it this far. Any moment now he expected to see some Middle Eastern guy jump from behind a rock or an old tree stump and finish him off. But so far there was no one.

Just as he was feeling like his plan might work after all and he could disappear into the trees, his foot caught something and he flew to the ground. Fifteen feet to his right, a flare shot into the air. "Oh, come on! What are the odds?" he said disgustedly as he jumped up and began running again.

Suddenly, wood from the trees around him began splintering up into his face. He could feel blood beginning to trickle down below his right ear. "Lord, help me!"

7:12 P.M. MDT

Just when Abdullah thought he had lost Riley, the flare went off. A smile spread across the assassin's face. He cut left and soon saw his quarry. Having abandoned his rifle back at the tree, Abdullah let loose with his assault weapon. Covington kept running.

They were going downhill now, both trying to keep their footing while running full-speed. Every ten seconds or so, Abdullah let off another burst. *If I could just get him on level ground!* The rough terrain was causing him to shake so much that he knew he could never hope to catch Riley with anything but a lucky shot. Time passed, and still Covington kept running.

Up ahead through the trees, Abdullah could see they were coming to another dirt road. *Perfect! That'll give me a flat place to stop and get a clean shot in.*

But then Riley did something unexpected. He burst through the tree line, jumped feetfirst as he reached the other side of the road, spun, and opened fire. Abdullah dove for a tree, hitting it with the full force of his speeding body. Something snapped in his side. More bullets whistled around him, forcing him to lie flat. When the firing stopped, he looked up to see Riley back on his feet and running away.

No! Abdullah tried to get up, but his broken ribs weren't the only damage. Pain screamed from his right calf, and when he looked down he could see blood soaking through his pant leg. He again tried to get up, but then dropped himself. Pine needles poked the back of his neck, and the scent of earth filled his senses. *Conserve your energy,* he thought. *You've got a long hike ahead to your car. You'll still get him. Remember, there's always Plan C.*

Reaching into his pocket, Abdullah pulled out an orange prescription bottle and dropped six Percocets into his mouth. *Just ride the wave. Soon enough, you'll be good to go.* Abdullah lay back while his brain turned off his pain sensors one by one. Soon he was asleep.

7:32 P.M. MDT

Riley ran for another ten minutes before he finally allowed himself to believe that nobody was following. Stopping, he leaned his body against a tree, gasping for breath. His lungs could feel every inch of the 9,000-foot elevation, and his muscles were screaming out in protest. He tried to walk off the cramps that were setting in, but his legs gave out from under him.

He lay on the rocky dirt, sucking deeply for air.

He assumed Skeeter and Khadi were all right. He hadn't heard any gunfire other than what had been fired at him. *Who would have believed that stupid plan would actually work?* He smiled weakly as he watched the sun dip below one of the high peaks. The sweat evaporating from his body reminded him that with the setting sun would come falling temperatures. Mustering all his strength, he pulled himself to his feet with the help of a nearby aspen.

He took one step, then another, then another. And soon he was slowly moving down the hill. *Downhill's the way to go,* he thought. *If I keep going down, I'll run into Silverthorne or Dillon Lake or something familiar. If I can find either one of those, I'll find safety and Skeeter and Khadi. . . . Yeah, and Khadi.*

Check another city off your "places I want to visit before I die" list, thought a frustrated Scott. Istanbul was one of those mystical spots that he had always dreamed of experiencing—the history, the architecture, the smells, the foods. He wanted to mingle with the people, drink their coffee, smoke a hookah, whirl with a dervish or two.

Instead, here he was in the middle of this ancient city, and the closest he'd probably get to the Hagia Sophia or the Grand Bazaar would be a postcard from one of the hundreds of kids selling them on the street. *Sort of like the way you experienced Prague. That was quite a fun little vacation,* he mused bitterly. Since that trip, he had been forced to change from sleeping on his left side to his right just so he could put his head down on the pillow.

This was the team's second night staking out mosques. The questioning of Kamal Hejazi's wife down in Cairo had been very profitable—particularly when she had been promised a new life in the United States for herself, her three remaining children, and her parents. Kamal had not been a very nice man, and his widow was convinced his activities were responsible for whatever had happened to her firstborn son.

She had told the CIA operative that Kamal had several times walked home with al-'Aqran following the *'Asr* prayers at a nearby mosque. Apparently, the old man was very faithful about his *'Asr* attendance and usually used the journeys to and from as opportunities to discuss business.

Scott shifted on the vinyl seats to try to get the blood flowing to his nether regions again. The air in the early '90s Mazda 323 hatchback was stifling, and by the looks of it, the air-conditioning hadn't worked since the turn of the millennium.

"Ugh," he said as he took a long pull from a glass bottle of warm Coke. He looked at his watch again. *'Asr is the late afternoon prayer, which means that in the next few minutes, somewhere in this huge metropolis, al-'Aqran will be walking out of one of the city's three thousand mosques—yes, that's a three with three zeros, folks!* That was another discouraging little factoid he had read about the former Constantinople, née Byzantium. Apparently the government was very adamant that Istanbul should be a Muslim city, so they had started putting up mosques everywhere. Half of the new mosques weren't even used. *Unfortunately, we have no clue which half, thus our chances of finding the right mosque hover just above an old-fashioned crapshoot.*

However, Mrs. Hejazi had given one more piece of information that narrowed the odds considerably. Her family had lived in the Eminönü district of the larger metropolis—the "old city" area on the west side of the Bosporus. Sometimes, after leaving a meeting with the leaders of the Cause, Kamal would call her on the cell phone to vent his anger. Whenever he called, she knew that she had a maximum of fifteen minutes to have his favorite food and drink ready for him before he walked in the door. Otherwise, he took his anger out on her in more physical ways.

When they had first arrived two nights ago, Scott and Jim had pulled out a map and determined how far a person could walk in fifteen minutes. Then they had drawn a wide circle around the Hejazi house—a circle that had extended to the edges of Eminönü, the neighboring Fatih district, and the Beyo lu district located directly across the inlet of water known as the Golden Horn.

Just like that, the three thousand mosques had been narrowed to 112—a formidable, but not impossible, number for the ten members of the team, along with the six CIA agents who had offered their eyes but not their guns for the operation.

Surprisingly, the CIA guys had been great. They had helped get the team acclimated right from the time of their arrival at Izmir Air Base, a three-hundred-mile drive south of Istanbul. A safe house had been prepared for the team, and the agents had provided vehicles, maps, and all the intel they could divulge.

Later that first night, over some bottles of Efes Pilsen, two of the CIA agents told about how they had graduated with four of the guys who had been killed when al-'Aqran had broken out of prison. All six of the men were looking for revenge, and they were counting on Hicks and Scott to do the job their superiors wouldn't allow them to do. *A little bit more time with these guys, and I'll have to change my opinion of CIA spooks.*

A knock on his passenger window almost made Scott lose all the warm Coke he had already drunk. He resisted reaching for the weapon he had tucked between the seats as he turned to look who it was. Immediately, he recognized the white-bearded man who had been sitting at the door of the shop Scott was parked in front of. The man was yelling something at him and waving his arms. Although Scott's Turkish was limited, it wasn't difficult to get the gist. This shop owner was tired of having Scott taking up his prime street-access real estate.

Scott waved without bothering to roll down the window, started the car, and moved up a couple of spots, making sure there was no angry old guy sitting in front of the shoe repair shop whose street parking he now occupied. *Good job keeping control. Pulling your weapon would not have been a good thing.*

Everyone had been on edge since the plans for the school attacks had been revealed. The possibility of a large-scale slaughter of innocent children and the ensuing societal and economic ramifications was difficult to even comprehend. Wholesale panic would combine with a passionate desire for revenge to create a perfect storm of anti-Arab backlash. Once that happened, who knew what the global impact would be.

At first when Hicks and Scott were discussing the possible attacks, they had thought that the Cause was committing a major blunder by planning school attacks during the summer. But then Gilly Posada, who had an elementary-aged son, had informed them of the school track system. In many schools across the country, the population of students had outgrown the available classroom space. As a result, the kids were divided into four tracks, each with a different school calendar. This meant that at any given time throughout the year, many elementary schools still ran at full capacity.

Hicks had contacted his superiors at Homeland Security, who were now trying to get warnings out to schools without causing hysteria. The safeguards at most elementary schools were so lax, it would be no problem for a gunman to enter and begin shooting. And even if there was an armed guard, most school district security personnel were not trained to handle a terrorist with an assault weapon. *Please, God, if You're really out there, help us stop this thing from happening!* Not for the first time, Scott wished he had the same kind of faith that Riley Covington had.

The doors across the street from Scott's car burst open. His fingers began drumming nervously on the cracked dashboard. He had parked his car on Ordu Cadessi in the Aksaray neighborhood of the Fatih district. Kitty-corner from him was the main entrance to the Pertevniyal Valide Sultan Mosque. The mosque itself was an enormous structure flanked by two tall minarets. Now prayer time was over, and people began streaming out of the front exit.

From the moment Scott had pulled up, the mosque felt right to him. It was nearly two centuries old—not one of the countless new buildings hastily constructed during the past three decades. Yet it also wasn't one of the really popular old tourist mosques, like the Blue Mosque or the Yeni Cami. *The New Mosque—a strange name for a four-hundred-year-old structure.*

But as the worshipers flowed out onto the street, Scott knew he was in the wrong place. *What is it? Think! It's not location. It's not architecture. What's bugging you?*

It's the people. They're too . . . urban. No, that's not right. They're too . . . comfortable? Well-off? Maybe that's it. Al-'Aqran has spent his life living from foxhole to foxhole. He's not going to hang around with the wealthy or the beautiful people. So where else? There's Sulukule, with its poor Gypsy population. But I've got to think that observing their coarse lifestyle would get on his nerves or at least offend his sensibilities. Balat? Right income level, but its Jewish roots would probably turn him off. Zeyrek? Maybe Zeyrek. Old buildings and ramshackle wooden houses. Perfect camouflage for an ugly, old, one-eyed man. What do we have going on in . . . ?

Johnson! He's in Zeyrek at the Eski Imaret Mosque. It fits perfectly—a thousand years old, run-down neighborhood, and to top it off, it started out as an Eastern Orthodox Church, which is pretty symbolic for the vision al-'Aqran has for the world. Gotta warn the boy!

But before he had a chance to speak, Chris Johnson's voice rang in his ear. "Velvet One, this is Velvet Eight. I've got a visual on Scorpion." Scott had decided for this operation to name al-'Aqran after the English translation of his name—the Scorpion.

"Velvet Eight, Velvet One," Hicks's voice replied. "Are you sure?"

"I never forget a face, especially one this mama-beatin' ugly. It's him." When the team had taken al-'Aqran into custody five months ago, Johnson had endured plenty of shifts guarding the man. Scott was sure of his ID.

"Velvet One, Velvet Eight. Ready to plant the dot."

"This is Velvet One. Do it and be careful, son."

"Velvet Two here," Scott broke in. "Give yourself a once-over. You sure you're still fully *hajji*-fied?" The CIA boys had given each of them very detailed disguises, but Scott was still extremely nervous about any of the team getting close enough to al-'Aqran to plant a GPS signaling dot on him.

"Dude, my mama wouldn't even know who I am."

"Lucky woman," Kim Li said from his position over in Horhor.

"Velvet One, radio discipline, boys."

Leave it to Jim to spoil good banter.

"Velvet One, Velvet Eight. I'm going in."

5:44 P.M. EEST

"Am I surrounded by fools? Must I get on a plane and go do everything myself? Tell me, you two, how am I to lead us in carrying

out the will of Allah if I can't get anyone to simply do what I ask?"
The loss of the warrior in the Washington, D.C., subway attack had
been a minor irritation. *Insha'Allah, it happens.* But the capture of
the Yamani girl and now the failure of the policeman to kill Riley
Covington were more than al-'Aqran could take.

On the old man's left side walked his young, trusted bodyguard,
Babrak Zahir—the tip of his spear, and the future of the Cause. On
his other side was Hamad Asaf—a friend for more years than he
could remember but lately struggling to accomplish even the most
basic of tasks. Each remained close to protect their leader from the
crowds of passing pedestrians. Al-'Aqran stopped suddenly, causing
Asaf to have to step back to avoid tripping.

"You must take care, my dear old friend," al-'Aqran said as he
examined a deep purple eggplant from a street vendor's cart. "It
seems your footing is getting a little more shaky of late."

Asaf nodded. "I am sorry, *sayyid.*" The three men began walking
again, ignoring the voices of the proprietors beckoning them from
the small shops they passed. "Our asset on Riley Covington says that
he has a foolproof plan he has been formulating. Covington will be
dead in forty-eight hours at the latest."

"Don't talk to me about foolproof plans," al-'Aqran said loudly,
striking the pavement hard with his walking stick. "Every one of his
plans was supposed to have been foolproof, but somehow Covington
still seems to keep besting the *fool's* plans! We will give this *asset* one
more chance. If he fails again, we will send Babrak over there to finish Covington and him."

"Yes, *sayyid.*"

As they continued to weave their way through the crowded
streets, al-'Aqran said, "Hamad, what is the schedule for the missions to the schools? You said that they are ready to go. Give me a
timeline."

Out of the corner of his eye, al-'Aqran watched as Asaf carefully
weighed out his words. *Either he is sufficiently scared of me, or he is
going to try to bluff. And if I catch him in a bluff, it will be the end of a
good, long friendship.*

Finally, Asaf answered, "A timeline is hard to give, *sayyid.* As I
told you before, we have everything ready to go. We are waiting right

now on the perfect timing. We are confirming that our target schools will all be full for our time of attack. Once we have that information, we will set a date, then wake our sleepers."

"Tomorrow," al-'Aqran said.

"What?" an alarmed Asaf responded.

"Tomorrow you will wake the sleepers. Tell them that the attack is set for a week from today. You have told me that everything is in place. Make it happen."

"But—"

"*Make it happen!*"

"Yes, *sayyid*, it will happen," Asaf acquiesced.

"See that it does," al-'Aqran threatened, "or else you and I will—"

Seemingly out of nowhere, a man bumped into al-'Aqran, almost knocking him over. The stranger reached out for the old man, catching him before he fell. "I'm sorry. I'm sorry," he kept saying over and over in Turkish.

Zahir grabbed the offender and roughly pulled him away. "Get your hands off him! What is the matter with you? I have a good mind to beat you in the street like the dog you are!"

The crowd had opened up, and Zahir was violently pushing the man when al-'Aqran called out, "Leave him alone, Babrak. He's . . ." There was something about the stranger that made the old man pause—a familiarity that seemed to shout from the deep recesses of his mind, though not loudly enough to be clearly heard. "He's apologized. Go in peace, friend."

Al-'Aqran watched as the man hurried off, disappearing into the mass of people that seemed to swallow him up. "Babrak," he said to the young man, "I have something I'd like you to do."

5:51 P.M. EEST

The tension was almost unbearable as Scott listened to the action on his earpiece. His leg was bouncing so violently from nervous energy that the whole car began squeaking. Scott closed his eyes when the contact was made—Johnson repeating "*Özür dilerim, özür dilerim*"— the Turkish words for "I'm sorry"—over and over. The sound of the confrontation filled Scott's head, and he visualized the action. An

Arabic voice began shouting at Johnson: "hands off . . . beat you . . . like the dog you are." Scott's Arabic wasn't good enough to accurately follow along. Then al-'Aqran spoke—there was no mistaking whose voice that was.

Finally, it was done. Scott began to relax.

Thirty seconds later, Johnson said, "Velvet One, Velvet Eight. The dot is planted. I'm just doubling around to my car, then I'll—*oomph*!"

Scott's eyes opened wide as the sound of a scuffle assaulted his ear. But as he listened, it began sounding less and less like a scuffle and more like a beating—and Johnson was definitely getting the bad end of it.

A voice sounded in the earpiece. Scott recognized it as the same one that had been screaming at Johnson earlier. At first the man yelled in Arabic, then Turkish, then, finally, heavily accented English, "Who are you?"

Johnson kept saying, "*Özür dilerim, özür dilerim!*" But the words sounded slurred now.

"Tell me who you are! Tell me!"

There was pleading now in Johnson's voice. "*Özür dilerim, özür—*"

The words were cut off by the other man growling something in Arabic. Johnson cried out; then Scott heard a sound that chilled him to the bone and would return to him every night for the next six months as he closed his eyes to sleep—a low, wet gurgling that lasted for about forty-five seconds. After that, there was only silence.

FRIDAY, MAY 29, 10:14 A.M. MDT
FRONT RANGE RESPONSE TEAM
   HEADQUARTERS
DENVER, COLORADO

"Thanks, Tara. And thank Evie for me too," Riley
said. He and Tara Walsh were walking through
the full parking lot outside of the building that
housed the FRRT. It wasn't until after returning
to Denver that Riley had realized his Yukon was
still up in the mountains. Driving a government-
issue vehicle was a good way to place a target on
his back, so Khadi had called the team of analysts.
All of them had quickly offered up their vehicles
for Riley's use—all except for Gooey, who for some
reason considered his 1986 Toyota Tercel hatchback a "classic."

   "Anything we can do to help—seriously." Tara
spoke with a smile, but Riley could see that any
happiness she may have been showing was forced.
"Are you doing okay, Riley? Khadi said you spent
the night in the woods."

   Last night had been miserable. He had hiked
at least six miles in the dark, and his face and arms
were covered with irritating little scratches from
low-hanging branches. At 3:00 a.m., when Riley
had finally met up with Khadi and Skeeter at a

trail lot by Dillon Lake, the joyous reunion had been brief. Skeeter had lost a lot of blood but had refused to go to a hospital until Riley was found. The ride down the mountain had been mostly silent with Khadi driving the Suburban, Riley nodding off in the passenger seat, and Skeeter stretched out in the back.

"Yeah, it was a longer hike than I thought. But I'm fine—no permanent damage."

Tara nodded.

It's either work or personal that's got her down, and if it's work, I want to know about it. Riley decided to go fishing a bit. "So, what do you guys in the Room of Understanding hear from Scott and Jim?"

Tara stopped and placed her elbow on the roof of a bright yellow Volkswagen Beetle. She took a deep breath. When Riley saw water form in her eyes, he began getting very nervous. "What's happened? Is it Scott?"

"No," she said with a wave of her hand. "Scott's okay—he's invincible. It's . . . I can't, Riley. You're not cleared for any of this. It's a breach of protocol."

"Listen, Tara, I don't want you to compromise any of your oaths. But given all that's going on, if Jim were here, what do you think he would say?"

"No, you're right, you're right! Jim's certainly one who believes in situational ethics." Tara took another deep breath. "Chris Johnson is dead. His . . . his throat was cut."

"Oh, man," Riley said, leaning against an SUV. His mind immediately flashed to a time when he and Johnson had gotten into a lighthearted argument about which was the best album by The Cars—the eponymous first one or *Candy-O*. Riley had really enjoyed the conversations he'd had with Johnson. The man had struck him as very intelligent, very well read.

Then he remembered something else, and Tara's mood made perfect sense. Scott had told Riley that there was the beginning of an office romance forming between the lead analyst and the very intelligent ops man. Scott, who for a long time had harbored an interest in Tara but considered her out of his league, had tried his best to mask his jealousy.

Reaching out his hand to Tara's shoulder, Riley said, "I'm so sorry, Tara. He was a good man."

"Of course he was a good man, but it always seems that the good ones are the first to go," she replied brusquely. She didn't pull away from his touch, but she didn't move closer either.

"I know. Trust me, I know."

"I know you do, Riley." Tara finally moved into Riley's embrace. She let out two sobs, then breathed in deeply to get control. "I just keep picturing him bleeding to death, alone, in some dirty alley in Istanbul."

Istanbul? How in the world did they end up in Istanbul? "Were they able to recover . . . ?"

Tara stepped back from Riley and returned to her place against the yellow Beetle. She tried her best to regain her professional air. "No, the police had surrounded the scene by the time anyone got there. Now the State Department is up in arms. It won't be long now until heads start rolling. Jim figures that in about twelve hours he and Scott will be taken into custody by their CIA contacts."

"Twelve hours? Is that enough time to get al-'Aqran?"

"Jim seems to think so. His words were, 'Al-'Aqran will be getting the grand tour of hell before you sit down to lunch.'"

Riley looked at his watch. *Lord, please protect these men as they go into battle against evil,* he prayed as he did the time calculations in his brain. "Thanks for filling me in. It sounds like a lot of stuff is happening, so I don't want to keep you. If you can just point me in the direction of the car, I'll let you get back to it."

"Oh, sorry. You wouldn't know. This is it," Tara said, stepping away from the Volkswagen.

"It is?"

"We figured, give Riley the one car that no one will be expecting him to drive."

Riley looked over the sunflower yellow Beetle with flower decals on the doors and a Free Tibet sticker in the back window. "I can honestly say you found it."

Tara handed Riley a set of keys hanging from a large peace symbol keychain with the bottom rim broken out so that, by holding it with the spikes positioned between her fingers, Evie could use it as a weapon to defend herself. "Evie said that she was sorry that the gas tank is so low, and she also recommended that you occasionally talk to the car for better gas mileage."

"I'll take that under advisement," Riley said as he used the key fob to unlock the doors. "Thanks again, Tara. Please let me know if there is anything I can do for you or for Chris's family."

"I will. But for now, you just worry about yourself." She turned to walk away, and Riley opened the car door. But just before he got in, Tara spun back around. "By the way, Riley, Khadi told me what you did up at the cabin—running right into the gunfire. That was either incredibly brave or insanely stupid."

Riley shrugged his shoulders. "Honestly? I'm beginning to think there's not much difference between the two."

Tara looked at him for a moment and then nodded. "Take care of yourself, Riley," she said and walked away.

7:20 P.M. EEST
ISTANBUL, TURKEY

"Who was he?" Al-'Aqran stood at the kitchen table surrounded by a hastily called meeting of his leadership team. "If you want me to leave with you—to run away from this man—I demand to know who he was!"

"But, *sayyid*, you were the one who recognized him," his friend Arshad Hushimi said. "Can you not tell us the identity of the man?"

"Are you not listening to me? I said I thought I had seen his face before. It would have been nice to be able to question him, but young Babrak's hastiness removed that option." He glared at the younger man, who refused to return his gaze.

Hamad Asaf spoke up from the seat to al-'Aqran's right. "If you will forgive me, *sayyid*. Perhaps we are asking the wrong question. Maybe instead of asking *who* bumped into you, we should be asking *why*."

"Finally, my friend, someone who is thinking," al-'Aqran said with satisfaction as he returned to his seat. "The rest of you, answer the man's question."

Hushimi answered first. "It seems that he was not trying to harm you. You yourself said he kept you from falling."

"I believe he was probably trying to steal from you," said Tahir Talib. "It is a common technique."

"Exactly," chimed in Hushimi. "Could he have been one of those piece-of-garbage, pickpocket Sulukule gypsies?"

Al-'Aqran shook his head violently. "What do I know of Sulukule and its gypsies? Besides, what do I have to steal? Think, you mules!"

Asaf broke the silence at the table. "If he was not taking from you, then maybe he was leaving something with you."

"Such as . . . ?"

Suddenly Asaf jumped to his feet. He began reaching into the old man's pockets.

Al-'Aqran tried to swat his hands away. "What are you doing, you fool?"

"I'm checking you for a tracker or a transmitter," he said, now running his hands up and down the long garment.

Babrak Zahir left the table and ran onto the balcony to look at the street, then quickly ran back in. He called as he passed, "Forget your searching. If they planted something on you, you will not find it. It will be too small."

At that moment, everything fell into place for al-'Aqran. He pushed Asaf away. "That face, those eyes—he was one of the men guarding me in Italy. A second group of soldiers showed up after I had been taken. He was one of them. I remember when he watched me, it seemed he never blinked."

"The Americans are here?" There was panic in Talib's voice.

A sound from outside caught al-'Aqran's ear. "Stop! I heard something," he yelled. But the sound didn't return.

"Quick—we don't have time to listen for phantoms," Zahir said, running for the sofa and the weapons that were laid on the floor behind it. "You must strip out of those clothes; then we have to get out of here! Talib, quit whimpering like an old woman and get *sayyid* a new set of clothing! You," he commanded, pointing to Hushimi, "help him get dressed."

Just as Zahir reached the couch, the front door burst open.

Al-'Aqran watched his young protégé almost put a bullet through the head of the neighbor boy. The boy cried out.

"Why are you here?" Zahir yelled, walking toward him but still not lowering his gun. "Answer me! Why are you here?" He grabbed the boy roughly by the neck.

The boy was trembling, and tears began to stream down his face. "I'm sorry! *Sayyid* asked me to tell him if strangers ever came around." The boy turned toward al-'Aqran. "I was on my balcony! They're here!"

"They're here? Who's here?" But before the boy could answer, the veteran of many battles realized what the sound he had heard a moment ago was. It was the familiar clicking of sound-suppressed gunfire. A grim smile spread across his face. "The Americans."

FRIDAY, MAY 29, 10:22 A.M. MDT
DENVER, COLORADO

Riley put the key into the ignition and cranked the starter. Immediately, his ears were assaulted by music at a volume that had to be pushing the capabilities of the car's standard-issue speakers. Fingers frantically pushed every button he could find on the stereo. A CD appeared; then the power finally shut off.

Riley pulled the CD out: *The Battle of Los Angeles* by Rage Against the Machine. *This girl is definitely a study in contrasts*, Riley thought as he tossed the CD into the center console, then quickly followed it with the fake daisy from the car's bud vase.

He thought about swinging the car around in the parking space so that the summer sun wasn't in his face. Instead, he just put the visor down and turned up the air-conditioning. He dialed a number on his phone, and Keith Simmons answered on the third ring.

"Listen, Pach, when you said there might be a little damage, I was thinking a broken window or two! But burning the whole place down? What happened?" Simmons was trying to sound angry, but Riley could hear the smile behind his voice.

"Would you believe a barbecue gone bad?"

Simmons laughed. "Nah, I've seen you barbecue. It certainly ain't that! Seriously, man, are you and Big Ugly okay?"

"I'm fine. Skeeter's in the hospital, but he'll be all right. Khadi Faroughi's there with him."

"Yeah, if that chick was with me, I'd be fine too."

"Watch it, *kemosabe*. Listen, Keith, I know you said on your message not to worry about the cabin, but still, I am so sorry. If I knew that the whole place would burn down—"

"You would have asked anyway. Come on, man, don't be telling me differently."

Riley winced at Simmons's comment. *Do I really have that kind of reputation?*

Simmons spared him from any more self-analysis. "But like I said, it's only stuff. Better than that, it's only insured stuff. A year ago, I would have gone all Donkey Kong on you—you know that. But *now* I know, my friend, that in this life there is more important stuff than *stuff*. So we'll rebuild it—maybe this time with an indoor sauna in the basement. Just don't go expecting an invitation to the housewarming," he finished with a laugh.

"Well then, God bless you, brother, because you certainly have blessed me."

"Hey, before you hang up, Z really wants to meet up with you."

"Afshin? What does he want?" The last thing Riley wanted right now was to talk to someone he hardly knew. He still hadn't had time to process what had happened last night, much less the news of Chris Johnson's death. At the moment, all he wanted to do was to find a dark place and brood.

"Who knows what's in the mind of a rookie? I wouldn't give him your cell number, so he just told me to please, please, please pass the message along."

Riley sighed angrily. "Do me a favor and text his number to me. I'll give him a call."

"Sounds good. So, can you tell me if you finished everything off up there?"

Not even close, he thought. "Unfortunately, no. But I do think we may have taken the upper hand."

"Good enough for me. Take care, Pach."

Riley put the car in reverse and squealed the tires backing out of the parking space. But then a text message beeped through on his phone. Sighing, he pulled back in. Sure enough, the message was from Simmons. *Fast fingers,* Riley thought as he dialed Afshin Ziafat's number.

"Afshin? This is Riley," he said when the rookie answered.

"Pach, man, I have been so worried about you. My church group and I have been praying up a storm for you. You doing okay?"

"Yeah, I'm fine. Thanks for the prayers." *Let's get this over with fast.* "So, Simm said you wanted to talk to me."

"Right, right. Hey, I'd really like to get together with you to, you know, to pray over you. God's really been placing you on my heart, and I think that if I could get a few of my buddies together and we could lay hands on you and pray—I mean it certainly couldn't do any harm."

Riley rolled his eyes. Normally he would have really been grateful for Afshin's offer, but right now it was just another source of irritation. "I appreciate it, Afshin. I really do. It's just that I'm still not the safest guy to be around." *Take the out. Come on, man, take the out.*

Unfortunately, it seemed that Afshin wasn't looking for any outs. "I know that, Pach. But God is greater than anything the world throws at us. Amen? My buddies and I aren't scared. I just really think it would be good if we could meet up with you."

Youthful enthusiasm and invincibility, Riley thought. "Listen, Afshin, you don't know how much I appreciate your prayers. It's just that—"

A call beeped through—Meg Ricci. *Thank you, Meg. Here's my out.*

"Hey, buddy, I just had a call come through that I need to take. I'll call you back and we'll set up a time."

"Sure, Pach. Please, sooner than later." Riley could hear the disappointment in Ziafat's voice. *That was weird.*

Now, speaking of weird . . . Riley switched over to Meg's call. "Hey, Meg, I was going to—"

"Riley, you have to help me! They have Alessandra! They say they're going to kill her if you don't come to the house!"

FRIDAY, MAY 29, 7:35 P.M. EEST
ISTANBUL, TURKEY

Scott could hardly hear Hicks's voice over the engine noise of the old delivery truck. The communication system was all set up, each man with a receiver in his ear and a mic taped to his cheek, but Hicks had said he didn't want to activate it until they were on site. He was going over the operational plan with the remaining eight members of the team one more time before they reached their destination.

Scott had helped develop the strategy and could visualize each step. Of course, with an hour's notice, they still had no idea what kind of building they were going into—a home, an apartment, a warehouse, a restaurant. However, Scott had already processed through those eventualities too.

As they bumped along the old roads, he tuned out Hicks's voice.

Scott scanned the faces of his team. Rage was in the eyes of every man. In fact, Scott had never seen the guys this worked up, and it frightened him. He knew each one of them was harboring an overwhelming desire for revenge against the people who had cut the throat of their friend, then left him to bleed to death in a stinking alley.

Revenge will cause people to think with their hearts and not their heads. They'll overcommit in the face of gunfire, and they'll worry less about civilian casualties. This has all the makings of a bloodbath on both sides.

I've gotta say something to bring them back down—something other than my typically obnoxious comments. So when Hicks finished his rundown, Scott spoke up. "Men, this is the time I usually say something stupid. But I know that right now, nobody feels much like laughing."

Everyone ignored him until they realized he was being serious.

"I just want to remind you to keep the goal in sight. This is about bringing down al-'Aqran—first and foremost. It's about saving hundreds, maybe even thousands, of American kids—kids like Gilly's little boy—who could be lost because of his plans. It's about meting out justice for the thousands of lives that have already been lost because of him. And if we get some revenge for Chris, that's just the gravy.

"Al-'Aqran is going to die today! This dude is so twisted, and the stuff he is planning is so heinous, we're not looking for an arrest; we don't want to put him back in a cell that he can escape from again. In the words of the great Apollo Creed, 'Ain't gonna be no rematch!' So keep sharp! Think with your heads! Follow the plan, and watch your buddy's back!"

A chorus of "Hooah," "Oo-rah," and "Let's roll" sounded from this hodgepodge of military backgrounds.

Hicks gave him a nod and a thumbs-up. "Okay, everybody, comms up! Give me a rundown."

"Velvet Two, check," said Scott.

"Velvet Three, check," said Jay Kruse.

On down the line it went. Scott's stomach clenched when Chris Johnson didn't answer for Velvet Eight.

"Velvet One, this is Runner." Immediately silence filled the van.

"Runner, this is Velvet One; go ahead," Hicks replied to the two CIA agents who had driven ahead to scout the target house. Two more agents were in the cab of the delivery truck, and the final two were in a tail car right behind the FRRT team. Although the agents' orders were to keep out of the action, they were dying to jump into the fray. "Please, give us an excuse" had been their comment to Hicks and Scott. Scott hoped the team wouldn't need them.

"Velvet One, it's a three-story building on the right side. Non-commercial. Solid door. Window bars. Alley on right only. Got two balconies each on floors two and three, so if it's a front-back, you've got four apartments on each floor."

"Any targets?"

"Just getting to that. You've got two guns at the front door. At least one more in the alley. And just a heads-up—if they've got any of those front apartments, you guys are going to be like fish in a barrel from those balconies."

"Got it. Anything else?"

"That's it. Bring these guys down hard, Velvet. Out."

All the team was looking at Hicks, who himself was looking down at the notes he was writing. Scott knew everyone was thinking about those balconies. In a battle, position was everything, and as of right now, it seemed like the bad guys had the position.

Hicks could turn their confidence either way here depending on how he reacted. When he had finished scribbling, he looked up calmly. "No different than what we thought, boys, except a few more stairs. We go in hard, and we go in fast. Logan, you got the target in the alley. Everything else goes as planned."

"Velvet One, this is Chauffeur. Ten seconds out."

"Tonight there's no mercy! Remember the schoolchildren! Let's do this thing!" Hicks pulled the black knit mask over his face, completing the intimidating all-black "walking shadow" look.

The rest of the team followed suit. Each man checked his sound-suppressed Magpul Masada assault weapon one last time. Posada chambered a shell into his Remington 870 Modular Combat Shotgun.

The truck screeched to a halt. Hicks and Matt Logan swung the rear doors open, and the team piled out. Scott could hear the sound-suppressed shots as he jumped out of the truck into a small pile of trash sitting in the gutter. To his right, Logan, Kim Li, and Steve Kasay jumped over a bloodied body and ran through the alley to the back. Straight ahead two more bodies lay askew on either side of the entryway.

The front door was open, and Velvet Team rushed in. Carlos Guitiérrez and Ted Hummel stayed by the door, looking back out while the rest of the team went to the first apartment.

When they reached the old wooden door, Hicks counted down with his fingers—three, two, one—then Gilly Posada blasted the hinges with his shotgun and Jay Kruse brought it down with his ram.

Scott and Hicks ran through the opening into a very sparsely furnished living room. Toward the back of the room next to a frayed red curtain used to split the room into two sleeping areas, a man stood shaking. Behind him were his wife and three young daughters.

"Lütfen, lütfen!" he was crying out: *"Please, please!"*

Scott approached the man and placed the barrel of his rifle square against the man's chest. *"Ariyorum bir—"* then he pointed to his eye—*"erkek.":* *"I'm looking for one . . . man."* He wanted to kick himself for not cramming more Turkish into his brain on the long drive up from Izmir Air Base. *Of all things, you can't even remember the word for eye, you idiot!*

The man started babbling and pointing up. Behind him, his wife was crying and his daughters were screaming.

Scott waved his hand in front of the man's face to get him to stop talking. When that didn't work, he gave a push with the barrel of his rifle.

The man shut up.

"Anlamadim! Nerede bir—" Scott pointed to his eye again—*"erkek.":* *"I don't understand! Where one . . . man?"*

The man pointed up. *Okay, he's upstairs. Now we're getting someplace.*

"Ross, hurry it up," Hicks said.

Scott waved him off. Gradually lifting his hand by levels, he said to the father, *"Bir, iki, üç?":* *"One, two, three?"*

"Üç, üç!" the man said, holding up three fingers. Then he used his hands to indicate the second front apartment.

"Teşekkür ederim," Scott said, patting the man on the cheek. *"Thank you."* He pointed to a back room, then indicated for the family to stay there.

The man nodded and hustled his family back.

"Velvet Team, Velvet Two," Scott said into his comm mic.

"Scorpion is in the third floor, front left apartment—repeat, third floor, front left apartment. Lead team is going up."

Hicks and Kruse were already at the stairs by the time Scott made it out the door. Posada waited to bring up the rear.

Automatic weapon fire sounded from upstairs. Hicks paused on the first step. "The balconies," he yelled. "Chauffeur, get yourselves out of here!"

"RP—!" Chauffeur called out, then an explosion ended his voice and blew in through the entryway. Debris rattled through the front hallway, and Scott heard it hit the inside of the apartment door next to him.

"Velvet Five and Seven, report in," Hicks called to the men at the front door.

Through his earpiece, Scott heard Hummel answer, "The truck took an RPG right into the cab. Guitiérrez got tagged with some shrapnel. He's not good!"

"Get him to safety, then stand your post!"

"Yes, sir!"

"From now on, only absolutely essential chatter on the comm!"

At the bottom of the steps, Hicks's eyes bored into each of his men. Then, abruptly, he turned his black-masked face and ran to the second level.

7:47 P.M. EEST

Babrak Zahir ran back in from the balcony and threw the smoking RPG tube into the kitchen. "Their truck is destroyed," he said to al-'Aqran as he met up with him by the front door.

"Good, good," the old man said. They had only the one RPG, so he had told Zahir to make it count. It sounded like the young warrior had followed his orders.

Al-'Aqran was alone in the apartment with Zahir. Hamad Asaf, Arshad Hushimi, and Tahir Talib, all armed with AK-74s, had gone out to meet the assault. Asaf and Hushimi were both veteran soldiers, and al-'Aqran knew they would be formidable foes. *Only that fool, Talib, looked like he wasn't sure which end of the gun to point at the enemy.* "Worthless," he grumbled.

Al-'Aqran looked at Zahir. *My life, entrusted into the hands of this child. Why couldn't his father be here with me? The two of us together could have taken on a whole army of Americans in our day. But that was a long time ago.*

Oh, Allah, I have served you faithfully over the years. I have suffered for you and have been tortured for you. I have killed in your name and for your honor. Now we are on the verge of doing something so glorious that your name will be praised throughout the nations.

I know you will take me in your time. Insha'Allah. All I ask, most benevolent God, is that you let me complete this mission, and that you don't let my life end at the hands of these motherless swine. Extend my time on earth, so that I may continue to do your will.

"Babrak, my son."

"Yes, *sayyid*." Zahir was pressed against the wall, looking out through a crack in the front door.

"Look at me, Babrak." Zahir obeyed. Al-'Aqran reached his hand around the back of the young man's neck and gripped him gently. "You know how I loved your father. He was a brother to me. I cannot remember weeping before your father's death, and I have not wept since." Gradually, he strengthened his hold, shaking him to emphasize his words. "These men who are coming are the ones who took your father's life in Italy. I know. I heard them brag of it afterward. These very men put the bullets into his body. If they make it this far, son, you remember that. You remember that, and you avenge your father!"

Al-'Aqran was gratified to see black hatred on the young man's face. "Don't worry, *sayyid*. Today I will restore my father's honor to him."

"Good boy," al-'Aqran said, clapping Zahir on the shoulder. "Make your father proud."

Gunfire began down the hall. While Zahir stayed by the door, al-'Aqran hobbled behind the wall of the kitchen.

Jay Kruse fell backward down the second flight
of stairs, blood pouring from his neck. Hicks and
Posada returned fire while Scott readied a flashbang
grenade. He pulled the pin, but before he could
throw it, a body fell from the landing above him
right on top of Posada, sending him down the stairs
and knocking the grenade out of Scott's hand.

"Cover up!" Scott yelled. Hicks and Scott squatted down, covered their ears, and closed their eyes
tightly. Still the concussion from the blast rocked
them. Scott fumbled for another grenade to send
upstairs to even the playing field.

The AK-74s opened up again. Splinters flew
all around him, some embedding themselves into
his cheeks and scalp. His ears were ringing and
his hands were shaking from the first flashbang,
but he finally found the pin on a second one and
tossed it up the stairway.

Hicks must have had the same idea, because
two explosions sounded, one right after the other.
Scott felt Hicks slap his arm to get his attention.

"I lead; you follow!"

Scott nodded.

Both men ran the final ten steps to the third

floor. A burst of gunfire from Hicks took out a dazed target in the middle of the hallway. On the landing to their right, a man dropped his gun, raised his hands, and pressed himself up against the wall. Scott put a round in the man's leg, and he dropped screaming. Scott used his hand to tell the fallen gunman to stay where he was; then he slid the man's AK-74 down the steps.

Scott and Hicks made their way down the hall, Hicks looking forward, Scott walking backward. Any moment, Scott expected a door to swing open and bullets to start flying. But except for the groans of the wounded man at the end of the hall, all remained quiet.

Scott quickly glanced to the front. *Just twelve more feet to the target door. Keep it going. Keep it going.* Suddenly, gunfire erupted. Scott dove for the ground as he felt something take a bite out of his left arm. He turned in the direction of the fire and let off a three-second burst. The target door shredded, and the gunfire behind it stopped. Quickly, Scott switched out his clip, then turned to check on Hicks.

Hicks was lying on the floor.

From the man's body position, Scott knew it wasn't good. *Oh no, not you, Jim!* He slid over to him, keeping his rifle trained on where the door used to be. Blood was darkening Hicks's black clothing in at least four places that Scott could see.

"Jim? Jim? You okay, man?" Scott checked for a pulse. It was weak but there. He shook Hicks's shoulder and gave his face a light slap. Hicks's eyes cracked open.

Then he spoke, and his words were so faint that without the microphone taped to his cheek, Scott never would have heard what he said. "Get moving, you idiot, before someone puts a cap in that fat gut of yours."

Scott grinned under his mask. "You got it, boss."

He hated to leave Hicks alone, but he had to finish the mission. He started moving forward, staying low to the floor.

"Velvet Two, this is Velvet Four; I'm coming up behind you." Scott was relieved to hear Posada's voice.

"Velvet Four, stay with Velvet One until I can get Velvet . . . Okay, this is stupid! Gilly, stay with Jim until I can get Li up here."

"Yes, sir," Posada said as he crested the top of the stairway.

"Li, break off your detail and get upstairs now."

"You got it, Velvet Scott."

As Scott slowly moved toward the door, his mind started racing. *Scorpion has to be in there, or else why would they defend it so strongly? But if he's in there, why is there no more shooting? The* hajji *in the doorway must have been the only guy—wait, check that—probably was the only guy. The old man's got to be in here. Remember who he is, though. He was a veteran soldier before you were even a gleam in your strung-out, heroin-addicted daddy's eye.*

Scott could see the shooter through the doorway. *There's no doubting that one is dead.* He moved a little farther forward, and when he finally reached the door, he peeked in.

7:50 P.M. EEST

So, this is the end, al-'Aqran thought. When he saw Zahir fall, he knew that his time was done. *I have served you for so long, God. Then I ask you for one thing, and you have said no?* The old man smiled. *Insha'Allah. What can I do if it is your will? One thing I can promise you, O Mighty One, is that when I finally go down, I will not go down alone. I came into this world fighting, I have lived my life fighting, I will die fighting!*

A footstep on the splintered wood of the door told him that they had come. He waited for two more footsteps. Then he reached around the corner of the wall and fired. A tall figure dressed all in black collapsed to the floor. Al-'Aqran ducked behind the wall. He knew there would be more. After a moment, he quickly glanced around the corner. The man was still there—a pool of blood spreading from his side.

Keep coming, you demon spawn of the devil! I'll send you to see the dark lord you serve, just like I sent this first one. Al-'Aqran hunched down, hearing his knees pop, and listened for his next victim.

7:51 P.M. EEST

"Scott, Scott, you okay in there?" Posada had been calling Scott for the past minute since the gunfire. So far, there had been no response. Posada wanted to go in, but he needed to keep pressure on the wound at the base of Hicks's neck.

Kim Li finally arrived up the stairs, and Posada waved him over. "Hold this here. I'm going to check on Scott."

"You got it," Li replied, grabbing hold of the bloody rag that used to be Posada's mask.

Posada left Hicks and started toward the door. Then a voice, barely audible, came through his earpiece, stopping him in his tracks. "Gilly, you there, man?"

"Right here, buddy."

"Move to the door, but don't come in."

"Yes, sir."

"Then go down to the floor, and on my go, start hitting the door fragments like footsteps."

"You got it."

7:52 P.M. EEST

Scott didn't know what parts of his body had been hit, but he knew it hurt like nothing he'd ever felt before. When he had assessed the situation, he recognized that al-'Aqran was poised to pick off the Velvet Team members one by one until they came in with strength. Even then, the stubborn old man would probably take out a couple more before he went down.

I can take this weasel out; I've just got to get him in the open. But if I make any noise, he'll be aiming right at me, which removes the "Olly olly oxen free" option. I just need a diversion, something or someone to draw his fire. That was when he called Posada.

"I'm in position," Posada's voice said into Scott's earpiece.

"Okay, ready, now."

A faint rustling noise started behind Scott. A moment later, the flashing barrel of the rifle appeared, followed by the face of al-'Aqran—the Scorpion. Scott's finger pulled back on his trigger, and a string of 5.56 mm rounds slammed into the old man's body, throwing him against the back wall, where he slumped to the ground.

Posada ran past Scott and retrieved the man's rifle. Scott tried to pull himself up, but his left leg wasn't working like it should. Looking around, he saw al-'Aqran's old walking stick.

"Gilly, is he dead?"

"No, the old man's a fighter," Posada said, leaning over al-'Aqran.

"Tell you what, bring me that walking stick, and then leave the room."

Posada raised an eyebrow as he walked over toward his friend. "Scott, are you sure you want me—?"

"That's an order!"

"Yes, sir."

Posada got the stick and helped Scott to his feet. "Call if you need me."

Scott just nodded his head. The pain in his side was making his head swim. *Focus, man, focus! You can do this!*

Slowly he made his way over to where the terrorist commander was raspily sucking in breath. Scott turned a chair from the table. The air whistled out of the cushion as he sat down. He pulled off his mask, removed the mic that was taped to his cheek, and nudged the old man with the barrel of his rifle.

Scott was gratified to see the look of recognition on al-'Aqran's face when he looked up.

Leaning his arm back onto the table just behind and trying to hide the wince of pain this nonchalant move caused him, Scott said, "Hey, Mr. Scorpion, we've got to stop meeting like this."

"Ah, the friends of Riley Covington, come to exact their revenge."

"Revenge? This isn't about revenge, old man; it's about justice."

Al-'Aqran laughed, but his laugh quickly deteriorated into a blood-spewing cough. He wiped his mouth with the back of his hand. "What do you Americans know about justice? We will see who is just when we stand before the one true, just God."

Scott shook his head. "That we will, and I'm guessing you are about five minutes away from seeing him. Now tell me about the school attacks before I use my knife to dig out your one good eye."

"What school attacks?" al-'Aqran answered. But Scott could see the surprise on the old man's face.

"I don't have time for your games," Scott said, wincing as he pulled his knife from his right boot. "You are thirty seconds away from me punching your one-way ticket to hell."

Again the laugh, but softer this time. "I may be on my way to hell. But at least if I am, I'll have the satisfaction of knowing that your friend Riley Covington will be joining me there within the hour."

Scott sat up quickly, sending lightning bolts through his body. He sucked in air, trying to get control of the pain. "You wish. Riley took care of your little boys up in the mountains."

Another coughing fit sprayed blood across the floor and onto Scott's boots. Scott was tempted to wipe them off on the man's scraggly beard. "Oh, I'm not talking about the mountains. Maybe if you get me to a hospital, I'll tell you a little more. Maybe we can even talk about your little children there too."

He's running a game! That's all he's doing; he's running a game, trying to buy more time. There's no way he's going to tell a thing. I'll find out about the school attacks and about Riley, but not from al-'Aqran. I'll get the info I need from the guy down the hall with the bullet in his leg. Scott slowly pushed himself to his feet.

A bloody smile spread across al-'Aqran's face. "How about it? You send me off to a dirty old prison and you get to save the lives of all those little fair-haired children. Deal?"

Scott shook his head. "Not this time, old man. I hate to tell you, but there ain't gonna be no rematch."

He pulled the trigger of his rifle twice, then slowly limped his way to the door.

FRIDAY, MAY 29, 10:58 A.M. MDT
PARKER, COLORADO

Oh, Lord, not little Aly!

Riley caught a glimpse of his pale face in the rearview mirror. *Cars are not designed to move this slowly,* he thought as he struggled to keep the VW Beetle at twenty-five through the small downtown district of Parker. *But the last thing I need right now is to have to explain to a cop where I'm going and why I'm driving this thing.*

Fighting a steadily losing battle with panic, Riley had eventually gotten the facts from Meg.

"Three men," she had told him. "They were dressed in black."

"Slow down, Meg," he'd said. "Tell me exactly what happened."

"I had just changed Aly in the living room, and I was throwing out her diaper. When I came back in, there they were. I don't know how they got in—I always keep the alarm on just like you told me. One of them was holding Aly, and she was reaching out for me."

"Did they say anything to you?"

"One of them came up to me and said, 'You tell Riley Covington to come over alone and unarmed. When he does, we'll trade you your little girl for him. We'll call you in an hour.' Then he pushed me, and I fell over the back of the couch. When I got up, they were walking out the door. Aly was screaming for me, Riley; she was screaming!"

"What time was that, Meg?"

"They just left! You have to help me, Riley! I don't know what to do!"

After checking the time on his watch, Riley had said, "You don't do anything except wait for me! I'm on my way over!"

He'd fired off a quick text message to Khadi's phone, then turned his own phone off and rocketed in the direction of the Ricci residence.

A mother pushing a running stroller suddenly appeared in front of him. Riley slammed on the brakes, skidding right up to a crosswalk. Angrily, the woman pointed to the flashing yellow lights indicating that someone was crossing. Riley waved his hand apologetically. *You bonehead! Get it together. If you can't even see the big flashing lights, how can you possibly expect to think clearly enough to get Alessandra back safely?* He accelerated and slowly made his way east.

Riley was exhausted—physically, mentally, emotionally. Even the adrenaline pumping through his veins was not enough to fully sharpen him up. He knew he was playing tired—and playing tired is a good way to get your head handed to you on a plate. The whole trip from downtown Denver had been one muddled thought after another. And now that he was three minutes from Meg Ricci's house, he still didn't have even a semblance of a plan.

Lord, this is going to have to be all You. I don't have this in me, but You promise us in the Bible that when we are weak, You are strong. So, give me Your strength. You also promise that if we lack wisdom, all we have to do is ask. So, I'm asking—give me Your wisdom, because right now I'm utterly clueless.

You know my heart, Father. I don't care what happens to me. "For to me, to live is Christ and to die is gain," right? I truly believe that. Just help me save Aly. Please, Lord, protect that precious little girl.

A chorus that he had sung in church about falling down and laying crowns popped into his mind, but he couldn't remember the words. So, he hummed a couple of lines, then faded into silence.

Just before Riley turned onto Meg's street, he pulled to the side, reached around to the small of his back, and pulled out a Ruger LCP .380. Giving it a quick once-over, he confirmed that he had a full six in the clip and one in the chamber. *Don't know how long I'll be able to keep this thing, but there's absolutely no way I'm going into that house unarmed,* he thought as he slid the pistol back into place. Slipping the car in gear, he made his turn and pulled up to his destination.

Before getting out, he scanned the neighborhood. *This whole thing could be a setup so that they can pop me on my way into the house. I don't see anyone . . . which means absolutely nothing.* Saying one more quick prayer, he got out of the car and hurried to the front door. Meg was waiting for him.

"Oh, Riley, you came," she cried out as she embraced him and sobbed. "I'm so sorry. I didn't know what to do."

"Of course I came. What else could I do?" Riley replied, holding her tightly. After a moment, he gently pushed her back so he could look her in the eyes. "We're going to get Aly back, Meg. Do you understand me? We will get her back!"

Meg tried to stifle her sobs. "Okay, Riley, I believe you. Thank you. Thank you so much."

Riley twisted his wrist to see the time. "Now, we've still got a half hour before they call. I want you to tell me again everything that happened when the men were here."

Meg nodded as she moved into the family room. She sat down in her late husband's leather chair; Riley sat on the edge of the couch across from her. The look on her face sent an uncomfortable feeling through his body. *Come on, let it go. You don't have time to be paranoid.* "Okay, Meg, start from the beginning. You were in . . . where? . . . Was it the kitchen throwing out her diaper?"

Suddenly, Meg's whole demeanor changed. She heaved a deep sigh, and the muscles on her face relaxed. Tears streamed from the corners of her eyes. Reaching down into the crevice next to her chair's large bottom cushion, she pulled out a handgun and pointed it at Riley.

"Riley," she said so quietly that he could barely hear her, "I'm so sorry. You have to put your hands up. Please, for Aly's sake, put your hands up."

At first, in his exhausted state of mind, Riley thought it was a joke. But just as quickly, the reality of the situation hit him. He dropped back into the couch. Lifting his arms, he held them up for a moment, then let them fall down to his side. All the fight had left him. Quietly, he said, "Meg. What are you doing, Meg?"

A voice broke in from the direction of the kitchen. "She's only doing what I've asked her to do. It's time I introduce myself to you, Mr. Covington. My name is Abdullah Muhammad, and I must tell you, you certainly are a hard man to kill."

FRIDAY, MAY 29, 8:05 P.M. EEST
ISTANBUL, TURKEY

"He's not looking good," Kim Li reported to Scott. "He's lost a ton of blood."

Scott looked down at Jim Hicks. He wanted to stop and do something—to let Hicks know that he was there with him. But his friend's words kept ringing in his ears. *Get moving, you idiot!*

"I want you to get him help as soon as the Turkish cavalry arrives! And you don't leave his side, not ever. You got it?"

As if on cue, the distinctive wail of the Turkish police cars sounded from outside.

"You got it, Scott."

Scott moved forward as quickly as he could, which wasn't saying much. The walking stick seemed to be doing the lion's share of the work. With every tap . . . shuffle, shuffle, he continued a trail of blood on the tile hallway. As he moved forward, his eyes remained fixed on the man by the stairs. For the first time in many years, Scott felt blind hatred.

The man must have seen it in Scott's eyes, because he clasped his hands together in front of himself and began whimpering while Scott was still fifteen feet away.

Go ahead and cry. You think that's going to get you mercy? You've already killed Johnson and Kruse and Guitiérrez and two good CIA men. My boss and mentor is bleeding to death, and my best friend is about to get killed by another of your people. "Do you really think you're going to get mercy?" Scott yelled out in broken Arabic. *"Do you?" Fat chance! What in the world are you thinking, you murdering piece of trash?*

Scott stood in front of the man and used the barrel of his rifle to swat the man's hands away from his face. "Look at me! You think those soft hands will stop my bullets? Look at me!"

The man slowly dropped his arms to his side.

In his earpiece, Scott heard Ted Hummel say, "Scott, the police are here, and they're wanting up bad."

Scott took his mic and pressed it back against his cheek, where it hung loosely. "Give me three minutes," he growled. He could hear the sounds of very unhappy voices in his earpiece and down through the stairway.

"How? They really want up!"

"I don't care how! You're a professional; figure it out!"

"Yes, sir!"

"What's your name?" Scott demanded, turning his attention back to the wounded man who was sitting propped against the wall.

"Talib. Tahir Talib," the man replied in a shaking voice.

"Tell me about the school attacks! Where? When?"

"I don't know."

"That's not the answer I want to hear," Scott yelled, kicking the bullet wound in the man's thigh.

Talib cried out, "I swear I don't know. That other man who was shot up here with me—he was to begin waking the sleepers tomorrow!"

"So you're telling me that the attacks are not scheduled to begin yet?" Relief flooded through Scott's body.

"Yes, *sayyid*. The process has not yet begun."

"You better be telling me the truth! Otherwise, I will find you in whatever pit of a prison cell they throw you into, and I'll dismantle you piece by piece. Now, tell me about Riley Covington! What are your friends preparing for him?"

"I . . . I don't—"

Scott raised his rifle and placed the end of the barrel on the bridge of the man's nose. Talib cried out, "Hakeem Qasim's widow! Her daughter is being used to draw Covington in!"

Scott was suddenly confused. The loss of blood was starting to make his head swim. He stepped back, catching his balance with the walking stick. "Is this the truth? Is it true?"

Talib's hands were back in front of his face. "It is, it is. I swear it!"

Again the rage took over. *These people will do anything and use anyone. Do any of them have the right to live? Does this piece of garbage really deserve to leave this building alive? Answer: 100 percent, unequivocally NO!*

Scott tucked his rifle under his chin and pointed it back at Talib's head. "Look at me! LOOK AT ME!"

Finally, Talib lowered his hands, resigned to his fate. Scott's finger gripped the trigger. Sweat was pouring down his face, and his whole body was shaking. "AAAH!" he screamed, and then turned and limped away leaving the man crying on the floor.

"Scott, you all right?" came Kim Li's voice from down the hall.

"Yeah," was all Scott said as he pulled a satellite phone out of a deep pocket in his cargo pants. "Hummel, I need two more minutes."

"I'm doing my best, boss."

Scott quickly dialed a number. *Come on, answer, answer!*

Riley's voice sounded before the first ring. "This is 303-8 . . ." *Of course he's got his phone off,* Scott thought as he dialed another number.

This time Khadi answered. "This is Faroughi."

"Khadi! I don't have time to talk! Is Riley with you?"

"No, he sent me a text saying he was going to Meg's house. Since then his phone has been off."

"No, no, NO, NO! Listen to me, Khadi! They've set a trap for him. They're holding Alessandra hostage to force Riley to come to them. You've got to get over there now—I mean, right this moment!"

Voices filled the stairway next to Scott, drowning out Khadi's reply. Turkish police began pouring onto the third level. Officers were yelling at him, guns were pointed. Scott dropped his weapon and raised his hands, and as he did, the room spun and he dropped.

"You're the guy from the mountains," Riley said as he watched the man limp into the room carrying a .40 caliber Smith & Wesson.

"Oh, you're bright . . . for a football player," Abdullah said sarcastically. "Although not so bright that you don't run out of a house directly into the line of fire. How did you know there weren't other guns out there waiting to take you down?"

"I didn't. I only knew it was me or my friends."

The man laughed. "Ah, the noble warrior! They warned me about you. Now, Meg, where is Riley's gun?"

"It's behind his back," Meg answered in a whisper.

"Good. Maybe your daughter will live through this after all," Abdullah said. Then to Riley, he ordered, "Stand up!"

Riley stood.

"Meg, throw your gun toward the front door, then get his gun and throw his there too."

Meg did as she was told. "I'm so sorry," she whispered to Riley when she reached behind him.

"Now, to the dining room." Riley followed Meg, with Abdullah taking up the rear. "Take up the plastic cuffs and secure Riley to the chair. Make them tight—I'll be checking."

Riley sat in a heavy wooden dining chair while Meg kneeled behind him. "Alessandra's locked in the basement. He's the only one here," she said quietly as she cinched Riley's wrists tightly to the chair.

"Good job, Meg," Abdullah said. "Now come back here."

Meg went and stood next to Abdullah. He brushed her cheek with the back of his hand. "You really are a lovely woman. I think I'll save you for later," he said as he dropped the butt of his gun down on her head.

"Meg!" Riley cried out as he watched her crumple to the ground. Then Abdullah turned toward him.

"You may wonder why I didn't just shoot you right off," Abdullah said, pulling out his cell phone. "My superiors like videos of my work, and I'm always happy to oblige. Besides, you made me work so hard, I kind of feel like you owe me a little fun." As he finished, he brought the gun hard across Riley's face.

Blood instantly filled Riley's mouth, and he felt the handgun's rear site cut a gash across his cheek.

"You managed to hurt me up in the mountains. And my vengeance is tenfold!" Again the gun came down on Riley's face.

Riley's vision grayed for a moment. *Alessandra! Hold it together for Alessandra!* Blood and saliva hung in long streaks from Riley's mouth. He spit out one of his lower molars. Taking as deep a breath as he could, he raised his eyes to meet Abdullah's.

"Ever the mighty warrior! A man of honor! Where's your God now, infidel?" Another blow rained backhanded across Riley's other cheek. Pinpoint lights burst throughout Riley's vision. *Please, Lord, one last time. Like Samson, give me one last time.*

"I asked you a question! Where is your God, and what is He in comparison to all-powerful Allah? Answer me, and I'll just put a bullet in your head now. Stay silent, and I can go on all day!"

Again Riley slowly raised his head. Trying to control his damaged mouth, he mouthed the words, "My God is my strength."

"Speak up, coward," Abdullah said, connecting with Riley's head farther back toward his ear. A ringing explosion burst in his head, and again Riley almost passed out.

Sucking in two gurgling breaths, Riley whispered the words, "My God is my strength."

This time, as Abdullah leaned in to hear Riley's words, Riley launched himself with power that only thousands of squats can give. His forehead connected with Abdullah's chin, causing blood to gush from the man's severed tongue.

As Abdullah stumbled backward, his foot caught the unconscious Meg's leg and he fell onto his back.

Riley gripped both sides of the chair and carried it with him as he shuffled to where Abdullah was laid out. Just as Abdullah was about to roll up, Riley jumped back onto the chair, letting the left rear leg drop just above the man's pant line. Abdullah screamed, pinned to the ground, the internal bleeding just beginning.

Riley felt the room spinning from his effort. A lightness in his head beckoned him toward the peace of unconsciousness. But as he felt himself slowly drifting away, his eye caught Abdullah lifting his gun toward Riley's face.

Too late.

Riley lifted the chair one more time. Then, crying out, he let every one of his 230 pounds drive the leg of the chair into Abdullah's chest, crushing the cavity's protective ribs and puncturing his heart.

11:17 A.M. MDT

Normally the trip from Parker Adventist Hospital to the Ricci home took six minutes. Khadi made it in three and a half.

By the time she turned into Meg Ricci's subdivision, she had two Parker police cars chasing her—lights flashing and sirens blaring.

Quickly she pressed speed dial 5 on her phone.

Tara Walsh answered.

"Tara, don't ask questions. I'm in Canterberry Crossing in Parker with two cops after me. Call them off now, or I'm going to end up with a bullet in my back!"

"Done!"

Khadi watched her rearview mirror as she wound her way up a hill. The cops weren't backing off. *Go away! There's not a chance these guys will let me make it to the door with a gun in my hand! What do I do?* Then, in a flash, everything became perfectly clear for her. *What else can I do? I just run into the line of fire for Riley like he did for Skeeter and me.* She glanced back into her mirror. *Hope you boys failed your marksmanship tests.*

Spinning around a corner, Khadi saw Evie Cline's yellow VW. She skidded to a stop right behind it. *Here goes,* she thought as she lifted her gun off the passenger seat and ran out the door. The police cars screeched in behind her, but they didn't get out of their cars. *Thank you, Tara,* Khadi thought as she ran toward the door.

She jumped a low hedge and was at the front door when she heard Riley's voice call out. Khadi burst through the door.

11:20 A.M. MDT

Riley had just tipped his chair over when he saw the front door open and Khadi's face appear over the family room furniture. "Go to the basement," he yelled. "Find Alessandra!"

Khadi continued to run toward him with her gun straight out in front of her. "Riley, sit rep!"

"One down and out! Clear up here! Now go find Alessandra! Stairs are out of the living room!"

Riley watched Khadi go and then closed his eyes. All that he could see from his position was an empty room and Abdullah's lifeless eyes. He wanted to check on Meg but didn't have the strength to pull himself over there.

Please, Lord, let Aly be okay! Please, Father, protect that little girl! A child's cry cut through the silence of the house, and a smile spread across Riley's face.

"Thank You," he said as he finally gave himself permission to give in to the soft darkness.

EPILOGUE

The long, brown mound hadn't had time yet to start sprouting grass. Memories flooded Riley's mind as he stared at it—some good, some not so good. *He was a good man, and his life definitely left a mark.* Kneeling, he picked up a small clump of dirt and bounced it up and down in his hand until it broke apart. He looked to his right, then reached out and put his arm around Scott, who was kneeling next to him.

"He never told me his middle name was Marion," Scott laughed, but there were tears running down his cheeks. "James Marion Hicks—oh, I would have had fun with that!"

Riley chuckled softly while he read the name on the headstone. He patted Scott on the shoulder, then reached down for another clump of dirt.

He and Khadi had gone together to see the artisan about the memorial. Khadi had read off the name to the proprietor, then had given Riley a hard elbow shot to the ribs when a laugh accidentally spilled out of his mouth.

Scott read the epitaph out loud: "*Hero and Beloved Friend. A Man Who Left His Mark.* Thanks for having them put that on, Riley. That's nice. That's really nice."

Scott had been tied up with the Turkish authorities for over three weeks, so he had missed the big battle with the people at Homeland Security. *I can't believe those weasels wanted to turn the funeral into a full-blown media circus,* Riley thought, *a military burial complete with dignitaries and multiple gun salutes. Yeah, that's just what Jim would have wanted. Let's hear it for Grandpa putting in a couple of calls to his star-shouldered friends to put the kibosh on the festivities.*

Instead, the funeral had been small, quiet, purposely out of the camera's eye. Riley had gotten his pastor to perform the service, and the only ones attending had been Khadi, Riley, Skeeter, the RoU team, and Hicks's thirty-nine-year-old daughter, Tyler, whom he had seen just once, and that from a distance. Riley had contacted Tyler's mother, who had given him permission to call her daughter. What had started out as a very awkward phone conversation had quickly turned into Tyler insisting on coming to the memorial service of her heroic father.

Riley had flown her in the day before the funeral, and when Tyler went home the day after, she had left with a carefully folded flag and the knowledge that her father had truly loved her.

Both men continued to kneel by the grave, lost in their own thoughts. Riley couldn't keep his mind from drifting back three weeks to when he had knelt in front of his father's grave, his mother on one side of him and his grandfather on the other.

Grandpa had put his arm around Riley's shoulders—as Riley had just done to Scott—and then Gramps had said softly, "Remember, son, we don't have to grieve like those who have no hope."

That was a tough moment, Riley thought, remembering how all the emotions over his father's death that he had been storing inside had finally burst out at that precious place. *But at least it brought some closure, right? Isn't that what they always say? It's time to move on? Yeah, right, who are you kidding about closure?*

It's gonna be a long time before that chapter of my life closes, he thought bitterly. *But Gramps was right about one thing—at least I'm going to see Dad again. That's where my hope comes from.*

The next week had been spent with Mom, making sure she was settled in her temporary home until the goat dairy she insisted on continuing could be rebuilt. The days working together to sort out

Dad's estate had been good; the nights talking with her had been better. He'd even taken a liking to a smoky chipotle pepper chèvre recipe that she had been trying out. *Go figure,* he thought, remembering the subtle burn on the back of his throat.

Scott slowly stood up, leaning heavily on an old walking stick he had brought back with him from Istanbul. "I think I'm ready."

"You sure?" Riley asked, quickly rising and helping him the rest of the way. "We got nothing but time."

"Yeah, I'm done. Besides," Scott said, loosening his tie, "this suit's a rental. I gotta have it back this afternoon."

Riley smiled. "I was going to ask you about that."

The two men walked leisurely back to the SUV, where Skeeter waited propped against the driver's side door. Khadi sat inside behind the wheel.

What else waited for Riley, he didn't know. The Mustangs had been leaving him messages again reminding him he had never been officially put on injured reserve, and that he *was* their franchise player.

We'll have to see. I'm not too sure if this Achilles injury has completely healed yet, he thought as he jumped up into the passenger side of the Suburban.

"Get moving, you idiot," Scott called from the backseat.

"What?" Riley and Khadi said in unison, turning around in time to see Skeeter give Scott a hard punch.

"Ow, Skeet," Scott said, rubbing his arm. "Don't worry, Khadi, I didn't mean anything by it. Just some loving words from an old friend."

"Give him another one, Skeet, just on principle," Riley said as he turned back around smiling.

As flesh connected with fabric in the backseat and Scott's yelp echoed through the vehicle, Riley caught Khadi's rich mocha eyes glinting at him. *Oh, Lord, have You ever created a more beautiful creature? She is everything I've ever wanted—everything I've been waiting for. If only she would see Your truth . . .*

His thoughts must have shown on his face, because Khadi grinned and said, "Why, Mr. Covington, I do believe you're staring."

Quickly recomposing himself, Riley turned to the front and said, "Drive the car, my dear Miss Faroughi. Just drive the car."

JASON ELAM is a sixteen-year NFL veteran placekicker for the Atlanta Falcons.

He was born in Fort Walton Beach, Florida, and grew up in Atlanta, Georgia. In 1988, Jason received a full football scholarship to the University of Hawaii, where he played for four years, earning academic All-America and Kodak All-America honors. He graduated in 1992 with a bachelor's degree in communications and was drafted in the third round of the 1993 NFL draft by the Denver Broncos, where he played for 15 years.

In 1997 and 1998, Jason won back-to-back world championships with the Broncos and was selected to the Pro Bowl in 1995, 1998, and 2001. He is currently working on a master's degree in global apologetics at Liberty Theological Seminary and has an abiding interest in Middle East affairs, the study of Scripture, and defending the Christian faith. Jason is a licensed commercial airplane pilot, and he and his wife, Tamy, have four children.

STEVE YOHN grew up as a pastor's kid in Fresno, California, and both of those facts contributed significantly to his slightly warped perspective on life. Steve graduated from Multnomah Bible College with a bachelor's degree in biblical studies and barely survived a stint as a youth pastor.

While studying at Denver Seminary, Steve worked as a videographer for Youth for Christ International, traveling throughout the world to capture the ministry's global impact. With more than two decades of ministry experience, both inside and outside the church, Steve has discovered his greatest satisfactions lie in writing, speaking, and one-on-one mentoring.

Surprisingly, although his hobbies are reading classic literature, translating the New Testament from the Greek, and maintaining a list of political leaders of every country of the world over the last twenty-five years, he still occasionally gets invited to parties and has a few friends. His wife, Nancy, and their daughter are the joys of his life.

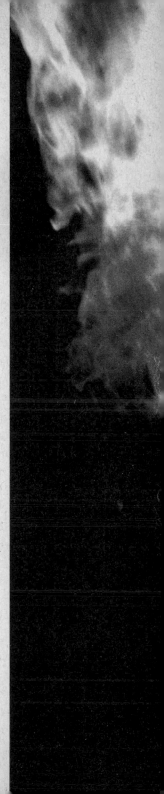

Hakeem Qasim picked up the small, sharp rock from the dirt. Tossing it up and down a couple of times, he felt its weight as he gauged his target. He glanced at Ziad, his cousin and closest friend. They both knew the significance of what he was about to do. Wiping the sweat off his forehead and then onto his frayed cotton pants, he cocked his arm back, took aim, and let fly. The rock sailed from his hand, across fifteen meters of open space, in through the driver's-side window of the burned-out Toyota, and out the other side—no metal, no glass, nothing but air.

"Yes!" the two ten-year-old boys shouted in unison as they clumsily danced together in triumph.

They had spent the better part of six days clearing this dirt patch, as attested by their cracked, blistered fingers and by the jagged gray piles in and around the old Corona. Hakeem took pride in the knowledge that his rocks were mostly of the "in" category, while Ziad's were mostly of the "around." But to have the final rock of the hundreds, if not thousands, that they had cleared from their newly created soccer field pass all the way through the car could mean only one thing—good luck.

Hakeem was the older of the two by seventeen days. Although he was small for his age, his wiry frame attested to his strength and speed. His uncle Shakir had told him, "You are like the cheetah, the pursuer." He wasn't exactly sure what his uncle meant by that, but he loved the picture it put in his mind. Often, when he closed his eyes at night, he dreamed of stalking prey out on the open plains. Hakeem the Cheetah—*watch out, or I'll run you down*. His complexion was dark, and his black hair was thick and wild. His eyes were a deep brown and had a feline intensity to them that he knew could be unsettling, even to his mother. "Hakeem, you have the eyes of the Prophet," she would say, sometimes with a shudder.

Ziad was the opposite of his cousin in build. Tall, square shoulders, large head—his father used to call him *Asad Babil*, the "Lion of Babylon," named after the Iraqi version of the Soviet T-72 tank. Ziad wasn't the brightest star in the sky, but he was a guy you wanted on your side in a fight.

As the boys scanned the dusty lot, Hakeem felt a tremendous sense of accomplishment, remembering what the field had looked like just a week ago. He glanced to his left, where he had tripped over a rock and badly cut his elbow—the impetus for their renovation. He unconsciously picked the edges of the scab; that rock had been the first to go.

A waft of lamb with garlic and cumin caught Hakeem's attention, awakening another of his senses. Well, his hunger would be taken care of soon enough. It was Friday, and every Friday (except for the day after the bombs had begun to fall last week) Uncle Ali came over for dinner. It was always a special event, because Ali Qasim was an important man. All the neighbors would bow their heads in respect as he drove by. Father would bow too, in spite of the fact that Ali was the youngest of the three brothers and Hakeem's father was the eldest.

Even now, Hakeem could see Uncle Ali's black Land Rover parked next to his house across the field. Beside it was the matching Land Rover that carried the men Ali called his "friends," although he never talked to them and all they ever seemed to do was stand outside the house looking around. There was a lot of mystery surrounding Uncle Ali.

Last month, in a day that Hakeem would not soon forget, Uncle Ali had invited the boy to take a ride with him. "Let's see how good my friends are," Ali cried as he hit the gas, burying the other Land Rover in a cloud of dust. They bounced down the dirt roads, laughing and yelling for people to get out of the way.

When they made it out to the main road, Ali had suddenly gotten serious. He reached into his *dishdasha* and handed Hakeem a small handkerchief that had been folded into a square. The boy's excitement grew as he opened one corner after another, discovering inside a bullet with a hole drilled just under the case's base. A thin chain had been threaded through the hole.

"Hakeem, this is a 7.62 mm round that I pulled out of an unexpended AK-47 clip that Saddam Hussein himself was firing outside of his palace."

Hakeem was still too afraid to ask what—or whom—President Hussein had been firing at.

"Feel the weight of it, Nephew. Imagine what this could do to a person's body. For centuries, the West and the Jews have tried to keep our people from worshiping Allah, the true God. You've learned about the Crusades in school, haven't you?"

Hakeem quickly nodded as he slipped the chain over his head. The cartridge was still warm from being kept against his uncle's chest.

"You know I'm not a very religious man, Hakeem, but I can read the times. Soon, because of their hatred of Allah, the Great Satan will come to try to destroy our country. But we don't fear, because Saddam will defend us. The mighty Republican Guard will defend us. Allah will defend us. And someday, our great leader may call on you to pick up a gun for him and fight against the West and defend his honor. Could you do it? Will you be ready, little Hakeem?"

Even now, as he fingered the long, narrow brass bullet hanging around his neck, thinking about how Uncle Ali's prophecy about the Great Satan coming to their land had been fulfilled only two weeks later, his own answer repeated itself in his mind. *I will be ready, Uncle Ali. I will fight for our leader. I will fight for our honor. I will fight the Great Satan!* Allahu akbar!

Suddenly, an ancient, peeling soccer ball bounced off the side of his head. "Nice reflexes, Cheetah," Ziad laughed. "What are you daydreaming about?"

"I was just thinking about Uncle Ali."

"I don't like to think about him. He scares me. People say he's friends with Uday. Could that be?"

"I don't know, Ziad. I think it's best not to ask too many questions."

"Yeah . . . I hope he leaves my mom alone tonight. I don't like the things he says to her or the way he looks at her."

Ziad was the son of Uncle Shakir, the second of the three brothers. When Shakir was killed three years ago while fighting in Iran, Hakeem's father had brought his brother's family—Aunt Shatha, Ziad, and Ziad's four-year-old sister, Zenab—into his own house.

The voice of Ziad's mother rang out from across the dirt field, interrupting their thoughts. It was almost time for *Maghrib*, the sunset prayer time.

"You realize that this will be the site of your great humiliation," Ziad taunted in the pompous language they used when teasing each other.

"Tomorrow, Ziad, your pride will be shown to be as empty as your mother's purse!"

That struck a little too close to home for Ziad, and he pounced upon Hakeem, quickly taking him to the ground. The boys laughed and wrestled, until the voice of Aunt Shatha came a second time—this time with a little more force and the addition of the word *Now!*

"We better get going. The field will still be here tomorrow," Ziad said. "I'll race you. Last one home's a goat kisser!"

"You got it! Ready . . . set . . ."

Ziad's forearm swung up, catching Hakeem right under the chin.

I fall for that every time, Hakeem thought as he dropped to the ground.

"Go!" Ziad yelled, bolting off to take full advantage of the lead he had just given himself.

Hakeem sat in the dirt for a few seconds, counting his teeth with his tongue. He was in no rush. He knew that no matter how large a lead Ziad created for himself, his cousin had no chance of winning. Hakeem would run him down, and then tomorrow he would make him pay on the soccer field for the cheap shot.

As he got up, he spotted his nemesis. Ziad was about halfway home, puffing with all his might. Beyond his cousin, Hakeem could see his mother and Aunt Shatha laughing and cheering Ziad on. Reclining on the roof were his father and Uncle Ali, shaking their heads and grinning. *Here's my chance to show Uncle Ali what his "little" Hakeem is made of.* Hakeem jumped up and began running at full speed.

Suddenly, the world became a ball of fire. The concussive wave knocked Hakeem off his feet. He lay flat on his back. Flames singed his entire body.

The first thing that entered his mind as he glanced around was *Look at all these rocks we'll have to clear off the field tomorrow.* The high-pitched ringing in his head was making it hard to think. As he slowly got up, a pungent smell hit his nose—a mixture of smoke, dust, and . . . what was that last smell? . . . Burnt hair?

What happened? Where is everybody? Ziad was running home . . . Mother and Aunt Shatha were at the door . . . and Father and Uncle Ali were on the roof. Hakeem looked around, trying to make sense of things and attempting to get a bearing on which way was home, but the dirt and grit in his eyes were making them water. Everything was a blur.

When he finally figured out which direction was home, he saw no roof, no door, no house, no Father, no Mother, no Uncle Ali, no Aunt Shatha, no Ziad. He saw smoke and dirt, fire and rubble. Hakeem stumbled toward where his home had been. He could only think of one thing: *Mama!* Now he began to feel the burns on his face, starting with a tingling and quickly growing to a fire.

Panic began to well up inside of him. *Mama, where are you?* Hakeem tried to call out for her, but all the heat, dust, and smoke had reduced his voice to a congested croak.

The ringing in his head began to subside, only to be replaced by a more terrifying sound—screams. Screams coming from all around him. Screams coming from within him.

People were running on his left and on his right—some carrying buckets, some covering wounds. Hakeem stumbled past a smoldering heap of rags that deep inside he knew was his cousin, but he couldn't stop—couldn't deal with that now. He had to find his mother. *Mama, I'm almost there!*

As he crossed his father's property line, he fell into a deep, wide hole. An exposed piece of rebar cut a long gash into his leg. Blood poured out, soaking his torn pants, but still he forced himself up.

Mama, I'll find you! Oh, Allah, help me! Allahu akbar, *you are great! Show me where she is! Don't worry, Mama, I'll save you!*

He grasped for handholds to pull himself out of the hole and felt something solid. He grabbed it and began climbing up the side of the crater. As he reached the top, he finally saw what he was holding on to. It was an arm—visible to halfway up the bicep before it disappeared underneath a massive block of cement and metal.

Hakeem instantly let go, falling back to the bottom. He twisted and landed on his hands and knees and began to vomit. As he hovered over the newly formed puddle, he could hear the screams all around him. He dropped to his side and rolled onto his back, closing his eyes tightly, trying to will himself not to look at the arm. As long as he didn't look up, didn't see the very familiar ring around the third finger of the hand, then maybe it wouldn't be true. Maybe he could just stay down here, and eventually his mother would find him. She would help him out of the pit, put ointment on his face, bandage his leg, hold him tight, and tell him everything was going to be okay.

But Hakeem knew that would never happen. He knew Mama would never hold him again. The distinctive ring he had glimpsed was one he had examined often as he listened to stories while lying in bed. It was a ring he had spun around his mother's finger as he sat with the women and children in the mosque, listening to the mullah condemn America and the Jews.

This has to be a dream, he thought. *Please, Allah, let me wake up!* Tears began and quickly turned into torrents. *I don't like this anymore; please let me wake up!* His heart felt like it would explode. He didn't know what to do. *Somebody help me! Anybody help me!!* He didn't want to look back up at the hand. He didn't know how to get out of the hole. He didn't know how he would stop the bleeding on his leg. He didn't know if he would ever stop crying. *Oh, Allah, please help me!*

Now his screams began again, and they continued on and on until finally Hakeem's world faded into an unsettled blackness.

2003
OPERATION ENDURING FREEDOM
BAGRAM VALLEY
HELMAND PROVINCE, AFGHANISTAN

His count was off. Second Lieutenant Riley Covington of the United States Air Force Special Operations Command was on watch at a perimeter security post. He had been lying at the top of a low rise, watching his sector, for four hours, and each time he had counted the boulders on the hill across the small valley, he had come up with thirty-six. This time, however, the count reached thirty-seven. *Keep it together, buddy*, Riley thought as he rubbed his eyes. He shifted slightly to try to allow the point of a rock that had been boring into his left leg to begin a new hole. *I have no doubt these guys scattered these rocks out here 'cause they knew we were coming.*

"You seeing anything, Taps?" Riley whispered into his comm. At the other security post, located on the opposite side of the harbor site, Airman First Class Armando Tapia was stretched out behind a small, hastily constructed rock wall.

"Everything's good to go," came the reply.

On this sixth night of their mission, Riley had chosen a less-than-ideal position to set up their camp. He didn't feel too bad, however; there were probably fewer than a half dozen ideal sites in this whole desolate valley. He was positioned on a low hill to the east of his Operational Detachment Alpha, and Tapia was planted to the north of the team. Rising on the south and west of the ODA camp were steep cliffs. If anyone wanted to approach their bivouac, they would have to come through one of the two security posts.

Typically, AFSOC missions were carried out singly or in pairs. The special-ops personnel were dropped in from high altitude to take meteorologic and geographic measurements, then silently evacuated. Very clean, very quiet. But Riley's team had lost three members in this area during the last two weeks. So it was on to plan B—take in a group and protect everyone's backside.

The moon exposed the barren landscape, eliminating the need for vision enhancement. Riley shifted again and flexed his fingers to keep the cool night air from cramping them. A scorpion skittered up to check out the rustle. Riley's number-two man, Staff Sergeant Scott Ross, said these creatures were called *orthochirus afghanus Kovarik*; Riley preferred to call them the "nasty little black ones." A well-placed flick sent the arachnid careering down the front side of the hill. *Time to start counting boulders again.*

Riley Covington knew that if he could survive this tour in Afghanistan, chances were good that by this time next year, the scenery around him would look a whole lot better. He was two years out of the Air Force Academy, where he had been a three-time WAC/MWC Defensive Player of the Year and, as a senior, had won the Butkus Award as the nation's top linebacker. He was six-two, rock hard, and lightning fast. His nickname at the Academy had been Apache—later shortened to "Pach"—after the AH-64 attack helicopter. *Hit 'em low, hit 'em hard, hit 'em fast!* Riley had sent more opposing players staggering to the sidelines than he could count. Once, a writer for the *Rocky Mountain News* had compared his hitting ability to Mike Singletary's, the infamous linebacker who had broken sixteen helmets during his college days at Baylor. He still felt proud when he thought about that comparison.

Two years earlier, Riley had been selected by the Colorado Mustangs in the third round of the Pro Football League draft, and commentators believed Riley had the possibility of a promising PFL career ahead of him. However, his post-Academy commitment meant putting that opportunity off for a couple of years. In the meantime, he had spent his last two thirty-day leaves in Mustangs training camps before rushing back out to wherever AFSOC wanted him next.

Riley's insides tensed as he came to the end of his count. *Thirty-four, thirty-five, thirty-six . . . thirty-seven . . . thirty-eight! Something is definitely happening here,* he thought.

WHOOMPF! The unmistakable sound of a mortar tube echoed through the valley below.

"Incoming!" Riley yelled as he opened fire with his M4 carbine at "boulders" thirty-seven and thirty-eight, causing one to stumble back down the hill and the other to remain permanently where it was.

A flare lit up the night sky as heavy machine-gun fire, rocket-propelled grenades, and small arms rounds targeted Riley's ODA. Riley looked to his left and saw an anticoalition militia approaching from the north, right over Tapia's position. Riley, seeing the size of the enemy force, let off a few more three-shot bursts, then bolted back down to the harbor site.

He took cover in a low ditch and scanned the camp. What he saw was not encouraging. Four of his ODA members were down—two with what looked like some pretty major shrapnel wounds. There was no sign of Tapia anywhere. The rest of his squad was scattered around the camp, pinned under the heavy barrage. One of their patrol Humvees had been hit with an RPG, and the large quantity of ammunition inside was cooking off. This situation was spiraling downward fast.

Movement caught his eye. It was Scott Ross, lying flat behind some empty petrol cans and waving to catch Riley's attention. Using hand signals, Ross indicated that his com was down and pointed back toward the second patrol vehicle.

Riley looked in the direction Ross was pointing and saw their salvation. Off to his left, about fifteen meters away, an MK19 automatic grenade launcher was mounted on its low tripod. Riley quickly signaled back to Ross to provide full-automatic cover fire, then rocketed out from safety and across the dirt. He almost made it. Something hit him in the hip, spinning him counterclockwise in midair.

He landed hard, gasping for air. As he tried to get up, a mixture of stinging and deep, throbbing pain dropped him down flat. He knew his men desperately needed him, but he couldn't move. Helplessness quickly overwhelmed him. *Lord, I can't stay down, but I don't know if I can get up! Give me what I need! Please, give me what I need!*

Ross was shouting at him, but the surrounding noise made it impossible for Riley to make out the words. Without the Mark 19, their chances were bleak.

Mustering all the strength he had left, Riley began pulling himself the rest of the way to the weapon. Bullets danced all around him, kicking up puffs of dirt into his face and clanging against the nearby Humvee. With each grab of the rocky ground, his adrenaline increased. Finally, the endorphins began to get the best of the pain, and Riley was able to get his feet under him. He stumbled forward, launched himself behind the Mark 19, and let loose.

It took him just under a minute and a half to empty the ammunition can of sixty grenades. The sound was deafening, and the explosions from the shells hitting the enemy positions lit up the night. Riley knew from experience that there was nothing to do but fall back in the face of that kind of fire, which was exactly what the enemy militia did. But RPGs and mortar rounds kept dropping into the camp.

Riley signaled for Ross to come and load another can of ammo on the Mark 19. Then he half ran, half staggered over to what remained of his ODA. The rest of his team huddled around him and he took a quick head count. Besides Ross, there were Dawkins, Logan, Murphy, Posada, and Li. *Not good.* They would be outnumbered if a second wave came.

"Posada, contact the command-and-control nodes in the rear and request immediate close air support and a medical-evacuation flight."

"Yes, sir!"

Riley drew his team close. "Okay, men, we have two options. We dig in here and try to hold off another attack, or we surprise them while they're regrouping."

"Tell ya what, Pach," said Kim "Tommy" Li, a man with an itchy trigger finger and way too many tattoos, "if there's gonna be target practice going on here, I'd rather be the shooter than the bull's-eye."

Riley laid out his plan. "Okay, then, here's how it's going to work: I'm guessing they'll feint another attack from the north, but their main force will come from the east, because that's where the Mark 19 is. They know that if they don't take the Mark out, they're toast. So, Murphy and Li, I want you to belly out to those boulders twenty meters north to meet their feint. Logan, you and Ross remount the Mark on the Humvee and get her ready to go head-to-head with their onrush. Dawkins, you and I'll hit the east security post. When you all hear us start firing, circle the Humvee around east; then everyone open up with everything and blow the snot out of these desert rats. Got it?"

An excited mixture of "Yes, sir" and "Yeah, boy" was heard from the men.

"Excellent! Posada, sweeten up our coordinates with command."

"You got it, Pach," Posada said as he pounded away on his Toughbook—a nearly indestructible laptop computer perfect for use in combat.

"We've got five of our guys down, with at least one probably out—that's unacceptable. Let's make 'em pay." Riley locked eyes with each member of his team and tried to draw from them the same courage he was attempting to instill. "Dawkins, don't wait for me to hit that security post with you! Ready . . . go, go, go!!"

Skeeter Dawkins was a good old boy from Mississippi. Fiercely loyal to Riley, there were several times when he had to be pulled off of fellow team members who he thought had disrespected their lieutenant. He was big, strong, fast, and knew only two words when under fire: *Yes* and *sir*.

Dawkins ran out ahead and was already in position by the time Riley got there and dropped next to him with a grunt of pain. Sixty meters out, Riley could see between forty and fifty well-armed enemy militia members prepping for another attack. "I'm guessing they're not done with us yet, Skeet."

"Yes, sir." It sounded more like *Yeah, zir*.

"Looks like they'll be feinting inside while rolling a flank around left. Must be boring being so predictable."

"Yes, sir."

The two men lay silently for a minute, watching the preparations of their enemies. Riley turned to look at the empty sky behind them. "Sure would like to see that air support come in right about now."

"Mmm."

"Skeet, anyone ever tell you that you ain't much of a conversationalist?" It was hard not to slip into a Mississippi drawl when talking with Skeeter.

Skeeter grinned. "Yes, sir."

The random actions of the enemy force suddenly coalesced into an organized forward movement.

"Looks like the Afghani welcome wagon's rolling again."

"Yes, sir."

"Skeeter Dawkins, you gonna let any of those boys through here?"

Skeeter turned to Riley. He looked genuinely hurt at his lieutenant's attempt to force an expansion of his vocabulary.

Riley laughed. Nothing like feigned confidence to hide what you're really feeling. "Don't you worry, airman. Just make sure you give them a gen-u-ine Mississippi welcome."

Skeeter smiled. "Yes, sir!"

Riley could hear the muffled sound of the Humvee starting up as he and Skeeter readied their M4s. Red dots from each of their M68 Close Combat Optics landed nose level on the first two attackers. Their fingers hugged the triggers.

The sudden whine of two Apache helicopters halted Riley's counterattack. The 30 mm cannons mounted on either side of the choppers strafed the enemy force. The ensuing carnage was hard to watch. One life after another was snuffed out in rapid succession.

When the last bad guy stopped moving, the Apaches turned and headed back to where they'd come from. Skeeter pulled Riley to his feet and helped him down the hill. Pain crashed through Riley's hip, and his left leg buckled. Kim Li rushed over and slipped himself under Riley's other arm.

"Well, Pach, it was a good plan," Li laughed. "Guess I'll have to take my target practice elsewhere."

Riley knew it was just Li's adrenaline talking, but he still had a hard time not laying into him. Too much blood had been spilled and too many screams filled the night air to be joking about killing just now.

Back at the harbor site, an MH-53 Pave Low was just dropping in to evacuate the team. Riley was eased onto a stretcher and carried the rest of the way. As he was lifted onto the helicopter with two dead and five injured, football was the furthest thing from d.